Always
REMEMBER US

A NOVEL

D1133763

A. M. Yallum

ISBN 978-1-68526-633-2 (Paperback)
ISBN 979-8-88644-529-9 (Hardcover)
ISBN 978-1-68526-634-9 (Digital)

Disclaimer: *Always Remember Us* is a work of fiction. Although its form is that of an autobiography, it is not one. Names, characters, places, and incidents either are products of the author's imagination or are used fictitiously. Any resemblance to actual events or locales or persons, living or dead, is entirely coincidental.

Covenant Books
11661 Hwy 707
Murrells Inlet, SC 29576
www.covenantbooks.com

To my Aunt Joanne and Uncle Joe, for embracing me at a crucial time in my life. For teaching me the value of family, sacrifice, and hard work.

To my Aunt Dorie, for showing me patience, unconditional love, and encouraging me to follow my dreams.

To my Aunt Palma and Uncle Bill, who were there from the beginning.

To all Marines. Semper Fidelis.

Chapter 1

Between and including the summers of 1967 and 1968, our transition into a better life occurred. But there are times that I wonder. The cost we paid for such a transition was steep, so to call what resulted from our calamity better is questionable. But you can be the judge of that. We lived on the outskirts of Pittsburgh in a small neighborhood called Larimer back then, and it was a strange time for us, and I sometimes wonder how any of us survived. I left Larimer as a boy and have never returned. Today, most neighborhood grocery stores, businesses, and homes have been torn down and are now nothing more than abandoned dirt lots neglected and choked full with weeds. I suppose this was inevitable, for even back then, the buildings and homes were aging and run-down and were dull from years of pollution that poured from the giant smokestacks of the steel mills that once defined Pittsburgh. Those who lived there before our time speak of Larimer with fondness. They said it was a good neighborhood then, where businesses thrived and children played freely in the streets far into the night.

Even when we lived there, we had a good school, and it stood tall with purpose and was full of life, given to it by the hopes and dreams of children. It stands abandoned now, and the halls and classrooms are badly in disrepair and loom eerily empty like an abandoned tomb. Plywood covers the windows, and the roof sags in places, making it look tired and wanly. Looking back, when my sisters and I lived there in our apartment with Joe and our mum, the decay had already begun, but we were too young to see it.

We sometimes speak of those years, and although most of our memories are undesirable, not all of them are bad because it was also a time of youthful discovery when summer days seemed to last forever. I would run shirtless all day in the sweltering heat, allowing the sun to bake my skin brown. Most parents didn't overprotect their kids, and as a result, we would disappear in the morning and would not reappear until supper or until the streetlights came on at dark. And we survived it without ever being run over by a car, kidnapped by strangers, or ripped apart by a pack of wild dogs.

Candy was a penny, and pop bottles were redeemable at any store for two cents. Strings, Popsicle sticks, and smooth stones had value. Games were simpler too. For hours we spun tops; shot marbles; played Jax or paddle ball; jumped rope; played hopscotch; mother may I; or green light, yellow light, red light stop. Lightning bugs were plentiful, and we caught them by the jar full. We mostly read comic books and Bazooka Joe bubble gum comic strips. And Dick Tracy, with his two-way radio watch, stirred our imagination like nothing else.

Still, there were darker times. But for the most part, we rarely speak of them now, mostly, I suppose, because there would be too much hurt to relive such remembrances, and although we don't begrudge our mum for anything, it would make her feel bad since it was her who had brought Joe into our lives. So we bury the painful memories inside, but they are always there, lingering in the shadows.

If there is an upside to our tragic family history, it is that the harsh glue of adversity holds stronger than any other. This adversity is the glue that held us together back then, and it is the glue that still binds us today.

Anyone with a lick of sense knows decisions and actions have consequences, and all these years later, I still wonder what would have been different if I hadn't pulled the trigger that day or if perhaps I had pulled it one more time. My sister Mindy says that was the day that changed everything for us, but thinking back, I have to disagree. It started, I'm convinced, the summer prior when I got into a fight with Lulu Johnson. If I hadn't instigated that confrontation, maybe none of what followed would have happened, including meeting

Honeymarmo and especially what happened to our sister, Doreen. I guess that's the thing about wondering; only God truly knows—certainly not me. It doesn't matter much because nothing will absolve me from the regret and guilt I still carry. Did I cause the tragedies, at least to some extent, or was I simply a victim like everyone else? As I said, you can be the judge of that.

It's funny how someone can look back at times of hardship and tragedy and, while being glad those times are long behind them, at the same time, miss them terribly. Life can be a mystery that way. I got into so many fights back then, and fighting for me came naturally, like spitting on the sidewalk. It was something I just did.

So let me start there.

*****

Mr. Cosenza's brand-new purple 1967 Lincoln Continental with its polished aluminum hub caps, chrome bumpers, and shiny trim glistened in the morning sun. I loved this car. I scampered down the two flights of stairs from our back porch to the graveled parking lot below, sliding my hands along the wrought iron railings, cleared the last four steps in one leap, then sprinted to the car. I caressed its side, flattened my nose against the driver's side window, and squinted to see inside. The immaculate, bright white leather interior tugged invitingly at me. I tried the door handle, but it was locked. Disappointed, I stepped back. "I'm going to get me one just like this someday," I muttered before finally sprinting across the parking lot toward Larimer Field.

The summer heat had arrived in Larimer, our small neighborhood outside Pittsburgh; it was early June. When I reached Larimer Field, I was panting; my hair was damp with sweat. I spotted my best friend, Donald, standing with several other black kids, all boys, and hurried to him.

"What's up, man, where've you been, Frankie?" asked Donald.

"I just woke up," I answered, searching beyond Donald. "Where's Ronald?"

Donald smirked. "Our mum caught him stealing money from her purse again, so she grounded him, then whooped him good."

I chuckled. "Did he cry?"

"Only when I slugged him."

"You slugged him?"

Donald nodded. "He called her a cuss name, and I told him I better not ever hear him call our mum a cuss name again, then I punched him." Ronald was Donald's twin brother. Donald was older by four minutes, and when Ronald stepped out of line, Donald often reminded him of that fact. I again snickered, then probed the crowd. I saw our friend Jan standing off to the side.

"Did you see Lulu yet?"

"Nuh-uh, Frankie, not yet," replied Donald.

"You think Jan has a chance?"

Donald shook his head. "No, I doubt it, man."

Our friend Jan paced as he scanned the outskirts of Larimer Field. Three boys abruptly appeared and climbed through an opening in the chain-link fence. The boy in front had an exaggerated gait. I grimaced.

When Lulu and the others reached us, Lulu strolled over to our friend. Jan was slightly taller than Lulu, lankier, and had a lighter complexion. Some said there was white blood in his family on his mum's side, but Jan never admitted it.

"You ready to get your feelings hurt, sucker?" Lulu sneered.

"Are you?" Jan shot back.

One of the boys with Lulu picked up a stick and scratched a starting line in the dirt. The other boy jogged out about fifty yards, turned, and waited.

"Let's do it, Oreo," said Lulu.

Jan expanded his chest. "I ain't no Oreo."

"Yeah, then what are you?"

"I'm the same as you," said Jan.

"Yeah, maybe on the outside!" retorted Lulu. Some in the crowd laughed.

"Man, you don't make any sense," said Jan.

4

"That's because what cents I had, I spent on your mama last night."

Jan clenched his fist as he glared at Lulu. Lulu stood his ground, daring Jan to do something about his insult. Finally, Jan unclenched his fist, then walked to the starting line, and Lulu trailed behind him.

"Lulu's such a punk," I whispered to Donald. We all knew he had goaded Jan into this race, and most everyone knew Jan didn't stand a chance.

Both boys placed their left foot on the line, bent their knees, and leaned forward, ready to spring. In the distance, the boy raised both hands into the air, then dropped his arms.

Both exploded from the line. Lulu took the early lead and quickly widened the gap between them. When they reached the finish line, Lulu had beaten Jan easily.

Jan and Lulu walked back toward us. Lulu raised his arms in victory as Jan sulked behind, his eyes downcast. When I saw the defeated look on my friend's face, I felt pity. My dislike for Lulu deepened, and a familiar urge stirred within me.

When he reached the starting line, Lulu crowed, "Any of you other suckers want to race me?" Most looked away.

I fought to suppress the growing urge inside. I had tried to stay clear of Lulu in the past. In fact, a couple of weeks back, I had walked into the boy's bathroom at school, where Lulu was robbing some skinny kid of his milk money. When Lulu gave me a threatening look, I turned and left. It wasn't that I was scared of Lulu; I just didn't know the boy Lulu was robbing, so I minded my own business, a lesson most of us learned early growing up on the streets of Larimer.

Now, as the urge inside got stronger, I stepped forward and immediately felt a sharp tug on the back of my shirt. "Come on, Frankie, not again," Donald whispered. I ignored him.

Now facing Lulu, I stared unflinchingly into his eyes. "Let's go. I'll race you," I said.

"Be for real, man, I ain't racing against no white, snaggle-toothed cracker!" said Lulu, spitting on the ground. His reference was to my two front teeth that had grown crooked. I felt my jaw tighten, and my left leg began to shake.

He's looking for a way out, I thought. I had to find a way to force Lulu to accept my challenge. Then, it came to me. I had to insult him, so I grinned impishly. "Well, your mama sure liked my teeth last night!"

Lulu lost his mind. His eyes bulged, and tiny drops of spittle flew from his mouth as he shouted threats and profanities at me. The group of boys shrunk back.

"I'm going to kill you, white boy, hear me?" he screamed, sticking his fist in my face. "Ain't no one talks about my mama and gets away with it. Especially no poor white trash like you, whose mama lives on food stamps."

"Look, man, I know you can probably whoop me in a fight, and you probably will," I answered, "but not until after we race—unless you're too scared?"

I stepped around Lulu's fist and walked over to the starting line. Lulu hesitated, then trailed behind me. I searched the field for a marker, and I spotted an old rusty can a little further away than the race Lulu had just run against Jan.

I pointed. "We'll run over there to that rusty can. First one there wins," I announced. "I mean, if it ain't too far for you?"

"Man, just gets to stepping, and when we get there, you best keep running," Lulu warned. I nodded at Donald, then placed my foot behind the starting line while Lulu placed his foot slightly in front of it.

From behind us, Donald yelled, "On your mark, get set, go!"

We both burst from the line. We stayed abreast the first few yards before I edged ahead. I glanced over my shoulder, and the contorted face of Lulu as he tried to regain lost ground gave me a burst of energy that catapulted me farther into the lead. I reached the rusty can well ahead of him.

In front of me was the open gate leading to Larimer Avenue and home. I told myself to keep running, and I knew I should, but the urge inside had now taken control. Instead, I stopped abruptly, spun, and before Lulu had come to a stop, unleashed the most brutal punch I could throw, hitting Lulu full force in the mouth. Lulu's bottom lip split open, and he stumbled back, collapsing in the dirt. Blood trickled down his chin.

"How'd you like that, creep?" I raged; my eyes flashed down at him. "If you ever call me a snaggle tooth again or call my friend an Oreo, I'm the one who will do the killing; you got me?"

Lulu sat stunned. He stared up at me; blood dripped onto his shirt. I circled to my right, and with a hard-snapping kick, caught Lulu on the left ear. He clutched his ear, yelped, then curled into a ball.

"Answer me, creep. You got me?"

Guttural sobs came from Lulu. I felt myself feeling sorry for him, but it passed quickly. I cocked my right leg to unleash another kick. "Yeah! Yeah! I got you!" Lulu cried out.

"Good," I said.

I glanced over at the crowd of boys who were now hurrying toward us. I again glared down at Lulu, pulled up some phlegm, and thought about spitting on him. Instead, I spat on the ground, then sprinted through the open gate leading to Larimer Avenue. Before disappearing behind a building, I looked back and saw someone helping Lulu to his feet.

I examined my bleeding knuckle, cut on Lulu's teeth. "You're so stupid," I scolded myself. I had made Lulu my enemy, which meant this was not over.

I ran the rest of the way home. At the rear of our apartment building, I hurried past the back door of Cosenza's store and climbed the two flights of steps. On our back porch, I held my breath and listened. All was silent. I had left the back door unlocked, so I pushed it open and slipped into the kitchen. I tiptoed through our apartment. When I reached my room, I ducked inside, cracked the door, and waited. Before long, from across the hall, I saw the door to my sister's room open.

"Pssst. Mindy, come here," I whispered. Mindy startled.

"Who unlocked your door?" my oldest sister whispered back.

"Never mind, just lock it for me, will you? If Joe finds it unlocked, he'll kill me."

Mindy pursed her lips. "Okay, hurry up and shut the door," she said. I gently pushed it shut, and Mindy set the hook latch in place.

"Thanks, Min."

"Shush," she answered. I heard the creaking of old floorboards as she tiptoed down the hall. I slid down the wall, crossed my legs, and waited.

Chapter 2

I stopped outside the front gate of Larimer Elementary School just as the late bell rang, then glanced in the direction of Larimer Bridge and the railroad tracks. Reluctantly, I looked back at the school's massive front doors. "At least it's the last day," I sighed.

Inside the classroom, everyone was already seated. I marched over to Mrs. Hathaway's desk and handed her my tardy note. She examined the torn piece of a brown paper bag, then read the note scribbled in eyebrow pencil.

"My mum couldn't find no paper or pencil this morning." I shrugged. "That's all she had to write with."

Mrs. Hathaway shook her head, then motioned me to my seat. I slid into my chair as my teacher tossed the note on her desk, opened the attendance book, and made a correction. I looked around the room. Donald and one of my Italian friends, Marco Constantino, were trying to get my attention.

Mrs. Hathaway stood. "Children, I have to run to the office for a few moments to pick up your report cards, and I need everyone to sit quietly in their seats until I return."

She stepped out into the hallway, and when her footsteps had faded, Donald and Marco slid out from behind their desks and hurried over to me.

"Man, Frankie, I heard you split Lulu's lip wide open," exclaimed Marco.

"Yeah, you should've seen all the blood," Donald said.

"What happened?" Marco's eyes widened. "How come you punched him?"

I shrugged, "I don't know. I guess he just made me mad."

"I heard Charles is supposed to wait for you after school today for what you did to Lulu," said Donald. My stomach tightened. Charles was Lulu's older brother. He was a grade ahead of us, much bigger, and had a dangerous reputation. I knew he would beat me in a fight.

"I ain't scared of him," I muttered.

"I would be," Donald said. "But that ain't all. I hear he's got a knife." The blood drained from my face.

"So what you going to do?" asked Marco.

"I don't know." I shrugged. "But I ain't running." Mrs. Hathaway's footsteps approached. Donald and Marco hurried back to their desks.

Mrs. Hathaway passed out report cards, and I reluctantly opened mine to see if I had graduated to the sixth grade. I looked on with relief as I counted four Ds and two Cs. I had made it. The morning dragged on, and then, at eleven o'clock, the bell rang, signaling the beginning of summer vacation. Everyone lined up at the door. Mrs. Hathaway led the class in two separate lines, boys and girls, down the polished marble hallway to the front double doors. She dismissed the girls first and then the boys.

Charles Johnson stood on the sidewalk outside the tall wrought iron fence surrounding the schoolyard. Lulu and another boy stood behind him. Charles and I locked eyes; he nodded, then slammed his fist into his open palm. My left leg began to shake. I briefly thought about running back into the school, but I remembered what I had foolishly said to Donald and Marco about not being afraid. Then, the school doors slammed shut behind me. With nowhere to escape, I gulped, then walked down the steps.

Halfway across the schoolyard, Donald, Ronald, Marco, and Jan appeared at my side.

"We're going to back you up in case they try to jump you," said Donald.

"Cool, man, thanks," I sighed, extending my open palm. Donald slapped me five. I felt better, but not much.

Outside the gate, I stopped in front of Charles. Donald, Ronald, Marco, and Jan moved strategically behind me.

"You think you're bad, don't you?" Charles scowled. "You're going to pay for sucker-punching my little brother."

"He had it coming," I said.

"Yeah, well, punk, what's going to happen next, you got coming, cause I'm gonna jack you up bad!" Charles retorted. He raised his fists.

Then it happened.

A yellow blur flashed through the air, attaching itself to Charles's back. It had arms and legs, and one of the limbs had wrapped itself around Charles's neck, clamping down on his windpipe. Charles coughed as he spun, attempting to dislodge the yellow blur from his back, but it was holding on tightly.

"Charles Johnson, you best leave my brother alone!"

I heard myself groan as I realized what was happening. It was Doreen, my older sister, who was in the same grade as Charles. She was wearing a pair of yellow pedal pushers, a yellow top, and black leather shoes with buckles. As Charles spun, Doreen's wiry legs constricted tighter around his waist. She tightened her chokehold before sinking her teeth into his fleshy earlobe.

Charles shrieked, then rammed Doreen into the metal bars of the schoolyard fence. The impact dislodged Doreen, and she landed on her backside. As Charles pawed at his ear, checking for blood, Doreen sprang to her feet.

Everyone stepped back to give them room. Doreen crouched, then edged toward Charles with fingers and nails outstretched like talons.

Charles backed away, still rubbing his ear. "I ain't fighting no girl."

Doreen's eyes flashed wild and fierce. "How's come, you chicken? Come on!"

Charles looked over at me. "For real, you have to have your *sister* fight your battles for you, sissy?"

I felt my face burn hot. "Ah, come on, Doreen," I protested, "this is my fight, so you just stay out of it."

"You're the one who's a sissy, Charles," Doreen goaded, ignoring me.

Charles moved toward her. "I'm warning you, Doreen, girl or no girl." At the same time, I stepped toward Charles. Then, a loud whistle blew from behind me.

"What's going on over there?" Mr. Harper yelled. Everyone turned toward the approaching gym teacher. "Break it up, and all of you get on home," he barked. "Go on now before I take all of you to my office and introduce you to my paddle." We all knew that Mr. Harper didn't give idle threats when it came to paddling.

Charles glared at me. "I'll see you soon, jagoff." He spun and walked off with Lulu and the other boy. Me, Doreen, and the others started down the sidewalk in the opposite direction.

"Doreen, you're crazy. Charles would've killed you," I informed her.

"I ain't afraid of no Charles Johnson," Doreen shot back.

"Yeah, but he's way bigger than you, and besides, you're just a girl," said Marco matter-of-factly. I knew Marco had just said the wrong thing and stepped quickly in front of him just as my sister lunged.

"Take it back!" she screamed. "You think I can't fight cause I'm a girl? Come on, let's go. Just you and me, Marco, right now!"

"All right, all right, I take it back, Doreen." I stayed between them until my sister calmed down. "I didn't mean nothing by it," said Marco.

"And don't you be telling Mummy that I was fighting neither, or else I'll have to tell her about your fight with Lulu," she threatened me.

"Don't worry. I ain't gonna tell."

"You best not." Then, abruptly, she turned and dashed off in the direction of a group of black girls jumping rope in the alley. Two long ropes were turning simultaneously, double Dutch, one girl on each end of the ropes. We all watched as Doreen got in line, and then when it was her turn, she jumped into the middle of the two rotating jump ropes with impeccable timing. The girls began to chant:

"Winston tastes good like a...
Ooh, aah, wanna piece of pie,
Pie's too sweet,
Wanna piece of meat.
Meat's too tough,
Wanna ride the bus,
Bus too full,
Wanna ride the bull,
Bull's too black,
Want my money back,
Clap! Clap!"

I was struck by how ordinary and harmless Doreen appeared, watching my sister with her yellow pedal pushers and black-leathered shoes with the shiny buckles. I shook my head.

Donald glanced over at me. "Man, your sister's crazy."

I was no longer cross with Doreen. How could I be? She had come to my defense at considerable peril to herself. "Yeah, I know that," I said.

We continued down the sidewalk with the jump ropes slapping the pavement in quick cadence and the gleeful laughter and chanting of the girl's rhyme fading behind us.

"Frankie, you need to watch your back, man. Charles and Lulu will be after you," Marco warned.

"Yeah, man, he's right," Donald concurred.

I nodded. "Yeah, I know that too."

Chapter 3

Joe Gallucci downed the last of his beer, thumped the empty bottle on the counter, walked through the dimly lit bar, then pushed the front door open. On the sidewalk, he squinted against the sunlight, pulled out a pack of Pall Malls from his shirt pocket, tapped the open end against his palm, and extracted a cigarette with his lips. His muscular forearms rippled and bulged as he struck a match and lit his cigarette. Joe snorted a stream of smoke through his hawk-like nose, then began to stagger down Larimer Avenue.

In the distance, a young black mother with her two young children walked toward him. When she spotted the large scary-looking man coming toward her and noticed how his bulky frame swayed, she snatched both children by their arms and quickly scurried across the street. Joe's lips curled into a cynical grin. He liked it when people reacted this way toward him.

When he reached the entrance to the apartment, Joe shoved the heavy door open and stepped inside. Inside the stairwell, he reached into his pants pocket and pulled out an old cellophane wrapper from a pack of cigarettes. He took two blue and orange capsules from the cellophane wrapper, popped them in his mouth, and then shoved the cellophane with the remaining pills back into his pocket before climbing the steps.

*****

I was sitting at the kitchen table, spreading peanut butter on a slice of bread, when my oldest sister, Mindy, walked into the kitchen.

14

"Where's Mummy?" she asked.

I pointed with my chin toward the open kitchen door. "She's out on the porch hanging clothes."

Mindy went to the kitchen door, peered out, then turned back to me. "I heard about your fight with Lulu and what you did to him."

"Yeah, you and half of Larimer," I retorted, taking a bite of my peanut butter bread. "Did you hear about Doreen?" I asked.

Mindy shook her head. "Nuh-uh. What?"

I took another bite. "She got in a fight today with Lulu's brother, Charles, and almost bit his ear off."

"Get out!" Mindy gasped. "What happened?"

"Me and him were about to go at it because of what I did to Lulu, but Doreen came out of nowhere, jumped on his back, and started fighting him."

Mindy's eyes widened. "Get out. She did not!"

I stuck my right hand in the air. "Honest to God. I ain't jagging you none, Min. I swear Doreen is getting crazier every day. It's like she ain't afraid of nothing."

Our mum, Rose Desimone, appeared in the doorway carrying a basket of dry clothes under her arm. She swept into the kitchen singing and set the basket on the table.

"Somebody loves me. I wonder who, I wonder who, he can be?"

"Wow, Mum, you sing so good," cooed Mindy.

"Yeah, Mum, you should be a singer or something. I'd buy your records—if I had any money," I added.

Our mum grinned at Mindy and me. "I wanted to be a singer when I was younger."

"Why didn't you? What happened?" asked Mindy.

"Life, sweetie. Life happened." Our mum said half-heartedly. "Have you seen your sister?" she asked, gently rubbing her stomach.

Mindy and I quickly exchanged glances. "No," we answered.

She pulled a shirt from the basket and began to fold it. "Well, I need yinz to go find her. A social worker from the relief office is supposed to come here tomorrow, and we have to get this apartment spic and span before she gets here. We need to get all of Joe's stuff out of here too." From the front of the apartment, we heard the door open.

"Maybe that's her," Mindy blurted out.

The door rattled as it slammed shut, then slow, heavy footsteps came toward us. Mindy and I clamped our mouths shut. Joe appeared at the entrance to the kitchen, and neither Mindy nor me dared look at him.

"Where's supper?" Joe grunted.

Our mum answered nervously, "Joe, it's too early. It's only two o'clock."

Joe scowled. "Did I ask you what time it was? I'm hungry now. Make me some supper."

Mindy and I sat motionlessly. Our mum took the clothes basket off the table and set it in the corner. "Go find your sister," she said to us. We both stood and stepped toward the door.

"Where do you think you're going, creep?" I froze. I glanced over, and Joe's black eyes bore into me.

"Oh, so you want to stare at me without permission, huh, bonehead? Get to your freaking room!" I snuck a glance toward my mum, and she looked away.

"What are you looking at her for?" Joe growled, clenching his teeth, revealing a sinister-looking gap between the front two. "I said get to your room." My room was to the front of the apartment. I moved quickly but cautiously in Joe's direction; my eyes glued to the linoleum floor. Joe blocked my way. As I tried to squeeze past his bulky frame, I accidentally brushed against him.

Joe grabbed a fist full of my hair. "Oh, so now you just want to assault me, is that it, creep?" I yelped as my hair roots ripped from my scalp. With only the balls of my feet touching the floor, Joe walked me across the living room and down the hallway. He kicked open the door to my room and flung me inside. I toppled across the floor and came to rest near the far wall. "Now, you stay in there until I say you can come out." I waited until Joe locked my door before I moved.

Slowly, I sat up and rubbed my head. The room blurred as tears welled up in my eyes. I felt the wetness on my cheeks, then tasted salt. I pressed my back against the wall, tilted my head up, and blinked hard. I hated my tears. They made me feel like a coward. I continued to stare at the ceiling waiting for them to stop and for the numbness that would follow.

*****

In the morning, I woke when my door was pushed open.

"Come on, Frankie, go get a bowl of cereal," my mum instructed, "then we have to hide Joe's things before the social worker gets here."

My stomach gurgled as I pulled a box of Cheerios from the cupboard. I filled a bowl and had finished devouring it when my mum came into the kitchen.

"Let's go. I need you to help me carry Joe's stuff to the empty apartment downstairs." Our apartment building had six apartments, three on the second floor, and three on the third floor. Two of the apartments on the third floor had occupants, including us, but the three apartments on the second floor had been vacant for as long as I could remember. The abandoned apartment directly below us had a busted door lock, and that's where my mum decided to hide Joe's things. I followed my mum to the front of our apartment, where she had stacked several boxes with Joe's clothes and belongings. Together we carried them down the stairwell and stacked them inside the abandoned apartment. It took three trips.

Shortly before noon, there was a knock. Mindy, Doreen, and I sat in the living room while our mum answered the door. She returned in a moment, followed by a lady in a gray tweed dress. The woman was middle-aged, had a pale complexion, wore a pair of dark-rimmed glasses, and had pulled her slightly graying hair tightly into a bun. She moved stiffly and carried a black satchel briefcase. It was a different lady than the one from the previous year. "These are my kids," our mum announced. The lady pursed her lips, lowered her chin, and peered over her glasses at us. Her expression was stern and businesslike.

"Good morning, children," she said aloofly. She perched herself on the edge of the couch, unbuckled her briefcase, reached inside, and pulled out a clipboard. She read silently to herself for a moment, then turned toward our mum.

"So, Mrs. Desimone, you have three children, is that right?"

"Please, call me Rose. But, yeah, that's right," our mum replied.

"And where is their father?" the lady asked.

"I don't know, somewhere in California, the last I heard," our mum answered. The lady scribbled something down.

"Does he give you any child support?"

"Nuh-uh, he doesn't give me nothing."

The lady frowned. "I see. Does anyone else live here besides you and your children?" she turned her attention toward me, Mindy and Doreen crammed together at the far end of the couch.

"No, it's just us," our mum lied.

The lady squinted curiously at our mum, who had been gingerly rubbing her slightly swollen stomach. "Are you by any chance pregnant?"

Our mum seemed to get nervous. She nodded. "About two months—I think," she whispered. The lady shook her head disapprovingly.

"Who's the father?"

"It's their father," our mum again lied.

The lady scowled. "I thought you said you weren't sure where he was?"

"I'm not. He showed up a couple of months ago for a while and talked about us getting back together. Then, he disappeared, and I heard that he had gone back to California, and that's all I know."

"Hmmm, I see," the lady said. We all sat in awkward silence as the social worker continued to scribble.

Finally, she looked up. "Well, your husband has a financial responsibility toward these children," she announced. "I will have Social Services try to find him and force him to meet those obligations. Now, have you worked over this past year?"

Our mum shook her head. "No."

Abruptly, the lady shoved the papers back into the briefcase and stood. "From what I can see, your apartment looks pretty clean. I need to inspect the rest of it."

"Sure," our mum said. We all stood, and as our mum led the lady through the apartment, my sisters and I trailed behind, trying to suppress our giddiness at how clever we had been in erasing any trace of Joe. When the lady wasn't looking, Doreen stuck out her tongue and made grotesque faces at her. Mindy and I covered our mouths and bit our tongues to refrain from laughing.

After inspecting the apartment, the lady retrieved her briefcase, and everyone followed her to the front door. "I will recommend that you continue to receive your relief checks and food stamps," she announced. "And being that you may be pregnant, once you confirm it with a medical note, I will ensure the paperwork gets processed for you to receive additional money and more food stamps as well."

Our mum's face lit up. "Thank you so much. That would be wonderful."

"No need to thank me, it's my job," the lady responded. "In the meantime, if you find out exactly where your husband is, you have an obligation to let us know."

"Oh, I will," our mum assured her. The lady turned and walked briskly into the hallway and descended the stairs, her footsteps echoing in the stairwell. We listened until we heard the street door open and shut behind her.

Our mum sighed with relief, then turned toward us. "Yinz did good, and it looks like we'll be okay for another year."

Our mum found us playing together on the back porch a short while later. "Come on. We have to move Joe's stuff back." We followed her single file. An unexpected gloom settled over us when we stepped into the abandoned apartment to retrieve Joe's things. We exchanged glances and seemed to read each other's minds as we wondered if, perhaps, we weren't the actual victims of our hoax.

*****

Rose stood over the hot stove, with her brown curly hair tied in a loose bun, and sweat dampened her forehead. She wiped the perspiration with the back of her wrist, picked up a handful of raw sliced potatoes, and dropped them into a pot of boiling water. Fried liver and onions, a meal she frequently cooked, crackled in a frying pan. On the back burner, a small pan of butter beans was simmering.

Next to the stove, a small fan, black with grease, circulated hot air. The lone window in the kitchen was pushed open, and not even the kitchen door, jammed wide by a wobbly chair, brought relief to the suffocating kitchen.

Joe appeared in the kitchen doorway from the living room. Rose, startled.

"You scared me."

"Where's the bonehead?" he asked.

Rose swallowed timidly. "The social worker came this morning, remember, so I let him out."

"Did you now?" Joe stepped toward her, his beefy hands dangled by his side. Before Rose could respond, she felt a heavy slap against her temple, causing her to stumble sideways into the stove. Joe stuck a finger in her face.

"When I say the little freak is not supposed to get out of his room until I say so, then he doesn't get out until I say so!" His lips curled over his clenched teeth. Rose stared at the floor. He continued to glare disgustedly at her deciding whether further reinforcement was necessary. Finally, he turned and walked from the kitchen.

Rose gently rubbed the side of her head. It hurt. She picked up a fork to jab into a piece of liver. Her hand trembled.

There was a time when Joe would never have hit her. When they first met, he treated her nicely and was even kind to her kids. She remembered when Joe had brought them to his uncle's farm in Gibsonia, where the kids petted and played with some farm animals. Joe had even taken all of them fishing on a small pond they had on the farm. Rose chuckled to herself as she flipped a piece of liver in the hot oil. That is all except for Mindy, who refused to kill a poor harmless worm by impaling it on a hook.

Sure, there was always a mean side to him, but he rarely showed it in the beginning, and his strong presence was one of the traits that attracted her to him. Rose knew he had a violent reputation on the streets and that he occasionally used drugs, but now she realized she had fooled herself into believing that she and the kids would always be safe from that side of him or that maybe it was possible to change his ways. There had always been some measure of fear, but he made her feel safe initially. Over time that changed. First came the verbal abuse, then later the physical violence toward her and her children. Now, his dominance was too powerful for her to fight. She tried to shield her children from Joe's cruelty as best she could, but she was no match for his domineering presence most of the time. Still, there were times when he would be kind to her and even be tolerable toward the kids, so she still held out some hope that maybe things could change. Despite his faults, she loved him. As a single mother with three kids living on relief, who else would be interested in her? It had been four years now, and with each passing day, she became increasingly trapped in his world. Rose set the fork down on the stove, walked over, and sat at the kitchen table. She caressed her stomach. Now, the baby would draw her in even further.

Mindy appeared in the kitchen doorway wearing a white blouse and light blue shorts with white socks pulled to her knees. Her hair was dirty-blond, and she was the only one of us that had blue eyes. Our mum would often tease her, calling her little miss prissy because Mindy would stare into a mirror for a long time, primping and brushing her hair. She was always quick to laugh, a trait inherited from our mum, and she loved to talk.

"Hi, Mum," she chirped.

Our mum looked up from her cooking. "Min, where have you been?"

Mindy immediately sensed something was wrong. "Me and Carletta were out roller skating. What's the matter, Mum?"

Our mum shook her head. "Nothing. I need you to set the table."

Mindy talked nonstop as she pulled out several mismatched plates and drinking glasses from the cupboard, some of which were old washed-out jelly jars. From a drawer, she snatched a fist full of tin forks and laid them next to the plates. With her task complete, she plopped down into a chair, still chatting away.

Our mum stepped away from the stove and interrupted her. "Did you see your brother?"

"Nuh-uh, I saw Doreen at the schoolyard, but you know Frankie. He can be anywhere."

Our mum walked to the open door and scanned the neighborhood. "I hope he gets home by the time supper's ready." Her voice dropped to a whisper. "Joe's already home."

Mindy's gay expression changed suddenly. She covered her mouth with her hand. When he was there, our apartment became a kind of dreadful mausoleum where we all spoke in fearful whispers. When Joe was home, we often experienced his wrath if we laughed too loudly or if he caught us talking above a whisper. Even then, when he was in a foul mood, he would sometimes accuse us of talking about him behind his back, usually resulting in some form of punishment. Either way, when Joe was in the apartment, the smartest thing to do was simply not speak above a whisper, and never in his presence.

"Go get your sister and tell her to get home for supper." Our mum sighed. "And for Christ's sake, if you see your brother, tell him I said he needs to get home right now."

"Okay, Mummy, but you know Frankie ain't going to listen to me." Mindy darted out the kitchen door.

As everyone sat down for supper, our mum stepped out on the back porch, shaded her eyes, and leaned against the railing. "Fraaankieee!" she hollered repeatedly. She scanned the neighborhood, but I was nowhere in sight. She sighed, then walked back into the kitchen.

Supper was almost over when I burst into the kitchen. Everyone was sitting at the table, including Joe. He was shirtless and was wearing only a pair of white boxers. Since it was rare for Joe to sit at the same supper table with us, I instantly knew he was there for me.

"So, creep, you think you can just waltz in here any time you feel like it, huh?" Joe's voice dripped with loathing. He stood. "You don't ever learn, do you?" I tore my eyes away from Joe's fierce gaze to the kitchen floor. I didn't answer; I knew better.

"Get to your room," growled Joe. I started through the kitchen. As I reached Joe, my body tensed, suspecting what was coming. My body lurched forward, and I crumbled to my knees as Joe's heavy hand thumped against the back of my skull.

"Walk faster, creep!"

Fear and humiliation gripped me. I scrambled to my feet and ran to my room. The kitchen went silent, and there was not even the clinking of silverware against plates. Joe turned to our mum.

"He gets nothing to eat tonight." Joe's penetrating stare kept her silent.

Inside my room, tears blurred my vision. I sat on the floor with my back against the wall, tilted my head up, and blinked rapidly at the ceiling. I repeatedly tapped my head against the wall. "Stop! Stop! Stop!" I whispered angrily as the first tears poured out. My head struck harder. "Stop! Stop! Stop! Stop!" I murmured louder. It wasn't until my tears flooded my ears that they finally stopped.

I heard Joe cross the hall a short time later before stopping outside my door. I held my breath, and Joe locked the door, and then his footsteps faded down the passageway. I sighed.

I looked around my empty room. There were two windows, neither of which had shades or curtains. One of the windows, the one on the right above the old steam radiator, was broken, and a large chunk of glass was missing. My room was completely void of furniture, except for a metal box spring bed with a bare urine-stained mattress. In the corner next to the door, which had no doorknob, was a cardboard box filled with used vacuum tubes from old televisions that Joe had collected and seemed to think had some value. It was junk. The old paint on my walls was peeling, and I watched as a cockroach scurried across one of the walls.

As the late afternoon light faded, I suspected that I would be locked in my room for a while—probably days. I listened through my broken window at my friends' voices and laughter as they played down the street. Hopefully, Joe would allow my mum to bring me supper before nightfall. I hadn't eaten since breakfast, and I was starving. Joe had dismantled the light switches, sockets, and electrical outlets in the room, so I was without electricity. Eventually, the afternoon light outside my window faded. No one had brought me food. I sat and rocked myself back and forth until my room disappeared into blackness. Alone, again, with only the darkness as my blanket, I fell asleep on the floor.

Chapter 4

Dawn's soft gray light crept through the window. I awoke groggily on the floor, uncurled, and shivered against the morning air. Standing, I stretched the stiffness from my body and rubbed my eyes. Three days had passed since Joe had locked me in my room. My stomach grumbled. On the second day, one small plate of food for breakfast was all that I had eaten. I lifted my shirt and sucked in my stomach. My skin stretched taut against my ribs, and it looked as if my belly button was pressing against my spine. I decided I would risk escaping to find some food. But I knew I had to make it back before Joe awoke.

I tiptoed over to the box of old vacuum tubes and pulled out a piece of cardboard. I pressed my ear against the door. All was quiet, so I pushed the cardboard into the space between the door and the door jamb and worked it through to the other side. Sliding it upward, I felt the latch hook, then gently lifted it from its locked position. The door swung open. I placed the cardboard back in the box, slipped out of my room, reset the lock, then crept through the apartment. I pulled open the kitchen door, stepped outside, and eased the door shut behind me. The sun had not yet come up. As I scanned our neighborhood, Shetland Avenue, with its Pittsburgh boxed houses stretched out before me in quiet silver-gray slumber. I knew I had to hurry. I rushed down the steps, raced across the graveled parking lot, ducked into one of the side alleys, and disappeared into the early morning hue.

Most of Larimer was fast asleep. I loved the early morning solitude; it made me feel as if Larimer belonged to me alone. Except for an occasional stray dog or alley cat, it was as if only I existed. I knew where to find the best gardens with the ripest tomatoes, fattest bell peppers, plumpest grapes, and the best fruit trees.

Only those I trusted most, like Donald, Ronald, Jan, and Marco, did I disclose the location of these prized gardens, and even then, I swore them to secrecy.

My stomach's gurgling grew louder as I walked, and my gnawing hunger pains worsened. I made a mental inventory of all gardens and settled on one on the northern edge of Larimer. An older stout Italian widow owned it. The garden showcased perfectly burrowed rows bursting with vegetables, and off to one corner of the yard was a cherry tree brimming with cherries, but I knew the fruit was still too green to pick. The backyard nestled up against a sloping hillside thick with underbrush that would help conceal me. Still, it would be risky as I had to climb over the four-foot-high chain-link fence that enclosed her yard. I began to jog.

I came to an abandoned house on Lenora Street, a half-block from the garden. Satisfied that no one was looking, I darted through the backyard and slipped over the hillside into the woods. Careful to keep my footing, I angled across the steep slope. When the Italian widow's yard was above me, I scrambled up the hill. I lay flat on my stomach outside the fence, peeked above the ridge, and probed the house and windows for any signs of life. Everything was quiet. My heart pounded as I scaled the fence and jumped into the yard. After a couple of steps, I stopped abruptly. In front of me, the entire vegetable garden had been trampled and smashed. Eggplants, tomatoes, and peppers lay rotting in the dirt. *What the...who would do something like this?* I thought, then, after a moment, it came to me. My anger bubbled up inside. I had shown the garden to only a couple of friends, and only one of them was stupid enough to be involved with this.

I heard a screen door shut. The widow wore a black dress, a black scarf covered her head, and she moved with incredible swiftness for someone of her age and short, thick stature. Before I could react, she had closed the distance between us.

She was gripping a broom and swung it angrily. Pain shot through my arm and shoulder from the impact. I took off running. I was almost over the fence when I felt a sharp stinging across the back of my legs, and then I was tumbling down the hillside.

"Look a' what a' you did a' to my garden! I know it was a' you, you a' bad a' boy!" she screamed in her thick Italian accent. I cowered behind a bush, afraid to move, hoping she couldn't see me.

"I know who a' you are. You a' that a wild a' boy. I know a' who you are." I lay motionless until the screen door again slammed shut. Then, I jumped to my feet and scrambled crab-like across the slope of the hill. As I reached the abandoned house's backyard, I started to run, and I did not stop until I got to Donald and Ronald's house.

*****

Donald's and Ronald's bedroom windows were on the second floor to the rear of the house. I reached their backyard and collapsed. I was spent and panting heavily; my chest heaved as I tried to catch my breath. It felt like my heart would explode. I lay motionless until my breathing slowed.

When I stood, my legs felt rubbery. I picked up a rock, tossed it toward an open window, and it disappeared inside, causing a loud clink that echoed through their bedroom. Donald's head appeared; his eyes were heavy with sleep.

"Frankie, what's up? What time is it?" he asked groggily.

"Never mind. Wake up Ronald, and meet me out back."

The sun now peeked above the rooftops. Donald squinted, rubbed his face, then nodded. "All right, we'll meet you there in a minute." He disappeared inside.

The twins emerged through the back door a few minutes later, Donald first, followed by Ronald. "What time is it?" Donald asked again, but I didn't answer.

When Ronald stepped into the backyard, I charged past Donald and tackled Ronald to the ground. I planted a knee firmly on Ronald's chest, grabbed him by the throat, and reared my fist to deliver my first blow. Before I could unleash my punch, Donald grabbed me from behind in a headlock and wrestled me to the ground.

"Get off my brother!" Donald yelled. "What's up with you, man?" He squeezed my neck tight while using his weight as leverage to hold me down.

Ronald staggered to his feet. "You're crazy!"

"Let go of me!" I shrieked.

"Nuh-uh, man, not until you promise to stop," said Donald.

My face was turning red from Donald's chokehold. I could hardly breathe. "I ain't promising nothing!"

Donald tightened his grip. Until I calmed down, there was no way he was letting loose of me. "Then, I ain't letting go," he informed me.

After several minutes, I surrendered. "Okay, I'll stop," I barked.

I felt Donald's grip loosen. He pushed off me and jumped defensively to his feet. I stood, glaring at Ronald.

"I know you did it!"

"What did I do? I didn't do nothing!" Ronald shot back. Donald and Ronald both looked perplexed.

"Don't lie. You know you did it, jagoff," I shouted. "The old Italian lady's garden…you tore it up."

The puzzled look remained on Donald's face, but instantly I saw the glint in Ronald's eyes. Donald turned toward his brother.

"I didn't—"

I abruptly cut him off. "You're a liar!"

Now it was Donald who recognized the guilt in his brother's eyes. "Man, Ronald, what did you do?"

"It wasn't me. It was Fat Ford," Ronald said. "I told him to stop, but he just started tearing everything up. There wasn't nothing I could do, Frankie, honest."

"You weren't supposed to tell no one about the garden in the first place," I yelled. "You gave me your word, man. You swore to God, crossed your heart, and hoped to die!"

Ronald knew he had betrayed a sacred trust between us and had lost a food source for me in the process, so he looked away. I moved toward him, but Donald stepped between us.

"I can't let you beat him up, Frankie. He's my brother," Donald said.

I stopped, then pointed at Ronald, "Stay away from me, jagoff." I spun and stomped off.

Behind me, I heard Donald scolding his brother. "Man, you're so stupid."

"I ain't stupid."

"You are too!"

I broke into a sprint once I was on the sidewalk. The gnawing hunger had returned. If I were to eat this morning, it would have to be soon.

Chapter 5

When I reached our porch, Larimer was stirring to life. A car accelerated up the street, front doors opened, and children began to appear in yards. I patted my stomach, partially satisfied with a couple of tomatoes and one green bell pepper. I pressed my ear to the door and heard one of the kitchen cabinets creak open. If it was Joe, I was as good as dead. Then, I heard someone humming the song Clementine. It was Mindy. I exhaled and eased the door open, slipping inside. Mindy startled.

"Frankie, how did you get out of your room again?"

"Shhhhh," I whispered. "Is Mum or Joe awake yet?"

"No, not yet. If Joe catches you, he's going to kill you. How did you get out?"

"Never mind, maybe I'll tell you later," I answered. "Min, do me a favor?"

She gave me a reluctant look. "What?"

"When I get back to my room, lock the door behind me."

"I don't know, Frankie. What if Joe catches me?"

I could see the fear on her face. "Come on, Min, he won't catch you. But if he catches me out of my room, you know what he'll do—like you said."

Mindy nodded. "All right, but hurry up." We both tiptoed through the apartment. I stepped inside my room, and Mindy set the hook-lock in place. I had gotten lucky it was Mindy that was in the kitchen and not Doreen.

"Thanks, Min," I whispered through the door.

"Shush," she whispered back. She tiptoed back to the kitchen. I looked around my room. Then, I walked over and slid down the wall facing my door and waited.

Soon, I heard everyone scurrying about, then heavy footsteps approached. My door swung open, and Joe stood in the doorway. Without thinking, I locked eyes with him. Joe came toward me like a slow-moving grizzly bear. He leaned over and smacked me hard across my temple when he reached me.

"Did I give you permission to look at me, you little freak?" Joe reminded me. My eyes darted to Joe's shoes.

"You see, I was going to be nice and let you out this morning, but now you can stay in here another day." He walked from the room.

"Lock the door, and the little imbecile can stay in there another day," Joe barked. I glanced up at my mum standing in the doorway. Our eyes met for a second, then she looked away and pulled the door shut. I slumped back against the wall and glared at the door as I heard my mum set the lock in place.

I finally heard Joe leave through the front door across the hall in the afternoon. I followed the sound of his shoes fading down the stairwell. I waited before moving about my room, making sure Joe was really gone. My bladder was full, and I had to pee badly. I stood by my door until I heard my mum's footsteps outside my door.

"Mummy?" My mum stopped. "Mummy?" I repeated louder this time.

"What is it?" My mum whispered back, even though Joe had been gone from the apartment for a while.

"Mummy, I have to go pee."

"Frankie, hush, I know you don't have to pee. You just want out, and you know I ain't supposed to let you out."

"Mummy, please," I begged as I squeezed my thighs together. It felt as if my bladder was about to burst.

"Frankie, I said—"

I punched the door viciously. "Mummy, I got to go bad!"

"Frankie, I can't. If Joe finds out, he'll kill me."

I knew I was close to wetting myself. I again slammed my fist into the door, firmer this time. "Let me out!" I shouted, "I said I have to go bad!"

"Frankie, hush up, I said!"

"No!" I screamed, "I said, let me out before I pee myself." I began to hammer the side of my fist into the door, rattling it on its hinges. My mum stood on the other side, wringing her hands. I stepped back.

With all my strength, I sent a kick crashing into the door. "Let me out! I said I have to go pee!" My mum continued wringing her hands. "Let me out! Let me out! Let me out!" I hollered indignantly, kicking the door repeatedly as hard as I could.

"Frankie, Stop! Okay! Okay!" I could barely hear her through my fury. "But you have to get right back in there when you're done, you hear me?"

I was panting heavily. "I know that!" I barked, "I just have to go pee, bad!"

My mum unlocked the door and pushed it open. "Hurry up before Joe gets back and catches you out of your room," she said nervously.

I sprinted to the bathroom just in time. I exhaled in glorious relief as I watched my urine stream bubble in the toilet water. I turned and walked from the bathroom toward my room when I had finished. Our pregnant cat Fluffy rubbed up against my leg in the hallway, and I bent down and picked her up.

"Hurry up, Frankie, before Joe catches us."

"How's he going to catch us?" I shot back. "He ain't even here." I walked back into my room, and my mum quickly shut and locked the door behind me. I laid down on the urine-stained mattress. The rank, musty odor no longer bothered me. I lay Fluffy down next to me and rubbed her fur. From deep within her, a low guttural purr vibrated against my hand. It felt soothing, so I lay next to her and closed my eyes.

I was startled awake. At first, everything seemed quiet. Then I heard Joe's ominous footsteps, and I pushed myself up on the bed and strained my ears.

From the kitchen, I could hear the clanking of pots and pans. Before long, I listened to the scraping of kitchen chairs as everyone sat down for supper. My mouth began to water as the smell of fried pork chops wafted through the apartment. More time passed. Then I heard someone scraping plates into the rubbish before being placed in the sink. The kitchen spigot gushed, and drawers and cupboards were pulled open and slammed shut. The radio clicked on, and the song "Bread and Butter" filled the apartment. Joe ordered the radio turned off, and everyone became quiet. I clutched at my stomach, and my hopes of eating supper had begun to fade with the afternoon light.

Then, I heard my mum's footsteps approaching. I perked up.

"Where do you think you're going with that?" Joe's gruff voice rang out.

"To Frankie," my mum answered. "He hasn't eaten since yesterday morning."

I held my breath, then my door opened, and my mum stepped inside, giving me a weak grin. She carried a plate with a fried pork chop, butter beans, applesauce, and a slice of buttered bread. I swallowed some spit. Then, the grin vanished from my mum's face when Joe's footsteps approached behind her. As he passed my room, Joe glanced disgustedly inside, then stopped abruptly. He was staring at my mattress. I glanced over to where Joe was looking. Fluffy had spread out lazily on the bed.

"How'd that filthy cat get in here?" Joe demanded, pushing past my mum and walking menacingly towards me.

"I asked you a question, bonehead. How'd that filthy cat get in here?"

"She must have come in when I let him out to go pee before," my mum interjected, knowing what was about to happen to me if Joe didn't get an answer.

Joe turned toward her. "Oh, you did? Ain't that nice. I guess you think you can just do whatever you want, despite what I tell you. Is that it?" he asked.

"No, Joe, he had to go to the bathroom," my mum stammered. She softened her tone so Joe wouldn't think her confrontational.

"What other sneaky things do you do behind my back when I'm not here, huh? Maybe you sneak some of those guys from across the street up here too when I'm gone? Do you? I saw men's footprints on the stairs, and I know they weren't mine."

"That's crazy. I can't believe you'd say that to me," my mum shot back.

"Who you calling crazy?"

"I didn't say you were crazy," my mum responded defensively. "I said what you're saying is crazy."

Joe stared coldly at her, and then he raised the back of his hand. My mum recoiled. I waited for Joe's backhand across my mum's face. But instead, he knocked the plate of food from her hand. It flew in the air and crashed to the floor. Food splattered everywhere.

Joe looked at me. "So you want to eat, freak? Well, go ahead and eat." I stood motionless, staring down at Joe's leather shoes. Joe reached over and wobbled me with a slap.

"Get down there on the floor and start eating," sneered Joe. Frightened, I dropped to my knees, and with my hand shaking, reached out, picked up a butter bean, and put it in my mouth.

"No, not with your hands, bonehead," Joe snarled. Not understanding, I didn't move. Joe moved behind me, placed the sole of his shoe on my back, and forced me down. My face was almost touching the floor.

"Lap it up, creep."

I lowered my face the rest of the way and slurped a small amount of applesauce. The depth of my fear was animal-like, and tears of shame and humiliation blurred my vision. I fought the urge to cry.

"How did you like it, creep? Tasty, right?" Joe asked. I nodded. "Good, you need to eat more, though. Your mother said you're hungry." Joe once again forced me down.

I continued to slurp and eat from the floor. Joe stuck a threatening finger in my mum's face. "When I say the little imbecile doesn't come out of his room, I mean he doesn't come out—for nothing!" My mum bowed her head submissively. "Now, clean this food up. I think he's had enough to eat. Don't you?"

My mum didn't answer, and Joe slapped her. "I'm sorry, I didn't hear you," he said sarcastically.

"Yeah," my mum mumbled, rubbing the side of her face.

"Yeah, that's what I thought you said. And get that filthy cat out of here," Joe ordered as he walked from the room. Without swapping looks with me, my mum obediently cleaned up the food from the floor, picked up Fluffy, then left, locking the door behind her.

I climbed on the bed and settled in for the night. It took a long time, but I finally fell asleep. In my dream, I was running away from Joe and my mum. They were chasing me, and a tall chain-linked fence blocked my way. I grabbed hold and began to climb. Partway up, my legs suddenly became sluggish, as if filled with cement. I panicked. The harder I pumped them, the heavier and slower they moved. Joe and my mum were now reaching up to grab me. Deep sobs shook me as I now churned my legs furiously, but this only caused my legs to move slower. Then, just as Joe and my mum grabbed hold of me, I jolted awake. My legs were pumping violently on the mattress, just like in my dream. I was crying, and sweat covered my brow.

I lay awake most of the night, and just before dawn, I finally drifted off to sleep again. This time in my dream, I was in my sister's room playing a game of Jax. My mum came into the room and told me to take a bath. In the bathroom, someone had filled our claw foot tub with water. I stripped, stepped into the bathtub, and slid beneath the hot steamy liquid. It felt spectacular, and my body went limp. As I soaked in hot water, I felt the need to urinate, so I did. An overwhelming sense of relief engulfed me as I let loose my bladder. The water seemed to get hotter. Then, for the second time, I woke suddenly.

On my mattress, I had curled myself into a tight ball. I felt wet heat as it soaked through my pants and shirt. The pungent smell of fresh urine overwhelmed me, and I jumped from the bed. The cool morning air seeped through my drenched clothes. I shivered as I looked helplessly around my room.

The apartment was quiet. All of my clothes were in my sister's dresser in their room. I would have to endure the odor and wet chill until someone could get me some dry clothes. I looked at the large wet spot on my mattress. As carefully as I could, I wrestled the mattress off the box springs and flipped it over. If Joe saw that I had peed the bed again, I would be in real trouble. The last time I had a bedwetting accident, Joe had shoved my face into the wet urine and had held it there while he raged, calling me a disgusting animal, and had threatened to take a board to me. I was relieved; no pee had seeped through to the other side. I tiptoed over to the door and sat, hoping that Mindy would wake first.

It didn't take long before I heard my sister's bedroom door open. I pressed my ear and cheek against the floor and strained to see under the door, and my heart sank. It was Doreen.

I watched as she quietly pulled the door shut behind her and tiptoed across the hall floor.

"Doreen?" I whispered.

"What?" she whispered back.

"I need some clothes. Can you get me some?"

"How come? What's wrong with the clothes you got on?" she asked.

I grimaced. I knew I had to tell her. "I peed the bed again."

"Ooolll, you better hope Joe don't find out," she warned.

"He ain't going to find out unless *someone* tells." I paused. "Will you get me some clothes?"

"What will you give me?"

"What?" She was blackmailing me. I knew this would happen.

"You heard me. What will you give me if I get you some clothes?" she insisted. I knew she had me over a barrel.

"Anything you want."

"Anything?" asked Doreen.

I felt my anger rising. "Yeah, anything!"

"Promise?"

"Yeah, promise," I said.

"Cross your heart and hope to die," insisted Doreen, making sure she closed every loophole.

"Doreen, I swear..."

"Say it, Frankie. Say, 'Cross my heart and hope to die,' or I ain't doing it," she said.

"Okay, okay. Cross my heart and hope to die."

"You didn't cross your heart."

"Yeah, I did, Dor. I crossed my heart and raised my right hand up to God," I lied.

"Frankie, you better not be lying."

"I ain't lying, I swear. Now, just get my clothes."

"Okay, but if I get them, you have to be my slave for an entire day when Joe lets you out." There, she had now exacted her price.

"All right, just get them."

"I mean all day, Frankie. And anything I say, you have to do it."

"I said I would, Doreen, I swear. Now just get me my clothes, please," I pleaded.

Satisfied, Doreen crept across the hall and disappeared into her room. She reemerged a moment later. I heard the latch on my door lift, and the door opened. Doreen reached in with a pair of pants, an old white T-shirt, and some underwear, and I snatched them from her. She quickly pulled and locked the door.

"Thanks, Dor," I said. I started to change. "Hey, what's this?" I complained, holding up a pair of white cotton underwear with small pink flowers.

"Those are Mindy's." She had been waiting for a reaction from me. "You don't have no more clean underwear in the drawer, and that's all I could find."

I held them out in front of me. After a moment, I concluded that these were better than nothing. "You best not tell anyone I'm wearing these," I threatened.

"Just remember your promise," Doreen reminded me. She continued down the hall. I wiped myself down with the dry portion of my old clothes, then changed, and I stuffed the soiled ones under the mattress until I could put them in with the dirty clothes later. Feeling better, I sat down on my bed and waited.

Joe coughed hoarsely, struck a match, and lit his cigarette. He looked over at our mum, who was stirring awake from her side of the bed. "Go make some coffee," he said. Our mum pulled on an old robe and left the room. Joe took a long drag from his Pall Mall, then exhaled as he swung his legs off the bed's side and stood.

From across the hall, I heard the creaking of bedsprings. A few moments later, the sound of Joe's bare feet made their way across the room, into the hall, then into the bathroom. The bathroom door didn't shut. Joe lifted the toilet seat, and I heard the hiss of his cigarette as he flicked it into the toilet, followed by the steady stream of urine.

Then, the door to my sister's room opened. Still groggy from sleep, Mindy scurried barefoot across the floor toward the bathroom, and her footsteps stopped abruptly.

After a pause, I heard Joe's gruff voice just above a whisper. "Get in here and shut the door."

I heard the bathroom door click shut, and then all was quiet. After several moments, the bathroom door reopened, and Mindy's footsteps scurried across the floor and disappeared into her room. Joe walked back to his bedroom. The smell of freshly peculating coffee filled the apartment.

The morning dragged on. Then, I heard Joe emerge from his bedroom once again, and he was wearing his shoes. Only when Joe was ready to leave the apartment did he put on his shoes. Even if Joe didn't let me out, I felt relief that he would be gone.

Joe's hard leather shoes stopped outside my room. I swallowed, then lowered my eyes to the floor. Joe fumbled with the latch, and the door banged open.

"Go on, bonehead, get out of here," Joe said. He walked back to his room.

I edged toward the door. Knowing Joe, it could very well be a trap. I stuck my head out the door. I heard my mum and sisters in the kitchen. I glimpsed Joe in the bedroom from the corner of my eye, standing in front of the mirror, combing his thick wet black hair. He stopped suddenly, walked over to his side of the bed, lifted the mattress, and pulled out a handgun. He examined it quickly before shoving it into his belt and covering it with his shirt. I hurried down the hallway, through the living room, and into the kitchen. My mum was at the table drinking coffee and smoking a Pall Mall while my sisters ate toast and drank milk.

My mum looked up at me. "Well, good morning."

I didn't answer. I looked over at my sisters. Doreen sported a mischievous look while Mindy sat solemnly quiet, staring down at the table.

"Make yourself some breakfast. There's Cheerios in the cupboard," my mum said.

I thought about running out the back door without eating before Joe changed his mind, but I was too hungry. I opened the cupboard, got a bowl, and checked for roaches. I pulled out the Cheerios and a bag of sugar from another cabinet and inspected them. There was none. I hated cockroaches and loved to squash them, but I wasn't allowed to in front of Mindy. She made me catch them, then free them outside. She said it wasn't their fault that they were cockroaches, and they were just trying to eat like anybody else, and they deserved to live like all of God's creatures.

"Frankie, how about making me a bowl too." I looked across the table at Doreen, who was grinning smugly at me.

"Get your own," I said. Doreen's grin vanished.

"Mummy, I have something to tell you," Doreen said loud enough for everyone in the apartment to hear. I knew she wasn't bluffing. Doreen never bluffed.

"I'm just kidding," I quipped. Our mum squinted curiously between us, and I reached for another bowl.

"What are yinz up to?" our mum queried.

A satisfied smirk appeared on Doreen's face. "Nothing," she said. Our mum shook her head, deciding not to pursue it further.

While I devoured my bowl of Cheerios, we all heard the front door open as Joe left. The tension in the apartment instantly deflated, and I was struck with a thought and got up from my chair.

"I have to go pee," I announced. I walked quickly to the front of the apartment and dashed into my room. I pulled my soiled clothes from beneath my mattress and carried them to the small closet outside the bathroom, where my mum kept the dirty clothes. I started back toward the kitchen, then stopped suddenly. I veered into my sister's room and gently slid open the bottom dresser drawer. There, clean and neatly folded, were several pairs of my underwear. I reached inside and touched them.

"I knew it," I mumbled. I pulled out a pair and heard footsteps in the hallway. I slid the drawer shut and hurried into the bathroom to change out of Mindy's flowered panties. I would make Doreen pay later.

Doreen and I sat at the kitchen table as our mum washed dishes, and Mindy stood quietly next to her, drying and putting them away.

Finally, our mum squinted down at her. "You're awful quiet this morning, Min," she said. "How come?"

Mindy shrugged. "I don't know."

Our mum reached out and stroked her hair. "Well, cheer up, and don't be so sad." Unexpectedly, our mum pulled her tight and playfully began to poke at her ribs. Mindy tried to pull away, but our mum was too strong. She began to tickle her unmercifully. Mindy slid to the floor to protect herself, but to no avail. She was soon giggling, which turned to laughter as our mum pinned her down. Not wanting them to have all the fun, Doreen and me quickly jumped on top of them and began to tickle our mum and each other. As we writhed jubilantly on the kitchen floor, I decided I would not get revenge on Doreen for making me wear Mindy's flowered underwear, and we all seemed to forget about Joe—even if it was only for a little while.

Chapter 6

The old hobo walked sluggishly alongside the railroad tracks. His hair and face were slick with sweat, and a trickle of it ran down the back of his neck behind his ragged coat collar, causing the skin between his shoulder blades to itch. He stopped, wiped his brow with his coat sleeve, then reached inside his collar and scratched. His face scrunched as he scanned the area, hoping to recognize something, anything, to gauge his location. He figured he was somewhere in Pennsylvania. Nothing looked familiar. Last night, he was chased from a boxcar by a railroad bull and had been walking ever since. Shading his eyes, he looked up at the sun almost directly overhead. He adjusted his twine sling tied to his blanket roll slung across his back, took a weary breath, and trudged onward. Thirty minutes later, a bridge appeared on the horizon. He perked up. This bridge was someplace that would give him shade from the blistering sun and where he could rest. He forced some vitality into his tired old legs, and now with a sense of purpose, picked up his pace.

*****

I loved being shirtless. The June sun felt warm on my face and shoulders as I walked toward Shetland Avenue, and it was great to be outside again. From behind me, my mum hollered my name from the back porch. I spun.

"Be home in time for supper," she yelled.

"Okay," I hollered back. I searched the neighborhood for Donald, Ronald, and Jan but couldn't find them anywhere. On Larimer Avenue, I turned east and jogged toward Larimer Bridge.

Larimer Bridge spanned a deep valley on the northeast outskirts of Larimer. At the bottom of the valley, Washington Boulevard, one of the busiest traffic thoroughfares in the area, stretched north and south. The thick steel railing of the bridge was chest high. Midway across, I stopped and pushed myself up on the tubular rail to where my stomach lay across the top. Precariously, I teetered forward as I watched the cars whiz by some hundred feet below. My insides went queasy. Once the thrill passed, I jumped down and continued across the bridge. Near the bridge's end was a hidden gorge, heavily wooded, where railroad tracks ran parallel to Washington Boulevard below. Here, an opening in the bridge paling led to a path that stretched to the bridge's underbelly.

I squeezed through and hurried down the dirt path when I arrived at the opening. I had always been fascinated by the bridge's underbelly constructed chiefly of cement. The transition from the hot summer sun to the perpetual shade beneath the bridge felt refreshingly cool on my bare chest and shoulders. A few yards further, at the bottom of the slope, lay the railroad tracks. I scrambled down the hill and walked the rails, hoping to find Marco.

Marco and I would often jump a slow train and ride it for maybe a mile before we lost our courage, then we would jump off before Larimer and home got too far away. I looked forward to the day I would jump into one of the boxcars and not lose my nerve. I would ride the train far from Larimer and far from Joe. It was only a matter of time; I was sure of it. I often sat alone under the bridge, imagining far-off places, new people, and adventures where I would no longer live in fear and maybe even someday become someone important.

Marco nor any of my other friends were anywhere around.

Disappointed, I walked back to the underbelly of the bridge. Then, from the corner of my eye, I glimpsed movement in the shadows where the bridge's cement arch rested against a massive concrete abutment. I snapped my head in that direction. There, crouched on his hams, was an older man, a hobo, staring directly at me. My muscles went rigid.

We stared at one another; then, I edged slowly toward the path. The older man finally grinned and gave me a nod.

"Howdy," he said.

I stopped. Instinctively, I quickly calculated the distance between the hobo and me and the distance to my escape route in case I needed to run for it.

"Cat got your tongue?" The older man chuckled.

I stood my ground, confident I could get away if I needed to. Emboldened, I turned fully toward the hobo. The older man was still squatting on the incline, his arms resting on his knees. He was lean of stature with a long sinewy neck. His long greasy hair touched his shoulder with streaks of gray in it. His leathery face had a matted gray beard, and his chin reached toward his nose as he grinned. His clothes were dirty and stained and were disagreeably mismatched. His trousers were too short, which left his bony ankles exposed, and the brown jacket he wore had rips in some of the seams. Next to him in the dirt was a rolled-up wool green blanket knotted tightly with some twine, long enough to be used as a sling. His eyes were hazel and were bright, almost liquid, and they glistened. Despite his rough and weathered exterior, he had a kind face.

"You a hobo?" I blurted out.

The hobo laughed, displaying a couple of missing teeth, and the ones that I could see were a grungy yellow. "Well, yep, I guess I am."

I continued to study him cautiously. "My friend, Donald, says hobos eat little children. Is that true?"

Again, the older man laughed. "Only the plump ones," he answered, looking me over. "You're a bit too scrawny for my taste, though," he added with a chuckle. "You'd probably give me indigestion."

I smirked, understanding the hobo was joshing with me. I liked his laugh. It was genuine, which put me at ease. "So what are you doing down here?" I asked.

The old hobo continued to smile. "Well, if you must know, I got here just a little while ago, and I kind of like it. I was just deciding whether or not I should move on or set me up a jungle for a while."

"Huh?"

"You know, a jungle—a campsite," the old man clarified.

"Oh, yeah," I said, pretending to understand what the hobo had meant.

"Seems like a good place, and I can use the bridge to stay dry if it rains. Mostly, I like to keep to myself, though, and wouldn't want to be bothered much." He then cocked his head to one side. "Do many people come down here?"

"Nuh-uh, not really. Mostly just me and some of my friends," I assured him.

The hobo scratched his beard thoughtfully. "I guess that would be jake."

"How long you been a hobo, anyway?"

My question amused the older man. "You sure ask what's on your mind, don't you?" He chuckled. "I like that. Well, let's see. I guess I've been on the bum for a long time now, maybe twenty years, probably more. I'm not really sure, though. After a while, it gets kind of hard to keep track." Without warning, he stood and shuffled down the embankment. I moved skittishly toward the path.

"Now, you ain't afraid of old Honeymarmo, are you?" the older man mused.

I raised my chin. "Nuh-uh, I ain't scared of no old hobo."

Honeymarmo laughed loudly at my bravado. He stepped slowly toward me with an outstretched hand. "Well, now that I told you my name, what's yours?"

Before grasping it, I inspected the hobo's hand to ensure it was safe. "Frankie," I said.

"Well, Frankie, I'm pleased to make your acquaintance." He pumped my arm.

"Me too."

Honeymarmo let go of my hand, returned to his squatting place, and plopped down in the dirt. I continued to stand awkwardly.

"Why don't you come sit down, Frankie, and keep me company for a spell."

I eased a little closer but not too close and sat down. Honeymarmo stared silently out at the railroad tracks.

"So why are you here in Larimer?" I asked.

"Larimer, huh, so that's where I am? Where exactly is Larimer, Frankie?"

"You mean you don't know where you're at?"

"I know I'm in Pennsylvania," Honeymarmo said. "Somewhere near Pittsburgh, I was thinking."

I nodded. "Yeah, you're in Pittsburgh."

"I thought so. As far as what brought me here, well, I just follow the tracks and go where the good Lord leads me." He squinted at me. "Well, now, that's a funny look. What's the matter, don't you believe in the good Lord, Frankie?" Honeymarmo asked pointedly.

"I don't know. I guess I never really thought about it." I shrugged.

"But you don't believe he leads or watches out for people?"

"No," I answered bluntly.

"Really? What makes you think that?"

"Well, he ain't never led or watched out for me," I assured him.

"So you don't think he cares about you?"

I shook my head. "No, I know he don't."

Honeymarmo bristled. "And how do you know that?"

"Because I've prayed to him before and asked him for help, but he ain't never helped me. If he cared about me, he would have helped me," I said coldly.

"Well, what kind of help did you pray for?" Honeymarmo asked.

I was getting tired of his questions, so I set my jaw. "I don't want to talk about it!" Surprised by my directness, Honeymarmo decided to drop the topic. We sat quietly, but I could see he was thinking.

"Frankie, you might not believe this, but I wasn't always a hobo. I lived a pretty normal life at one time—had me a wife and daughter too. It was a long time ago, though, back when I was a young man." Honeymarmo finally said, breaking the silence between us. "They were my whole world, and they were both so beautiful."

"Really?" I asked skeptically, finding it hard to believe that someone who looked like this old man would actually have a family. "So what happened to them?"

Honeymarmo squinted down at the dirt, searching for words. "Well, one day, my little girl got sick. She was only five years old. Then, a couple of days later, my wife got sick too. We just thought it was a bad cold or something. They got a lot sicker after a few more days, so I called in a doctor. It turned out they both had come done with diphtheria." Honeymarmo paused; a pained expression crossed his face. "Our little girl went first. And just a couple of days after that, my wife died. In about a week, I went from being the husband of a wonderful wife and the father of a beautiful little girl to having nothing. My life as I knew it was over, just like that, and the sadness in me was so deep that I couldn't talk to anyone for weeks. The truth be told, the grief has never really left me, Frankie, and probably never will."

"That's messed up!" I said, now believing what he was telling me. "What were their names?"

"Clara and Becky." Honeymarmo smiled warmly. "Clara was my wife, and Rebecca—we called her Becky—was our little girl."

I shook my head as a thought came to me. "I don't get it. How can you say God cares about you or anyone when he let your wife and daughter die?"

The old hobo fell quiet again, searching for more words. "It's funny you would say that, Frankie. You know, for the longest time, I did blame God. My wife and I prayed for our little girl, but he took her anyway. Then, to rub salt in the wound, he turned around and took my Clara. He didn't answer my prayers either. I was mad at him for the longest time. When you lose something, like a family, something that is your whole world, it's easy to blame someone or something else or just give up on life. That's what I did. I just shook my fist at God. After about a year or so, I found myself on the road. I guess I wanted to hide from the world, and what better place to do that than on the open road where no one knows you."

Honeymarmo picked up a twig and snapped it in two. "When you're on the road, Frankie, you spend a lot of time alone with only your thoughts to keep you company. You find that you have a lot of time for soul-searching. Eventually, you realize you can fool other people, but you can't ever fool yourself, not if you're honest." The older man locked eyes with me. "You see, Frankie, God wasn't responsible for my family's death, especially my little girls'—I was."

"You? How was it your fault?" I asked incredulously.

"Because it's true. When it comes right down to it, I was responsible. You see, I knew that I should have vaccinated our daughter with the diphtheria vaccine, but I kept putting it off. My wife even reminded me a few times, but I always seemed to come up with some excuse as to why we couldn't do it just then—I thought there would be plenty of time to get it done later. My parents had vaccinated me as a boy, but Clara's parents never got her vaccinated. We were supposed to get the vaccination for both my daughter and wife, but I kept delaying it. So you see, Frankie, it wasn't God who was responsible for their death. It was me. My decisions killed my own family. I guess I've been punishing myself ever since."

"Yeah, but God could have still saved them if he wanted to, but he didn't," I interjected bitterly, mostly because I didn't want to be wrong about it being God's fault.

"You know, I thought about that too, Frankie. But you see, God has given each of us free will, free choice, going back to Adam and Eve. Free will has consequences, good and bad, and we live with the cost of our choices every day. Adam and Eve used their free will to disobey God, and we've had to live with the consequences of their decision ever since. We're to blame for our choices, which often affect others around us, especially those we love. There are billions of people on this earth making billions of decisions every day, some good, but many bad, and God is not in the business of correcting or making right every bad decision people make." Honeymarmo fixed his gaze on me again. "No, Frankie, if things are bad in your life, then chances are it's because of choices that you or others around you have made, but never blame God."

Finally, acknowledging he may have a point, I nodded. "I guess I never thought about it like that before," I said, "and I sure am sorry for what happened to your family, but I don't think you should blame yourself. You didn't do nothing wrong on purpose. It was just one of those bad things that happen."

"Thank you, Frankie." Honeymarmo grinned. He stood, walked over to his blanket roll, pulled out a book, returned to where he was sitting, and read silently.

"What are you reading?" I asked.

"My Bible." He held it up for me to see. "Have you ever read any of it?"

"No, I heard of it, but I ain't never seen one."

Honeymarmo's eyes widened. "You mean to tell me you've never seen a Bible before?"

I shook my head.

"Well, what about in school?" asked Honeymarmo.

"They don't have Bibles in schools. One of my teachers told us they used to, but they outlawed them or something," I informed him.

"They outlawed them?" Honeymarmo exclaimed. "Huh, I never heard of such a thing. You know, Frankie, God's word is light. It's what gives us our morals and values, and it's what guides us to make good decisions in this world. Without it, there is nothing left but darkness and chaos. You can never replace God's Word with anything better—not never!" Honeymarmo frowned. "Huh, ain't that something—outlawed! I'll tell you something, Frankie, if what your saying is true, there will come a day when the schools in this country will regret taking God's Word from the classroom—mark my word." He handed me the Bible. I took it from him and gave it a once-over. It was different than the books at school, and I was surprised at how small the print was and how fragile the pages were. It read kind of funny too.

I handed the Bible back to Honeymarmo. Honeymarmo took it and mostly read silently to himself but occasionally read some of it to me. He read to me about God's Son, Jesus, and what he had done for me on the cross. Finally, the energy of my youth returned, and the promise of a long summer day got the best of me. I stood abruptly.

"I have to go now," I informed the old hobo. Honeymarmo put down his Bible and stood as well.

"Well then, it was nice meeting you, Frankie," Honeymarmo said. He extended his hand, and we shook. I started up the path, then stopped and turned back.

"Thanks for not eating me for lunch," I joked.

"Well, just stay away from those mashed potatoes and gravy, and you'll be fine." Honeymarmo laughed.

I chuckled. "If I come back tomorrow, will you be here?"

Honeymarmo's smile widened. "Probably."

I scurried up the path to the bridge, where I began to jog toward Larimer Avenue. For the very first time, I wondered if maybe this old hobo was right. Perhaps I had been wrong about God and the notion that God didn't care about me.

Honeymarmo watched as his new friend walked up the path and disappeared. There was something about the boy. Beyond his unkempt hair covering his eyes and his crooked front teeth, there was something different about him. He liked him, for sure, especially his sense of humor, but there was something else, something he couldn't quite put his finger on. He was troubled somehow; the flash of anger in his eyes had told him that much. Still, he seemed like a good kid. *Yeah, there's something else there*, Honeymarmo thought. He gave a glance upward. "Maybe I will stick around for a while," he said out loud.

Chapter 7

I burst into the kitchen just as our mum placed a plate of fried chicken thighs on the kitchen table for supper. "Is Joe home?" I whispered to my sisters, who were already seated at the table. "Nope," they answered.

I plopped down in a chair, picked up a juicy piece of chicken, and bit into it; grease trickled down my chin. After supper, Mindy and Doreen cleared the table and almost immediately started arguing over whose turn it was to wash the dishes. Our mum clicked on the radio and turned up the volume to drown them out. Dion and the Belmonts singing "A Teenager in Love" crackled from the old radio, which seemed to halt the squabbling, temporarily, as they both began to sing along. I sat quietly, thinking about Honeymarmo and things we had discussed. I debated whether I should pull Mindy to the side and tell her about the old hobo I had met with the funny name. When the song ended, my sisters again began to fight, so I decided against it.

My sisters and I spent the rest of the afternoon on the back porch with our mum, playing "Mother May I?" and "Green Light, Yellow Light, Red Light, Stop," until the sun dipped over the horizon. We pulled the old wobbly kitchen chairs onto the back porch, sat together, talked, and watched the neighborhood kids play in the fading summer daylight. Usually, we would be amongst them, but now we were content to shout out to our friends from the porch and engage them in conversation. I pulled one of the chairs to the far end of the porch and watched below as the Cosenza brothers played boccie ball with other Italian men on their boccie ball court. I laughed as the Italian men argued and shouted good-naturedly at one another in Italian. I wished I could speak Italian to understand what they were saying.

The streetlights soon flickered on, and mothers began appearing on their porches, calling for their children to come in for the night. Shouts of protest echoed along the street as the children were not ready for the summer day to end. But eventually, the children vanished from the sidewalks, yards, and porches as nightfall chased them inside for the night.

Soon our neighborhood was swallowed up by blackness, except for puddles of light from the streetlights. Chirping crickets and the flickering glow of lightning bugs filled the warm night air creating calmness. Together, Mindy, Doreen, me, and our mum sat peacefully in the night with only the yellow glow from the kitchen's open door behind us.

"I wish it could always be like this," I said.

"Yeah, me too," Mindy and Doreen chimed in. We all looked at our mum, who smiled thinly and only stared out into the darkness.

Finally, our mum stood, then disappeared into our apartment to run a hot bath, and one at a time, Mindy, Doreen, and I took turns soaking in the old cast-iron bathtub. We emerged from the bathroom with wrinkled fingers and toes, and our faces scrubbed pink with the fresh smell of Lux soap still clinging to our skin and hair. Before bed, we relished a special dessert of butter and grape jelly spread on a slice of bread. I layered the creamy butter so thick that it hurt my teeth when I bit into it. Afterward, we washed the sweetness from our mouths with a cup of cold milk. It was a rare night for us all, and as we settled into our beds, I knew that my sisters shared the same hope as me; that in the morning when we woke, Joe would still be gone.

*****

"Ya-huh, she is too!"
"Nuh-uh, she is not!"

I sat up and rubbed my eyes. Our mum stomped into Mindy's and Doreen's room from across the hall. "Mary, mother of God, will you two *stop* your fighting!" she screeched. Mindy and Doreen fell silent, and our mum left the room. A moment later, the fighting reignited. I knew this loud commotion meant that Joe was not in the apartment, and I hurried across the hall.

Mindy was sitting on the bed, humming, pretending to read a *Betty and Veronica* comic book. She was ignoring Doreen, who was sitting on the floor, screaming at her. The more agitated Doreen became, the louder Mindy hummed, drowning her out. Finally, filled with rage, Doreen rose to her feet.

"What are yinz fighting about?" I interrupted. They both stopped and looked over at me.

"Frankie, who's prettier, Betty or Veronica?" Mindy asked, emphasizing Betty's name. Doreen immediately objected.

"That's not fair. I heard the way you said Betty, and Frankie always takes your side." Doreen seethed.

Mindy continued to sit calmly on the bed, waiting for me to answer.

I sat down next to Mindy. I knew Veronica was Doreen's favorite *Archie* comic book character. "Betty's way prettier," I said.

Doreen's face flushed hot. "You're a liar!" she screamed. "I hate yinz both!" Mindy and I both bristled. We knew our sister and understood all too well the danger we were in when she reached this level of rage. Although overmatched, Doreen sized us up. I was sure she was calculating whether the few licks or scratches she would inflict would be worth the thumping she would get in return. "Yinz both make me sick," she finally hissed, "and don't yinz think this is over, jagoffs!" She stomped from the room. Mindy and I exchanged glances and breathed a sigh of relief. Although we had avoided Doreen's wrath, for now, she had put us both on notice.

"You best watch your back," I warned my oldest sister.

"I will. Same for you."

Mindy continued to read her comic book. I heard our mum coming out of the bathroom and met her in the hall. Her face was ashen, and her eyes were damp and bloodshot. She was holding her stomach.

"You okay, Mummy?" I asked. She nodded, placing her hand on my shoulder as she walked to her bedroom.

"I'm going to be fine—just a little upset stomach from the baby. I need you to run over to Martha's store for Mummy and see if Phyllis will give me a couple of bottles of ginger ale and a pack of Pall Malls on credit," she said weakly. "Tell Phyllis I'll pay her when our check comes in next week."

"Okay." I raced out the door and ran down the steps. I pulled open the heavy doors and stepped out onto the sidewalk when I reached the bottom. Our apartment building housed two Italian grocery stores. To the right was Cosenza's, and to my left was Natalutti's, owned by our landlord, Dorothy. I turned left.

At the corner, I looked in all directions. It had been a few years since the streetcars had stopped running on Larimer Avenue, but the streetcar tracks were still there. The intersection was clear, so I darted catty-corner over to Martha's store.

The front door to Martha's store faced the corner and was wedged open. I strolled inside and immediately veered to my left toward the candy display. I pressed my nose against the glass, taking in the shelves loaded with penny candy. There were red licorice whips, Mary Jane's, Bit-O-Honey, watermelon slices, Bazooka Joe bubble gum, candy dots on sheets of paper, sweethearts, pixy sticks, little wax pop bottles with juice, wax lips, Tootsie Rolls, suckers, jawbreakers, Swedish fish, and much more. My mouth watered. I wished I had money. I stepped back from the case and looked around the store. I spotted Phyllis sitting on a stool at the end of the counter. She was a heavyset Italian lady with a friendly plump face and loose, saggy jowls. She was looking directly at me.

"What do you need, Frankie?" she asked pleasantly. I strolled over to her.

"My mum sent me over to get a couple of bottles of ginger ale and a pack of Pall Malls."

"And did your mum give you any money?" Phyllis asked dryly.

I shook my head. "Nuh-uh, she asked if you could put it on her credit. She'll pay you next week when the relief check and food stamps come in."

Phyllis grimaced. She got up, reached underneath the counter, pulled out a notebook, set it down, and opened it. She studied it briefly then looked across at me.

"Tell your mum that she already owes me $17.75, and she hasn't paid me anything in over a month." I hung my head. Phyllis sighed, then pulled out a pencil. "Tell your mum I said after today, I can't give her no more credit until she pays some of this bill."

"Okay," I mumbled.

"Go on and get your ginger ale," Phyllis said with a flip of her hand. I stepped over to the old red Coca-Cola cooler and lifted the lid. Several different types of bottled pop were in the cooler, and I quickly found the ginger ale. I pulled out two green bottles and set them up on the counter.

"It's awful early in the morning for your mum to be drinking pop," Phyllis said as she snapped open a brown paper bag and placed the bottles inside. She reached behind the counter, retrieved a red pack of Pall Mall cigarettes, and dropped them in the bag.

"She woke up this morning with a stomach ache," I said. "I think she was throwing up."

Phyllis stopped and pursed her lips disapprovingly. She shook her head again. "Your mum can barely feed you three kids as it is. How in the world is she going to feed another baby?" I shifted on my feet uncomfortably. I figured Phyllis was mad because my mum owed her so much money. Phyllis slid the bag across the counter. "Is there anything else your mum wanted?"

Before I could stop myself, I blurted out, "Oh yeah, I just about forgot, she wanted me to get fifty cents worth of penny candy too." I swallowed and fought to keep a serious face. Phyllis squinted and probed my eyes. I added for good measure, "She said maybe it would help make her stomach feel better." Satisfied, Phyllis walked to the glass candy case and opened a small brown paper bag.

"Any particular kind she wants?" she asked.

"No, she just told me to pick some out for her."

I pointed to several candies and watched Phyllis drop them into the small bag. Afterward, she placed it inside the larger bag.

"Don't forget to tell your mum what I said," said Phyllis as she again scribbled in the notebook.

"I won't." I snatched the bag from the counter and bolted from the store. The road was clear of traffic, so again, I ran catty-corner across the street to our apartment building and ducked into the stairwell. Setting the bag down on a step, I pulled out the small bag of penny candy. *Man, I should have asked for seventy-five cents' worth*, I thought to myself, shoving the bag down the front of my pants and hiding the bulge with my loose shirt. Picking up the big bag, I ran up the steps.

I put one of the ginger ales in the refrigerator in our kitchen. I pulled a bottle opener from a drawer and popped off the lid of the other bottle. I took a short swig before bringing it to my mum along with the Pall Malls.

I found her lying on the bed with a wet rag on her forehead. "Phyllis said to tell you that she can't give you no more credit until you pay some of what you owe her." I handed her the pop. "I put the other bottle in the fridge," I said.

"Mummy, why are you going to have a baby if you can't afford it?" My mum was in the middle of a swallow when ginger ale spewed from her mouth and nose, and she began to choke.

"Where did you hear that?" she asked hoarsely, trying to clear her windpipe while wiping her face.

"Phyllis said she don't see how you're going to feed another baby," I informed her.

"Well, Phyllis needs to mind her own business, especially around yinz kids," my mum snapped irritably, then she lay back on the bed and covered her face with the wet rag, so I crept from the room to find Mindy. I found her sitting on the back porch, playing a game of Jax.

"What are you on?" I asked. Mindy smiled as I sat next to her.

"Sevensies," she answered. She had all the Jax in her fist and scattered them skillfully in front of her. Then, with the little red rubber ball in the same hand, she tossed it gracefully into the air and, with great skill, swooped up a handful of Jax, then caught the ball after one bounce in the same hand. She looked over at me, grinned widely, and held out her open palm without looking.

I counted them out loud. "One, two, three, four, five, six, seven." Mindy giggled. There was hardly anyone who could beat her in Jax. I had tried several times but never succeeded. Doreen was a decent Jax player who I could win against on occasion. She had defeated Mindy once the previous summer. After the win, Doreen refused to play Mindy again. It was her way of having permanent bragging rights as she asserted herself to be the all-around Jax playing champion. It didn't matter that it was a fluke or that Mindy had beaten her a thousand times before. Doreen knew that if she played Mindy again, she would lose, and there was no way she would jeopardize her self-proclaimed title as Jax champion by agreeing to a rematch.

"Where's Doreen?" I whispered.

Mindy's eyes opened wide. She knew I was about to share a secret, and we had lots of secrets between us. Mindy loved me; she had told me so many times and trusted me more than anyone. She knew she could tell me anything, and I would die before I would betray her trust, especially if she asked me not to. On the other hand, Doreen was a blabbermouth who wouldn't hesitate to use any of Mindy's secrets against her if a disagreement or dispute arose. She was vindictive that way. There were times that Doreen hadn't even needed a reason; she tattled and betrayed Mindy's trust just for spite—that's why she no longer told her secrets to Doreen, only me. And I always returned the favor.

Mindy leaned forward. "I don't know. Why?"

I looked cautiously over my shoulder. Satisfied we were alone, I reached down the front of my pants and pulled out the bag of candy. I opened it and showed Mindy. Her face lit up.

"Frankie, where'd you get that?"

"Promise you won't tell?"

"You know I won't," Mindy reassured me with a punch to my shoulder.

"When I went over to Martha's store to get some ginger ale and cigarettes for Mum, I lied to Phyllis and told her mum wanted fifty cents' worth of penny candy too. I lifted the bag so my sister could inspect it further. "It worked. She gave it to me."

"Get out. You're not supposed to do that!" Mindy said reproachfully. "If Mummy finds out, you'll be in so much trouble, Frankie."

Mindy was right, but at the moment, I didn't care. I pulled out four pieces of candy. "Want some?"

Mindy squinted thoughtfully, then nodded. "Here you go, and remember, don't say nothing to Doreen," I cautioned, handing her two pieces. "You know she'll rat me out."

"I know that," clucked Mindy, seemingly miffed that I would even caution her. We shoved one of the candies into our mouths. We heard the clattering of patent leather shoes running up the metal steps as we started to chew. Quickly, we stuffed the other piece into our mouth, and I shoved the bag back down the front of my pants. With cheeks bulging, we chewed furiously. Doreen's head appeared at the top of the steps. We stopped chewing, and Mindy and I looked stone-faced at one another. Doreen stopped when she saw us.

"What yinz doing?" she asked. She no longer seemed angry at us from this morning.

Mindy and I knew we were in a pickle. If we opened our mouths to speak, Doreen would realize we were eating candy and demand to know where we had gotten it. Mindy and I shrugged our shoulders, and Doreen's eyebrows knitted together suspiciously.

"What do yinz have in your mouths?"

Doreen had busted us, and we knew it. It started with Mindy. A glint of infectious laughter appeared in her eyes. I tried to suppress mine, but I could feel the giddiness overtaking me. Mindy and I struggled to keep our mouths shut as the laughter grew inside us. Our chests and stomachs began to convulse as we fought to keep the laughter under control. It was useless. In a moment, we both found ourselves lying on the porch, rolling around like a couple of roly-poly bugs, laughing while making obscene guttural noises as we tried to keep our mouths shut so as not to spit out our candy.

"What's so funny?" demanded Doreen. She became suddenly defensive and irritated as she suspected we were laughing at her. "I said, what do you have in your mouths? What are yinz laughing at?"

Doreen's voice grew louder. Each time Mindy and I made eye contact, our laughter deepened, and we knew we couldn't look at one another anymore, especially if we had any hope of stopping.

I choked on my candy as I gasped for air. My side ached. Doreen was now sure we were laughing at her. I tried to stop laughing long enough to tell her different, but it was hopeless.

"Forget you, forget you both—yinz are both jagoffs. We'll see who gets the last laugh. I'm going to tell Mummy." She scowled, stomping off into the apartment, yelling for our mum.

Mindy was the only person who could make me laugh this hard. I knew I had to get away from her if I were to stop. I stood, motioned to inform her of my departure, and scampered down the steps. Mindy sat on the porch, wiping her eyes, fighting to control her pee. Laughing this hard always made her have to go pee. On Shetland Avenue, the giddiness finally left me, and I was able to chew and swallow my candy. It was early, but it seemed like the start of a perfect day.

Chapter 8

Shetland Avenue stretched north and south through Larimer. Shetland's north end ran past our apartment ending at Lenora Street, which ran east and west and wrapped around Larimer's northern outskirts. Beyond the backyards of the houses on Lenora Street, Larimer sloped off into a steep wooded hillside that eventually emptied into Negley Run Boulevard. This wooded area was a favorite place where the neighborhood kids liked to explore and play, and was where I decided to look for Donald and Ronald. I shuffled down a dirt path and saw them standing by a large rose of Sharon bush. Each of them carried a washed-out jar with nail holes punched in the lid. Inside the jars were menacing-looking bumble bees. They heard me approaching, jerked their heads in my direction, then Ronald quickly turned away.

"What's up, man? Where have you been?" asked Donald.

"Locked in my room again," I replied. Donald was one of the few I had told about Joe. Since second grade, we had been best friends, and I trusted him more than anyone outside Mindy.

"What a jagoff." Donald scowled.

"Yeah," I concurred. Ronald said nothing, and I sensed the awkwardness between us. I reached down the front of my trousers, pulled out my bag of candy, and I gave two pieces to Donald.

"Wow, thanks, man," Donald said, squinting curiously at me. I pulled out two more and held them out for Ronald.

"Here you go." I grinned amiably to ease the tension. Ronald reached tentatively for the peace offering.

"Thanks." They shoved the candy into their mouths.

"Sorry about the other day," I said.

"We're cool," Ronald answered. We sat down on the dirt path, and they both updated me on their hunt for bees throughout the morning.

We caught bees a while longer until eventually we grew bored and decided to walk back to our neighborhood, searching for something else to do. We set up rusty cans in Donald and Ronald's back-yard to sharpen our rock-throwing skills. Eventually, that too lost its excitement. Then, we sat lazily in the grass, thinking of something to do next, then I remembered Honeymarmo. Briefly, I considered telling Donald and Ronald about the old hobo. Maybe I could tell just Donald, but ultimately, I decided to keep Honeymarmo a secret—at least for now.

"Well, I got some things to do," I announced, rising to my feet.

"What do you have to do?" asked Ronald.

"Just somethings for my mum," I lied. "I'll see yinz later." I left them sitting in the grass.

Ten minutes later, I squeezed through the railing opening and scampered down the path that led under the bridge. Honeymarmo lay stretched out on his back, his head resting on his blanket roll, his eyes shut tight. I cleared my throat. Honeymarmo's eyes shot open, and he cocked his head sideways in my direction. The startled look fell away when he recognized me. The twinkle in his eyes that I remembered appeared.

"Well, if it ain't Frankie," said Honeymarmo, grinning widely. I responded with a smile. It made me feel good that the old hobo had remembered my name. "And you came to visit old Honeymarmo, did you?" He struggled to his feet and walked stiffly toward where I stood. He shook my hand. Then, we walked up the slope and sat in the dirt.

"So what've you been up to since I saw you last, Frankie?" Honeymarmo asked.

"I been locked in my room, mostly," I said, not sure why I had just confided to this old hobo I hardly knew. Maybe it was because he seemed so friendly, and after all, he had shared his story about his family with me. I felt my cheeks flush. Honeymarmo squinted curiously.

"Who locked you in your room?"

"Joe. He's my mum's boyfriend," I said. "He's a real jagoff."

Honeymarmo seemed to study me harder. "Does he do anything else to you besides lock you in your room?"

I hadn't expected him to start asking me questions, and I felt a little uncomfortable. "Yeah, I mean, sometimes he beats me too. But I'm used to it."

"You're used to it? No one should ever get used to being beat, Frankie," Honeymarmo said. I shrugged indifferently.

"What about your mother?"

"What about her?"

"Well, don't she say or do anything about this Joe fellow hitting you and locking you in your room?"

I shook my head. "Nuh-uh, I mean, she doesn't want to get cracked in the mouth. She don't say nothing because mostly she knows better."

"Huh," grunted Honeymarmo. He watched as I pulled my knees to my chin and stared solemnly toward the tracks, avoiding eye contact. "It's all right, Frankie. It ain't nothing to be embarrassed about. It certainly ain't your fault that this Joe fellow does those things to you." I sat quietly for a moment longer, then glanced at Honeymarmo.

"Yeah, but sometimes I do stupid things, things I know I shouldn't do. I don't mean to, but it seems like I just can't help it," I confessed.

"What do you mean? What kind of things?"

I shrugged. "I start fights, lie a lot, and sometimes steal things— stuff like that. Sometimes things pop in my head, and even though I know it's wrong, I just do it anyway."

Honeymarmo shook his head. "Maybe so, but everyone struggles with that, Frankie—I mean everyone. It's a condition of the human heart. None of us are perfect, and we all do bad things at times, but that alone doesn't make a person bad, including you. You're still young, so you still have time to learn how to control those urges before they become too strong in your life, before they take over completely. It sounds to me like, maybe, you just need someone in your life to teach and correct you properly."

"That don't work none," I clucked. "Joe always tells me I never learn my lesson. Then he beats me more."

"There are other ways than that, Frankie. said Honeymarmo. "Beating someone out of anger or hatred doesn't accomplish anything. As a matter of fact, it usually has the opposite effect. To be taught to do the right things and be effective, discipline must be done with love when necessary. Does that make sense to you?"

"Some, I guess."

"I know someone who can help you with this—someone who loves you and will always be there for you, no matter what."

I knew I wasn't aware of any such person, so I shot the old hobo a doubtful look. "Who?"

"God, Frankie, that's who."

I went quiet. I had never given God much thought before, and when I did, I had always thought of him as this powerful being that lived in the sky that would strike me down with lightning if I did something too terrible. I squirmed uncomfortably, and I think Honeymarmo sensed my uneasiness.

"So this Joe fellow, does he beat you often?" Honeymarmo asked.

I shrugged. "I don't know," I mumbled. I wasn't evasive; I honestly didn't know what would be considered more excessive than usual. Honeymarmo leaned back on his elbows.

"You don't like him much, do you?"

My jaw muscles tightened as I clenched my teeth. "He's a jagoff, and I can't stand him! I hate him. I hate his guts! Every day I wish he'd die!" I blurted out angrily. Honeymarmo seemed startled at my sudden outburst.

"Well, Frankie, maybe you have a right to hate this Joe fellow," Honeymarmo said softly. "The fact is there are some people, along with other things in this world that makes it hard not to hate." He paused. "I know what it's like to hate. There was a time in my life that I was filled with nothing but hate. It seemed like I was mad at

61

the whole world and everyone in it. But you know what I eventually figured out, Frankie?"

"What?"

"I figured out that to carry that kind of anger and hatred around is just poison. It poisons you and everything around you. If you carry it around long enough, it will destroy all the good in you. And you know what else?" I shook my head. "It can eventually make you the same as whatever it is that got you to hate in the first place. You become no different. Hate will destroy you and everything you love or care about. At some point, Frankie, you're going to have to deal with the hate and anger you're holding inside of you because if you don't, it will do a lot more harm to you than anything this Joe fellow ever will. One day you'll get away from all of this, including your situation with your mom's boyfriend, but Frankie, you can never get away from yourself."

I listened as Honeymarmo spoke, but my anger and hatred wouldn't allow reason to get a foothold. *This old hobo has no idea what he was talking about,* I thought. Not knowing who Joe was or what Joe was capable of, how could he understand? Joe caused me to live in fear every day. And every day, he made me feel like a coward, and it made me ashamed. Anger, hatred, and fear were woven together so tightly in my life; I couldn't distinguish one from the other most times. When I was around Joe, I felt worthless.

"Why do you think you get in fights?" Honeymarmo asked.

Not knowing, I shrugged. "Mostly to let people know I ain't afraid of them, I guess."

"You mean the way you're afraid of Joe?"

It suddenly felt like this old hobo was attacking me, so I glared grudgingly at him. It was as if he was rubbing my face in my own weakness and cowardice, and I resented him for it. "I ain't afraid of Joe! I ain't afraid of nobody!" I snapped defensively.

"I believe you ain't afraid of nobody else, but I also believe you are afraid of this Joe guy, and you know what, Frankie? That's okay. You're a kid, and he's a grown man. There's no shame in that."

I fidgeted uncomfortably in the dirt. I was regretting coming here. But at the same time, I saw the truth in what Honeymarmo was saying, even though I didn't like it.

"You know, Frankie," Honeymarmo continued, ignoring my anger, "God really can help you get rid of your fear, and anger, and hate."

"Yeah, how?" I asked sarcastically.

"Well, the first step is getting to know him," Honeymarmo said.

"Yeah?" I smirked, "and if I got to know God, would he kill Joe for me if I asked him to? Maybe strike him down with lightning or something?"

Honeymarmo frowned. "God doesn't work that way, Frankie. The Bible says his ways aren't our ways, but—"

"Then I don't want to get to know him," I said, cutting him off. "If he cared about me like you said, then he'd kill Joe dead!" Honeymarmo studied my angry face as he searched for something to say, but nothing seemed to come to him. So instead, we just sat quietly until, eventually, the anger ebbed from me.

Honeymarmo finally broke the silence. This time he didn't talk about God. He instead told me stories about his life as a boy and his experiences on the road being a hobo. Sometimes I interrupted him to ask questions, but mostly I just stretched out lazily under the bridge and listened with fascination. Honeymarmo was a good storyteller. Despite his rough weathered skin, dirty mismatched clothes, greasy hair, scruffy beard, and yellow teeth, I was fascinated by him. Except for his ragged appearance, he seemed like any other person. The more Honeymarmo talked, the more I liked him, and I no longer felt resentment; to the contrary, I began to like him even more. He was the only adult to ever talk to me like a grown-up. I pulled out some of my candy and shared it with him as we waited for a train. Before long, we heard a distant rumble. Then, the train got louder, and when it reached us, the thunderous roar from the grinding wheels and clanking of steel as the boxes rattled on the rails was deafening under the bridge. For me, it was thrilling, and I felt sad when it eventually had passed.

After a while, I felt the tug of the warm summer day. I stood. "I have to go now." I saw the disappointment on Honeymarmo's face and felt both a twinge of guilt and was sorry for him.

"Well then, thanks for visiting old Honeymarmo. I hope you'll come back and visit again soon."

"You going to stay down here much longer?" I asked.

"I'm not sure." Honeymarmo shrugged. "When I hear the tracks calling me, then I'll pack up and go. It could be tomorrow. It could be next week or longer. I just don't know."

"Okay, hope I see you later," I said. I scurried up the path toward home.

Honeymarmo followed his new friend up the path with worried eyes. He knew that if someone kicked a dog long enough, at some point, the dog would turn on the person doing the kicking. And based on the flashes of hatred and anger he saw in the boy, he couldn't help but think that time was not far off. He was curious about what this Joe fellow looked like and if he was as cruel as Frankie was telling him. He had known men like this before and thought he had a sense of Joe. Maybe he would find out for himself.

*****

On the porch below ours, Doreen was playing hopscotch. She was still carrying a grudge against Mindy and Frankie and was content to play alone. She hated how Frankie and Mindy were close and had secrets between them. They hardly ever shared any with her. Whenever she fought with either of them, they always took sides against her. And she knew they talked about her behind her back. What happened this morning with the comic books and Frankie again siding with Mindy, plus Frankie and Mindy laughing at her on the porch, was more than she could take in one day. The more she thought about it, the more she seethed. With a chunk of red brick as her marker, Doreen tossed it, then jumped into an open square. As she played, she spotted Frankie in the graveled parking lot, walking toward the back of Cosenza's store. Doreen eased slowly behind the stairs so as not to be seen.

Near the bottom of the steps that led up to the apartment was the back door to Cosenza's Italian grocery store and meat market leading to the butcher shop. Every morning, a fresh layer of sawdust was spread on the butcher shop floor to soak up the blood from butchered meat, then swept outside at the end of the day. I stood on the sawdust and inhaled deeply. I loved the smell of it.

Someone had stacked empty fish crates next to the door, along with discarded food and meat boxes. The ripe smell of fish, meat, and fat permeated the air, attracting swarms of flies. As I stepped closer, I detected the faint scent of vanilla and anise coming from some of the other boxes that once held Italian cookies. Sometimes, I got lucky and found a damaged pack of cookies that the store couldn't sell.

I began to rummage through the boxes, and I found nothing, so I straightened to leave.

My head exploded with pain. I think I shrieked. Brilliant specks of white light swarmed before my eyes, and I clutched the top of my head in agony before dropping to my knees. Everything blurred. Warm sticky wetness oozed through my hair and fingers and down my face. I blinked hard when the liquid reached my eyes. I wiped the wetness away, and that's when I saw that blood covered my hands. I heard the clicking of hard-heeled shoes running away from the porch above me. It was hard to focus as my surroundings became foggy. My heart was thumping, and my breathing became panicked. Now, the world around me began to spin, so I reached for the ground to steady myself. My hand brushed up against what felt like a brick.

Then, through the fog, I heard whistling. I squinted in that direction. A door slammed shut, then Mr. Cosenza, wearing a white butcher's apron, was stooping over me. That's when everything faded away. I felt a jarring motion as someone carried me up the steps.

"Rose! Rose!" Mr. Cosenza screamed.

"Oh god! Oh god! What happened?" My mum screamed from somewhere far away. I again went limp, and then, there was only darkness.

Someone was wiping my face with a wet rag. I opened my eyes and blinked. The large crack that ran through our living room ceiling came into focus. I felt strangely relaxed as I lay on the couch. Calmly,

I looked around and noticed I was only wearing underwear. My mum was kneeling over me. She stroked my hair while she inspected the wound on my head. The fog was gone, the spinning had stopped, and I realized that my mum was talking to someone. It was Mr. Cosenza.

"Are you sure, Rose? That gash on his head looks pretty nasty. He definitely could use some stitches, and it wouldn't be a problem. We could put him in the car and run him down to the hospital."

"I think he'll be okay, Tappo. The bleeding stopped, and he's waking up now." My mum said, biting her bottom lip. Tappo was Mr. Cosenza's nickname. "If he gets worse, I'll send Mindy or Doreen down to get you."

Mr. Cosenza nodded. Rose stood and escorted Mr. Cosenza through the living room. "Okay then, I'll be downstairs in the store if you need me. Don't let him sleep for the next few hours in case he has a concussion," Mr. Cosenza warned.

"I won't," Rose promised, "and thanks, Tappo, for everything." I listened as Mr. Cosenza's footsteps crossed the freshly mopped kitchen floor, reached the porch, then faded down the back steps. My mum reappeared in the living room, her face tight with worry as she looked down at the floor.

"Mindy, mop over Tappo's footsteps he tracked in. Hurry up. If Joe comes home and sees them, he'll probably accuse me of having a man up here and crack me one across the mouth." Mindy quickly obeyed her mum.

My mum again knelt beside me. "Frankie, what happened?" Her voice was trembling. "Who did this to you?"

"I don't know, Mum. I was standing by Cosenza's back door, and then I felt a bad pain in my head. That's all I remember."

"How do you feel now? Is your head still hurting?" she asked worriedly.

"A little, I guess."

"Tappo said you're not supposed to sleep, so try to stay awake. If the pain gets worse, let me know right away, and I'll have him drive us to the hospital. If we have to do that, I just hope Joe doesn't find out," she muttered nervously.

"Okay," I said.

I looked around the living room. Mindy had finished mopping and stood near the kitchen passageway, gnawing on her bottom lip. I gave her a weak smile. I scanned further and noticed Doreen standing by the window in the corner. She avoided eye contact with me as she shifted nervously. My eyes made their way down the length of her body until they came to rest on her black, buckled shoes.

Chapter 9

My wound healed slowly, and Doreen avoided me as much as possible. She suspected I knew that it was her that had nearly killed me, and she nervously anticipated my revenge. I knew it was wrong, but I found it deliciously gratifying to be the sole source of Doreen's paranoia. I bided my time and waited for an opportunity to present itself so I could settle the score.

During this time, our cat, Fluffy, had kittens. It happened in the morning. I, Doreen, and our mum were sitting at the kitchen table when we heard Mindy shriek as she rushed through the apartment.

"Fluffy had her babies! Fluffy had her babies! Come and look!" she screamed. Everyone followed her to the dirty clothes closet. Inside, an exhausted Fluffy lay in the corner with nine kittens snuggled up against her flabby stomach. She raised her head, squinted, then managed a faint meow before resting her head back down on the dirty clothes.

Our mum turned to me. "Frankie, go downstairs and get me a clean box from behind Cosenza's."

I dashed through the apartment and down the back steps. Behind Cosenza's store, I rummaged through some boxes until I found one suitable. I sprinted back and handed the box to my mum, and she lined it with old rags then gently placed fluffy and her babies inside. My sisters and I stared in awe at the miracle of new life and the picturesque scene of motherhood.

"They're so cute," Mindy cooed. Doreen reached in and caressed one of the kittens.

"You're not supposed to pet them yet, Doreen. They're too young," our mum scolded. Doreen jerked her hand back, and our mum looked around. "We have to find a place for them."

"How about my room?" I suggested. "They'll be out of the way, and they won't bother Joe." Our mum considered my idea.

"Okay," she agreed, carefully picking up the box with Fluffy and the kittens and carrying them into my room. She faced the three of us. "Now remember, none of yinz can pick them up for at least a couple of weeks." We all nodded.

"Fluffy made a real mess in the clothes closet. I'll have to wash all these clothes now. Doreen, I need you to start sorting them out. Mindy, hang clotheslines while I get the washing machine ready," our mum instructed.

"I always have to sort out the clothes. How come I never get to hang the clotheslines?" Doreen complained.

"Cause you're too short," Mindy reminded her.

"Nuh-uh, I am not!" Doreen shot back.

"Ya-huh, are too."

Our mum kept the washing machine in the bathroom. It was cylinder-shaped with wheels, and it had a rubber hose that drained the dirty water into the bathtub. When turned on, it shook and rattled noisily. It was yellow and white, and the top had two stacked motorized rubber rollers where wet clothes were hand-fed between to wring out the excess water before being hung up to dry.

Our mum brought out baskets of washed clothes to Mindy and Doreen, who hung them on the clotheslines. I lay on the floor in my room next to Fluffy and her kittens. The loud hum of the washing machine reverberated throughout the apartment.

The front hallway door opened, and Joe's large frame loomed menacingly in the doorway. Because of the rattling washing machine and slurping from the hose as it drained in the tub, no one had heard his footsteps in the stairwell. He stepped into the apartment and looked disgustedly at the hanging laundry. His eyes settled on Mindy and Doreen.

"Get out of my sight," he growled. Mindy and Doreen, sitting cross-legged on the floor, sprang to their feet and scurried to their room. Joe slammed the door shut. Our mum appeared in the hall. I lay motionless on the floor, and I could see them both from my vantage point. Joe faced our mum, and I held my breath, hoping Joe would not look in my direction.

Joe pointed to the hanging laundry. "What's all this?"

"Fluffy had her kittens in the clothes closet this morning, so I have to wash them. It was a mess, and I didn't want the clothes to get ruined," explained our mum.

Joe grimaced. "Go get me something to eat," he finally said, turning from her toward their bedroom. *Oh, please God, don't let him turn around*, I thought to myself, knowing that if Joe didn't see me, I could sneak down the passageway and escape out the kitchen door. Then, Fluffy, who had climbed from the box and now sat next to me, decided to meow. I glanced down, and Fluffy was staring up at me. She meowed again. "Shush," I whispered. I looked up, and Joe was staring directly at me. He strolled over, stood in the doorway, and looked disdainfully between Fluffy and me and the box full of kittens. He reached in, pulled the door shut, and locked it without saying a word. I slumped against the wall and glared at the door. My teeth clenched.

"I hate you! I hate your guts!" I muttered under my breath toward the door and Joe. Then, Fluffy meowed again. My eyes flashed angrily at her. It was her fault. If she hadn't meowed, I would have been all right; I would have been able to slip away. Angrily, I reached over and slapped her. Fluffy bolted across the room, searching to escape, but there was no place to go or hide. She turned toward me, arched her back, then hissed. I felt no remorse, and I didn't care if I had hurt her. I just stared at her. Then, I realized I was grinning.

*****

It took two days before I mustered enough courage to escape. Early morning always offered the best opportunity not to get caught. I pulled the piece of cardboard from the old box, worked it into the crack between the door and the door jamb, and slid the cardboard up until I lifted the hook latch out of its locked position. A couple of minutes later, I was sprinting across the graveled parking lot away from our apartment.

*****

Joe woke early with a hacking cough, sat up, swung his legs off the side of the bed, stood, and walked over to the dresser. He tapped the open end of a cigarette pack twice against his palm, extracted a cigarette with his lips, struck a match, then lit it. A thick plume of smoke snorted from his hawk-like nose. His coughing stopped. Grabbing an ashtray from the dresser, he walked from the room. Fifteen minutes later, he emerged from the bathroom. He was almost to his bedroom when he stopped, turned, and walked across the hall to the creep's room. He unhooked the latch, pushed the door open, and stepped inside.

Joe scanned the room. *The bonehead had gotten out, and he couldn't have done it alone,* he thought. One or both of his sisters had to have helped him. Maybe their fear of him was waning and needed to be reinforced. If respect and fear of him were to be maintained, the little brats, all of them, would have to pay. He reemerged from the room angrily, but his footsteps were heavy with purpose this time. He walked directly to Mindy's and Doreen's bedroom.

As the two snored, he reached down, grabbed each of them by the hair, one in each hand, and yanked them from the bed. "Don't pretend to be sleeping!" he growled, dragging them from the bedroom. "You little sluts think I'm stupid, don't you?"

As their hair ripped from their scalp, their grogginess vanished, and they whimpered from the pain. Their eyes were now wide with panic and confusion. Rose was still in bed sleeping and was jarred awake by her daughters' distraught cries as Joe dragged them into their bedroom. His powerful forearm muscles bulged as he lifted them by the hair to where only the balls of their feet touched the floor. He flung them across the room, and they crumbled to the floor in a heap.

Joe stomped from the room and reappeared a moment later, carrying a thick wood board. When Mindy and Doreen saw it, they began to cry, knowing what was coming next. As Joe stepped toward them, their cries turned into terror-filled sobs.

"No, no! Please! Please! Please!" They both begged.

Rose, still confused, started to protest, but Joe menacingly showed her the back of his hand. "Shut your mouth!" he barked. Rose recognized the dangerous tone and, fearful of his slap, or worse, shut her mouth obediently. Joe turned back toward Mindy and Doreen; his tight lips stretched across his clenched teeth with the sinister gap as he raised the board.

*****

On Larimer Avenue, I turned right and quickened my pace toward East Liberty. It took me about ten minutes before reaching my destination a block before East Liberty Boulevard. My mum called this the bad part of our neighborhood, mainly because it usually occurred here when something terrible happened, like a stabbing or shooting. Larimer had gotten its notorious reputation from this area, where most bars were. I had spied Joe here many times, standing around on the corners or frequenting the bars.

This early in the morning, the streets were quiet. I hurried past several bars, crossed the road, and slipped down an alley. I arrived at the rear of a small Italian bakery and made my way to some old garbage cans located directly across from a bread delivery truck. I crouched down behind the garbage cans and waited. Before long, the bakery's back door opened, and a short, stocky man with hairy forearms appeared. He had a flour-smudged face and wore a dirty white apron. He walked to the rear of the bread truck and noisily jerked up its rolling metal door. He disappeared back into the bakery, and I heard the rattling of a bakery cart rolling across the concrete floor. The baker reemerged in the alley, pushing a cart loaded with fresh Italian bread packaged in white paper sleeves. He placed the trays of Italian bread on metal racks in the back of the truck. I inhaled deeply. The smell of fresh-baked bread saturated the air. My stomach tightened, and my mouth watered with anticipation.

Once empty, the man wheeled the cart back into the bakery. I sprang from my hiding place and darted toward the truck, barely breaking stride as I reached inside, grabbed two loaves of bread, and accelerated into a full sprint up the alley.

"Stop, you thief," a man's voice with a thick Italian accent rang out. I heard someone running behind me.

"You come'a back'a here," shouted the man. "If I catch'a you, I'm'a gonna break'a you neck." My legs pumped faster. I reached Larimer Avenue, veered right, and sprinted toward home. Knowing I couldn't stay on Larimer Avenue for long, I ran for one whole block, crossed the street, and ducked down a side street. I cut through a yard to another side street, through another yard, and into an alley. Then, with my legs now burning and my lungs feeling like they would burst, I collapsed to the ground behind a large overgrown rose of Sharon bush next to a garage and listened for someone still chasing me.

All I heard was my labored breath and blood pounding in my ears. I was too spent to move. Gradually, my breathing grew shallow, and my heartbeat slowed. I mustered the energy and courage to peek out from behind the rose of Sharon bush but saw no one. Cautiously, I stood and stepped back into the alley as I broke off a chunk of Italian bread and shoved it into my mouth. It was warm, and the soft doughy texture melted deliciously over my tongue. I broke off an even bigger piece and again shoved it into my mouth until my cheeks bulged. Tenderly I chewed, savoring the flavor as I walked in the direction of our apartment.

*****

"Which one of you little sluts did it?" Joe snarled.

Mindy's and Doreen's eyes were shiny with terror.

"I'm only going to ask you one more time," he warned, pointing the board directly at them. "Which one of you little whores let the creep out of his room?" Mindy and Doreen stared back vacantly. When neither answered, Joe moved quickly toward Mindy first, grabbed her wrist, yanked her off the floor, and dangled her out in front of him with only her toes touching the floor.

"No, please! Please! I didn't—" She screamed. The board flashed savagely through the air and repeatedly found its mark on Mindy's thighs and backside. As it impacted her bare flesh, it made a sickening slapping sound that echoed through the apartment. Immediately, deep purple welts began to appear on her white fleshy legs. The onslaught continued for a full minute. Finally, when his arm tired from holding her, Joe let go, and Mindy collapsed to the floor like a rag doll. Her tormented sobs were so deep that they sucked the breath out of her. Her lungs gasped desperately for air; she grasped the back of her legs and buttocks and crawled toward Doreen.

"Please, no! Please, no! Please, no!" Doreen cried as he turned his attention to her. Tears streamed down her face as she begged him not to beat her. Joe snatched her by the arm and lifted her high into the air. Again, the board flashed angrily through the air, repeatedly finding its mark. Since Doreen was lighter, Joe prolonged his brutal onslaught because he could hold her in the air longer. Primitive sobs erupted from deep inside her. Finally, he dropped her to the floor, and she dragged herself across the floor to Mindy. Sporadically, she sucked for air between sobs. The sisters huddled together, crying uncontrollably. The entire apartment reverberated with the sounds of their tortured howls and screams. Rose squirmed helplessly on the bed.

"Now, I'm going to ask you again. Who let the bonehead out?" Joe asked, stepping toward them. Mindy's and Doreen's pain was so great that they could only answer with strangled cries. Their lungs still fought for oxygen.

Joe leered coldly down at the two of them; his thin lips curled cruelly. "So you still don't want to answer me, huh?" He reached down, grabbed Mindy by the wrist, and the second round of savage beatings commenced.

After the third round of beatings, Joe decided maybe the little brats didn't have anything to do with the bonehead getting out of his room, or else they would have confessed by now.

"Go on, get out of my sight." Barely able to stand, Mindy and Doreen struggled to their feet. Their legs and buttocks burned hot and stung like the stabbing of a thousand needles. They limped to their room. Their breath still came in spasms, and they couldn't control their sobs.

Once they had left the room, Joe walked over to the dresser, pulled out a cigarette, and lit it. He turned to Rose, still holding the board, pointing it at her.

"Did you know he was gone? Huh? Did you let the little creep out?" he asked accusingly.

"No, I didn't let him out, Joe." Her voice quivered. His black eyes bored straight through her.

"I better not find out that you did. Now go make me some coffee." He tossed the board on the bed next to her, turned, and opened a dresser drawer. He pulled out a shirt.

Rose slid out of bed obediently and walked shakily to the kitchen. She rinsed out the coffee pot and filled it with water. As Rose scooped coffee into the brew basket, coffee grounds spilled over the stove. She held her hands out in front of her, and they were quaking violently.

Chapter 10

I t was still early morning, so all was quiet. I decided to see if Honeymarmo was still under Larimer Bridge, so I maneuvered stealthily through our neighborhood. I ducked behind several bushes and hedges to stay hidden from our apartment, knowing if Joe saw me, I'd be dead. I had already devoured the first loaf of bread and started on the second. After eating some of the second loaf, I pressed my hand against my swollen stomach, and I couldn't eat another bite, so I wrapped up the rest.

I reached the gap in the bridge railing, squeezed through, and scampered down the path. Honeymarmo was curled on his side, sleeping in the dirt with his head on his blanket roll. My footsteps startled him awake, and he sat erect. He grinned when he saw me.

"Well now, good morning Frankie," he said, "You're up and about early this morning, aren't you?"

I nodded. "Yeah, I guess so." I walked over and handed Honeymarmo the wrapped-up bread.

"What's this?" asked Honeymarmo.

"It's some fresh-made Italian bread," I answered. Honeymarmo opened it and took a deep whiff.

"Now, where would you get this so early in the morning?" he asked. I hadn't prepared for the question, so I had to think fast.

"Some men at the bakery up the street gave it to me," I lied.

"They gave it to you? Just like that?"

"Well, no, not just like that," I said, shuffling uncomfortably. "I help them load their truck in the morning sometimes, and they give me a couple of loaves of bread for helping them. That's why I'm up so early." I grinned to better sell my lie. Honeymarmo smiled back. "Anyways," I continued, "I couldn't finish two whole loaves, and I didn't want to throw the rest away, so I thought you might want it."

Honeymarmo smiled appreciatively. "Why, thank you, Frankie." He closed his eyes, bowed his head, and said, "Thank you, Lord, for this bread and for Frankie who brung it. Help me also, Lord, to always be mindful that this is the bread that will only sustain my body, whereas you are the true bread that has given me life everlasting. Amen."

As Honeymarmo shoved a piece of bread into his mouth, I felt a rare twinge of guilt. I turned my back to the old hobo and pretended to be interested in something further down the tracks.

Honeymarmo gave a gratified sigh. "I have to say that was about the best punk I've ever eaten." I turned back around and lowered myself in the dirt. The guilt from before had passed. I picked up a stick and began scratching the ground.

"Did that Joe fellow have you locked up again?"

I nodded. "Yeah." I felt his probing eyes. I saw Honeymarmo reach into his bedroll and pull out his Bible from my peripheral vision.

"You know, your situation with this Joe fellow reminds me of a story from the Old Testament," he said.

"What's that?"

"What's what? You mean the Old Testament?" I nodded, feeling suddenly stupid like I did at school when I didn't know the answer to a question that everyone else knew. "Well, the Old Testament is the oldest part of the Bible," explained Honeymarmo. He seemed to sense my embarrassment. "Shoot, that's all right," he quickly added. "The truth is most grown-ups don't know the difference between the Old Testament and New Testament either.

"Anyway, there's this story in here about this boy who would one day become a great king." He began to thumb through the pages. "This boy's name was David, and he was just a lowly shepherd. One day the army of Israel—that was where he was from—went to war with this other tribe called the Philistines. Now, this other tribe had a fierce warrior who was a giant of a man that no one had ever defeated in battle before. This giant's name was Goliath, and he was eight or nine feet tall." I watched in amazement as Honeymarmo stretched his hands up toward the sky to elaborate on Goliath's enormous stature.

"Wow, that's even bigger than Joe," I quipped.

"Way bigger!" Honeymarmo said. "Anyway, every day Goliath would walk down into a valley and challenge the soldiers of Israel to fight him, but none of them would go because they were all too afraid. But David, you see, had a special relationship with God, so he wasn't scared at all. He trusted that God would help protect him, so when he saw that not even one soldier had enough courage to fight Goliath, he marched right down into the valley to fight him himself." Honeymarmo paused. He leaned back on his elbows, stretched out his legs, crossed his bare ankles, and stared up into the rafters.

"So what happened?"

Honeymarmo gave me a wink. "Well, when Goliath saw David coming, he almost busted a gut laughing, thinking this must be a joke. You see, David was so scrawny he couldn't even lift a shield or wield a sword, so he had nothing with him to fight Goliath except for an old slingshot."

"Get out!"

"No, it's true," said Honeymarmo. "So while Goliath stood laughing at him, David pulled out his trusty slingshot, found three smooth stones, placed one of them into his slingshot, took dead aim, then let the stone lose. Well, sir, God guided that stone, and it hit Goliath so hard right between the eyes that Goliath dropped dead right there on the spot."

"Get out. You mean he really killed him?"

"Yes, sir, dead as a doornail." Honeymarmo sat back up. "Then, David walked over to Goliath, and even though he could barely lift it, he picked up Goliath's sword and cut the giant's head clean off. He lifted up the head and held it up for all the Philistine army to see. When they saw it, they got so scared that they all ran away, and David, because of his faith and trust and his love for God, gave the army of Israel a great victory."

"C'mon, is that story true?" I clucked skeptically.

"Yep." Honeymarmo nodded emphatically. "If it's in the Bible, then it really happened."

I rubbed my face and stared thoughtfully out at the tracks. "Joe is kind of like Goliath, ain't he?"

Honeymarmo grinned at my inference and nodded slightly. "You might say that."

"Are you saying I should challenge Joe like David did Goliath?" I asked, a little confused at the comparison.

Honeymarmo's grin vanished. "No, Frankie, that's not what I'm saying. You see, David first trusted God, and with God on his side, he achieved a great victory in his life. With God on his side, he was able to find the courage and a way to defeat his enemy. Frankie, God seeks you out every day. You just have to respond to him, then trust he will be there for you too."

"I don't know." My forehead wrinkled, and I squinted in thought. "Like I said already, God ain't never helped me before."

Honeymarmo placed his hand gently on my shoulder. "I think God will help you, but first, you have to give him a chance. You have to seek a relationship with him. Frankie, God is not a rabbit's foot that you rub, hoping he will grant your wish. God wants a real relationship with you through his son. When that happens, then anything is possible. There are lots of ways God can help you out of your situation if you trust him, but first, you have to allow God to help change you so you can make better choices." Honeymarmo paused. "Just promise me you'll think about it some more."

"Okay, I will," I promised. Honeymarmo grinned wide.

"Good." He extended his Bible. "I want you to take this." At first, I stared at it, not sure I wanted to take it. "Go on, it's okay," Honeymarmo assured me. "You can bring it back in a day or two." I took it from him, and at that moment, I felt a closeness and trust toward Honeymarmo like I had never experienced with another adult before.

Chapter 11

I gripped the Bible tightly while walking around with it the rest of the morning. On Shetland Avenue, I plopped down on the curb as I considered places to stash it. After a few moments, an idea came to me. Jumping to my feet, I sprinted toward one of the vacant apartments where I lived. I reached the second-floor porch winded, slid open a window, and climbed inside. I searched around and settled on a spot under the kitchen sink to hide the Bible. I gathered some old newspapers strewn about and covered it up. I climbed back through the window, pushed it shut, and walked quickly to the stairs that stretched up to my apartment.

"Frankie!"

I spun to face my mum, standing at the top of the stairs. Her eyes flashed angrily at me, and instantly I knew Joe had discovered me gone. As she started down the steps toward me, I glanced over my shoulder to flee, a tactic I had used in the past to avoid immediate punishment but decided against it.

Displaying anger did not come naturally to our mum, and efforts to discipline us made her uncomfortable. As she reached the landing, I sensed something was different this time.

"You little jagoff, how did you get out of your room?" Her voice was trembling with anger. "You're in so much trouble!" I shut my mouth and said nothing, feeling a sharp sting from her slur.

"What am I going to do with you? Do you know how much trouble you caused?" she scolded me. She reached out and gripped my arm.

"Joe found you gone this morning, and he beat your sisters black and blue because he thought they let you out of your room." It was easy for me to envision the beating session I knew all too well, and I felt my face flush hot.

"Frankie, how did you get out of your room? I know your sisters didn't let you out. You tell me right now," demanded my mum, "and don't you lie to me." All I felt was my hatred and anger for Joe for what he had done to my sisters. Her threats and warnings meant nothing to me, and I knew I wouldn't tell her how I had gotten out.

I jerked loose from her grip. "I just pulled the door this morning, and someone had already unlocked it," I lied.

My mum frowned. "Oh, for Christ's sake, don't go there with me! I said, don't you lie!"

"I ain't lying!" I shouted. "Maybe Joe forgot to lock it last night after he checked up on me. For real, Mum, he was so high he could hardly walk."

"You know Joe didn't leave it unlocked."

"How do I know that?" I snapped. "How do you know that, Mum, huh? How do you know he didn't do it on purpose?"

"What? Joe wouldn't—"

"Joe, wouldn't what?" I interrupted. "Joe wouldn't do something like that? Huh? Is that what you're saying? I'm saying he did, and he did it just so he could have another reason to beat us."

I could see my mum thinking now as she stared at me. "I don't believe—," she started to say, but I again cut her off.

"Oh, come on, Mum, you don't believe what? Huh? You don't believe Joe would do something like that? Oh yeah, I forgot, he doesn't need a reason to beat us. He can just do that whenever he feels like it, can't he, Mum?" I had taken dead aim with my accusation, and by the wounded look on my mum's face, it had hit its target.

I watched the anger drain from my mum as she reached for the railing and sat weakly down on one of the steps. I did feel some remorse for my words and even had an impulse to comfort her, but I couldn't bring myself to do it.

"Get on up to your room," my mum finally murmured feebly.

I ran up the steps, and then I heard my mum in the kitchen a short while later from my room. She turned on the spigot, and I heard her crying over the sound of gushing water.

I decided to look in on my sisters. I crept across the hall and peeked inside their bedroom. Mindy was lying on the bed sleeping with her back to me; angry red and dark purple welts covered her legs. Doreen leaned against the metal radiator staring out the window. She turned to look at me as I stepped through the door.

We stared at one another. "I'm sorry I got yinz in trouble," I said.

Doreen shrugged. "It don't matter. Even if I knew how you got out, I wouldn't have told him nothing—even if he killed me dead." She grimaced. "I hate his guts."

I turned to leave, then stopped. "Doreen, I ain't going to get you back no more for what you did to me with the brick."

Doreen grinned impishly. "I don't know what you're talking about, and even if I did, you couldn't anyway even if you tried," she quipped.

"Whatever!" I snickered. At that instant, I felt close to Doreen. Although, mostly, she was hard to figure out. There were times when I despised her, primarily because of her aversion to reason, her natural mean streak, and her spiteful ways. Then, there were times like this that I felt affection for her as much as I did for Mindy, maybe even more. She was a mystery to me. At times she was willing to risk life and limb to come to my aid as she did with Charles, but then there were those times when she could inflict serious injury like dropping a brick on my head. Yet despite it all, I was glad she was my sister. There was no person better to have on my side if I needed someone to be there for me in a pinch. *She sure is fickle,* I thought.

Once in the hall, I stood for a moment, then hurried into our mum's room and walked to the other side of the bed where Joe usually slept. I lifted the mattress and stared down at Joe's pistol. I reached down and stroked it, debating within myself. Finally, I pulled my empty hand back, lowered the mattress, and walked away.

As I reached my bedroom door, I felt queasy with fear, knowing what was coming. I could turn and run, and no one could stop me, but I knew that if I did, Joe's retribution could once again fall upon my sisters and my mum. Besides, my escape would only be temporary. My shoulders slumped, and I sighed as I pushed open my door. I sat in the corner on the floor with Fluffy and her kittens, waiting for Joe to get home to administer my beating.

*****

I jerked my chin up off my chest and looked around the room groggily. I had drifted off to sleep, but something had woken me. Joe's footsteps echoed in the stairwell as he climbed the steps. In the hallway, the front door banged open, then rattled shut. Joe walked directly to my room and pushed open the door. I averted my eyes to the floor but could feel Joe's fierce gaze boring into me. Leaving the door open, Joe turned and walked into his bedroom and was returning when my mum intercepted him in the hall.

"No, you ain't doing it," she said.

Joe stopped abruptly. "What did you say to me?" His voice was menacing as he dared my mum to repeat herself.

My mum stood her ground. "I mean it. You ain't beating him." Then, I heard the loud smack. My mum gasped as she stumbled back and fell to the floor. She then staggered to her feet and stormed into her bedroom. I heard dresser drawers opening and slamming shut as my mum emptied them of her clothes and stacked them on the bed. Joe stood frozen, seemingly undecided about his next move. Finally, he walked into their bedroom.

"What do you think you're doing?" he demanded. My mum didn't answer. She sniffled, then pulled an old suitcase out from under the bed and began to pack.

"Oh, so you're not talking to me now, is that it?" Joe asked sardonically. My mum again ignored him. "I said, what do you think you're doing? Where do you think you're going?"

"I'm leaving! Me and the kids are going to my sister's." Her tone carried a coldness I couldn't remember hearing before, and it seemed to confound Joe.

"Oh, come on." His voice softened a bit. "Just because of that little smack? What do you want me to say? I'm sorry? Okay, I'm sorry." The door to their room shut, muffling their conversation. Eventually, the conversation stopped altogether.

A couple of hours passed before their bedroom door opened. Joe's bare feet approached. I stiffened, expecting the worse. My door pushed open, and Joe stood in the doorway in his boxers, staring down at me. My mum appeared at Joe's side wearing her old tattered robe. Joe grinned crookedly, but his black eyes remained stolid and cold.

"Go on out and play, bonehead," he said. Although I was afraid to move, I stole a glance toward my mum, and she grinned warmly at me.

"Go ahead, Frankie," she said, "It's okay." I stood cautiously.

"Yeah, go ahead, Frankie," snickered Joe mockingly. "It's okay." He stepped to one side to let me pass. I squeezed between him and the door and tensed for the smack to the back of my head. It didn't happen, so I raced down the passageway to the living room. My mum followed me, and Joe went back to the bedroom. In the kitchen, my mum stopped me and asked if I wanted something to eat. I shook my head. I needed to get out of the apartment as fast as possible before Joe changed his mind. So I dashed out the kitchen door and started down the steps.

"Frankie?" my mum yelled after me, and I turned and looked up at her standing at the top of the steps. "Be home before the street-lights come on."

"Okay," I shouted back. I sprinted down the remaining steps, never looking back, and disappeared into the familiar embrace of Larimer.

Chapter 12

For the next few days, my room remained unlocked. I woke in the mornings and moved freely around the apartment, while Joe mostly stayed in his bedroom drinking coffee, smoking cigarettes, and blowing his nose incessantly into a dirty hanky that he always carried with him. Despite my newly found freedom, I remained leery; I understood all too well that my current situation was only temporary. It didn't take long for Joe to prove me right.

I had emerged from my room to go to the bathroom. Joe was in the hallway and moved intentionally in my path, so I attempted to walk around him. Joe again stepped in front of me. He was naked except for a pair of boxers, and he held a lit cigarette and a cup of coffee. I glanced up into a hate-filled glare and froze, except for my left leg, which began to tremble.

"Did I give you permission to look at me, freak?" Joe growled. I stood still, afraid to answer. "I asked you a question, jagoff."

"No," I finally mumbled.

"So what are you looking at?"

"Nothing."

"Oh, so I'm nothing now, is that right, huh?" Joe's coffee-stained teeth clenched as he waited for a response. I stood silent. Joe leaned forward and whispered harshly into my ear. "You think you own this place now, don't you? You're the king, right? You just come and go as you please. Is that how you think it works, freak?" I didn't answer. "What did you say to your mum, huh, you little loser?" His hot breath stunk of coffee and cigarettes. I raised my eyes and found myself staring at a crude bird tattoo on Joe's enormous chest, only inches from my face. "Oh, I see, you just ignore me now since you think I'm nothing, is that it? It doesn't matter. Whatever it was you said, you'll never turn her against me. You see, she'll never want you as much as she wants me. You know that, don't you, jagoff?" Joe reached out and jammed the hot cherry of his lit cigarette into my cheek.

"Uhhhh!" I cried out as I recoiled back and brushed the hot ash off my face. I cupped my hand over the fresh burn.

"How about being a little more careful, bonehead, and watch where you're walking," Joe grunted callously. "I hope you accidentally walking into my cigarette didn't burn you too bad." He gave a low guttural laugh showing the gap between his front teeth, which made him look even more menacing, then shoved past me, almost knocking me down. I stood there in the hallway for a few seconds, gently touching the raw burn on my cheek before gathering enough nerve to move. I hurried to my room. I thought hard about it but eventually decided not to tell my mum about what happened, mostly because, in the end, I knew nothing would change, and it would only make things worse for all of us.

*****

I left the apartment shaken, and the burn on my cheek had started to blister. Unable to find any of my friends, I found an old rubber ball in the alley across the street and began throwing it against the wall of an abandoned garage. I pitched the ball too high against the wall on one throw, and the ball ricochet over my head. It sailed over some hedges behind me and landed under a pine tree in someone's front yard. I walked around to the sidewalk, pushed open the gate, and slipped into the yard. I spotted my ball and dashed for it.

"Hey, what are you doing?" It was a girl's voice.

I startled and jerked my head in the direction of the porch. She sat on her porch glider, smiling down at me, and I immediately recognized her. Like most of the kids in my neighborhood, she was black, had shiny, thick hair that came to her shoulders, and wore a white headband. Her smooth brown face was radiant, and her large doe-like eyes reflected a glint of amusement as she stared at me.

I didn't answer her.

"Your name is Frankie, isn't it?" she asked. Her voice was soft. I nodded.

"You don't talk much, do you?" She laughed.

"I don't know." I shrugged stupidly.

"I bet you don't even know my name," she asked playfully.

"Yeah, I do," I replied. "It's Bunny." I mainly had seen her at school on the playground, but she rarely came outside to play with the other kids in the neighborhood.

"Well, how come you never talked to me before?" Bunny asked teasingly.

"I guess because I heard you were stuck up," I answered bluntly. Her eyes widened to match her smile, and then she laughed loudly again. It was an infectious laugh.

"You're funny," Bunny said. "Do I seem stuck up to you?"

"I don't know, not really, I guess." I shoved my hands uncomfortably in my pockets.

"You can come up here on the porch," Bunny said invitingly. I picked up the ball and climbed the steps. Bunny patted the space next to her on the glider, and I timidly sat down. I began to fidget in the seat. I wanted to talk, but I couldn't think of anything to say.

"What happened to your face?" she asked concernedly.

I gingerly touched the cigarette burn. "I accidentally got burned by a cigarette, that's all," I mumbled.

"Does it hurt?"

"Not really. I've had worse," I said. I think Bunny sensed something in my tone, so she decided not to pursue it further.

"You know, we were in Mrs. Piper's class together way back in first grade," she informed me.

"Get out. I don't remember that."

"It's true, and I remember you used to always get in trouble and would have to stay after school." Bunny giggled.

"I still have to, sometimes." I grinned.

"Well, I guess some things never change."

"No, I guess not." We both laughed. Truthfully, I loved her laugh, and I found myself sneaking glimpses of her brown, liquid eyes, smooth face, full lips, and perfect teeth when she wasn't looking. I had to fight to keep from staring at her. Bunny loved to talk, and I admired that she was so good at it. Soon, her easygoing nature had drawn me into her world, and I found myself talking effortlessly with her. We talked about anything and everything, and none of it was annoying, not like it was with most girls I had chatted with in the past. According to Bunny, we had a lot in common. I hadn't thought about it, but it must have been true since Bunny said it.

Without warning, the screen door opened, and we both found ourselves looking up at Bunny's mom. She was pretty like Bunny, except older. Bunny's mum studied me.

"I was wondering who you were talking to, Bunny," she finally said. "So who's this?"

"Mom, this is Frankie. He's in my class at school," Bunny lied, which instantly made me like her even more.

Bunny's mum continued to squint down at me. "Aren't you that boy who lives in the apartment across the street?" She pointed up toward my back porch.

"Yeah, that's me," I replied.

"I thought so," Bunny's mum said. She continued to stare. I squirmed. "Well, Frankie, did you eat yet? If not, I was just going to fix Bunny her lunch, and you're more than welcome to join her," she said. Bunny bumped my leg with her knee.

"No, I didn't eat yet," I informed her. I was starving.

"Well, come on then, I'll fix you a plate too." She held the screen door open for us. We both slid off the porch glider and walked into the house. Bunny's mum made us chipped ham sandwiches with cookies and a tall glass of ice-cold milk in the kitchen. Bunny and I sat across from each other, watching each other eat, occasionally giggling at one another. Even watching her eat, especially how she took such small delicate bites, made me mushy inside.

After lunch, we went to her room to play. It was spectacular. She had curtains and a bedspread that matched her pillows. She had spotless white furniture, and her dresser had a lamp and pictures and knickknacks, all neatly arranged. I had never seen anything like it before. We sat on a big throw rug on the floor next to Bunny's bed, and she taught me how to play Parcheesi. Finally, her mum came in and told her to clean her room.

"Maybe Frankie can help you," her mum suggested, smiling at me.

"Okay," I agreed after mulling it over. After Bunny's mum left the room, we began picking up and putting away Bunny's things.

At some point, we found ourselves kneeling on opposite sides of Bunny's bed. We lifted the bedspread edges and laughed as we spied one another across the floor underneath the bed. We seemed to read one another's minds, and we crawled under the bed and met in the middle. It was cool under her bed, and we stared at one another in the semidarkness. Her face had an ethereal glow that made me warm inside. Then, without warning, Bunny leaned forward and kissed me full on the lips. It only lasted a couple of seconds, but the touch of her soft lips against mine made my entire body tingle. My heart raced, and I stopped breathing for fear that the glorious feeling surging within me would go away if I exhaled.

"I like you," whispered Bunny.

"I like you too," I whispered back.

After a few seconds, Bunny pouted. "Aren't you going to kiss me back?" she asked.

I eagerly leaned forward and reciprocated, giving her a quick peck on the lips. It felt awkward. We lay there, tenderly staring at one another, until we heard the creaking of floorboards as Bunny's mother walked across the living room floor. We darted out from under the bed just before her mother stepped into the room.

"Bunny, you and I need to go do some shopping, so I'm afraid Frankie will have to go now," she announced pleasantly.

"Yes, ma'am," Bunny answered as her mum left the room. Bunny and I stared at one another the way two people do who share a secret. We walked to the front door. The truth was, I didn't want to leave.

"Can I come over again?" I asked.

"You better," she teased. She turned to make sure her mum wasn't looking, then gave me a quick kiss on the cheek. I seemed to float through the front door and down the front walkway until I finally stood outside the gate. I felt warm inside, yet scared like I did when I teetered precariously on the railing of Larimer Bridge a hundred feet above the ground. I looked at Bunny one last time, we waived at one another, and then with a burst of energy, I sprinted up the street.

*****

I decided to retrieve Honeymarmo's Bible the next day and risk sneaking it into my room. I knew if Doreen saw me with it, there was a good chance she would try and steal it when I wasn't around. I knew I could trust Mindy, though. I found her playing hopscotch with her best friend, Carletta, just up the street. I hollered out to her from the back porch, and when she spotted me, I motioned her over. She said something to Carletta, then ran over to me.

"What's up?" she asked.

"C'mon, follow me."

"Where are we going?"

"Just come on, I want to show you something," I said. Mindy followed me to the second-floor porch of our apartment building. We climbed through a window into the abandoned apartment and made our way into the kitchen. From under the kitchen sink, I retrieved the Bible.

"I found this the other day," I lied, holding it out for my sister. I wasn't sure if I was ready to tell her about Honeymarmo, if at all.

Mindy's eyes were wide with anticipation. "What is it?" she asked, taking the book from my hand and turning it face-up. The words *Holy Bible* and a large cross reflected up at her in gold etching. I looked over at my sister's face thinking she would be impressed, but instead, I became alarmed by her expression. Her eyes filled with tears, then became angry; her bottom lip began to quiver. Without warning, she flung the Bible across the room against the wall.

"Min, why'd you do that?" I blurted out. Mindy didn't answer but instead stared back at me with anguish as she fought to keep her emotions under control. I had never seen her like this before. Then, her stomach heaved as she began to sob. She spun abruptly and ran toward the open window.

"Min, what's the matter?" I yelled after her just as she climbed through. I watched as she rushed down the back stairs. I just stood there in the empty kitchen, distraught and confused at my sister's painful expression and emotional outburst. I walked over, picked up the Bible from the floor, and dusted it off. It didn't seem to be damaged. I inspected it closely to see if maybe there was something I hadn't seen before that would make my sister react the way she did, and I saw nothing. It didn't make sense. I shoved the Bible down the front of my pants, covered it with my shirt, then climbed through the open window, closing it behind me.

In my room, I shut my bedroom door, pulled out the Bible, and sat on the floor next to the box where the kittens snuggled inside, fast asleep. I caressed the cover curiously, still trying to figure out why it had made Mindy so upset. I opened it, thumbed through the pages, and found a maple leaf marking a Bible page called Judges. I began to read. It was all about some powerful guy named Samson. Before long, I was fully engrossed in the story and found I couldn't put the book down. It read a little funny with peculiar words like *thee* and *thou* and other unfamiliar phrases, but I soon finished the story. I leaned back against the wall and allowed my imagination to take over. This story was different than the comic book superheroes I usually read about in comic books. Maybe it was because Samson felt like a real person. After all, Honeymarmo said it was true if it was in the Bible. I began to wonder what it would be like to have such strength, and I even pondered whether God would consider making me that strong. Why wouldn't he, especially if I promised God that I would only use such strength for good? I bowed my head and prayed.

I sat in my room and waited. When I had given God what I believed to be sufficient time to answer my prayer and fill me with Samson's strength, I stood, walked over to my closet, and stood in the doorway as if I were standing between two giant pillars. I spat generously on each hand then rubbed them together. Taking a deep breath, I placed my palms firmly against both sides of the door frame and pushed with all my might. My face soon turned purple as the blood vessels in my face filled with blood. The bones in my forearms began to ache from the strain. Finally, at the point of exhaustion, I exhaled loudly as my body went limp. I felt light-headed as I rubbed my throbbing forearms while carefully examining the door frame. Nothing had moved. For whatever reason, it appeared as if God wasn't ready to give me Samson-like strength just yet. I made up my mind that I wouldn't give up that easily. I would just have to keep after God until God relented. So I paced my room and prayed some more.

As I waited, I replayed the story of Samson in my mind. I bent down and picked up an imaginary jawbone. The Bible said that Samson used the jawbone of a donkey as a weapon. I began to wield the imaginary jaw bone around my head, but instead of fighting thousands of Philistines like Samson, I readied myself to battle Joe. I crouched, ready for his attack. Joe charged me, and I smashed him in the face with the jaw bone sending Joe flying across the room.

"Get up, weakling!" I yelled. Joe struggled to his feet and charged again. This time, I leaped to the side and drove the jawbone hard into Joe's stomach. As Joe bent over in pain, gasping for air, I sent him flying against the far wall with an uppercut.

"Your strength is no match for me, creep," I crowed. Joe got up slower this time, and when he again charged, I picked him up over my head and spun him around and around until I grew dizzy. The room was now spinning wildly, so I stopped suddenly and body-slammed Joe hard to the floor. I felt winded and drained of energy as Joe lay at my feet. Wearily, I picked Joe up one final time and, with the last of my strength, threw him out the broken window. I collapsed to the floor, completely exhausted.

"Water!" I cried out, rolling around feigning thirst. "I need water!" I clutched my dry, parched throat. Just then, my bedroom door flew open, and Doreen stood in the doorway.

"Mummy sent me to find out what's going on in here. What are you doing? How come you're making so much noise, and who are you talking to?" She looked around the room. "There ain't even no one here."

Sprawled out on the floor, I rolled over a couple more times, then gazed up at my sister with desperate eyes. I swallowed dryly. "Water!" I begged. "Save me, Dor, I need water!" With an outstretched hand, I dragged myself across the floor toward her. When I reached Doreen, I clutched her ankle, and Doreen shook my hand loose and jumped away from me.

"You're so weird, Frankie," she exclaimed. She ran from the room and yelled, "Mummy, I think Frankie done lost his mind!" I crawled from my bedroom, through the hallway, and into the bathroom on the verge of death. I pulled myself feebly up on the sink, turned on the spigot, and gulped mouthfuls of life-giving water.

*****

Fluffy's kittens were growing fast. They had gotten too big for fluffy to nurse, so she spent less time in my room. One morning, as I lay on the floor with them, my mum came carrying a milk bowl. The kittens circled her feet, meowing loudly, rubbing their soft fur against her ankles. She set the bowl down, and they swarmed it, pushing and nudging each other for position as they lapped greedily at the milk until it was gone.

"We're going to have to get rid of them. They're getting big now, and there's no way we can keep all these cats," my mum announced.

"Aww, how come?" I protested.

"Joe don't want all these cats here anymore, and besides, we can't afford to feed them all."

The kittens had once again surrounded my mum and were rubbing against her ankles and legs, meowing hungrily. She called out for Mindy and Doreen, and they appeared in the doorway.

"I need yinz to talk to all your friends and see if any of them want a kitten," she said.

"Okay," they answered as our mum left the room.

"I have an idea," Mindy announced. "We can make a sign saying 'free kittens,' and we can stand on the corner and give them away."

"I get to make the sign," insisted Doreen. "I have the best handwriting."

"You're crazy. You do not," Mindy clucked. "You write like you're still in kindergarten."

"I do not!"

"You do too!" They walked from my room, slapping at each other.

I stretched out on the floor and watched as the kittens searched the room, looking for mischief. Working my fingers like giant spider legs, I walked them slowly across the floor toward a tiger-striped kitten. It tensed, arched its back, and instinctively pounced on my hand, rolled on its back, and began biting and scratching me furiously. I busted out laughing while I tussled with it on the floor before I finally shook it loose. Other kittens that were watching wandered over to get in on the fun. They attacked, and I playfully fought off several at a time. One of the kittens I had named Snowball because she was pure white suddenly pounced on my bare foot. "Hey, not so hard!" I laughed as I shook Snowball loose. Most of the kittens were now in full assault mode, attacking from every direction, and I laughed even harder at their antics. Eventually, they got bored and quit, except for Snowball, who purred and rubbed her face and whiskers against my side. I picked her up and set her on my chest, where she curled up in a ball to sleep. She felt warm and soft. I decided I would give her to Bunny. I closed my eyes contently.

Then, I felt the heavy vibration through the floorboards. Joe appeared in the doorway. He scanned the room before his truculent eyes settled on me. He was carrying something, he threw it at me, and it landed on my leg.

"Pick up the cats and put them in there," Joe said coldly. I stared blankly at the empty pillowcase on my leg.

"Now, freak!"

I pushed myself up and began to pick up the kittens, placing them inside the pillowcase. When I reached for Snowball, she pounced on my hand playfully, flipped on her back, then bit and scratched me.

"Snowball, stop it!" I whispered, and I shook her loose inside the pillowcase. Just then, Fluffy walked into the room. She looked inquisitively up at me as if asking, "What's going on? What are you doing with my babies?"

Joe snatched the pillowcase from my hand, grabbed me roughly by the scruff of the neck, and walked me toward the bathroom. Mindy and Doreen were already waiting, and Joe shoved me toward them. I rubbed the back of my neck while exchanging bewildered looks with my sisters. The pillowcase full of crying kittens writhed as if it had a life of its own. Joe spun it several times to seal it shut. He tugged off his shirt, stepped over to the bathtub, and dropped to one knee. The tub was full of water. It was then that I gasped, and my eyes widened with horror as I realized what was happening. Mindy and Doreen cupped their hands over their mouth to stifle a cry. Joe's lips curled into a grin just before his muscular arms plunged the writhing pillowcase deep under the water. The cries of the kittens stopped. Joe showed no emotion as the drowning kittens fought for life. Tiny bubbles broke the water's surface as the kittens exhaled and fought for their last breath of air. The entire ghastly scene was over in a little more than a minute. Joe stood, pulled the pillowcase from the water, and held it over the tub as water gushed out. When it had slowed to a trickle, he tossed the soggy, lifeless sack at my feet. It landed with a wet sickening thud.

"Open it," Joe sneered, staring directly at me. Obediently, I picked it up and untwirled the pillowcase. "Now, take one out."

Shaking, I set the pillowcase down, reached inside, and pulled out one of the kittens. It was Snowball, and she was soaked and lay limp and lifeless in my hand. The musky smell of wet fur, along with something else, assaulted my nostrils. Snowball's little pink tongue protruded grotesquely from her mouth.

"Go ahead, creep, play with the nice kitty now," grunted Joe. I stood dumbfounded, not understanding.

"What, are you stupid? You heard me. Go ahead and pet it, imbecile!" I obediently began to stroke the top of the dead kitten's head.

"All of yinz," commanded Joe. Mindy and Doreen reached over and began to pet the lifeless kitten; tears poured down Mindy's cheeks, and she was sobbing.

"You sick little retards, is that how yinz little monsters get your kicks, playing with dead cats?" A demented grin crossed Joe's face as he grabbed his shirt and a towel from the towel rack.

"Go find a garbage can somewhere and get rid of them," he ordered while drying his arms as he left the bathroom.

When he was gone, I looked over at Mindy. She was still crying as she stared at the lifeless sack. I then looked over at Doreen. She showed no emotion. Fluffy wandered into the bathroom as I placed Snowball back into the wet pillowcase. She sniffed the pillowcase, then looked up at me and meowed accusingly. I felt numb as I lifted the pillowcase off the floor. It was heavier than before. I would find a place to bury them instead of throwing them in the garbage. The three of us walked glumly from the bathroom in a single file. The soggy pillowcase rubbed against my right leg. A widening water spot spread on my pant leg, and the dampness seemed to penetrate through my skin into my bone. The musky smell of wet fur was overpowering, but again, there was that other smell I didn't quite recognize. When I was almost through the apartment, it dawned on me. I felt myself grimace, then held my breath to avoid the pungent stink of death.

Chapter 13

The following morning, I scampered down the path leading underneath Larimer Bridge. Honeymarmo's bedroll was in a corner next to the abutment, hidden from sight, but he was nowhere around. I adjusted the Bible in my waistband, then descended to the bottom of the ravine so I could fool around on the railroad tracks while I waited for Honeymarmo to return. I walked along, balancing unsteadily on one of the narrow rails pretending it to be a tightrope a thousand feet off the ground. I teetered onward with my arms outstretched, imagining that one slip would send me plunging to certain death. With deep concentration, I fought to keep my balance.

There was some movement to my left. At first, I thought it might be Honeymarmo, but when I jerked my head in that direction, I found myself staring into the vengeful eyes of Charles Johnson. Immediately, I knew I was in trouble. I jumped from the rail and spun to flee in the opposite direction. Lulu and another boy named Clarence blocked my way. I froze. The three boys moved quickly to surround me, cutting off all avenues of escape. Charles and Clarence held large sticks while Lulu gripped a heavy rock larger than his open hand. My heart began to race as panic set in. In desperation, I lurched toward a small opening between Charles and Lulu, only to have them quickly cut me off. I stepped back, realizing they had me trapped.

"Where do you think you're going, cracker boy?" Charles sneered. My head swiveled fitfully between the three to see and repel the first one that attacked. I raised my fists. The circle tightened. I grappled for something, anything that I could say to stop them.

"Yinz are only brave when there's three of you," I exclaimed. "How about fighting me one at a time?" It was a long shot, but challenging them to a one-on-one fight was the only thing that came to mind. I also suspected that Charles would demolish me in a fair fight, but it would probably be better than the alternative I now faced. Charles stopped and held up his hand to signal the others to halt their advance. He and I stood face-to-face a couple of paces apart.

"You want to fight me?" Charles hissed. "All right then, I'm hep with that, white boy. I'm going to beat you so bad your mama ain't going to recognize you when I'm done." Charles dropped his stick, then reached into his pocket and pulled out a large folded pocket knife. "Then, I'm going to carve you up good." My left leg began to shake.

Charles stepped toward me as we glared at each other, and I stiffened. Then, Charles broke eye contact for a fraction of a second, gave a flickering glance behind me, then nodded. Before I could react, I felt the stinging impact of a thick stick cracking across my back, causing me to yelp in pain as I dropped to my knees. In a flash, before I could protect myself, Charles took a step forward and landed a solid kick to my face. I collapsed to the ground just as all of them swarmed me. Instinctively, I curled into a ball, buried my chin into my chest, covered my face, and clutched the back of my head. Relentlessly, the kicks and punches rained down on me. One of the blows stung my ear, while another took away my breath as it crashed against my ribs. Then, a sharp pain exploded in my upper back between my shoulder blades as Lulu's rock found its mark.

I shrieked in agony, but the assault continued. Now, I curled myself tighter into a protective ball in survival mode. Knowing I was defenseless, I expected Charles to plunge the knife somewhere into my body. *I can't just lie here and die*, I thought. I uncurled myself and made another attempt to escape. The barrage of punches and kicks worsened. I felt a blunted blow to my stomach, then a fist smashed into my mouth, and then once again, I collapsed, curling back into a protective ball. That's when I knew for sure that I was going to die.

Then, from off in the distance in the direction of the bridge, I heard someone yell. The kicks and punches seized. Cautiously, I peeked from between my arms. Honeymarmo was running toward us, his arms waving wildly, his face twisted and demented, his eyes were wild, and he had something in his hand.

"Drop that, or I'll carve you up!" he screamed. A large, heavy cobblestone hit the ground next to my head with an ominous thump. I glanced up and saw that Lulu had dropped it.

"He's got a knife!" Clarence yelled. They all took off running.

"You better run, or else I'll kill all of you!" Honeymarmo shouted. He was close enough now to where I could get a good look at what the others had seen. The sun glistened off the blade of a menacing-looking knife that Honeymarmo wielded above his head. I glanced across the railroad tracks just as the three of them disappeared into the woods.

Battered and weak, I pushed myself to my knees just as Honeymarmo reached me. I cringed in pain as Honeymarmo helped me the rest of the way to my feet.

"Are you all right?" Honeymarmo asked worriedly, examining my bruised and bleeding face. I nodded.

"Your mouth's bleeding," Honeymarmo informed me. "Who in tarnation were those boys, and why were they beating you up like that?"

"Just some punks from school," I mumbled, spitting out blood.

Honeymarmo continued to stare at me, waiting for further explanation, but I stood mutely. Realizing I had no intention of elaborating further, at least not now, Honeymarmo shook his head.

"Well, that one punk was about to smash your head in with that cobblestone there if I hadn't shown up when I did." He pointed at the ground, and I glanced down at the large cobblestone, then back up at Honeymarmo. "And that other kid, the bigger one, was holding a knife, and I could have sworn he stabbed you with it."

"No, he didn't. Don't worry. I'll get them back. They're a bunch of jagoffs," I sneered. Honeymarmo saw the hate in my eyes, then again shook his head.

As we stepped off in the bridge's direction, Honeymarmo shoved the knife into a leather sheath that hung from his belt and then grasped my arm to help steady me, and he decided not to press me further. Once underneath the bridge, we sat quietly for a long time.

Gradually, my anger ebbed, and I remembered why I had come. I slipped up my shirt and pulled Honeymarmo's Bible from my waistband. That's when we both noticed the jagged puncture hole in the cover.

"Here you go," I said. "Charles must have stabbed it with his knife. Sorry."

Honeymarmo rubbed his thumb over the hole. "That's okay, son, it wasn't your fault. I'd rather there be a hole in the book than have a hole in your stomach, right? And besides, it goes to show you that it's true."

"What's true?"

"That the Word of God can save lives." Honeymarmo grinned.

Despite my pain, I grinned at his corny joke. "I guess so."

"You can still hold on to it for a while if you'd like," Honeymarmo offered.

"No, I'm done with it," I said. Honeymarmo took it from me, and we both went quiet again.

Finally, I broke the silence. "I liked the story about Samson, but I couldn't hardly understand some of it."

Honeymarmo grinned. "Yeah, it does take some getting used to," he said. "So you liked the story of Samson, huh? What was your favorite part of the story?"

"I don't know," I answered, "I guess I just liked how strong he was and how he beat up anyone that messed with him. If I had that kind of strength, I bet no one would mess with me, especially those punks today."

Honeymarmo chuckled. "Probably not," he said.

I grinned at Honeymarmo. "I prayed to God and asked him to make me strong like Samson. But he didn't. I guess I knew he wouldn't, but I thought I would ask anyway."

Honeymarmo laughed out loud. "Did you now? Well, sorry to hear that, Frankie. But there's something you need to understand about God. You see, God doesn't always give us what we want, but mostly he'll give us what we need. Sometimes, Frankie, what we need may be the opposite of what we want."

"Yeah, but it sure would have been nice if he made me that strong, especially today. I'd say I needed it," I joked.

Honeymarmo chuckled again, then held up his Bible. "Anyway, just let me know if you want to borrow it again." He placed it in his lap.

Again, we sat silently; Honeymarmo seemed content with waiting for me to speak first again. My adrenaline was waning, and I began to feel the full effects of the beating I had absorbed. It caused me to fidget uncomfortably.

"I was going to bring you a kitten," I finally said.

"A kitten?" Honeymarmo queried. "Well, I'm not sure I could do much with a kitten, living on the fly the way I do, but I do thank you for the thought. Where'd you get a kitten at anyhow?"

"Our cat Fluffy had kittens, and there was one with stripes, just like a tiger. I was going to give it to you, but it's dead now," I said solemnly.

"Dead? What happened to him?"

"Joe killed it. More than that, he killed all of Fluffy's kittens. He drowned them all in the tub."

"Why, that's awful. Why would he go and do something like that?" asked Honeymarmo.

"Our mum says he done it because our cat Fluffy couldn't feed them no more on account of them getting too big. She said we couldn't afford to feed them neither. She said Joe didn't want them to starve to death. But that ain't true. That ain't the reason. He did it because he's just a mean jagoff, and he likes doing stuff like that. He likes doing mean things, and he's getting meaner every day." I picked up a twig and snapped it in half. I felt Honeymarmo's gaze.

"Honeymarmo, can I ask you a question?"

"Yeah, sure, Frankie."

"Do you think Fluffy's kittens went to heaven?"

Honeymarmo leaned forward, resting his elbows on his knees. "Why, it wouldn't surprise me at all if they did," he said. "I mean, animals don't have souls like you and me, but they're God's creatures, aren't they? I'm sure God brings some of them to heaven when they die, especially the ones we loved, so one day we can enjoy them again, just like we did here on earth."

I perked up. "You really think so?"

"Why, sure. The way I see it is your kittens were innocent little creatures, so God would have no problem bringing them into heaven," he explained, his voice softening. I felt relief wash over me as I contemplated what Honeymarmo had just told me. "Have you given any thought to what we talked about before, about seeking a relationship with God?" Honeymarmo asked.

"I guess I thought about it, some," I replied.

"You know, Frankie, the most beautiful thing of all is that when you decide to trust God and trust in what his Son, Jesus, has done, you are adopted by God as his child, and he becomes your Heavenly Father forever. Did you know that?"

I shook my head.

"You see, most people think since God has made us in his image, we are naturally his children, but the word of God says differently. It says because we are born sinners, we are children of darkness and wrath. It is only through our willingness to trust and be obedient to him, and the washing away of our sins, do we become children of God," Honeymarmo explained.

"So I'm not one of God's children?" I asked.

"Not until you chose to become one. God has given you free will, so becoming his child or going to heaven is a choice you have to make, and no one can make that choice for you. You have to believe that the sacrifices God and his Son made for you are real."

"What if I'm not ready to make a choice?" I asked.

Honeymarmo squinted at me thoughtfully. "Deciding not to make a choice, Frankie, is making a choice."

I looked over at the Bible lying in Honeymarmo's lap and then back up at him. Although I felt a longing to believe what Honeymarmo was telling me, I felt a nagging resistance inside.

"There's something that don't make sense to me," I said.

Honeymarmo gave me a curious look. "What's that?"

"Well, if God loves everyone like you say and only allows people into heaven who accepts him and his Son Jesus, then what about the Indians?"

"The Indians?" asked Honeymarmo with bewilderment. "What about the Indians?"

"What I'm saying is, if they ain't never even heard of God and Jesus, it ain't their fault, so why would God not allow them into heaven, especially if he loved them like you say? That don't seem right," I added.

Honeymarmo grinned with approval.

"That's an excellent question, Frankie, an excellent and important question indeed." Honeymarmo leaned back on his elbows. "I think God does adopt some of them as his children and does allow them into heaven, even if they never heard of him or Jesus," he explained.

"Well then, that doesn't make sense neither," I said.

Honeymarmo pursed his lips. "A serious question deserves a serious answer. I'll explain the best I can as to why I believe it's true and why it does make sense, but first, let me say that God is a powerful spirit who spoke, and the heavens with the stars, moons, planets, and everything else, including our Earth, came into existence. It's hard to wrap our puny minds around such a thing, so believing something beyond our comprehension takes faith. Now, let me ask you a question. Is lying or stealing wrong?"

"Everyone knows lying and stealing are wrong," I clucked.

"How about murder, is murdering someone wrong?"

"That's stupid. Everyone knows that too," I said.

"Okay, well, let me ask you this: did someone have to teach you lying, and stealing, and murdering someone is wrong?" asked Honeymarmo.

I paused thoughtfully. "I don't know. I mean, not really, I guess. You just know it."

"That's right, Frankie, you just know it. No one had to teach you those things are wrong. Have you ever asked yourself why?"

I shook my head.

"Because they're God's laws, and God has written his laws into the hearts of all men, which includes you and me and the Indians. That's why we know that we shouldn't lie, cheat, steal, murder, or do other bad things. We didn't have to be taught that those things are wrong because our heart already knows it."

I wrinkled my forehead and slumped back in thought. "Huh!" I grunted.

"And there's something else—God has revealed himself in nature and in all of his creation. When we look at the stars at night, or a sunrise, or a sunset, or trees and flowers, or the vast ocean, or the birds as they migrate each year at the same time in perfect formation, there's something inside all of us that says there's someone more powerful than us in the world controlling things. That, Frankie, is God revealing himself to us. Do you have any idea what I'm talking about?"

I nodded slowly. "Sometimes, when I climb a big tall tree, or watch the clouds, or stare up at the stars at night, it makes me feel small."

Honeymarmo chuckled. "I ain't never heard anyone put it better than that," he said.

I perked up. "So what about the Indians?" I asked.

"Frankie, the way I read the Bible, two main issues concern God regarding people. We are either obedient or rebellious. The Indians you talk about, and there are others like them across the world who have never heard about God or his Son personally, but they know God's laws of right and wrong because it's already written in their hearts. They recognize that someone or something has created what they see and experience every day. For those who try to be obedient to what God has placed in their hearts, I believe God will show them his mercy and wash away their sins. He will allow them to enter heaven as his children, not because of any works they have done but because of their obedience." Honeymarmo gave Frankie a stern look. "But those Indians that are not obedient to what God has placed in their hearts and reject him and his handiwork in creation, God will reject."

"I guess that makes some sense," I said.

Honeymarmo nodded. "At some point, Frankie, you have to make a choice. You have to choose sides. It's a hard thing to do, trusting God, I mean. Do you know what that's called?" asked Honeymarmo.

"No. What?"

"That's what God calls faith."

I sat quietly, formulating a question. Then, I looked over at Honeymarmo. "So if I accept Jesus and what he done for me, and God adopts me as his son, does that mean I won't have any more bad things happen to me? Does that mean God will protect me from Joe?" I asked sincerely.

"I don't know, Frankie," Honeymarmo admitted. "Maybe he will, and maybe he won't. The Bible says it rains on both the just and unjust. You see, we live in a corrupted world, and God's children are subject to the same laws of sin as everyone else. We will get sick, and we will experience death, and we will suffer injustices from both man and nature. Even though God has given us his grace, and we become his children, we are still sinners and will always be sinners on this side of heaven. The difference is God has forgiven us. As God's children, there will be times that he intercedes for us as we struggle to stay within his will, but our hope is not in this world, Frankie, but is in eternity with him. I know that's a hard thing to understand, but faith is trusting God even when you don't understand everything."

I took a deep breath and exhaled. I understood some but not all of what Honeymarmo said. As we talked, I felt a kinship with this old hobo and found I could speak freely with him as I had never spoken to another adult before. I mean, I could tell him anything without the fear of him belittling or judging me. Then I noticed the leather knife sheath hanging from Honeymarmo's belt. There was green etching on the sheath that took the form of a deer.

"That sure is a nice knife. Where'd you get it?"

"This? I've had this quite a while. I got it from an old road dog I traveled with a few years back. He was a German who had come over from Germany and had a hard time finding work and all. I guess the memory of the war was still too fresh in some people's minds. He had a thick German accent but spoke good English. Anyways, when we parted ways, he gave it to me as a gift to remember him and our time spent traveling the rails together. He was a good guy, and I've often wondered whatever became of him."

"You think I can hold it?" I asked.

"Why, sure, just be careful you don't cut yourself. It's very sharp." Honeymarmo pulled it from the sheath and handed it to me.

"Wow, this is something." I turned the knife slowly in my hands, inspecting it. Its blade was about five inches long, had a brass blade guard and an aluminum bird's head pommel. There was the letter *H* carved into the handle. "What's this handle made out of?"

"That's a stag handle. It's made of deer antler," Honeymarmo answered, amused at how enamored I was with the knife. He handed me a piece of wood. "Here, you can do some whittling on this. Just be careful."

"Really? Thanks, I will." I took the wood and began shaving thin strips.

For a good part of the afternoon, we basked in one another's company. Honeymarmo even read things to me from his Bible as I whittled away. Finally, it grew late, and I knew I had to get home for supper. I handed the hunting knife back to Honeymarmo. He took out a hanky from his pocket, wiped the blade and handle, then shoved it back into the sheath. "Always clean your knife after you use it," Honeymarmo said. We both stood, then we walked over to the path.

"Honeymarmo?"

"Yeah, Frankie."

"Thanks for saving my neck from them jagoffs before."

Honeymarmo laid his hand gently on my shoulder. "Frankie," he said warmly, "I know you're mad about what happened with them there boys today for what they did to you. I know you want to get back at them. But those kids are dangerous, and you need to stay away from them. Sometimes the best thing to do is swallow your pride and just move on. That doesn't make you a coward. Maybe eventually, you can even learn to turn the other cheek and forgive them. Like I said, I see a lot of anger in you, and you have to learn how to let that anger go, Frankie, or else one day you'll find yourself hating the world and everyone in it. It will poison your soul. I've seen it. It will consume your life, and in the end, it will destroy you and keep you from becoming the person that God wants you to be. Do you understand what I'm saying to you?" he asked gently.

I nodded. "Yeah, I think so."

"Good. Just think about it." He smiled again, and his eyes shone with light from somewhere deep within him. I couldn't help but return his smile. Then, a thought struck me.

"Does that mean Joe too?" I asked.

Honeymarmo nodded. "That means especially Joe. Maybe not so much for his sake but for yours."

"So if Joe decided to accept Jesus, then God would allow him into heaven too, even after all the bad things that he's done to me and my sisters and my mum?"

Honeymarmo nodded. "That's right, Frankie, if he was sincere and meant it, and he changed his ways, God would forgive him." Inwardly I recoiled, as I turned and ascended the path knowing full well that there would never be any forgiveness for Joe. I would always hate him. I felt a sudden resentment toward God at the idea that God would even consider forgiving Joe for everything he had done to us. It wasn't right. I decided that there would be no forgiving Charles, Lulu, or Clarence. Forgiveness was out of the question because another confrontation with the three of them was inevitable. I was sure that they had already begun to spread the story of what they had done to me, and before long, every kid in the neighborhood would know what happened, and the expectation would be for me to settle the score. I could not just let this pass because others would take it as a sign of weakness if I did. And any perceived weakness would make me vulnerable to future attacks from others. By the time I reached Larimer Avenue, my heart had hardened against some of those things Honeymarmo had tried to teach me, especially about forgiveness. I wanted no part of it. So without compunction, I began to plan my revenge.

*****

As Honeymarmo walked up Larimer Avenue, he pressed close to the buildings, hoping Frankie wouldn't spot him. Just up ahead, Frankie hurried along. After a couple of blocks, Frankie reached an intersection, turned right, and disappeared. Honeymarmo sped up, and as he approached the corner, he glanced at the street sign, and it read Shetland Avenue. Across the road was a sizeable red-bricked building that housed a couple of grocery stores and had apartments on the top two floors. At the intersection, he looked in the direction Frankie had gone.

Honeymarmo didn't see him anywhere. He turned right also, and when the rear of the building across the street came into view, Honeymarmo saw Frankie climbing metal stairs leading to the apartments on the third floor. From the third-floor porch, his young friend disappeared inside an open doorway.

"So this is where you live," Honeymarmo whispered.

From across the graveled parking lot, Honeymarmo heard the sounds of some kind of construction. The boy reemerged, looked in the direction of the hammering, stomped down the steps, and sprinted across the parking lot toward Larimer Field.

Honeymarmo turned, walked back to the corner, crossed Shetland Avenue, and stood in front of the apartment building. He looked up at the address above the door on the sidewalk outside the apartment building entrance, and it read 557.

He paused for a moment, then looked around and noticed an alley next to the school a little way up the street, so he crossed Larimer Avenue, walked briskly to it, and waited. He knew it was a long shot, but his curiosity and concern had gotten the better of him. He hung back in the alley just far enough to not be noticed from the street. A little less than an hour later, he saw him.

Joe sauntered down the street toward the apartments. When Honeymarmo saw his massive muscular frame, broad-boned forehead, brooding eyes, and hawk-like features, he instantly knew who he was. In all his years traveling the rails, Honeymarmo had come across just about every type of person imaginable, including some that were just plain evil. Now, as he watched Joe making his way down Larimer Avenue, his senses and instincts told him this was the same type of danger. Honeymarmo, who did not easily succumb to fear, felt a shiver inside.

Joe pushed open the door under the address that read 557 and disappeared inside. Honeymarmo filled with sorrow, and his spirit sank. "Oh, Frankie, you poor kid! You ain't a big enough dog with big enough teeth for this one," he murmured. When Frankie had told him about Joe, Honeymarmo thought he had some notion about the guy's nature, but now he realized how wrong he was. Seeing Joe, he was scared for his little friend.

Finally, Honeymarmo stepped out of the alley and walked down Larimer Avenue toward Larimer Bridge. A few minutes later, he sat in the dirt under the bridge. He lay back, stretched out his legs, crossed his bony ankles, and clasped his hands behind his head. Then, for a long time, he stared up into the rafters, deep in thought.

Chapter 14

When I arrived in the parking lot behind our apartment, the pain and soreness from the beating I had taken earlier had worsened. I gingerly climbed the back stairs, still pondering my revenge. When I stepped into the kitchen, no one was there. I opened the refrigerator, but there was nothing inside to eat. As I considered whether to risk going to the front of the apartment and maybe running into Joe, I heard hammering coming from outside. I drifted out on the back porch and spotted several Italian men scurrying about Larimer Field. Some were building large wooden platforms, while others erected large rod iron archways strung with lights. I was so excited that I never noticed Honeymarmo across the street. I scampered down the steps and sprinted across the parking lot until I reached the tall chain-link fence surrounding Larimer Field. The platforms could only mean one thing; tomorrow would be the Italian summer festival of Saint Rocco. Many Italian families who had moved away from Larimer would return, maybe even some of my own family on my father's side, most of which I hadn't seen in years. I turned, willing to risk running into Joe, and sprinted back to the apartment to tell Mindy and Doreen.

"For Christ's sake, Frankie, what happened to your face?" my mum exclaimed as I burst into the kitchen.

"I got in an accident," I lied, surprised that my mum was now sitting at the kitchen table.

My mum grimaced dubiously. "Don't go there with me. You're lying. You were fighting again, weren't you?"

"Mum, I swear to God, I was swinging on a rope over the hill, and it went right smack into a tree."

My mum examined my bruised face more closely. "You sure you ain't lying to me?" she insisted, and I sensed an opening.

"C'mon, Mum, why would I lie about something like that?" My mum studied my face harder. I didn't blink. "I swear, I almost knocked myself out cold, and more than that, I ain't never swinging on that rope again."

"Good, because them rope swings are just too dangerous," she finally said. "Now, go wash your face—and make sure you use soap."

"Okay, I will," I said, hurrying toward the bathroom.

*****

It was late afternoon, and I sat outside the Larimer Field fence with Mindy and Doreen the following day. We watched in amazement at the wooden platforms built in only a day. One of the platforms held a live band that played Italian songs, and people, primarily Italian, gathered around it to dance and sing and laugh. The platforms had light bulbs strung overhead, and tall wrought-iron archways covered with strings of lights were everywhere. When night arrived, the brightness from hundreds of bulbs illuminated the entire field, transforming it into a magical gala complete with food, live music, singing, and laughter.

I inhaled deeply, savoring the aroma. There was nothing better than the smell of cooking Italian sausages with onions and peppers or grilled hot dogs. There was also pizza, casseroles full of pasta, Italian pastries, and various other Italian foods. My sisters and I watched outside the fence as more families arrived, and the festival took on a life of its own. It was an extravaganza of lights and excitement and delicious aromas, causing our stomachs to gurgle and mouths to water. Stacked high just inside the fence were scores of wooden soda pop cases, and I pointed out to my sisters the assorted flavors of cream soda, ginger ale, Pepsi, black cherry, orange, and root beer. I had never seen so much food and soda pop in my life, and it was spectacular.

Each year, we rarely ventured beyond the fence, and those few times we did, the close-knit Italian families mostly ignored us. I can't be sure why. Maybe it was because we weren't full-blooded Italians like them. But it didn't matter, because we never had money to buy anything anyway. We would beg our mum to take us, but she always resisted our pleas. I suspected it was because the food vendors didn't accept food stamps. I wasn't for sure, though. So now, like other years, we sat in both wonder and envy of the marvelous sense of family and belonging amongst the Italian families as we watched them celebrate, yearning to be part of it.

Our father was an Italian from the old neighborhood, and he knew all of the Italian families in Larimer, and they knew him. When he left us, he moved out west to California. Our mum wasn't Italian but was a mixture of Irish, German, and English. She often joked with my sisters and me, telling us we were a "Heinz 57" mix, a little bit of everything. We never understood the joke, but my mum would laugh, so we laughed along with her so that she wouldn't feel stupid. Most of our family on our father's side didn't bother with us, and I thought it was because we were poor and because of Joe. Our mum would always remind us that we weren't supposed to tell anyone that Joe lived with us. Still, I suspected most people in Larimer, especially our Italian relatives, already knew.

As the festival got into full swing, Mindy, Doreen, and I sat outside the fence, hoping someone would invite us to be part of the grand celebration and perhaps even share with us something to eat.

"Look!" Mindy suddenly shouted, pointing into the crowd. "That's Aunt Connie."

"Where?" Doreen asked, straining her neck.

"Right over there, with that girl and boy." Being the oldest, Mindy often remembered relatives that Doreen and I didn't recognize. "I think those are our cousins, Sofia and Anthony."

"Are you sure?" I asked.

"Aunt Connie!" Mindy yelled as loud as she could. "Aunt Connie!" Mindy jumped to her feet and began to wave her arms excitedly. Our aunt Connie was standing next to one of the platforms, talking to another Italian woman. Mindy's voice rose above the noisy crowd and a man playing the accordion and singing an Italian song from the old country. Our aunt Connie looked in our direction, smiled pretentiously, then waved. She turned back toward the lady and whispered something.

"Aunt Connie!" Mindy persisted gleefully. "Aunt Connie, it's me, Mindy!"

Once again, our aunt Connie turned toward us. She sighed, whispered something to the lady, and began to walk toward the three of us. Mindy either didn't notice or didn't care about her apparent indifference. But I noticed.

"She's coming over," Mindy giggled excitedly. Doreen and I remained silent.

"Well, hello, Mindy," our aunt Connie greeted when she reached the fence. "My, aren't you getting big." She looked down at Doreen and me sitting in the dirt. "Now, don't tell me this is Doreen and Frankie!" she exclaimed.

"Yep, it sure is, Aunt Connie," Mindy chirped.

"My, my, haven't the three of you grown. Why, I bet I haven't seen yinz for a couple of three years now," Aunt Connie declared, still looking down at Doreen and me. As I looked up at her through the chain-link fence, I felt suddenly small and unimportant. I looked away—the girl and boy we had seen with her earlier appeared by her side.

"Hi, Sofia. Hi, Anthony." Mindy waved happily. They waved weakly back at her and said hello in a voice barely audible.

"So how's your mum doing?" our aunt Connie asked.

"She's fine. She's going to have a baby," Mindy blurted out. She had elected herself the spokesperson for the three of us, which suited Doreen and me just fine. Our aunt Connie looked suddenly stunned, and she paused before responding.

"Oh, uh, that's nice. Well, yinz tell her I said hello. By the way, I just talked to your father last week." Doreen perked, scrambled to her feet, and stood next to Mindy.

"Did you really, Aunt Connie? Is he still in California?" Doreen asked wide-eyed.

"Of course, Doreen."

"Did he say anything about me?" Doreen asked.

"Why, yes, he did, Doreen. He said if I saw you make sure I tell you that he loves and misses you, all of yinz, very much," she added. No one was better at lying than me, and I immediately saw through our aunt's clumsy attempt. I looked up at both my sister's glowing faces, and it was apparent they were swallowing her fib. My eyes narrowed skeptically as I again looked at our aunt Connie.

"Did he say if he was going to send for me?" Doreen's asked. Her question certainly caught me off guard, and it almost staggered our aunt Connie. She struggled uncomfortably for an answer.

"Well, Doreen, your father's kind of between jobs right now, but once he finds one and saves up some money, it wouldn't surprise me one bit that he sends for you." Doreen's eyes widened further. When our aunt Connie glanced down at me, I smirked brazenly, and her eyes darted quickly away.

"Well, we got to run now. It was so good to see you three again, and please don't forget to tell your mum I said hello." They turned and walked away.

"She's so nice," Mindy said. "I'll be back. I'm going to tell Mummy Aunt Connie said hi." She ran off toward our apartment. Doreen again plopped down next to me.

"Did you hear what Aunt Connie said, Frankie?" Doreen asked. "I bet by next year, when Daddy finds a good job, that he'll probably send for me to go live with him." She beamed. "If he gets a good enough job, I'll bet he'll send for you and Mindy too."

I couldn't help but wonder how my sister could be so stupid. She was usually pretty smart about these things, and it wasn't like her to have someone fool her so easily. As much as I relished any opportunity to frustrate or anger Doreen, as I looked into her eyes and saw them shiny with hope, I couldn't bring myself to tell her that it was all a lie. So, I just nodded. We turned our attention back to the festival, and before long, Mindy rejoined us. Together, we watched the other children laughing, eating, and running care-free through the crowd as they played tag and other games. The Italian men shouted, laughed, and drank homemade Italian wine as they sang, danced, and played boccie ball. Families filled the platforms, and they too sang and danced to songs from the old country.

The night grew late, and the three of us pressed against one another, not for warmth but companionship and a shared dream of one day belonging to such a world. The joyous celebration on the other side of the fence unfolded before us like a scene from a fairy tale. Then, from somewhere behind us, our mum's voice rang out through the darkness, calling us in for the night. Mindy and Doreen stood to leave, but I didn't move.

"Min, tell Mummy I'll be up in just a little bit. I want to see the fireworks from here," I informed her. Mindy and Doreen ran across the graveled parking lot, disappearing into the night. I was not ready to leave because, deep down, I still held out hope for the possibility of someone inviting me in to join them, mostly to eat. Soon the night sky exploded with brilliant fireworks, and afterward, as my eyes lids grew heavy, I once again heard my mum calling to me through the darkness. I ignored her until, gradually, the lights from the festival grew hazy, and I could not fight my weariness.

"Frankie?"

I opened my eyes sleepily. My mum stood over me as I lay in the dirt outside the fence. The coldness from waking up caused me to shiver. I looked around, confused. The festival had thinned of people but still had plenty of life left in it. "C'mon, you have to come home now," my mum whispered. She helped me to my feet, and we walked through the pitch-black parking lot. Off to the right, three floors up, a soft yellow glow seeped out of our open kitchen door, like a beacon guiding us home. Fully awake now, I looked over my shoulder one last time.

The music and the lights still called out to me, as did the people and all those delicious foods, and although I had not tasted so much as a single morsel, it didn't matter. For in my imagination, I had savored it all. I had danced on the platforms to the music and had run wild through the crowd, laughing jubilantly with my cousins and the other Italian children. It was wonderful.

"Isn't it a great festival, Mum?" I yawned.

"Yeah, Frankie. It sure is."

Chapter 15

The next day, just as quickly as they had built them, the same men took down the wooden platforms. The field, once again, was empty. Me, Ronald, Donald, and Jan met on the boccie ball court next to Cosenza's store.

"So what yinz want to do?" I asked.

"How about going to the basketball court and playing basketball?" Jan suggested holding up a dilapidated rubber ball.

"Okay, anything's better than just sitting here," Donald replied. Everyone agreed.

Together, we walked to the basketball court on the far end of Larimer Field. We chose sides, me and Jan, against Ronald and Donald. Since it was difficult to get a true bounce out of the tattered rubber ball, we only pretended to dribble.

As we played our modified version of basketball, we noticed a boy leaning against the fence at the far end of the court. We stopped and strolled over to him. As we reached him, I instinctively sized him up. He was black and was the same size and built as me.

The boy nodded friendly-like as we stopped in front of him. "What's up?" he asked.

"What's up with you, man?" Donald replied. I said nothing.

"What's your name?" Ronald asked.

"Leroy."

Donald squinted and cocked his head. "Don't you go to our school?" Leroy nodded.

"Yeah, I remember seeing you around the playground," Jan recalled.

"So where do you live?" Donald asked. "I ain't seen you around here before."

"Over on Mayflower Street," Leroy answered. "I'm not usually allowed to leave our street, but my mum went to Wilkinsburg to visit my auntie, so I snuck on over here," Leroy explained.

Leroy had just given me an opening. "For real, man, you just do whatever your mum says? Are you a mama's boy?" I asked. Everyone's mood instantly changed. Leroy seemed confused at my verbal assault.

"Where's Wilkinsburg?" Donald asked quickly in an attempt to derail the tension I had created.

Leroy had heightened his defenses. "It's on the other side of East Liberty somewhere," he said, ignoring me; being ignored only reinforced my resolve.

"How about answering my question, creep. You a mama's boy?"

Leroy's eyes hardened, succumbing to the inevitable. He looked directly at me. The others began to fidget.

"Frankie, ain't no reason—," Jan started to say.

"Shut up, man!" I warned, and Jan looked away. I turned my attention back to Leroy, who now stood defiant.

"No, I ain't no mama's boy," said Leroy.

"I think you are. I think you're a sissy," I goaded him. Ronald, Donald, and Jan shrunk back, leaving us to further size one another up.

"I ain't no sissy," Leroy said, expanding his chest as his fists came up defensively. "Take it back," he demanded. As Leroy's fists came up, I felt the familiar stir within me. My stomach churned, and my left leg began to shake. I took a couple of steps back, raised my fists, and said, "Come on! How about making me take it back, punk!"

I suspected Leroy might back down for a moment, but unexpectedly he charged with his head down, trying to tackle me to the ground. After realizing Leroy's mistake of taking his eyes off me, I grabbed Leroy in a headlock that stopped his momentum cold. I tightened my grip as Leroy's arms flailed wildly, trying to punch me. I pushed Leroy's head down and sent a knee crashing upward into Leroy's face. Leroy stumbled back, falling to the ground. A trickle of blood appeared from his left nostril.

"Stay down, punk," I warned. Leroy sat dazed, his eyes filled with tears. Then, he shook his head, his eyes narrowed, and he scrambled to his feet. He raised his fists again, charged at me, and I braced myself. Leroy kept his eyes on me this time, and one of his punches caught me on the temple. We both threw haymakers at one another, some connecting before we stepped back to regroup. Leroy had learned from his mistake, and I knew I would have to be more careful now.

This time it was my turn to attack. I moved in quickly, snapping jabs to keep Leroy off guard. When I was close enough, I leaped to Leroy's left, grabbed a handful of his shirt, and spun him, tearing most of his shirt from his torso. The maneuver had rendered Leroy off balance and had exposed his back to me, which allowed me to grab him in a bear hug from behind. I lifted Leroy off his feet and slammed him to the pavement. The back of Leroy's head bounced off the cement with a sickening thud. I followed up with two kicks to Leroy's ribs, causing him to gasp for air. I backed away.

"Now, stay down, creep. Give up yet?" I asked angrily, my left leg still shaking from the adrenaline.

"You best stay down, Leroy," warned Donald, "ain't no sense in getting your head busted open."

Once Leroy's breath returned, he staggered slowly to his feet. A knot had appeared on the back of his head, and his eyes were still defiant. With blood still trickling from his nose, Leroy raised his fists and took a step toward me.

"I said, take it back," he snorted. I stood in disbelief.

I again raised my fists. "You still have to make me, punk," I reminded Leroy. Without hesitation, Leroy charged. We again showered punches down on one another. After several seconds, we stepped back to assess the damage. Our breathing was labored. Leroy's nose was bleeding heavier and had smeared across his cheek. I felt warm blood trickling down my chin. I touched my lower lip, where it had been split open. When I pulled my hand away, my fingers were sticky with blood. I licked over my wound. Staring at one another, we both began to circle in an attempt to gain an advantage.

This pause gave me time to calculate my next move. Leroy was more dangerous than I had anticipated, and he was incredibly courageous, but it was clear he lacked experience, and I knew I had to use that to my advantage. I suddenly rushed him, swinging high, which forced Leroy's hands up, allowing me to tackle him to the ground. I now sat on Leroy's chest. Pressing both knees into Leroy's arms, I managed to connect with three well-aimed punches to Leroy's face before Leroy bucked me off. I jumped to my feet and stood over Leroy as he struggled to get up. I still held the advantage. When Leroy was almost to his feet, I grabbed him by the back of his torn shirt and spun him in a full circle before letting go. Leroy, again off-balance, tumbled awkwardly across the basketball court. He gave a pitiful grunt as he hit the pavement and rolled. His forearm had been scraped raw, and beads of blood appeared on the wound. A blot of blood seeped through Leroy's torn trousers over his left knee.

"Stay down there," I panted. This time I did not call Leroy a punk.

Sluggishly, Leroy got to one knee, and I could hear Ronald, Donald, and Jan muttering behind me. Then, Leroy got to his feet despite the exhaustion and pain from his wounds. He faced me and raised his chin insolently into the air, breathing heavily, his broad nostrils flared. He again raised his fists.

"I ain't no sissy, and I ain't no mama's boy. Take it back," he warned. As I looked into his proud, defiant eyes, I realized nothing short of unconsciousness or death would prevent Leroy from coming at me, time and again. As he stood fearlessly in front of me, blood smeared across his face, a knot on the back of his head, his arm and knee scraped raw, and his shirt almost completely ripped from his torso, the anger drained from me. Now, as I faced Leroy, I felt respect and, yes, even fear. I lowered my fists. Leroy watched my hands drop to my side and cautiously probed my eyes for any sign of deceit or trickery.

"All right, we'll call it a draw. I take it back," I conceded. I was relieved when Leroy lowered his fists. Ronald and Jan immediately slapped us on the back, congratulating us on a good fight, while Donald stood silent. Leroy and I continued to stare at one another, saying nothing. Our eyes and our expressions, at that moment, communicated everything we wanted to say.

"C'mon, let's get back," Donald finally said.

The four of us left the basketball court. I trailed them through the opening in the chain-link fence, stopped, and looked back at Leroy standing alone on the basketball court. Our eyes locked, and with some humor, Leroy cringed as he reached up and gingerly rubbed the knot on the back of his head. I grimaced and gently pressed my fingers against my swollen bottom lip. Then, I turned and raced to catch up with the others.

Once we reached Shetland Avenue, Donald, Ronald, and Jan played catch in the street with the scruffy rubber ball. I sat alone on the curb, watching them as I waited for the pain in my lip to subside. Donald came over and sat down next to me. He awkwardly shifted on the curb as he stared down into the gutter. Finally, he sucked a long breath.

"Frankie, you know for real we been boys for a long time now, ever since second grade," he began, "but I got to tell you, what you did to Leroy today was wrong, man. He didn't do nothing to you. Lately, it seems like you want to fight everyone. It's like you enjoy it or something, and you're getting meaner and looking for trouble all the time now." He paused, waiting for me to respond.

"Yeah, but at least I wasn't afraid, was I?" I clucked.

"What are you talking about, Frankie? Ain't no one ever said you were afraid of nothing," Donald remarked. I went silent.

The thing was, I knew Donald was right. I didn't understand why I had started a fight with Leroy, especially since I didn't know him. But there was something inside that sometimes just seemed to take control of me. I had no answer or defense to what Donald was saying, so all I could do was shrug.

"My mum says that the other parents around the neighborhood are saying that you're wild—that you're dangerous. Some of them say they see you roaming the neighborhood at all hours of the morning and sometimes at night, mostly by yourself, and they think you're just looking for trouble. She thinks you're a bad influence on me and Ronald," Donald said. I turned fully toward him.

"Is that what you think?" I asked pointedly.

"No, man, I told her that you weren't wild or dangerous." Donald searched the gutter for words before looking back over at me. "Don't get mad, but I told her about Joe. I know I promised never to tell anyone, but I had to make her understand so we could still loaf together. I told her how mean he was to you and why you were out so early in the mornings. I had to let her know it wasn't because you were looking for trouble." I could hear the tightness in Donald's voice as he confessed his betrayal. For some reason, I didn't care, and I just listened.

"My mum and dad told me and Ronald they didn't want us to loaf with you so much. Man, Frankie, you got to stop fighting all the time, or else..." Donald's voice trailed off uncomfortably.

I sat quietly, digesting what Donald was telling me. Then, I cocked my head toward Donald. "So what are you saying? You don't want to be my friend no more?"

"No, we'll always be boys, Frankie," Donald said. "But if you don't stop fighting all the time and doing some of the other things you do, we just won't be able to hang out together as much, especially around my mum and dad, or else Ronald and I will get in trouble." The tone in Donald's voice was remorseful.

I became sullen. I felt hurt because I had never done anything against Donald's mum or dad. Sure, I sometimes got into fights when I probably shouldn't and did other wrong things, but did that make me a bad person? I thought of the familiar urge growing inside me when I confronted Leroy, and I did nothing to stop it. Perhaps Honeymarmo was wrong; maybe I was just no good. Maybe I was a bonehead and a creep, like Joe said. Unexpectedly, my eyes began to sting, so I turned from Donald to blink away the wetness before Donald could see it. Then, I felt my anger returning. My vision cleared, and I stood abruptly.

"All right," I said. "I'm going to go before your mum or dad sees you sitting here with me."

"No, it's okay for now, man," Donald assured me. "Besides, they ain't even home right now."

I plunged my hands into my pockets and stepped away from Donald. "I have to go do something. I'll catch yinz later." I walked in the direction of Larimer Avenue, not knowing where I was going or where I would end up. I accelerated my pace, knowing that my friendship with Donald, and maybe even the others, had somehow changed.

Chapter 16

My hunger for revenge against Charles, Lulu, and Clarence consumed me. As I worked on a plan, I knew that my revenge had to create enough fear within them that the very idea of reprisal against me would be unthinkable. Finally, I settled on a plan, so all I had to do now was wait for the right opportunity to present itself, hoping I had the guts to go through with it. It would take some luck to avoid getting caught, and it would be dangerous, but in the isolation of my room, I studied on it for a long time while also building up my courage. I knew I had to execute my plan soon before Charles, Lulu, and Clarence got to me again. So I put the word out to my friends to find me if they spotted the three of them somewhere together.

The opportunity presented itself a few days later. I was in the kitchen arguing with Doreen about superheroes, a subject she knew nothing about. Doreen had the opinion that Spiderman could defeat Superman in a one-on-one fight. After lifting myself from the floor from busting a gut laughing, I explained to her that Superman could fly, had heat vision, super breath, super speed, and had superior super strength, plus he had a steel body. In contrast, all Spiderman could do was shoot stupid webs from his wrist.

"Yeah, well, what about kryptonite?" Doreen insisted.

"Get out of here, Doreen. Spiderman man ain't going to carry no kryptonite around in his back pocket just in case he gets into a fight with Superman. That's so stupid."

"I ain't stupid," Doreen hissed.

"I didn't say you were stupid. I said what your saying is stupid," I clarified.

Doreen was having none of it. "Take it back," she demanded, "I ain't stupid."

"I ain't taking nothing back," I said, not backing down. "Because you are stupid." I saw the rage ignite in Doreen's eyes and immediately knew I had gone too far.

Then, from outside, I heard Jan yelling up at me from the parking lot below. I sighed with relief, then carefully backed out of the kitchen onto the porch while reminding Doreen how lucky she was that Jan had shown up when he did. I knew better than to turn my back on my sister, so I stood sideways as I glanced over the railing to speak to Jan.

"Yeah, Jan, I'm up here. What's up?" I shouted.

"Frankie, come here!" Jan hollered. I hurried down the two flights of steps.

Jan was excited when I reached him. "Frankie, I was down on the hillside behind the cat lady's house, and Charles, Lulu, and Clarence are down there swinging on the bull rope. I just wanted to let you know like you asked, man."

"How long ago?" I asked.

"Just now," Jan said. I felt my stomach tighten.

"Okay, thanks, man," I said, slapping him five. I ran back up to the apartment.

Even though my heart was racing, I tried to keep calm as I casually stepped into the kitchen, where Mindy had started peeling potatoes. I walked through the apartment to see where everyone else was and what they were doing. Joe had left early in the morning, hopefully, for the rest of the day. My mum was in the bathroom with the door shut, and Doreen was reading a comic book in her bedroom. I slipped into my mum's bedroom and quickly walked to the far side of the bed where Joe slept. Carefully, I lifted the mattress. An unfolded newspaper covered a portion of the metal springs, and on top was a box of bullets and a loaded handgun. I picked up the gun. It was hefty, and my hand trembled from the fright and euphoria of holding it. Carefully, I eased the loaded gun inside my waistband,

cinched my belt, then covered it with my loose shirt. I smoothed out
the covers on the bed and walked swiftly from the room and through
the apartment. I walked nonchalantly past Mindy in the kitchen,
stepped out onto the back porch, and stepped carefully down the two
flights of stairs. I dared not run with the heavy weapon stuffed down
the front of my pants for fear that it would dislodge and fall to the
ground. Instead, I walked at a brisk pace to the cat woman's house on
Lenora Street, occasionally and discreetly, adjusting the loaded gun
in my waistband as I went.

When I reached the cat lady's house, I hurried through her backyard and disappeared over the ridge. After walking a short distance
in the woods, I stopped and listened. Sure enough, just a little further down the hill, I heard voices. I studied the terrain then slid off
the dirt path, creeping stealthily toward the sounds. It was Charles,
Lulu, and Clarence, like Jan said. I stooped behind some dense jagger
bushes for concealment about ten yards away from them. The three
took turns swinging out over the steep hillside on a thick hemp bull
rope tied to an overhanging tree limb.

I took several deep breaths to calm myself before gathering the
courage to pull the gun from my waistband. I found a small gap in
the bushes to see through. A large drainpipe made of corrugated steel
jutted out of the sloping ground a little way up the hill behind them,
and I figured I could hit it without shooting and killing one of them.
Charles had just retrieved the dangling rope and was bringing it up
the hill to hand it off.

I dropped to one knee and pointed the gun. But as the drainpipe came into view, the gun, as if I had no control, swung to the
right until I found myself staring down the barrel at Charles. As
Charles came into focus, the image of him holding a knife flashed
through my mind. My anger ignited as I remembered the beating
I had taken. My teeth clenched, and I squeezed my eyes shut as I
pulled the trigger. The trigger didn't budge. I dropped to the ground
and rolled over on my back. I was breathing hard from panic, not
because of Charles, Lulu, or Clarence but because of what I had just
almost done. The alarm I felt seemed to take my anger away. I lay still
until calm and my senses returned.

I promptly examined the gun, noticing a small switch on the side that read "safety." I clicked it off and once again raised myself to one knee, this time taking dead aim at the drainpipe. Just as Lulu pushed off, I jerked the trigger. The explosion was deafening, and a spent cartridge ejected and landed next to me. Charles and Clarence immediately went rigid. The bullet ricocheted in the dirt in front of the drainpipe, and I fired again. Charles and Clarence both bolted down the steep hill. Clarence, who was in front, tripped, and Charles stumbled and fell on top of him.

Charles screamed, "Don't kill me! Don't kill me!"

Clarence cried out, "Don't shoot us! We didn't mean it!"

Lulu had swung out over the steep hillside and was near the highest point when he heard the explosions. Fearing for his life, he panicked and let go of the rope, plummeting some fifteen feet to the sloping hillside. He landed awkwardly and tumbled down the hill grunting in pain.

My ears were ringing. I had not expected the gunfire to be so loud, and the force of the recoil had almost made me drop the gun. As the three of them scrambled and dove into the brush for cover, I quickly picked up the spent cartridges, turned, and ran back up the hill, hoping not to be seen. My entire body was shaking. Panting hard, I reached the crest of the slope, and just before stepping back into the cat lady's backyard, I shoved the gun down the front of my pants and covered it with my shirt.

I hurried through the yard and out to the street. I suspected others had to have heard the shots. Sure enough, a few elderly residents were standing on their porches, debating what they had heard. I did my best to look innocent and was careful not to look directly at them.

"I'm telling you, it sounded just like gunshots," an elderly man was saying.

"Hey, you!" the same man shouted. I maintained my pace, then, careful not to turn entirely, glanced over my shoulder.

"Who me?" I asked.

"Yeah, you! Did you hear a gunshot?"

I shook my head. "No, I saw some kids lighting cherry bombs down over the hill," I lied as I strode further away. The man turned and shouted to a lady on the porch across the street.

"There's nothing to worry about, Emma," he said. "Some kids are lighting off cherry bombs over the hill."

"Well, I wish I knew who they were," she snapped angrily. "I would go tell their mums. That about scared me to death."

I didn't hear the rest of their conversation as I hurried away. It seemed like it took forever before finally arriving at the bottom of our apartment steps. I ascended rapidly, crossed the porch, and stepped into the kitchen. There was no one there. Trying to maintain my composure, I walked into the empty living room and stood still. I heard muffled voices. Creeping down the passageway to the front of the apartment, I crossed the hallway to my sister's room and listened through the closed door. Both my sisters were inside having a singing contest. Mindy was in the middle of her rendition of "Tears on My Pillow."

I slipped quietly past them and peeked into our mum's room, and she wasn't there. Then, I heard her out in the stairwell, talking with someone. I pulled the gun from my trousers and hurried into the room. I lifted the mattress and placed the pistol back on top of the newspaper. I patted my pants pocket to ensure the spent cartridges were still there. They were. I would bury them in Larimer Field when I got the chance. I smoothed over the covers and hurried into my sister's room, where I would nominate myself as the judge for their singing contest. Of course, I would choose Mindy as the winner, but more importantly, they would be my alibi if I needed one.

Chapter 17

T he next day, in late morning, Donald, Ronald, Jan, and Leroy, found me as I sat lazily in the dirt with my back against the chain-link fence on Larimer Field. Leroy had been hanging out with them regularly for about a week.

"Charles sent word he wants to meet you here on Larimer Field," Leroy informed me. "He said maybe at noon? I hear he's afraid to come into our part of the neighborhood, and he's waiting up the street for an answer."

I considered the location. Larimer Avenue would have plenty of people around at noon, so I doubted that Charles would be stupid enough to try something. No, I concluded that there was only one reason to meet with me now; to call a truce.

"Okay, let him know I'll be here waiting at noon," I instructed, "and tell him Lulu and Clarence need to be with him."

"All right," said Leroy, "and we'll make sure he knows we'll be here too, in case they try something."

I objected, "No, man, yinz can wait across the street in the schoolyard if you want, but I have to meet the three of them alone."

"But, Frankie—," Jan started to protest. Donald elbowed him into silence.

"All right, man, if that's how you want it," Donald said.

"Go let them know that Frankie will be here at noon, waiting," Donald instructed. Leroy, Jan, and Ronald took off running. After they had gone, Donald faced me.

"You did it, didn't you?"

"Did what?" I asked innocently.

"You know what, Frankie," Donald persisted. "I knew it was you the second I heard about it." Unable to deny it under Donald's accusing gaze, I gave him a furtive grin. There was no regret in me; I did what I had to do. "Man, Frankie, you could have killed one of them!" Donald's accusatory tone made me bristle.

"Donald, man, you weren't there that day at the tracks," I said. "I'm telling you, for real, they tried to kill me, and I'm not jiving you none. If that guy hadn't come along when he did and scared them away, I'd be dead right now. I'm lucky to be alive." I paused. When I had told Donald about being jumped by Charles and Lulu and Clarence, I had made up a story about some random stranger happening by, and he had chased them away. I still hadn't told Donald about Honeymarmo.

"And I'll tell you something else, when they were over the hill, swinging on the rope, and I was hiding behind that jagger bush with the gun in my hand, I almost shot and killed Charles. I swear to God I did, but I didn't because when I pointed the gun at him and pulled the trigger the first time, the safety was on. But the other times, I just fired the gun at a drainpipe and then took off out of there. I'm so lucky the safety was on. That scared me more than anything."

Donald listened intently. He at first seemed uncertain but then seemed to reconcile something within himself. "So what are you going do now?" he asked.

I grinned. "You'll see," I said. "Before they get here, you guys can hide on the basement steps across the street at the school."

Donald nodded. "Okay, man, but you better be careful."

It was just before noon, and I stood nervously on the sidewalk in front of Larimer Field. I glanced across the street and saw Ronald's head poking out from above the steps descending to the school's basement. I waved for him to get out of sight, and Ronald's head disappeared. I saw the three cross the street near Martha's store a few moments later, coming toward me. I noticed with some satisfaction that Lulu was limping. I bit my bottom lip to keep from laughing, turned, and walked several yards onto the field to wait. When they finally stopped in front of me, I noticed the difference in their attitude. Gone was the aggression, and there was now a consolatory and even amiable demeanor in its place.

Charles stepped forward and cleared his throat. "We know it was you, man! We want a truce. We came to say we were sorry about jumping you at the railroad tracks and that we ain't going to come after you no more."

"I don't know what you're talking about, man," I said. "I didn't do nothing, and even if I did, you couldn't prove it anyway!"

"Aw, come on, Frankie, we said we're sorry. We just want to forget everything and maybe even be friends." He turned toward the other two. "Don't we?"

"That's right," Clarence agreed.

"Yeah." Lulu grimaced.

"See?" Charles said. "We don't want no more trouble. If you agree, then it's over."

I pretended to consider their proposal. "I don't know. I mean, yinz jacked me up pretty bad," I reminded them.

"Man, we said we were sorry!" Lulu interrupted. Charles silenced him with a look.

"Yeah, just like Lulu said, we said we were sorry," Charles repeated.

"Well, I guess we could be friends now," I said in a conciliatory tone. Their faces relaxed. "But somehow, it just doesn't seem fair to me," I added. Their faces tensed. Inwardly, I was deriving pleasure by toying with them.

"What do you mean, what doesn't seem fair?" Charles scowled.

"That I get jumped and almost killed by you three. Man, you tried to stab me," I reminded him. "I mean, what about me? I think it's only fair that I get yinz back in some way, so we're at least even before we can become friends."

Charles's squinted. "Get us back, how?"

I shrugged, then scratched my chin. When enough time had passed, I snapped my fingers as if a solution had suddenly occurred to me. "I got it," I said eagerly. "How about if you let me punch one of you one time in the face, then I'll consider us even. That's only fair."

Clarence immediately protested. "No way, you ain't punching me in my face!"

"You're crazy if you think I'm going to let you punch me in the face," Charles objected.

Lulu was shaking his head vigorously and waving his hands. "Hell no, man, nuh-uh!"

"All right, have it your way. It's your funeral," I said as I turned and strolled toward the open gate.

Just before I reached it, Charles shouted out to me, "Wait! Wait! Just hold on a minute!"

Feigning impatience, I stopped and crossed my arms across my chest. Charles turned to the other two, and they began to whisper heatedly at one other. Clarence and Lulu shook their heads ardently, but after a moment, they stopped. Finally, Charles turned back toward me.

"Just one punch, right?" he asked.

It took all of my strength to maintain my composure. "Yeah," I reassured him, "just one punch, and then I'll consider us even for what you did to me. I won't even punch my hardest. Afterward, we can be friends, and everything will be cool between us."

They exchanged glances, and all nodded grudgingly. "Okay," Charles acquiesced, "let's get this over with. I'll be the one," he said reluctantly. With a sense of purpose, I strolled back toward them. I positioned myself directly in front of Charles. Charles sucked a deep breath, braced himself, and stuck out his chin. He was squinting hard. I couldn't resist the temptation of having a little fun at Charles's expense, so I reared back and feigned a quick punch. Charles instinctively flinched away.

"No way," I protested, "there's no flinching. If you flinch, I get another punch on account I won't get in a clean shot." Anger flashed into Charles's eyes, but he quickly regained his composure because of what he believed to be at stake.

"All right, all right!" he relented, "just hurry up, man!" Once again, he resumed the position. I again reared back, but this time with all the force I could muster, I let loose a punch that crashed into Charles's jaw.

Charles stumbled back, yelped in pain, stomped his foot, and let loose with several cuss words. He cupped his chin and began to rub his jaw. He sucked in air through his teeth and spat out a small amount of blood.

"I thought you weren't going to punch your hardest?" he complained.

"I didn't," I lied.

"Whatever. We cool?" Charles asked resentfully.

"Yeah, man, we're cool," I assured him.

The three pushed past me toward the open gate with everyone in agreement. As the three of them walked down Larimer Avenue, it was almost comical to watch them as Charles gingerly rubbed his chin. When they had disappeared around a corner, I darted across the street to where Donald, Ronald, Jan, and Leroy were hiding. When I reached the cement steps and looked down, Leroy, Jan, and Ronald were rolling on the ground, laughing their fool heads off.

"Frankie, you're about one crazy dude," Leroy applauded. I grinned, acknowledging Leroy's comment as a compliment.

"So you saw me punch Charles?" I asked.

"Man, Frankie, I ain't never seen nothing so funny in my life," Ronald quipped.

"Me neither." Jan laughed.

"Yeah, it was pretty funny," Donald added, but he wasn't laughing.

Chapter 18

In Youngstown, Ohio, Marcus Logan sat alone in his backyard near his neighborhood's outskirts in Hazelton. He had just turned seven and would be entering the second grade this next school year. His mum affectionately referred to him as Little Marcus, and his dad was Big Marcus. He had carefully set up miniature green and tan toy soldiers on the ground, which he strategically placed in opposition to do battle. Now, as he sat in the overgrown grass knocking over the plastic soldiers one at a time mimicking machine gun fire and mortar explosions, he decided the green plastic army would win this time.

His mother, Candy Logan, a beautiful thin-framed woman in her late twenties with almond-shaped eyes, smooth black skin, and high cheekbones, stood in the kitchen, looking out the screen door across the back porch. She smiled warmly at her son as she watched him play. She pushed open the screen door and stepped out onto the wooden porch.

"Little Marcus?"

"Yes, Mom?"

"Stay in the yard. I have housework to do. You hear me?"

"Aw, Mom, can't I go over to Gino's for a little bit?" Marcus protested. Gino was his best friend who lived across the alley three houses down.

"No, you can't. I told you I have housework to do for now. Maybe when I'm done, we can go visit."

Marcus frowned. "Aw, Mom," he sniffled from a slight summer cold and wiped a trickle of snot from his upper lip with the back of his hand.

"Don't 'aw, Mom' me, and use your hanky like you're supposed to," his mother reminded him. He pulled a hanky from his pants pocket and wiped his nose. Candy walked back into the house, leaving her son to play war with his little plastic soldiers.

Later, as Marcus sat near the fence, resetting soldiers for another battle, a looming shadow appeared on the ground in front of him. He looked up over his shoulder. A rugged-looking white man wearing old dirty clothes stood just on the other side of the fence, staring down at him. He was also wearing a funny hat, and he was grinning, friendly-like.

"Well, howdy. What's your name?" the man asked pleasantly.

"Marcus."

"Well, hello, Marcus. Who's winning, the tan or the green army?"

"The green. I like green," Marcus replied.

"Well, so do I," chuckled the man. "Looks like we have something in common." The man widened his grin. "It sure is hot, ain't it?"

Marcus nodded, "It sure is."

"Well, I was just on my way to the store to get me an ice-cold soda pop and some candy. Do you like soda pop, Marcus?"

Marcus nodded again. "I like orange Crush."

"No kidding," the man chuckled, "orange Crush is my favorite too." The man paused. "Say, Marcus, do you have any money? We can maybe go get an orange Crush and some candy together."

Marcus shook his head. "No, I ain't got no money."

"Well, shoot, Marcus, I'll tell you what. Here, hold out your hand." Marcus did what the man asked. The man gently grabbed his hand and pressed something into his palm. Marcus pulled his hand down and looked at it.

"It's a fifty-cent piece!" Marcus proclaimed with delight.

"Ain't nothing like a nice shiny fifty-cent piece to make someone happy." The man giggled. "So now there's no reason we both can't walk to the store and get us an ice-cold orange Crush and some candy."

Marcus looked up at the man, then down at the bright shiny new fifty-cent piece, then up again at the man. "I don't know, mister, my mom said I was supposed to stay in the yard," he said hesitantly.

"Well, that's because moms always worry. But since you're with an adult, heck, she won't mind. And besides, we'll bring her back an ice-cold soda pop, and some candy too." The man with the funny hat chuckled. "Boy, oh boy, Marcus, Won't she be surprised?" he asked excitedly.

Marcus furrowed his eyebrows in thought, then smiled widely up at the man. "Yeah, she sure will."

"Well, then, let's get going."

Marcus tightened his grip on his shiny new fifty-cent piece, jumped to his feet, and walked through the back gate to where the man stood. They started up the alley together.

"Hey, the store is the other way," said Marcus.

"Why, of course, it is, I know that," answered the man, "but I know a shortcut that will get us there and back faster." He again grinned at Marcus, who nodded and smiled back. They reached the edge of a wooded area and disappeared into the trees.

It was almost an hour later, as she stood near an open window cleaning an upstairs bedroom, that Candy realized she no longer heard the sounds of make-believe war coming from her son. She poked her head out the window and peered into the backyard. It was empty. That was odd since she hadn't heard the screen door slam shut. Little Marcus never did anything quietly. She hollered his name out the open window, and there was no response. She pulled her head inside and began walking through the house, yelling for him. Only an eerie silence answered her.

She pushed open the screen door, walked briskly through the backyard, out the gate, and up the alley toward Gino Martinelli's house. She fought to control the rising anger within her. It was not like Little Marcus to disobey her, but she would make sure it never happened again when she got hold of him. She arrived at the

Martinelli's backyard, opened the gate, strode across the backyard, and knocked on the back door.

In a moment, an Italian woman opened the door. She wore a dark house dress and wiped her wet hands on a towel.

"Candy? Won't you come in." Mrs. Martinelli smiled warmly, motioning for Candy to step into the kitchen.

"Sorry to bother you, Maria, but I've come for my boy. I told him to stay in the yard, but he didn't listen. Wait until I get hold of him." Candy Logan grimaced.

Maria Martinelli gave Candy a queer look. "I'm sorry, Candy, but I haven't seen Little Marcus today. Gino's not even home. He went downtown with his father this morning, and they're still not back yet," she said. Candy Logan felt the queasiness deep in her stomach for the first time. Maria saw the worry appear in her eyes. She set the towel down on the kitchen table.

"Don't worry, Candy. I'm sure he's probably somewhere close. Come on, I'll help you find him." They both hurried out the back door. They split up to search in opposite directions in the alley, hollering Marcus's name, and other neighbors heard them yelling and inquired what was going on. Soon, several neighbors, including some of the kids, walked the neighborhoods, expanding their search, all shouting Marcus's name. Without any sign of her son, each passing moment brought a foreboding and sickening dread within Candy. Tears poured down her face as she shouted out Marcus's name.

After a while, Candy frantically dialed for the police, and then she called Big Marcus at work. Several police cars, along with Big Marcus, arrived to join them in the search. For the rest of that day and night and the next couple of days, the entire community continued its efforts to find Little Marcus, which expanded to other areas around Youngstown. Still, nothing. It was as if Little Marcus had vanished from the face of the earth.

Chapter 19

Wanting as fewest people to know about my revenge with the gun, I swore everyone to secrecy, and except for Ronald, I was confident they would all keep my secret. However, I did receive some assurance from Donald that he would make sure his brother wouldn't blab. Donald said this in front of his brother, so there would be no doubt about the consequence, which was good enough for me. The truth was that Charles, Lulu, and Clarence were still dangerous, but I was confident that I was safe as long as they thought themselves in mortal danger. If I were crazy enough to shoot at them once, I would certainly do it again. I would have to be careful.

At first, it appeared as if I had been successful with my revenge and firing Joe's gun without consequence. But then, a few days later, a squad car pulled into the graveled parking lot behind our apartment.

Doreen was sitting on the back porch when it showed up, so she was the first to see it. Two police officers climbed out and looked up in her direction.

"Mummy," she announced into the kitchen, "there's a cop car down there."

Our mum dried her hands on a towel and walked out on the porch. "I wonder how come." She watched as the two policemen walked across the parking lot toward the back of Cosenza's store. "Something must have happened at Cosenza's," she speculated. At the bottom of the steps, the policemen stopped abruptly, turned, and started up the stairs.

"They're coming up here!" Doreen exclaimed. Our mum froze as she watched them get closer. When they reached the second-story landing, she turned and quickly walked back into the kitchen.

I was just finishing breakfast and was shoving a piece of Town Talk bread into my mouth when our mum walked back inside the kitchen. She looked nervous.

"Policemen are coming up the steps," she announced, giving me a reproachful look. I went pale.

Our mum, Mindy, and Doreen started busying themselves by clearing the kitchen table. I faced the opened kitchen door when the police officers suddenly appeared on the porch. They looked intimidating in their dark blue uniforms. Everyone stopped what they were doing, and I felt a powerful urge to run. But before I could, the bigger policeman knocked on the door frame.

"Excuse me, ma'am," the policeman said politely, "may we come in?"

Our mum stared numbly. She had a plate in her hand, and the water gushed from the spigot behind her. Mindy, who was rinsing dishes, shut it off.

"Ma'am, may we come in?" the policeman repeated.

Our mum smiled nervously. "Sure. What's this all about?" The two of them stepped into our small kitchen.

"Ma'am, we're here about a boy named Frankie. We understand that he lives here. Is that right?" The more prominent police officer asked pointedly.

When I heard my name, I began to choke on my last swallow of bread. The two police officers looked over at me and then turned their attention to our mum.

Our mum stammered nervously. "Yes, that's Frankie. He's my son." I began to fidget uncomfortably. The two policemen exchanged glances.

"Ma'am, what's your name?" the other policeman asked.

"Rose. Rose Desimone," she answered nervously. The policeman scribbled something down on a notepad.

"I see. Well, let me ask you this, ma'am, do you own a gun?"

"A gun? Goodness gracious, no! Why do you ask?" The policeman ignored her question.

Then, the smaller policeman looked directly at me. He quickly examined his notepad, then said, "So you're Frankie?"

All eyes in the small kitchen fixed on me. I skittishly averted eye contact with the policeman, then nodded.

"Son, did you shoot at those boys?" I didn't answer. "I asked you a question. Did you?"

"I didn't shoot at nobody," I blurted out. "I don't even have no gun." I peeked over at my mum, who was staring at me in utter bewilderment. I looked down at the table again.

After an awkward pause, our mum broke the silence. "Mary Mother of God, what did you do, Frankie?" I didn't answer. She looked over at the policemen.

"What did he do?" she demanded.

"Yeah, what did you do, Frankie?" Doreen chimed in.

"Yinz, hush up," our mum barked.

"I didn't even say nothing," Mindy protested.

"Hush," our mum warned sharply. She again turned toward the policemen.

"Well, apparently, it started with your son here getting into an altercation with three black kids down by the railroad tracks."

"There wasn't no altercation, them jagoffs jumped me, and I didn't even do nothing to them!" I interrupted, setting the record straight.

"Anyways, from what we were able to gather, so far, someone tried to shoot these boys the other day, and they claim it was your son." The police officer watched me as he spoke, and I didn't flinch.

"What?" my mum gasped, staring down at me. "Why would they think it was you, Frankie?" she asked, giving me a stiff slap to the back of my head, and I cringed away.

"How should I know? I said I didn't do nothing," I grumbled.

Our mum looked back toward the police. "He says he didn't do it. Did anyone see him?"

"No, ma'am," the bigger officer said. "The fact is nobody saw him do it or can even identify him as being there when the alleged shooting incident occurred. We searched the area and couldn't find any evidence, like shell casings and such. We talked to some of the neighbors in that area, and a couple of them said that someone might have been lighting off cherry bombs in the woods nearby."

"Well, that's what must have happened then," our mum rationalized. 'These boys heard the cherry bombs go off, and they thought someone was shooting at them."

"Yes, ma'am, that may very well be true, but the fact is your son also punched one of the boys in the face. We have witnesses to that," the shorter police officer said indignantly, and he stared directly at me. "Son, you can't go around punching people in the face."

"He said I could."

"He let you so that you wouldn't shoot at him again," the officer said, trying to keep his composure.

"He's a liar. I didn't shoot at no one," I insisted.

"Maybe you did, maybe you didn't, but this is a serious accusation, and we have to check out everything. You understand?" he added, looking over at our mum.

Doreen could no longer contain herself. "Frankie, who'd you punch in the face?" she asked excitedly.

"Charles."

"Nuh-uh, get out of here." She giggled. I glanced harshly in her direction to shut her up, but there was such approval in Doreen's eyes I grinned instead. My mum reached over and again slapped me stiffly in the back of his head.

"Don't you be smirking!"

She looked back at the policemen. "Is he in trouble?"

The bigger policeman looked sternly at Frankie. "Well, since this kid was stupid enough to give him permission to punch him, and we can't prove he shot at them, I don't see much we can do—at least not at this time." I slumped further down in my chair. "We're still going to investigate further, though," he persisted.

The two police officers exchanged exasperated looks and communicated something with their eyes. Finally, the bigger policeman again addressed our mum. "We'll be going now, but we'll be in contact if anything else comes up." He closed his notepad. "Thank you for your time, ma'am," he said, doffing the bill of his hat. They walked single file out the door.

"You're welcome," our mum shouted after them.

As they headed down the steps, our mum turned angrily toward me. "I can't believe you, Frankie. You're in so much trouble," she hissed. I sat with my arms folded across my chest.

"You did it, didn't you? You used Joe's gun, didn't you? And don't you lie to me! You could've killed someone. And what do you think Joe would do if he found out about this, huh?" she asked. I perked up when my mum said "if" instead of "when." There was hope that she would not tell him. Needing to know for sure, I looked pitifully up at her.

"You're not going to tell him?" I asked.

"Christ, if I do, there ain't no telling what he'll do, but I can almost promise that you'd spend the rest of the summer locked up in your room." I could see the anguish in her eyes, and I gave her a remorseful look. Finally, she shook her head. "I won't tell him. But if he finds out about this, and if he finds out that I knew you took his gun and shot it, both of us will get smacked around, or worse," she warned. I breathed a sigh of relief.

"Sorry, Mummy," I said, and I meant it this time.

"Frankie, what am I going to do with you?" my mum pleaded. "If I would've told those policemen that we had a gun in the house and it belonged to Joe, and the welfare people found out, we could lose all our benefits. Then what would we do?"

"I won't do it no more, Mum," I promised, "I swear."

Our mum ran her hand through her thick black curly hair, picked up a plate off the table, and slowly walked toward the sink. "I don't know what I'm going to do with you, Frankie," she said weakly. "You're always getting in fights, you won't listen, and you even steal from me, your own mother," she said morosely. I gave her a perplexed look. "Oh, don't give me that look. Don't think I don't know about you putting the candy on my credit over at Martha's store and telling Phyllis it was for me!" I knew I was busted, so I gave no defense. I gave Mindy a furtive glance, and her expression told me she was as surprised as me that our mum found out. "Go on and get out of the

141

kitchen so your sisters can clean up," our mum said glumly. I got up and walked outside on the back porch. Doreen followed me while Mindy remained to help our mum rinse dishes.

"Did you really punch Charles in the face?" Doreen beamed.

I nodded. "Yeah, I don't know what I was thinking," I said, feeling relieved for my narrow escape and glad for the compassion my mum had just shown me.

"Jeez-o-man, Frankie, did you make him bleed?" Doreen asked; her face was aglow at the prospect.

I looked disgustedly at my sister. "Doreen, you're sick."

"Yeah, yeah, but did he?" she persisted eagerly.

I nodded. "Some," I gloated.

Doreen was giddy with excitement. "Nuh-uh, get out! Man, oh man, Frankie, I wish I was there to see it," she cackled.

"Doreen, get in here and empty the rubbish, and the floor needs swept too," our mum yelled.

"All right, Mummy." Doreen gave me an approving wink, turned, and hurried off to do her chores.

I sat on the porch for a long time, reflecting on what had happened. It occurred to me that I seemed to have escaped punishment on so many levels. Joe could have been home, and today's entire situation with the police coming to our apartment could have ended disastrously. I shuddered at the prospect. I thought of all the scenarios that could have unfolded. The policemen could have searched the apartment and found the gun, but they didn't. My mum could have committed herself to tell Joe everything, but she promised not to. Even my lie to that old guy about some kids lighting off a cherry bomb seemed to work out in my favor. But staring down the gun's barrel and feeling the resistance of the trigger made me ponder most. What if it had fired? I shuddered at the very thought.

For things to work out in my favor to this extent was not the norm for me. Trouble usually followed me like a lost puppy. There was something different about this, something that seemed almost orchestrated. There were too many things in play to be just dumb luck. I began to think about Honeymarmo. I tilted my head back and rested it against the brick wall as I stared up at the blue sky.

It was strange, but it seemed as if I saw it for the first time, even though I had stared up at it a thousand times before. Then it struck me. I wondered if God, at that very second, was staring down at me. Compelled, I bowed my head.

"Thank you, God. I believe in you, and I believe what your Son Jesus has done for me, and I'm sorry for what I did. Help me to be a better person, and please don't let Joe find out what I did," I whispered reverently. I then stood and walked into the kitchen, where my mum was wiping down the stove with a dishrag. I wrapped my arms around her waist and laid my head against her bosom in a rare show of affection. I squeezed and gave her the kind of hug that I hadn't given her in a very long time.

"I'm sorry, Mummy," I whispered contritely. My mum's initial surprise was evident as she at first didn't move or respond. Then, after a brief pause, I felt her arms embrace me. We stood that way for a few seconds until, finally, we let go of one another. With a warm smile, she reached out and muffed my hair.

"You need a haircut. I can hardly see your eyes," she said, brushing my hair away from my eyes.

"Yeah, I know," I responded. I turned and dashed out the kitchen door to see if I could find Honeymarmo.

*****

I scampered down the trail next to Larimer Bridge. When the bridge's underbelly came into view, I spotted Honeymarmo squatting on his hams with his back to me.

"Honeym—," I started to shout but stopped abruptly. As the squatting hobo turned his head, I realized it wasn't Honeymarmo. The hobo stood. He was shorter and stouter than Honeymarmo, and heavy stubble cast a dark shadow over his face making him look unfriendly. His dark piercing eyes immediately put me on edge. The hobo wore an old black suit jacket with a gaping hole in the left elbow, dirty brown trousers, and large black shoes. On his head sat a worn and crumpled fedora.

"Frankie!" A voice echoed further up the hill where the bridge arch rested against the cement abutment. I jerked my eyes toward Honeymarmo, who was standing near the top of the slope, and he shuffled down the incline towards me.

"Well, what have we got here?" the stranger cackled in a husky voice as he looked me over head to toe. "Well, you old wolf you." He gave Honeymarmo a crude wink. "I see you done got yourself a little lamb." He cackled again. The stranger grinned widely at me, but his eyes remained cold and scary.

"Frankie here is a local yokel, and he ain't no lamb," Honeymarmo interjected sharply as he reached my side. "He's a good kid and a good friend of mine."

"Sure, sure," said the scary-looking hobo, "I bet he is. I bet he is indeed." He smiled crookedly. A couple of teeth were missing, and those remaining were grungy brown with black decay near the gums. "Well, where are my manners." He reached a hand out for me to shake. "They call me Grub."

Reluctantly, I reached out and shook. Grub's hand was thick and calloused, and it felt as if I was grasping a piece of steel. I stood mute as Grub continued to stare roguishly at me.

"Grub here just happened by this morning and decided to visit for a while," Honeymarmo explained. He exchanged a cautious glance with me.

"Well, you know this is the first time I ever been to the Big Smoke, and it ain't all that bad," Grub said, "and it's getting better all the time." I gave Honeymarmo a searching look, and Honeymarmo grinned thinly at me.

"The Big Smoke is what we hobos call Pittsburgh," Honeymarmo explained.

"Well, why don't we all just cop a squat and get acquainted," Grub suggested. He plopped down in the dirt. Honeymarmo gave me a nod, and we joined him.

"So Frankie, is it? Why, that's a real hobo name. You sure you ain't no hobo like us?" Grub teased. I shook my head. "I'm just joshing you." Again Grub cackled. "You go to school, boy?"

"Yeah, but it's summer vacation now," I answered.

"Let me guess. I bet you're going to be in the sixth grade next year."

"How'd you know that?" I asked, obviously impressed.

"Why, hell, I know all about school. I graduated sixth grade myself, you know. But then I figured that them knowledge boxes were just a waste of time. It's just another way for the government and society to control you. No, the real education and learning, Frankie, comes from being on the road in the real world because it teaches you about life and people and about surviving. That's where I got my learning, and I'll match it against any bookworm any day of the week," Grub crowed.

"Living on the road is also a guarantee to end up poor, and when you reach the end of your life, you have nothing to show for it— no work, no home, no family, no money, nothing," Honeymarmo argued passively.

Grub bristled. "Yeah, well, at least I've been free, and I ain't spent my life beholding to no one." He scrunched his thick, furry eyebrows. "And I certainly don't dance to the tune of others like some puppet on a string."

Honeymarmo had made his point, so he placated his next remark to avoid escalating the argument. "Well, I suppose there's something to be said for that."

"You're damn right," Grub barked indignantly. We sat in awkward silence for a moment.

Finally, Honeymarmo once again spoke. "A few years back, I traveled the rails for a bit with a hobo named Dakota Dave. He was nice enough to me, but he was a mean old dog to most folks. There was something about his eyes that just naturally warned a person to tread carefully. He had spent some time in prison and always claimed that's where he got his hardness and dislike for people in general. I got to say, Grub, you got that same look in your eyes. Have you ever been to the big house?"

Grub gave Honeymarmo a curious look, then grinned, obviously impressed at his powers of observation. "I sure have. Twice, in fact," he bragged.

"What for?" Honeymarmo asked.

"Well, let's see. The first time was for almost beating a bull to death with a club. He was a mean son of a bitch, almost killed me when he pulled me from one of the boxcars in Cleveland. Laid my head wide open with his club." Grub took off his fedora and pointed to a spot on his head. All I saw was dirty, greasy hair. "Well, I took that club from him and gave him a taste of what he was dishing out. Damn near killed him. They got me for assault and battery. They tried to charge me with attempted murder, but it didn't stick. I did a little more than a year for that one."

"What about the other time?" Honeymarmo asked.

Grub grinned impishly. "That one happened in Kansas City. I was broke, down on my luck, and damn near starving, so I decided to jackroll some drunk guy. A guy's got to eat, you know! Anyway, just when I finished jackrolling this guy in an alley, got damn near fifty bucks, a couple of do-gooders happened by and wrestled me to the ground until the cops got there. I did almost a year for that one."

"Yep, a man has got to eat, I suppose," Honeymarmo said.

Grub suddenly reached down and rubbed his stomach. "Speaking of starving, you got any food? My bindle is bare."

"I got a couple of cans of beans," Honeymarmo said.

"Well, you think you could share one with an old road dog?" Grub asked, giving a pitiful but hopeful look.

"Why, sure," Honeymarmo said. "Maybe you can build a fire and heat them up some."

"Sure thing, I'll get my banjo and dig a pit." Grub stood and limped up the slope to his bindle shoved on top of the abutment. He pulled out a small shovel and hobbled back to Honeymarmo and me.

"You hurt?" I blurted out. Grub grimaced.

"Just a little. I got an infection in my big toe from these here damn shoes. They're just too big for me." He plopped back down in the dirt and pulled off his left shoe and sock. His big toe was swollen and red, and pus oozed out from under his dirt-encrusted toenail. I cringed.

"There's a hospital down the street, not too far from here," I informed him.

Grub looked over at me as if I had said something exceedingly stupid. "Don't this boy know nothing?" he asked Honeymarmo. "Boy, hospitals just wait for hobos like us to come in so they can slip us the black bottle. Ain't no way I'll ever go to no hospital."

"What's the black bottle?" I asked.

"You ain't never heard of the black bottle?" Grub asked incredulously, giving me a dumbfounded look. "Why, the black bottle is poison, son, poison."

"Poison? Get out. Hospitals don't poison no one," I exclaimed.

Grub's black eyes flashed angrily, and his tone took on an aggressive air of bellicosity. "Are you calling me a liar, boy?" he growled, leaning toward me.

Honeymarmo quickly interjected, "Now, don't get your feathers ruffled, ain't no one calling you a liar. He just ain't never heard of it before." Grub seemed to weigh Honeymarmo's explanation before he settled back.

Grub intermittently leered over at me as he eased his sock and shoe back on. "Well, let me tell you, I've known two bums that have gone into hospitals for less than what I got here, and both ended up on a slab at the city morgue. Hospitals get paid secretly by rich folks and the government to poison us because we're considered a scourge on society. They know they can't control us like others, so they slip us the black bottle any time we go to the hospital to get rid of us. That's the truth, boy, and you can take that to the bank," Grub proclaimed matter-of-factly. He picked up his shovel and began to dig a firepit before continuing. "They don't teach you that at that knowledge box you go to, do they? That's because they keep you ignorant and teach you only those things they want, so they can control you and your life."

Once Grub dug the firepit, he stood and limped over to the edge of the woods on the other side of the bridge. He returned in a few moments, carrying a crumpled-up brown paper bag and an arm full of sticks and twigs. He knelt next to the pit, placed the crumpled sack in the center, and, starting with the smaller twigs, began to stack them in layers around the crumpled paper, making a tepee which gradually got bigger as he overlaid the taller sticks on top of the smaller twigs. Once he had finished constructing the tepee, he pulled out a pack of matches from his jacket pocket, struck one, and lit the crumpled bag. It immediately ignited, and flames licked up over the wood setting it ablaze. He shoved the matches back into his jacket pocket, felt around, and produced a handful of old cigarette butts. He fingered through them, picked out a nice plump one, shoved the rest back into his pocket, placed it between his lips, picked up a lit stick from the fire, and lit it with a series of exaggerated puffs.

"I think the fire is ready for them there beans," he announced. Honeymarmo stood, and I stood with him.

"I have to go now," I announced.

"Go? What for? Why don't you stay so we can get better acquainted?" Grub pleaded. He gave me a wily grin. As I looked into Grub's black eyes, I felt the hairs on my arms stand erect.

Honeymarmo picked up on my uneasiness. "He says he got to go," Honeymarmo said, nudging me toward the trail. "I'll see you again soon." I could hear the tightness in Honeymarmo's voice.

"Yeah, we'll see you again soon, Frankie," Grub cackled, giving me another disturbing wink.

I turned and sprinted up the trail, and for some reason, I ran back to my apartment without stopping.

Chapter 20

I t had been more than a week since I had last seen Bunny, and I couldn't stop thinking about her. I would stroll past her home, hoping to find her on the porch or in her yard, but had no luck. Discouraged, I finally mustered the courage to visit her. It was late morning, and I nervously made my way up the walkway and knocked on the front door, and Bunny's mother opened it.

"Is Bunny here?" I asked without giving a proper greeting.

Bunny's mum looked amused. "Well, good morning, Frankie," she said.

"What's up?" I responded awkwardly.

"Wait here a moment, and I'll get her for you." She disappeared inside, leaving the door slightly ajar. I shifted my feet nervously. *What if she doesn't want to see me?* I thought to myself. My stomach knotted. Then, the door flung open, and Bunny appeared with her infectious smile and shiny brown eyes that seemed to be reserved just for me. I relaxed, and the unsettling feeling in my stomach faded.

"Where have you been?" Bunny asked, feigning indignation. It was clear she was glad to see me, although I couldn't imagine why. She was wearing yellow shorts and a pink shirt, and a white band held her tight ponytail in place.

I cleared my throat. "I walked by a few times, but you ain't never outside." Although I didn't think it possible, Bunny's smile widened, making her look even more beautiful. She reached out and gently touched my arm, causing my heart to flutter. Bunny turned and shouted into the house.

"Mummy, me and Frankie are going to sit on the front porch."

149

"Frankie and I," her mum corrected her.

"Frankie and I are going to sit on the front porch," Bunny repeated, rolling her eyes at me.

"Okay," her mum answered, reappearing, "but just for a little bit."

"Yes, ma'am." Bunny pulled the front door shut. She and I strolled over and sat down on the porch swing. She scooted against me, and my arms and legs tingled. I had the urge to touch her hand but was afraid. I had been anxious to see her, but now didn't know what to say or do. My mind searched for a topic, but nothing came to my mind. The longer I sat in silence, the more panic-stricken I became, mostly fearing Bunny would grow bored or, worse, regret that I had even stopped over. Then, mercifully, Bunny spoke first, breaking the awkward silence.

"What's the matter, don't you like me no more?" she asked. The question caught me off guard.

"What? Yeah, of course, I like you," I assured her. "I'll always like you, Bunny." I was relieved to have something to say finally. Bunny nibbled on her bottom lip, then looked down into her lap.

"Yeah, I know you like me, Frankie, but do you love me?" she asked. The question confused me because I could have sworn that I had just told her that I did.

"Yeah, that's what I just said," I tried to clarify.

"No, you said you'll always *like* me," she corrected me. "You didn't say you'd always love me." Bunny's lips puckered into a pout. My heart sank. Everyone knew when you told a girl you liked her it meant you loved her; apparently, everyone except Bunny. I rubbed my face.

"Of course, I do, Bunny," I reassured her. There, I had said it. I gazed at her beautiful face waiting for her smile to return. The pout remained, and my confusion deepened.

"You have to say it. You have to say the words 'I love you,'" Bunny said sulkily. "But only if you truly mean it." As I stared into Bunny's doe-like eyes, my innards seemed to melt like butter under the hot sun.

I cleared my rapidly drying throat. "I love you, Bunny," I muttered clumsily, tugging at my collar. My words seemed to have been spoken by someone else. I waited painfully for her response. Her brilliant smile immediately reappeared, and her eyes lit up. I breathed a sigh of relief as Bunny gently caressed my arm.

"You're so silly, Frankie," she chuckled. My brain turned to mush. The confusion I felt deepened beyond anything I had ever felt before. *Silly? Why am I silly?* I thought. *Because I said I loved her? She made me say it.* My mind raced, and I felt foolish. Bunny didn't seem to notice. She began to chatter about all kinds of things, and I did my best to follow along. But I couldn't seem to concentrate. So I decided to say as little as possible so as not to make Bunny pout again and to avoid suffering the indignity of experiencing even more confusion or foolishness—if that were even possible.

"Frankie...Frankie!" Bunny shouted.

"Oh, uh, what?" I answered, realizing I hadn't heard what Bunny was saying.

"So do you?" she asked.

"Do I what?"

"Do you want to come?" she asked impatiently.

"Come where?" I asked.

"Frankie, haven't you been listening?" Bunny snapped irritably.

"Yeah, I was," I lied. "I just didn't hear you, that's all."

Bunny looked at me skeptically. "The movies," she finally said. "My mum is taking me to the movies tomorrow in East Liberty, so how about I ask her if you can go with us?"

I nodded. "Okay."

Bunny jumped up and ran into the house. A moment later, she was back and plopped down next to me. "My mum says you can go with us," she giggled happily. "She said it cost fifty cents to get in. The show will start at one o'clock, so we'll have to leave about 12:15, so we can catch the bus."

"Okay, I'll be here about twelve," I promised, rising to my feet. Bunny frowned.

"You ain't going to leave yet, are you?" she asked. It was hard to resist her siren call, and especially those large, beautiful, pleading eyes.

"I'm sorry, but I have to, Bunny. I have to do something for my mum, but I'll see you tomorrow," I assured her. I turned and walked briskly from the porch, leaving Bunny watching after me. On the sidewalk, I faced home, pondering where I would get fifty cents. I knew I couldn't get it from my mum; she never saved more than a few cents after spending whatever she got from relief on food, cigarettes, and rent. That's why she had credit at the neighborhood stores, and most times, that was barely enough.

*****

I rummaged through the garbage behind Cosenza's store until I found it. I carefully examined the burlap sack making sure there were no holes. It would do nicely. I turned and scanned the graveled parking lot in front of me. I could get two cents for each empty pop bottle I returned to the store. To my disappointment, I didn't find any. I sighed. At this rate, it would be a very long day. I strolled over to the alley across the street with the burlap sack in hand and began searching through the labyrinth of alleyways crisscrossing through all of Larimer.

I kicked through the tall grass and weeds that grew wild out-side the backyard fences and searched through every empty field I came across. I climbed the drain pipes of garages, scanned their flat tarred-covered roofs, and even searched old abandoned houses. The entire north side of Larimer snuggled on top of a sloping hillside, and after reaching its crest, I calculated what would be a reasonable dis-tance a pop bottle would travel if heaved. I scrambled down the hill to that distance and walked along the slope the entire length of the woods, searching under bushes and looking around every tree until eventually, I had worked my way back up the hill.

Afterward, I walked back toward Larimer Avenue then turned east toward Larimer Bridge. I shuffled down the path alongside the bridge toward the railroad tracks, and neither Honeymarmo nor

Grub was there. I made my way to the tracks and began to walk south for about half a mile, searching for bottles, without having any luck. I walked in the opposite direction for about the same distance before turning back toward the bridge. Once there, the shade felt inviting, but I didn't stop to rest. Instead, I shuffled back up the path.

I opened up my sack before reaching the top of the path, looked inside, and counted seven pop bottles. One was full of dirt, and I knew no store would accept it, so I chucked it into the woods. I had been working diligently, scavenging through the neighborhood for more than two hours, and six good pop bottles were all I had to show for it. I sighed dejectedly. I would never get my fifty cents at this rate.

"Well, Frankie!" I turned, and on the trail stood Honeymarmo. I had been so deep in thought that I had not even heard him approach. Honeymarmo flashed his infectious grin as he closed the distance between us.

"I thought maybe you had gone," I said.

Honeymarmo reached out and placed his weathered hand on my shoulder, and I noticed that it was trembling. Honeymarmo turned his gaze toward the tracks below.

"Yeah, it seems as if I have been getting a bit restless lately, but I ain't had the hankering to leave just yet," he said pensively.

"You okay, Honeymarmo? Your hand is shaking awful bad."

Honeymarmo again grinned. "Well, I have been a little under the weather lately. It seems as if I've been more tired than usual, and I've been nauseous some, but I'm sure it will pass. So what have you been doing since I saw you last?"

"A whole lot of stuff," I said. Then a thought struck me, and I looked past Honeymarmo down the trail. "Where's Grub?" I asked edgily.

"He said he was going to do some panhandling around town." Honeymarmo grimaced. He looked sternly at me, and his countenance turned somber. "I'm not sure I trust that one. He has a bit of a bad streak in him. I've been trying to talk to him about God, but he doesn't seem very receptive. He's a strange one. Do me a favor and stay away from him, Frankie, unless I'm here, okay?"

"Okay," I promised. My sense of urgency to scrounge for pop bottles temporarily waned, and together me and Honeymarmo descended the path.

We reached the underbelly of the bridge and sat in the dirt. Honeymarmo stood and walked to his bindle, then returned carrying a piece of wood. He pulled out his stag-handled knife and handed it to me. "Here you go. Whittle on this. It's a nice piece of pine."

He again plopped back down in the dirt and watched as I began to carve the piece of wood. Thunder rumbled in the distance. We looked up at the sky.

"I hope it don't rain," I commented. "I hate the rain."

"Well, I think it may pass," Honeymarmo said, observing the fast-moving clouds. Then, he seemed to study me. "Why would you say you hate the rain?" he asked.

"Because I just do. I mean, what good is it? You can't do nothing when it rains, and if you're outside, you just get all wet and have to stop playing. If I'm at home, and it rains, Joe just locks me in my room longer. It's worse being locked up when it's raining. It makes me sadder."

Honeymarmo scratched his beard. "When I was a boy, my grandmother used to say the rain was God's tears. She said when the world became more sad than happy, God would send his tears to wash away enough of the sadness until there was once again more happiness than sadness in the world." Honeymarmo chuckled. "I used to believe that for the longest time." He stared intently at me. "Isn't there anything you like about the rain?" he asked.

I thought. "Yeah, I do like the way it smells when the rain stops," I admitted.

Honeymarmo smiled. "You know why that is, Frankie?" I shook my head.

"It's because the rain washes the air clean, and it washes everything clean. But it does a lot more than that."

"What do you mean?"

"Well, what do you think?"

"I don't know. I guess it helps the grass and trees, and flowers and stuff grow better," I surmised.

154

"That's right. Without rain, Frankie, there'd be nothing but desert. Gardens and crops wouldn't grow to feed us, and there would be no fresh water to drink because there would be no rivers or streams. Rain is the life source of this earth that keeps everything alive, including you and me." Honeymarmo motioned all around us. "Sometimes, Frankie, you have to look at the world beyond how something affects just you. Sometimes, an inconvenience to you may be critically important to someone or something else. Always try to look beyond yourself and consider others. A selfish person will always think of themselves first and foremost." Honeymarmo locked eyes with me. "You're not a selfish person, Frankie, are you?" Honeymarmo asked.

I dropped my head. "I don't think so," I mumbled.

"Good," Honeymarmo said. "Never hate something good, Frankie, and never hate for selfish reasons."

"Okay," I agreed, "I'll try to remember that."

I updated Honeymarmo on what I had been up to, telling him about Bunny and my revenge on Charles, Lulu, and Clarence. I knew I risked disappointing my friend, mainly since I had ignored Honeymarmo's advice, but for some reason, I felt compelled to tell Honeymarmo everything.

"Do you know what grace is?" Honeymarmo asked when I had finished. Although I had heard Honeymarmo mention it before and had heard it expressed by others, the truth was I wasn't sure what it was.

"Not really," I admitted reluctantly, hoping Honeymarmo wouldn't think me stupid.

"Grace, the way I see it, is showing kindness or forgiving someone even if you feel in your heart, for whatever reason, they don't deserve it." I quickly deduced he was speaking of my recent revenge.

"I know you didn't want me to get back at Charles and Lulu and Clarence, but you just don't understand," I said. "If I didn't do something, the next time they caught me alone somewhere, they would have killed me, for sure."

"I think I know that now," Honeymarmo admitted. "But let me ask you this. Is there anything that's keeping you from forgiving them now?" The question made me squirm as I stared into the dirt. Honeymarmo had no idea what he was asking of me, and I didn't answer.

"Just think about it, Frankie," Honeymarmo said. "Forgiveness has a way of eliminating hate. And when hate is gone, goodness will flourish. Right now, your heart is hard, but you have to find a way of allowing the roots of grace and forgiveness to penetrate it. It is the only way you will find any true peace or fulfillment, and in the end, that is what will set you free."

"Okay," I mumbled. Honeymarmo smiled at me approvingly.

"There's something else I wanted to talk to you about," Honeymarmo said. "The other day, when you were here with Grub and me, he was talking about school being a waste of time. Do you remember?"

"Yeah, I remember."

"Well, you don't listen to that nonsense. You're smart, only I still don't think you know it. You are, you know. Concentrate on school and get a good education if you can, because along with having God in your life, a good education will give you the confidence and ability to dream, and dreams pursued can take you a long way in this life. Promise me you will study hard." Honeymarmo gazed with expectation into my eyes.

I nodded. "Okay."

"The only other advice I will give you besides that is that no matter how much education you get, never think you are better than anyone else, never become prideful, and never become smarter than your own common sense. Okay?"

"I'll try not to," I promised.

"Good, because I have faith in you." Honeymarmo once again became ebullient, and his eyes lit up. "So what's in the sack?" he asked inquisitively, changing the subject.

"Pop bottles. I have to get some money so I can go to the movies with my girlfriend Bunny tomorrow. I've been looking just about everywhere for them," I said.

"Girlfriend, huh?" Honeymarmo mused. "So how you doing so far?"

"Not so good." I sulked, explaining how unproductive my search had been. If I were to collect enough bottles, I knew I would have to be on my way. I handed the knife and piece of wood back to Honeymarmo. Honeymarmo wiped down the blade and handle and shoved the knife back into its leather sheath. I stood abruptly and looked up at the sky. Honeymarmo was right; the clouds had moved on. "I have to get going now," I said. Honeymarmo stood and warmly muffed my hair. I walked over to the path leading up the slope. Honeymarmo shouted after me.

"Frankie, thanks for visiting, and remember what we talked about, especially what I said about staying away from Grub." I nodded as I turned up the path.

Much of what Honeymarmo said seemed to gain a foothold, and I would have no problem staying clear of Grub. For the first time, I considered the possibility of actually forgiving Charles and Lulu and Clarence, as Honeymarmo had suggested. I was also glad that Honeymarmo hadn't asked me to forgive Joe this time. For me, that would be the equivalent of forgiving the devil himself. Hating Joe was one of the few pleasures I had, and I would never let Honeymarmo take it from me, no matter how close we had become. *No*, I thought to myself as I reached Larimer Avenue; *with or without God, that kind of grace was not and would never be in me, no matter how much Honeymarmo tried to convince me otherwise.*

*****

I reached my apartment's back stairs, carrying my nearly empty burlap sack, and plopped down on the third step. I was tired. The day was waning, and I had not yet found nearly enough pop bottles to pay my way at the movies with Bunny. I was desperate, and desperate times called for desperate measures. I knew where there were lots of empty pop bottles, but I would have to steal them, and it would be risky to get them by myself. There would be consequences if caught. For my scheme to work best, I would need an accomplice. Because of her disposition and virtuous character, I immediately ruled out Mindy. No, I would need to find someone bold and daring

yet someone who had the type of compromising principles and eth-
ics that would allow them to justify their illicit activity for a price. I
needed to find Doreen.

I found her sitting on the front stoop of our apartment building
on Larimer Avenue. She was fussing with a pair of steel roller skates,
the kind that slid over one's shoe. One of the skates was lying next to
her, and the other one was on Doreen's foot, and she was tightening
it with a steel key.

"Where did you get the skates?" I asked engagingly.

I was standing to her right, and the sun shone behind me.
Doreen squinted up at me. "I traded for them," she said. "I gave
Connie-Mae three of my *Betty and Veronica* comic books, four Lotta
Dots, and my Chinese jump rope."

Sensing an opening, I quickly gave her a compliment, "You
done good, Doreen."

"No, I didn't. I got gypped!" Doreen scowled. "This skate won't
stay tight and keeps coming loose and falling off my shoe. And one
of the wheels on the other skate doesn't turn anymore. You just wait
until I catch Connie-Mae! I'll get my stuff back," she threatened. I
had no doubt she meant it.

"You ain't seen Jan or Donald or Ronald around anywhere, have
you?" I asked nonchalantly.

"Nuh-uh," she answered, tinkering fervently with her skate. I
waited to give her the chance to ask why, and she wasn't biting.

I began to look anxiously up and down the street for effect. "For
real, they better get here pretty soon before it gets too late for us to do
it," I muttered. Doreen stopped what she was doing, shaded her eyes
with her hand, and squinted up at me again.

"What do you mean? What are yinz going to do?" she asked.

"I ain't supposed to tell you, Dor, it's a secret, and I swore on
Mum's life that I wouldn't tell no one," I said dismissively. I knew
Doreen hated for anyone to be privy to a secret not shared with her.
"But it's something that's gonna make us a whole lot of money," I
added. There, I had baited the hook with a secret and with money,
two of Doreen's greatest weaknesses. I decided to tease the line just a

bit to give her more incentive to bite. I glanced down at her doubt-fully. "Besides, ain't nothing no girl can do anyway."

Doreen jumped to her feet. "I can do anything you can do," she bristled.

"Ha! I doubt it. This takes guts, and I think you'd be too scared," I said, looking past her.

"I ain't no scaredy-cat!" she clucked. She took an aggressive pos-ture to gain my attention. I knew I had her, so I stopped searching up and down the street and turned my full attention on her. Finally, I took a deep breath as if coming to an important decision.

"All right, Dor, I'm going to trust you, but if I tell you, that means you got to do it with me. I mean, Donald, Ronald, and Jan will be mad at me for getting all this money without them, but that's their problem for not being here like they said they would. Besides, you're my sister," I added for good measure. I knew she wouldn't back down. Not now.

"So what do we have to do?" she asked.

I knew I was taking a chance because, typically, the only secrets Doreen ever kept were the ones she didn't know about. "Come on," I said. "I'll tell you on the way." Together we walked up Larimer Avenue for a couple of blocks, crossed the street, and made our way to the alley behind Carver Street.

*****

"Yes, sweetie, can I help you?" the elderly woman asked. She was standing in her front doorway, looking down at the little girl standing on her porch, seemingly on the verge of tears. Doreen gave the woman a pitiful look.

"I'm looking for my little puppy who ran away this morn-ing," Doreen sniffled. I'm scared he might get run over by a car or something."

"Now, now, don't you cry, sweetie. It'll be okay," the woman said sympathetically. "I haven't seen a puppy, but tell me his name and what he looks like."

Doreen sniffed as if fighting back her tears. "Well, he's black and white, and his name is umm…Spot."

"Okay, I promise that I'll keep an eye out for him, okay?" the elderly woman said.

"Okay, and thank you so very much. If I don't find Spot, I'll come back again to check." Doreen smiled feebly, then turned and walked from the porch.

"You do that, and good luck finding your puppy, sweetie," the elderly woman yelled after her. Doreen waved as she walked next door to the next victim's house.

As soon as I heard Doreen's knock and the sound of voices on the front porch, I darted through the backyard and leaped onto the porch. The back door was ajar, and I could hear Doreen. I picked up the empty pop bottles by the backdoor and set them carefully in my burlap sack. There were six altogether, and I took them all. Lifting the sack carefully so the bottles wouldn't clink together, I crossed the wooden porch and sprinted across the yard. I counted four green Fresca bottles and six Pepsi bottles on the back porch of the next house. I waited patiently for the knock and the muffled voices as Doreen once again went through her lost puppy routine.

Before launching our scheme, Doreen and I walked through the alley spotting the back porches with the pop bottles to strategically target those houses. When we were confident that Doreen could identify the homes from the front, we briefly went over her skit, and although I was not much of an acting critic, I could honestly say that Shirley Temple had nothing on Doreen. She was a natural.

In less than an hour, even before we had finished looting all the porches we had targeted, my burlap sack was so jam-packed and heavy that I could hardly lift it. The last three houses we targeted, I had to set the bulging sack down in the alley and carry the pop bottles back in my arms. With two houses still left to go, I knew I couldn't tote anymore. I wanted to tell Doreen that we had gotten enough, but I found myself in a predicament where I couldn't risk carrying the sack out to the street, nor could I leave it unattended in the alley for that length of time. My only recourse was to abandon Doreen to finish her performances without me.

As I walked home with the burlap sack slung over my back, I found myself chuckling out loud as I pictured Doreen knocking on those last doors, thinking I was still there, going through her lost puppy routine for no reason.

I plopped down on the bottom step with my arms and back, aching from carrying all that weight, and opened the burlap sack. It was bursting with empty bottles, and I quickly removed ten bottles and hid them in an old box under the steps. It wasn't long before I spotted Doreen approaching.

"I was looking all over for you. How did you get here so fast?" Doreen asked as she came running up to where I sat, counting the pop bottles. I decided to change the subject.

"Spot?" I asked dubiously.

"Well, I didn't know she was gonna ask me the stupid dog's name, and that was the only name I could think of," Doreen said defensively.

"You're lucky we didn't get caught."

"Well, we didn't—so there!"

"Never mind!" I said. "Help me count these." Doreen hesitated as if considering questioning me further but decided against it. She plopped down on the ground; her eyes were wide with greed. Together we counted the bottles. There were twelve-quart size pop bottles worth five cents each and thirty-six regular pop bottles total.

"That's one dollar and thirty-two cents!" Doreen giggled. Then her eyebrows narrowed. "How about me? How much do I get?" I looked at her thoughtfully, then scratched my chin.

"Well, let's see now. Since it was my idea, and I did all the work and took all the risk getting the bottles, I'd say twenty-five, no, thirty cents would be fair." Doreen folded her arms and wrinkled her forehead.

"I won't take less than forty cents," she announced. "And if you don't give it to me, I'll tell Mummy what we did, even if I get in trouble for it."

I frowned as if being ripped off. I thought for sure Doreen was going to demand at least half. "Okay," I finally said. "You win. Forty cents, but not a penny more." Doreen giggled as we placed the bottles back in the sack. She followed as I lugged the bulging burlap sack over to Martha's store. Inside, we set the bottles down one at a time on the counter so Phyllis could count them.

"Where'd yinz get all these?" Phyllis asked suspiciously.

"We been searching and hunting bottles for a couple of three days," I replied. "Mostly, we found them in the alleys and on the hillsides where people just throw them away." Phyllis considered my answer, and then, seemingly satisfied, one by one, she began to set them down behind the counter as she counted them out loud. Doreen and I exchanged a gratified glance.

We sat on the curb outside the store, and I counted out one dollar and thirty-two cents. I held out forty cents for Doreen, and she reached for it, but I quickly pulled it back.

"You did really good, Dor, but you have to swear you won't tell nobody what we did."

Doreen stared at the money. "Don't worry, I ain't stupid, you know." I dropped the coins into my sister's outstretched hand. Doreen jumped up and ran into the store. A few minutes later, she reemerged, a smug grin stretched across her face, and she was carrying a small brown paper bag stuffed with forty cents' worth of penny candy.

"How about giving me a piece?" I asked.

"Forget you! You got more money than me. Go buy your own candy," Doreen yelped. I already knew she wouldn't give me a piece, but I had to try. Doreen stuck her tongue out at me, and then she reached into the bag, pulled out a strawberry licorice lace, and slowly fed it into her mouth, making obscenely delicious noises to tease me as she ate. As I debated whether I should spend some of my money on candy, I suddenly saw Doreen's facial expression change. Her eyes narrowed fierce-like as they fixed onto something up the street.

I followed my sister's gaze to a black girl playing hopscotch on the sidewalk toward the back of our apartment building on Shetland Avenue. "Connie-Mae, you jagoff, you gypped me! I want my stuff back!" Doreen shrieked. Lickety-split, Connie-Mae took off running. Doreen looked for traffic then took off in a full sprint after her.

Connie-May had a full half-block lead on Doreen, but she would be lucky to make it to the safety of her house before Doreen caught her.

With satisfaction, I looked down at the money in my hand. I counted three quarters, a dime, a nickel, and two pennies. Then, unexpectedly, I was struck by a pang of guilt. I brushed the feeling aside and instead focused on the fun I would have with Bunny at the movies the next day. I thought about buying some candy and saving it to share with her but decided against it. As I stood, the guilt returned, and it was harder to shake this time. Then, I began to think about both Honeymarmo and God for some reason. As I made my way across the street to retrieve the other hidden bottles, I had the nagging and uncomfortable feeling that someone was watching me. I swallowed, then glanced upward.

Chapter 21

I spent the better part of an hour soaking in a hot bath and scrubbing myself pink with a thick bar of Lux soap. My mum pulled a pair of pants and a red shirt from the laundry closet and washed them for me to wear.

After I dressed, I hurried toward the kitchen, anxious to go, but my mum abruptly halted me.

"Hold still!" she scolded, grabbing me by my shoulder. She held me steady as she dug the tip of a comb into my scalp and dragged it through my wet hair, etching a perfect part.

"Ouch, that hurts!" I complained. "Hurry up, Mum, I gotta go!"

"You got plenty of time," my mum mused. She lifted my chin and looked me squarely in the eyes. "You better be on your best behavior, you hear me?"

"Yeah, yeah, I will," I promised.

"You sure Bunny's mum is going to pay for the movies for you?" When I had asked if I could go to the show with Bunny and her mum, my mum said she couldn't afford it. I obviously couldn't tell her that I already had the money because then she would have demanded to know where I had gotten it, so I told her Bunny's mother had insisted on paying my way.

"Yeah, honest, Mum, she says she does it all the time for Bunny's friends that go to the movies with her," I explained.

"Well, okay then, I guess it's all right." After she combed my hair and inspected behind my ears, I tore loose from her grip, darted across the porch, and started down the steps. "Remember what I said, and make sure you say thank you to Bunny's mum!" my mum yelled after me.

"I will!" I yelled back.

Bunny's mum opened the door and stood looking down at me as I stood on the porch. She smiled approvingly. "Well, don't you look nice today?" she said, pushing the door wide for me to enter.

"I should. My mum made me stay in the bathtub for almost an hour," I complained. She chuckled.

"Did she? Well, come on in. Bunny's in her room, and we're just about ready to go."

I squeezed by her and walked straight toward Bunny's room across the living room. Bunny was sitting on her bed, coloring in a book. When she saw me come through the door, her face lit up. Whenever she looked at me this way, it made me feel warm inside and full of worth.

"Frankie!" she cried out happily as she sprang from the bed. As she stood in front of me, I looked demurely down at her feet.

"Mummy?" Bunny cried out.

"Yes, Bunny?" her mum yelled back from inside her bedroom upstairs. Bunny grinned cunningly. "We leaving soon?"

"In about five minutes." But before her mum had finished her sentence, Bunny had leaned forward and kissed me full on my lips. I realized she hadn't been concerned about when we were leaving; she just wanted to find out where her mum was in the house to make sure it was safe to kiss me. I blushed. Bunny absolutely captivated me. I was intrigued by her boldness and her carefree way of expressing herself. And to be honest, I wondered what it was that she saw in me. Whatever it was, I was glad.

She looked at me with anticipation. It wasn't until later that I realized Bunny was expecting me to kiss her back. But being blissfully ignorant of such things, I just stood awkwardly staring at her feet until she mercifully grabbed my hand and walked me over to her bed, where we both sat down and began to color until it was time to go.

The truth was I had never been to the movies before. We rode the bus, and as we stood outside the ticket booth at Regents Movie Theater, I was anxious to get inside.

"Are you sure you have enough money?" Bunny's mum asked.

"Oh, sure!" I replied, pulling the money out from my pocket and holding it up for her to see. "My mum gave me plenty so I could get popcorn and stuff."

"Well, that is a lot of money. I should probably get you to pay for us," Bunny's mum mused. I think she must have seen the panic cross my face because she quickly added, "I'm just teasing you, Frankie." I breathed a big sigh of relief.

We paid at the ticket window, and at the entrance, an older boy in his teens with pimples snatched the ticket from my hand and tore it in half. I gave the boy a fierce look and felt my fist tighten. Then, to add insult to injury, this pimple-faced teenager handed me back only half of my ticket that I had paid fifty cents for, keeping the other half for himself. I felt my left leg begin to shake as I sized him up, debating the most advantageous place to land my first punch.

"Move along." The teenager scowled impatiently. Luckily for him, Bunny nudged me through the entrance toward the snack counter. When I stepped into the lobby, I froze as if in a trance. The lights illuminated a bright red carpet, and the sound of popcorn popping was like music, as its buttery aroma filled the theater. On some of the walls, there were big colorful movie posters. It was wonderful. We got in line at the snack counter, and Bunny's mum insisted on buying the popcorn and drinks for both of us. She even bought us a box of Milk Duds to share during the movie.

Bunny and I raced down to the front row of seats, but Bunny's mum insisted that we not sit so close to the screen. I was in awe at how gigantic the white screen was, and I couldn't imagine how a picture could fill up the whole thing. We settled on a row closer to the middle of the theater and centered ourselves in the seats. Bunny sat between her mum and me, and she and I shared a large box of popcorn while her mum had her own smaller box. We sat and waited for the movie to start.

When, at last, the lights dimmed, and the picture burst on the screen, and I saw and heard it for the first time, I was awestruck. I had only watched movies before at home on our old black-and-white television with its fuzzy reception. Now, as I stared in amazement at the bigger-than-life screen with the images exploding out at me in brilliant technicolor, it was purely magical. My mouth gaped open, and my eyes widened to absorb everything before me. At that moment, I was so enthralled, so captivated at what I was experiencing, that everything around me seized to exist, and I forgot all about Bunny sitting close beside me. Finally, I was shaken from my spell when Bunny playfully poked me with her elbow.

That afternoon, the movie at the matinee was a return movie entitled *Mary Poppins*. Bunny and I spent that afternoon munching popcorn, drinking pop, and eating Milk Duds. We would stealthily allow our fingers to caress, sometimes for several minutes, as we dug into the box of popcorn together. As I pressed against Bunny, I convinced myself that nothing in the world could ever be better than this, and I wished that the movie and the day would never end. I would have been content to sit in the dark, next to Bunny, for the rest of my life.

Then, it was over. Bunny gently pulled her warm hand out of the empty popcorn box away from mine as the credits rolled on the screen. The lights turned on, and everyone in the theater, including us, stood and filed out of the theater. I couldn't remember ever being so sad about having to leave a place in all my life, and strangely, as we walked from the building, it felt almost as if I were leaving a part of myself behind.

On the way home on the bus, Bunny and I sang, "A spoon full of sugar helps the medicine go down, the medicine go down, the medicine go down. Just a spoon full of sugar helps the medicine go down, in quite a delightful way." Then we giggled and laughed, and even Bunny's mum chuckled. At that moment, I felt full. Not so much from popcorn or candy but from a fullness of joy and life, and yes, even love.

*****

When I got home and walked through the kitchen door, my mum was sitting at the kitchen table crying, her eyes were bloodshot, her bottom lip puffy, and a welt had formed on the right side of her face. In an instant, all the carefree giddiness I had felt from an afternoon of wonder, happiness, and love evaporated. My mum looked up at me hopelessly and gave no pretense at a smile. Clear snot dripped from her nose. Then, I heard Joe's heavy footsteps, and I braced myself.

Joe slowly and deliberately came toward me, and I could do nothing to oppose his size and brute strength. His eyes were depraved and glazed from the effects of some drug, and as he jerked me up by my arm and by my hair, all I could do was tense my body to prepare for whatever would come next.

"Well, did we have fun at the movies, freak?" Joe asked. He dragged me through the kitchen and living room, and when we reached the passageway that led to the front of the apartment, Joe lifted me off the floor and heaved me down the hall. My body twisted as I soared through the air, and when I landed on my back, my head whipped back and bounced off the dense wood floor with such force that I recoiled almost into a sitting position. The hallway spun rapidly, and I found myself unable to focus. My head swooned with the droning of a thousand bees. Then, Joe lifted me off the ground, and once again, I was airborne. This time, the left side of my rib cage absorbed the full impact of my landing as I smashed into the floor. I heard myself grunt as my wind left me. Frantically, I gasped for air. Then, I again was yanked up by my hair and dragged to the doorway of my room. Still gasping for air, Joe flung me across the room. I rolled and tumbled before coming to a stop near the wall, my crumpled body sprawled in an unnatural position. I was unable to move; my lungs fought desperately for oxygen. I thought for sure I was going to suffocate and die.

Then, mercifully, a short gasp of air made its way into my lungs, and then another, then still another, until gradually, my lungs slowly began to fill again. I dared to look around only to find Joe towering over me, which meant this wasn't over. I watched Joe's right leg lift from the floor in a deliberate motion and snap toward my face. The tip of Joe's leather shoe struck me hard on the right temple, and specks of light swam before my eyes. Joe continued to stand in front of me. I lay entirely motionless now, the right side of my face pressed against the floor. Then, mercifully, I watched Joe's feet turn and stroll toward the open door. My face felt the vibration of Joe's heavy footsteps along the wooden planks. Joe pulled and locked the bedroom door shut. I felt a warm froth slowly gather under my tongue until it eventually filled the inside of my cheek and trickled out the corner of my mouth. The droning in my head grew louder. It was a while before I gathered the strength and nerve to move. Woozily, I sat up. I was overcome with a strong urge to cry, but my tears would not come—I wouldn't let them.

I sat on the floor, motionless, for a long time. The pain was too great, and I was afraid to make any noise that would bring attention to myself. I knew the slightest sound or commotion in Joe's current state of mind could evoke another assault.

As my adrenaline began to wane, I now felt the total result of Joe's brutal attack. I found that I could not lift my arms without a stabbing pain shooting through my side and back. The back of my head throbbed, and along with the droning, searing pain was intensifying in my forehead. I was weak and suddenly nauseous. I staggered to my feet and made it to my window just as the vomit came. It smelled like spoiled popcorn.

Afterward, I slid down the wall and stared impassively across the room. My stomach had settled some, but the rest of my body still hurt.

"Frankie? Frankie?"

"What?" I finally answered irritably.

"Are you all right? Are you hurt?" my mum whispered through the door.

"Go away, Mummy!" I said coldly. I didn't want to talk to her or anyone else, so I laid down on the floor and closed my eyes.

"Frankie?" my mum whispered again. I would not answer. "I'm sorry," my mom said. "I'm sorry."

I heard her footsteps fade away. The earlier part of the day with Bunny and her mom no longer seemed real. I closed my eyes, and although it took a very long time, sleep mercifully overtook me, temporarily washing away the numbness and the pain.

Chapter 22

A couple of days had passed before my mum unlocked my door to let me out. By then, the more severe injuries inflicted by Joe had become tolerable, and the less severe wounds had mostly healed.

She stepped into my room, carrying a plate of bacon and eggs with a piece of toast. "Look, I made you some dippy eggs, just how you like them," she said, handing me the plate. "Joe said you could come out of your room today. I also ran you a hot bath for when you're done eating, and I put clean clothes in the bathroom for you."

I didn't respond. I sat on the floor and devoured my first food in two days while my mum watched. When I finished, I stood and handed her back the empty plate.

"How are you feeling?" she asked contritely.

"How do you think?" I snapped sarcastically. My mum reached over and pushed the hair away from my eyes, but I jerked away.

"Go take your bath," she said softly. "It'll make you feel better."

Without saying a word, I limped past her toward the door.

Joe had already left the apartment for the day, so I soaked in the hot tub until the water turned cold. Afterward, I dressed and went to the back porch. The warm morning sun felt magnificent, and I ran as fast as my pain would allow, down the back steps and across the graveled parking lot toward Shetland Avenue. My mum stood in the kitchen doorway and watched until I disappeared.

"How come Frankie don't have to empty the rubbish or help clean up like we do?" Doreen complained as she wiped down the kitchen table.

"Don't worry about it missy. That's none of your business. Now you hush up!" Our mum gave her a stern look. "I got clothes to wash. Go get Mindy, and both yinz go clean your room. Then go separate the colors and whites," she said. Doreen half-heartedly obeyed.

I searched the neighborhood, but there was no trace of Donald, Ronald, Jan, or Leroy. I considered heading toward the tracks to find Honeymarmo when, instead, I decided first to visit Bunny.

In the alley next to Bunny's house, I hurried along, anxious to see her. As I reached the hedges next to the large pine tree in Bunny's front yard, I heard voices coming from Bunny's porch. I stopped and parted the overgrown hedge to get a better view. There was Bunny, and snuggled up close to her sat Bruce, another boy from the neighborhood on the porch glider.

"So I whooped both of them!" I heard Bruce exclaim.

Bunny stared admirably at him. "Get out. At the same time?"

"Yep," Bruce bragged.

"You're so strong, Bruce. Make a muscle." Bruce tugged back his sleeve and strained his bicep as Bunny squeezed it. "Wow, it's so big," she cooed.

My heart sank. I felt the brutal sting of jealousy. As I watched, the pain of betrayal washed over me. I loved her, and Bunny had even made me say it. I had opened my heart to her and had trusted her. Now, I felt foolish and vulnerable, naked for all the world to see.

My jealousy turned to anger as I watched, which quickly became loathing for Bunny and Bruce. I churned with contempt as I watched Bunny laugh, and it was a laugh I had believed to be only for me. *She's a liar, a big fat liar*, I thought.

I knew I should walk away, but instead, I felt the familiar stir inside me. I ran alongside the hedges until I reached the sidewalk, threw open the front gate, and strode angrily toward Bunny and Bruce.

Bunny and Bruce heard the metal gate bang open and watched as I approached them. Bruce stood as if to greet me, oblivious to the fury that I was feeling. Bunny noticed, and I landed my first punch. Bruce cupped both hands over his right eye as it exploded with pain. My second punch glanced off Bruce's head, causing him to stumble off balance. I rushed in, lifted Bruce off his feet, slammed him to the porch, jumped on top of him, and delivered several more punches. Bunny jumped off the glider and grabbed my arm.

"Stop, Frankie! Please stop! You're hurting him!" Bunny cried out.

I shook Bunny's hand from my arm and glared up at her. "How big is his muscle now?" I seethed.

The front door flew open, and Bunny's mum appeared. "What's going on out here? Frankie, what are you doing? Get up off him, now!" she yelled. I stood and stepped back.

Bruce struggled to one knee. He began to cry. "Why'd you do that? What did I do to you?" I didn't answer.

Bunny's mum helped Bruce to his feet and hugged him to her side. "I think it's best you leave now, Frankie, and you don't need to come around here or see Bunny again. You hear me?" I turned toward Bunny.

"Why'd you make me say it? Why did you make me say that I loved you when you didn't even love me? Why?" My eyes filled with anguish. Bunny couldn't hold my stare and cast her eyes to the porch.

"You heard me, Frankie, you need to go now," Bunny's mum repeated.

I sucked a deep breath to calm myself. "I'm going, and you don't have to worry, Bunny, because I never want to see you again. Not never. I hate you. I hate your guts!" I seethed, then turned and walked away.

I didn't know what to do next. On Larimer Avenue, I sat on the curb in front of our apartment building. This pain was different from any Joe had ever inflicted, and in some ways, it was worse. I tried to convince myself that I only told Bunny I loved her because she tricked me into it. But I knew I was lying to myself. Everything about her fascinated me, and my love for her was genuine. Maybe that's why it hurt so much. Feeling isolated, alone, and rejected, I stood and wandered through Larimer's streets, searching for something but not knowing what. Finally, I decided I would find Honeymarmo. Maybe he had an answer; perhaps he could make me feel better.

*****

I moped quietly down the trail. When the bridge's underbelly came into sight, I looked around but saw no one. As usual, it felt cool here in the shadows. Disappointed that Honeymarmo wasn't here, I turned to leave.

"Well, if it ain't, Frankie," a gruff voice rang out. I bristled, then turned in time to see Grub appear from behind a bush on the other side of the bridge, and in his hand was a nearly empty green wine bottle.

Grub staggered toward me. "I thought maybe you were the cops," he said, grinning ear to ear like a predatory cat; his eyes were bloodshot and glazed.

I remembered Honeymarmo's warning about Grub and thought about running. But I didn't. "Where's Honeymarmo?" I asked.

"Well, I think the old Bible thumper went up to do some pan-handling. But he should be back soon," Grub quickly added. "Why don't you come and keep old Grub company for a while until he gets back." He sat down, patted the ground next to him invitingly, and then set the wine bottle down between his feet. At first, I was uncertain, then, again ignoring Honeymarmo's advice, I hesitantly edged toward Grub. Grub seemed to sense my uneasiness. "You ain't afraid of me, are you? Why, I'm about as harmless as a fly," he said, forcing a laugh to put me at ease.

Not wanting Grub to think me scared, I feigned a smile and eased myself down next to him. Grub held me in place with a penetrating stare, then again grinned wide.

"That's right," he cooed. "So, Frankie, do you like trains?"

"They're all right." I shrugged.

"Have you ever been on one?" he asked.

"Sure, me and my friend Marco jump them sometimes and ride them for a little way."

"That's all, just a little way? So you ain't really been no place special on one?"

I shook my head.

Grub became suddenly animated. "Why then, you don't know what you're missing." He beamed. "There's a whole wide world out there filled with all kinds of new and exciting things to do and see." He gave me a playful nudge with his elbow. "I can tell you're one of those brave souls that love new things and adventures, aren't you?"

I shrugged as I considered Grub's compliment. "Yeah, I guess."

"Why, sure you are," Grub continued. "I bet you ain't afraid of nothing. I knew that the first time I set eyes on you. I said to myself, now there's a young man who's got courage." He again nudged me and cackled. "I got good instincts about these things." I nodded to acknowledge Grub's point. "Why, I bet the next time you jump a train, instead of just a little way, you wouldn't be afraid to go ten miles, or twenty miles, or even ride a train all the way to the ocean, would you?" he asked.

I swallowed hard at the prospect. "Nuh-uh," I lied.

"I knew it." Grub cackled loudly, slapping his knee. "Say, Frankie, have you ever been to the beach before?" Grub asked, almost as an afterthought.

Again, I shook my head. "I ain't never been nowhere outside Pennsylvania," I responded.

"Why, that's a dirty rotten shame," Grub said sympathetically. "Ain't nothing like being near the ocean with the fresh salty air, and the sand, and the seagulls. It's a sight of beauty, I tell you, a true Indian Valley if ever there was one. And the people are real nice there too. Why, a man can panhandle at some places near the ocean and almost get rich." He looked at me sorrowfully and shook his head. "And you ain't never been. What a dirty, rotten shame."

I sat listening to Grub's description of the ocean, and as I painted a mental picture, I felt suddenly inadequate, like I was missing out on life itself.

Grub suddenly sat up straight and gave me another nudge. "Hey, I got me an idea!" he said. "We can go to the beach, you and me together. We can jump one of these trains right here, and we'd be there before you knew it."

The bravery and curiosity for adventure I had experienced a moment before deflated, and I felt suddenly uncomfortable at such a prospect. Then, I felt panic. I fought to push it back, so I searched for any excuse. Nothing came to mind, so I did what I did best—I lied. "My mum is sick, real sick," I said, "and the doctor said she might not have long to live, and she needs me to help take care of her."

Grub gave me a skeptical look. I crossed my heart and raised my right hand to God. "I ain't lying."

"Well, I'm sorry to hear that, Frankie, but don't you have brothers or sisters?" Grub asked cunningly.

I nodded and answered before thinking. "I have two older sisters."

"See, there you go. You have two older sisters to help take care of her. Now, on the other hand, you're the man of the house, ain't you?" he asked cleverly. I nodded. "Well then, the best thing for you to do would be to provide your mum money to help her in her time of sickness. That's what the men of the house do. And like I already told you, at the beach, them nice rich people practically throw money at you, and I'll make sure that you have plenty to send back home to her." Frantically, my mind raced as I searched for another excuse, another lie, but nothing came.

Grub unexpectedly reached into his jacket pocket and pulled something out. He scooted closer and pressed up against me. "Open your hand," he said. Feeling trapped, I reluctantly did what Grub asked. Grub reached over and pressed a fifty-cent piece into my palm. "That's for you," he said seductively. "Ain't nothing like a nice shiny fifty-cent piece to make someone happy." Slowly Grub closed my hand around the large coin while at the same time giving my fingers a rough caress. My panic deepened, and I attempted to yank my hand away. Grub only gripped it tighter. I began to squirm. Finally, Grub let my hand go, and his left hand dropped to my knee, squeezing it. Full-blown fear now gripped me.

"There's a lot more where that came from," Grub whispered as he shoved his hand back into his jacket pocket as if to pull out more money. "Why, I have two nickel notes right here." He patted the inside of his jacket pocket. "You ain't afraid of ole Grub, are you?" Grub's hand slid from my knee to my inner thigh. As Grub squeezed, his grip felt like a vice. He leaned his face close to mine, and his grizzled chin felt like a wire brush as it scraped against my face. I jerked my head back and strained to pull away.

"It's okay," Grub said. "Ole Grub is here to protect you. Why, I would never hurt you." Grub's hot putrid breath that reeked of decay, cigarettes, and cheap wine assaulted my nostrils. I grimaced then held my breath. I felt nauseous. "You're going to go on the road with ole Grub, and I'm going to take good care of you. Yes, sir, you're going to be my little lamb, and I'm going to make sure nobody ever hurts you," he purred. I turned my head to exhale and suck a breath of good air. I increased my struggle, but Grub only pulled me tighter.

"I'll make sure you have everything you need, and all you have to do is be nice to ole Grub when I need you to be nice to me. That's all! But if you don't want to be nice to ole Grub, and you fight me, well, who knows," he whispered fiendishly in my ear. Grub's hand slid further up my thigh. Feeling completely helpless, the world around me blurred through swollen tears. I continued to struggle desperately against Grub's deadly clutch.

Then, I saw something flash through the air from the corner of my eye, followed by a loud hollow thump. Grub's grip went limp; he reached for the back of his head as he slumped to the dirt groaning in agony. I looked up, and towering above us, gripping Grub's shovel, stood Honeymarmo. I almost didn't recognize him. I had never seen this side of him before. His eyes were crazed, and his chest heaved. I blinked the tears from my eyes, then realized the sound I heard was the shovel impacting the back of Grub's skull.

As Grub lay squirming in the dirt, Honeymarmo brought the shovel down hard against Grub's head for the second time. Grub's moaning seized, and he lay motionless on the ground next to the wine bottle.

"Get away from him, Frankie," Honeymarmo said coldly. I rolled to Grub's left, then scrambled to my feet. Honeymarmo took a step forward and stomped on Grub's right hand. Grub instinctively jerked his hand to his chest, telling me he was still alive. I saw for the first time the large unfolded pocket knife Grub had been holding, lying in the dirt. Honeymarmo kicked it away.

Honeymarmo continued to glare down at Grub, his eyes cold and distant, and the joyful glint that was usually there was gone. Honeymarmo turned toward me. "He didn't hurt you none, did he?"

I shook my head. "No, I'm okay. He just scared me a little," I said, looking back down at Grub.

"It's my fault, Frankie. I'm sorry. I knew he was a bad seed from the start, and I should have never let you meet him the other day. I should have better warned you to stay away from here until he had moved on. I thought maybe if I could teach him a little about God, he would understand the need for forgiveness and perhaps be willing to change. I know now there's no changing him. He's a wicked man with a hard heart who has allowed evil to corrupt him for too long. I was just throwing pearls before swine." Honeymarmo sighed. "I'm sure he's done this before, and I need to make sure he never hurts anyone again. You best get on home now, Frankie."

"What are you going to do?" I asked.

"Never you mind, you just need to get!" Honeymarmo replied sternly. He had never spoken to me like this before, and it troubled me. I hesitated.

"Maybe he's learned his lesson. Maybe you can just let him go and make him leave if he promises never to do anything bad like this again," I said.

Honeymarmo gave me a long hard look. "No, Frankie, evil doesn't change for the better. Evil only becomes more evil. If I were to let him go, and he hurts another kid, or worse, and he would, how would that make you feel knowing you could have stopped it?"

"Not too good," I muttered.

"Me neither," Honeymarmo said, "but that's exactly what would happen. It's okay to forgive bad things done against you, and you should, but never side with evil. Good should always side with good." He glanced down at Grub, then up again. "Only evil sides with evil, Frankie. It'll be okay. Now, you need to get on home, and it's probably best if you don't tell anyone about this, okay?"

"Okay," I agreed. The truth was I couldn't get out of there fast enough. For some reason, I thought about Bunny and her betrayal of me, and it no longer seemed to matter. I turned and started up the trail, then felt something in my closed fist. It was Grub's fifty-cent piece. I felt repulsed, as if the coin was contaminating my entire being, so I dropped it in the dirt and wiped my hand on my trousers. I turned back. I watched as Honeymarmo stepped closer to Grub, who was still sprawled out on the ground, barely moving. Honeymarmo's knuckles were white as he gripped the shovel tight with both hands.

"Honeymarmo, it wasn't your fault, and I should have listened to you," I said. Honeymarmo looked over at me, and for just an instant, his face became placid, and I saw the old friendly glint reappear in his eyes.

He grinned. "Make sure you come back and visit in a couple of days, but not before," he said. Then, as Honeymarmo looked back down at Grub, the old familiar glint vanished, and his eyes once again grew scary cold.

Word quickly spread throughout the neighborhoods that someone had murdered a hobo in the woods near Larimer Bridge. A couple of days later, I found Ronald, Donald, and Jan hanging out at Larimer's school playground. Ronald was entertaining the others in his usual jocular manner by giving his best impersonation of James Brown. He held a pretend microphone and sang "I Got You" while imitating James Brown's signature dance moves. Donald and Jan were laughing.

"Get down, Ronald," I encouraged as I plopped down on the steps next to Jan and Donald.

"Let's see you do a split," Donald shouted.

"Yeah, do it," Jan pressed him. Encouraged, Ronald gave a final off-key shriek into his fist, spun, then dropped into a full split. The crotch seam on his trouser ripped open, and Ronald's eyes opened wide. The comical look on his face, coupled with the sound of his ripping trousers, silenced everyone. Then, simultaneously, everyone burst into laughter.

"Man, Mom is going to be mad at you," Donald squealed.

Ronald pulled himself up and strained his neck to see his backside. The tear in his trousers had fully exposed his underwear. Everyone laughed harder. "Man, that ain't funny." Ronald frowned, but the infectious nature of everyone's laughter soon had him laughing as well.

For the rest of the afternoon, Ronald walked around with his pants split wide; it didn't seem to embarrass him in the least. He would intentionally make sure that strangers on the street got a good glimpse of his underwear so all of us could get a good laugh at the people's shocked expressions.

Eventually, we found ourselves at Martha's store. Between us, we scraped together enough for a cold bottle of pop, and we dared Ronald to go into the store and buy it, which he gladly accepted. We positioned ourselves just outside the front doors and watched as Ronald strolled inside, pulled an ice-cold bottle of orange Crush from the ice cooler, and set it on the counter. Phyllis rang it up, and Ronald slapped his change down, except for a purposely dropped nickel. Stepping back, he turned away from Phyllis, spotted us outside the door, gave us a mischievous wink, then bent at the waist to pick up the coin. When Donald, Jan, and me, saw the shocked expression on Phyllis's face, we collapsed to the sidewalk laughing.

"Ronald, does your mum know you're walking around with your backside hanging out?" Phyllis grimaced. We couldn't hear Ronald's response above our laughter. Ronald stepped through the doorway sporting a grin. We all took off running.

At Larimer Field, we plopped down along the chain-link fence. Ronald loosened the bottle cap with his penknife and popped it off. He started to raise the bottle to his lips.

"Don't backwash," Donald warned.

"Man, shut up. I don't backwash." He tilted the bottle's mouth on his bottom lip and poured a swallow. I was next in line, and Ronald handed me the bottle. I wiped the bottle mouth with my shirt, touched it to my bottom lip, and took a big swig. Afterward, I handed the bottle to Donald. Donald grabbed it from me and examined the orange pop for anything foreign.

"Man, just drink it," everyone shouted. Satisfied, Donald wiped the bottle's mouth with his shirt, pressed the bottle mouth to his bottom lip, and tilted it up, before handing the last of it to Jan. Jan gulped the last big swallow, stood, and heaved the empty bottle. With our thirst temporarily quenched, the four of us rested lazily against the fence.

"So who do you think did it?" Jan asked, breaking the silence.

We all gave him a bewildered look. "Did what?" Donald inquired.

"Killed that hobo the other day?"

"I don't think it was anybody from Larimer," Ronald said.

"What do you think, Frankie?" Jan asked.

"Man, how would I know?" I snapped.

"You don't have to bite my head off, man. I was just asking," Jan responded. I stared silently at the dirt.

The day grew hotter, then in the distance, coming from Shetland Avenue's direction, we heard the distinct ringing of a bell. Ronald sprang to his feet. "It's the Italian iceman!" We all cranked our necks in the general direction of the clanking sound.

"Man, I wish we had some more money," Jan grumbled. We all stood and strode toward the opening in the fence and the ringing bell. In the gravel parking lot behind my apartment, we saw old man Monterosso slowly making his way up Shetland Avenue pushing his hefty wooden cart. He stopped, reached inside, pulled out a large handheld bell, rang it a few times, tucked it back inside the cart, and waited for customers to arrive. Kids disappeared into their houses to beg their mum for a dime.

"Come on, I got an idea," I said. Together, we ran to the bottom steps of our apartment. "Wait here. I'll be right back." I sprinted up the steps and disappeared inside. In a moment, I reemerged and stomped back down the steps. I held up my fist with the end of a dollar bill sticking out. Ronald, Donald, and Jan stared at me curiously.

"Where'd you get that from?" asked Jan.

Ronald grinned approvingly. "You done stole it from your mom's purse, didn't you?"

"I didn't steal nothing," I responded. "Let's go!" We ran across the gravel parking lot in the direction of the Italian ice cart. Old man Monterosso was an Italian man, medium in stature, but was stout for his age. His only distinguishing feature was his bigger-than-normal ears. He spoke little English, had a thick Italian accent, and was usually pleasant but not overly friendly. The cart he pushed was cumbersome and big enough to carry two vats full of Italian ice, one strawberry flavored and the other lemon. A large handheld bell was on a shelf at the back of the cart. I loved to watch him scoop Italian ice into a small cone-shaped paper cup that came with a flat wooden spoon. He sold them for ten cents each. There was nothing better in the world than the taste of old man Monterosso's creamy homemade Italian ice on a hot summer day.

Me, Donald, Ronald, and Jan waited for our turn. I was in front and held up the dollar partially tucked into my fist so old man Monterosso could get a good glimpse. "I'm buying one for everyone," I announced. Old man Monterosso spotted the dollar, grinned, and said in his thick Italian accent, "Okay, what a'flavors?"

He filled the paper cones, handed them out, then wiped his hands on his apron. "That's a'forty centsa." I gave him the crumpled-up bill.

Old man Monterosso set it down and reached into his apron pocket to pull out a hand full of coins to count my change. He stopped abruptly, then picked up and unfolded the dollar bill to examine it closer.

"Hey, this 'a no real'a money!" he shouted angrily, waving the bill in my direction. "This 'a no good!" I bolted toward the alley. Donald, Ronald, and Jan, who had already begun to eat their ill-gotten Italian ice, immediately realized what was happening and tore out after me.

"Come'a back here, you a'thief! You son of a beech!" Old man Monterosso shouted at the top of his lungs. "You a' no good, boy! You son of a beech! I'm a'gonna tella' your mother! All of you a'no good boys!"

His shouts faded as we sprinted up the alley. I was far in the lead, running as fast as my legs would carry me until we all were out of the Italian iceman's sight and reach. When I was sure I was safe and was confident that no one had followed us, I stopped and waited for the others.

"Man, I can't believe you gave him fake money, Frankie. You're such a jagoff," Donald snapped.

"It was Mindy's," I snickered. "She fooled me with it pretty good the other day, and I thought for sure it would fool old man Monterosso. I only wish he would have given me the change before he realized it was fake."

None of them seemed amused. "Man, that's not funny, Frankie," Ronald grumbled.

Donald scowled. "Yeah, if our mom finds out about this and tells our dad, man, we're going to get whooped good. We're already not supposed to loaf with you no more."

"Your mom ain't going to find out," I clucked.

"How do you know that? Huh?" Donald snapped back. For the first time, I realized how upset my friend was.

"Because he don't know who you or who your mom is," I reasoned.

"Yeah, but what if someone we know saw us, and they tell our moms?" Jan said. I hadn't thought of that. I shrugged.

"And you know Marco and his older brothers are going to be looking for you now since the Italian iceman is their grandfather," Ronald reminded me.

I hadn't thought of that either. Since Marco was one of my good friends, I would have to find Marco first and invent some lie to tell him. I noticed that everyone still had their Italian ice except for Ronald.

"Where's your Italian ice?" I asked him. Everyone looked at Ronald.

Ronald shook his head and then grimaced. "Man, I got so scared I just dropped it and ran." Despite our predicament, we all laughed.

"Here, have some of mine." I handed my Italian ice to Ronald as a peace offering.

We all drifted further up the alley. "Man, that was stupid, Frankie!" Jan said. The rest nodded in concert.

*****

I stepped into the kitchen, and Doreen gave me a smug grin. I knew immediately I was in trouble.

"Mummy, Frankie's home!" Doreen shouted.

Our mum shut off the spigot and spun from the kitchen sink. She swiftly closed the distance between us and snatched my ear. "Ouch!" I cried out as she yanked and pulled me through the kitchen and into the living room, where she firmly pushed me down on the couch.

"You little jagoff! So you want to steal from Mr. Monterosso, do you? Yeah, I know what you did. Marco's mum came by a little while ago, and I had to give her forty cents to pay for what you stole. Do you think we're rich? You think I have forty cents lying around to spare? Well, we don't. More than that, if Joe finds out, what do you think he'll do to you? Maybe I should tell him?" my mum threatened angrily.

I sat pouting as I rubbed my ear. I knew I had done wrong and even deserved the tongue-lashing I was receiving, but when my mum threatened to tell Joe, I felt a deep resentment toward her. I folded my arms across my chest.

"Go on, tell him!" I seethed. "I don't care, let him kill me. You'd probably like that anyway, wouldn't you?"

My mum bristled at my indictment. "Frankie, you don't say stuff like that. I don't want to see you get in trouble," she assured me. "I just don't know what to do with you anymore. You keep doing these things, and I'm afraid something bad is going to happen to you, or us, because of it." She stared indecisively at me, then sat on the other end of the couch. She buried her face in her hands. "I just don't know what to do with you anymore," she muttered. "I just don't know what to do."

I looked over at my mum and felt regret. She was right. I had again done something stupid without regard to how it would hurt someone else, but why couldn't I seem to stop myself. Something inside made me do these things, and I didn't understand it, nor could I seem to control it. I could tell my mum I was sorry and mean it, but I also knew it would only be a matter of time before I did something like this again. I hung my head with guilt. Then, Honeymarmo came to mind, and what he had told me about free will, and choice, and selfishness, and how God could help make me a better person. Maybe later, I would pray for help.

Later, I found out that Donald's and Ronald's mum did find out about what had happened, and they both got a whooping from their dad, and he grounded them for a week. At first, they had steadfastly denied any involvement, but someone said that the britches of one of the boys running away had a split in the back. When their mum saw Ronald's britches, well, they couldn't deny it further, especially Ronald, who sang like the proverbial canary. Donald's and Ronald's mum and dad made it clear they were never to loaf with me again, and except for random encounters, they didn't.

*****

With Donald and Ronald no longer allowed to associate with me, I found myself alone on Larimer Avenue in front of my apartment building a few days later. I tried finding Honeymarmo earlier in the day but had no luck. In the direction of Larimer Bridge, a block away, a mob of boys had gathered on the sidewalk. I heard them shouting, but they were too far away for me to understand what they were saying. I drifted toward them, realizing I knew most of them as I drew closer. They seemed to be yelling at someone across the street, and one of the boys heaved something in that direction. A couple of the boys broke away from the group and sprinted toward me. It was Marco and his neighbor, a boy named Gino from the Italian side of Shetland Avenue. I stood my ground and clenched my fists. I was ready to fight, thinking maybe they were coming after me because I stole from Marco's grandfather.

"Come here, Frankie, hurry up," Marco shouted excitedly as he and Gino got within a few yards of me.

"Come where?" I asked distrustfully.

"Just c'mon," Marco panted. I still didn't move.

"I thought you'd be mad about your grandfather," I said bluntly.

"Hell, I ain't mad about that," Marco said. "My mum and dad were pretty mad, but my brothers and I thought it was funny. Besides, your mum paid my mum the money." I knew Marco was telling me the truth.

"So what's going on?" I inquired.

"Just come on, man!" Marco repeated.

"Here, take this," Gino said, handing me a good-sized stone. It was smooth and felt hefty in my hand. We took off running toward the crowd of boys who had now worked themselves into a frenzy.

"Go on, get out of here, you jagoff!" Marco's older brother Dino shouted from the front of the crowd.

"Yeah, hit the bricks! Go back to where you came from!" someone else in the crowd hollered.

From the back of the crowd, I tried to gain some sense of the situation. My first inclination was that some kid from a neighboring borough had wandered into Larimer, and Marco's brother and the rest of the boys were chasing him off. The agitation from the mob was contagious, and I felt myself getting caught up in the excitement.

"Okay, everyone got their rocks?" Dino shouted. From the rare of the group, I held up my smooth stone along with everyone else.

"Okay, on the count of three. One, two…" The entire mob of boys reared back. I could not yet see our target, so I pushed my way to the front of the crowd so my aim would be accurate. My adrenaline surged, and as my eyes settled on our target, I froze. There, cowering in a doorway, his arms raised defensively to protect himself, crouched Honeymarmo. I stared at my friend wearing his dirty, mismatched clothes, frightened for his life.

"Three!" Dino yelled. Everyone let loose their rock except for me. Honeymarmo cringed and ducked away to protect himself from the onslaught. From my vantage point, it appeared that all of the stones had bounced off the building and plate glass windows around Honeymarmo without a single one hitting him. Honeymarmo, realizing that the barrage had ended, peeked out from between his arms. He was scared. Then, he spotted me. I immediately saw the recognition in his eyes. Honeymarmo's fear dissipated, his arms lowered, and the gentle glint in his eyes, I had come to know, and love, appeared. He was glad to see me.

Then, Dino, seeing the recognition on the hobo's face when he looked at me, and seeing I still gripped my rock, faced me. "Do you know that dirty old bum?" he asked accusingly. Everyone's eyes were now on me. I swallowed.

"No, man, I don't know him!" I clucked defensively.

186

"Well then, throw it. What are you waiting for?" Dino asked.

"Yeah, throw it, Frankie!" several boys in the crowd shouted. "Hurry before he gets away!"

I don't know why I did it, but I reared back and heaved the rock toward Honeymarmo. Everyone erupted into cheers as it sailed across the street and found its mark, striking Honeymarmo just above his right eyebrow. Blood instantly began to ooze and drip from the wound. I watched in horror as it trickled into Honeymarmo's eye, down the right side of his face, and into his grey whiskers. Honeymarmo stared with bewilderment at me; the translucent light in his eyes that I had come to trust and love faded. The pain and anguish that took its place caused me to cup my hand over my mouth. I felt sick inside. "Oh god, oh god, what did I do?" I mumbled under my breath as the image in front of me seared itself into my consciousness. Honeymarmo reached up, rubbed the blood from his eye, and pressed his hand against the wound to stop the bleeding; a shadow of melancholy and defeat crossed his face. He gingerly pulled his hand away to inspect the blood.

Again, we exchanged looks. Then, it was as if Honeymarmo recognized the shame and remorse in my eyes. He lowered his head to shield his eyes from me in the hopes of lessening my shame and embarrassment. I knew what he was doing. Even in that moment of my betrayal, I understood that Honeymarmo's sole concern was for me. Slowly, Honeymarmo turned, his head hanging wearily. He stepped from the doorway, and as he walked away, I felt a powerful urge to run across the street and throw my arms around my friend and tell him I was so very sorry, but I found that I could not move. Instead, I stood and watched, sure that I had now severed our friendship. But the worst part was I had no idea why.

"Great shot, Frankie!" Marco and Gino shouted, laughing and slapping me on the back. Everyone jubilantly congratulated me.

"Come on, let's get out of here," someone yelled. We all took off, running toward Shetland Avenue. A little way up the street, I slowed and turned back to catch a glimpse of Honeymarmo. I didn't see him anywhere. "I'm sorry," I whispered. "I'm so, so sorry." Then,

I heard Marco call my name, so I turned and rushed blindly toward them all.

*****

Honeymarmo shuffled slowly down the path leading under the bridge. He felt tired, more tired than he could ever remember feeling before. He dropped down in the dirt, and his bones welcomed the rest. He pressed his hand against the wound above his eye, and he pulled it down to look. It wasn't bleeding like before, but there was still blood.

"Oh, Frankie," he moaned sadly. He could only imagine his young friend's guilt and shame for what he had done; he had seen it on his face. It made him sad, and he felt even more tired now. Honeymarmo sat for a long time. Finally, he forced himself to his feet, then slowly shuffled up toward the abutment where his things were stashed and pulled out his old Bible and a pencil. He again sat down in the dirt and began to write; his hand was shaking. After he had finished, he sat quietly, staring out at the horizon. He figured now was the time to move on, even though his tiredness hadn't left him. But first, he had one more thing to do. He slowly walked up the path toward Larimer Avenue. About thirty minutes later, he returned. He retrieved his bindle and waited. There seemed to be almost no energy left in his legs, and his nauseousness had returned. *Hopefully, a slow-moving train will come along soon,* he thought. If it did, he wondered if he would even have the strength to jump aboard.

Chapter 24

J oe sunk his teeth into the leather belt wrapped around his bicep, then pulled it tight. Once the veins in his muscular forearm swelled, he found one to his liking and jabbed in the needle, slowly plunging the heroin into his bloodstream. His body went limp, and the room faded away. He was sitting on the floor and slumped back against the wall.

"Give me the needle, man," he heard someone say. A tall, lean, black man extracted heroin from a spoon on the coffee table and eased the needle into a naturally bulging vein in his forearm. After a soft gasp, the hypodermic needle dropped to the floor, and he eased back against the wall next to Joe.

An hour later, the two of them made their way up Larimer Avenue toward Meadows Bar and Grill. Inside, they sat on bar stools and ordered a couple of drafts. The black man discreetly handed Joe a sizeable white pill when the mugs arrived. Joe looked down at the Quaalude, tossed it into his mouth, and washed it down with a mouthful of foamy beer.

"All right, Boots, I owe you," Joe said. Boots understood that Joe was a man of few words, so he didn't respond. After a couple of beers, Boots leaned toward Joe.

"How about we go back to my place and do some more smack?" he whispered. Joe nodded.

Outside, Joe felt the need to relieve himself. Not wanting to return to the bar, they turned into a dark alley, where both of them urinated next to some trash cans. Afterward, they turned and met face-to-face with two black men, holding switchblades.

189

"Give us the drugs and money," the bigger of the two men demanded. Joe's black eyes went cold, and he stepped in front of Boots staring directly at the bigger man who had made the demand.

"All right, it's in my right pocket, but if you want it, you have to come and get it," Joe said calmly.

The bigger man at first seemed indecisive. "Go on and get it from his pocket," he nervously instructed his partner. The other man edged skittishly toward Joe; his knife was outstretched. Joe raised his hands submissively. As the man reached for Joe's pocket, Joe unleashed a lightning-quick punch that caught the man flush in the face, lifting him off the ground and knocking him unconscious before he hit the pavement. The other man charged, lunging with his knife, and before Joe could react, the knife plunged into his stomach. Joe grimaced, stepped back with his right foot, and unleashed a punch that dropped the man to the ground. Now standing over him, Joe reached down and grabbed the front of the large black man's shirt, lifting him off the ground to deliver another blow. The man reached up and again jabbed the knife into Joe's gut. Joe's second punch shattered the man's left eye socket. The man went limp. "Come on, stab me again, jagoff," Joe snarled. His third punch broke the cartridge in the big man's nose. The fourth punch broke out three of his front teeth. His fifth punch bent his nose to one side, and the sixth punch fractured his right cheekbone. The man's face swelled into a mangled, bloody mess.

"Joe, man, I think you killed him," Boots exclaimed, grabbing Joe's arm. Joe stood erect. He looked around, walked over to a round metal trash can, picked it up, carried it over to the man he had just beaten, raised it over his head, and with all the force he could generate, slammed it down on the unconscious man's head.

"Oh, damn, man. We need to get out of here," Boots said nervously.

Joe looked down at his stomach and blood-soaked the front of his shirt, and he grunted. "Yeah, all right."

A little way down Larimer Avenue, the heroin, Quaaludes, alcohol, and blood loss took full effect, and Joe's legs weakened. He became dizzy, and he fought to keep from collapsing. Boots did his best to prop him up as they walked, but it became increasingly difficult. When they reached the front of Joe's apartment, it took all of Boots' strength to help him up the flights of stairs, and as they got to the apartment door, Joe collapsed to the floor. Boots rapped on the door in a panic, then sprinted down the stairwell and ran up Larimer Avenue as fast as his legs would carry him.

Our mum was in her bedroom, sitting on the bed watching television. She stood, walked to the old black-and-white TV, lowered the volume, and listened. It sounded like a knock at the door, and she stepped into the hallway just as I appeared from the living room.

"Did you hear a knock?" she asked me.

"I thought I did," I answered.

She walked to the door and listened. "Is someone there?" she asked. There was no answer; then, she heard a groan. "Who is it?" Another groan.

She unlocked the door and cautiously peeked into the stairwell.

"Oh my god, Joe! Joe! What happened?" my mum cried as she saw Joe in his blood-soaked clothes. He was struggling to get to his feet. Mindy and Doreen, who had heard the commotion from the kitchen, appeared in the hallway.

"Frankie, help me get him inside!" our mum cried in a panic as she rushed to Joe's side. I hurried into the hall, and we both strained to prop Joe up. We managed to get him to his feet, and my legs almost buckled under his weight as we helped him to the bedroom. A trail of bloody footprints followed us. Inside the bedroom, he collapsed on the bed.

"Was he shot?" I asked.

"I don't know!" our mum cried. "Joe? Joe? What happened?"

Joe forced his drooping eyelids open. "A couple of jigaboos tried to rob me," he said. He grabbed his shirt and pulled it up to expose his stomach. "One of the jagoffs stabbed me," he grunted, "so I crushed his skull in." Our mum gasped when she saw the gaping wounds.

"We have to get you to the hospital," she sobbed.

"No, no hospital. Just clean it up and stop the bleeding," Joe said. He shut his eyes. Our mum ran her fingers through her hair.

"Frankie, close the door, then help me get his clothes off," she finally said. "Mindy, Doreen, go fill a pot of hot water and some tea towels and set them outside the door. Get the rubbing alcohol, too. Then, you two wait in the kitchen." Mindy and Doreen sprinted through the apartment to do what our mum had asked.

An hour later, Joe lay completely naked on the bed. Our mum had torn strips from an old sheet and wrapped them tightly around Joe's waist to hold the rags she had used for dressings in place. She began washing the blood from the rest of his body.

At first, I didn't notice it, but it suddenly appeared as our mum washed the blood away from his groin area. Initially, I didn't react because the significance of what I was looking at hadn't yet dawned on me. Then, like a bolt of lightning, it hit me. I gasped.

"What? What's the matter?" my mum asked.

I slowly shook my head. "Nothing!" I said. "Do you need me anymore?"

"No, go ahead, I'll finish up here," my mum answered. She dunked a rag into the basin of red-tinted water, wrung it out, and continued to wipe Joe down.

I hurried from the room. I had to find Mindy.

*****

I found Mindy sitting with Doreen at the kitchen table. "Min, I need to talk to you," I announced.

"What about?" Mindy asked.

"Just come here. I'll tell you in my room," I said.

"What do you need to talk to Mindy about?" Doreen asked.

"None of your business," I snapped.

"Ah, come on, I won't tell no one. Is it a secret? It is, isn't it?" Doreen persisted. "You can tell me. I won't tell no one."

"No, I can't because you're a blabbermouth!" I blurted out.

"I am not!" Doreen objected.

"C'mon, Min, it's important," I said. Mindy stood and followed me to my room, and I shut the door behind us.

"What is it?" Mindy asked, squinting at me curiously.

"I saw it, Min," I said.

"Saw what?" Mindy chirped.

"I saw Joe's tattoo, down on his private parts area," I answered.

Mindy's expression turned somber. Her eyes filled with anguish before darting away.

"That day in the empty apartment when you got mad and threw the Bible, it wasn't because of the Bible, was it? It was because of the cross that was on it, just like the cross tattoo on Joe's private parts. That's it, isn't it, Min??" I asked.

"Shut up!" my sister snapped.

I ignored her. "Min, what did he do to you?"

"I can't, Frankie, I just can't! I'm so ashamed! And if I were to tell anyone, he would kill me, Frankie, he said he would!" She began to sob.

"Mindy, if you can't tell me, you have to tell Mum. She has to know, Min," I pleaded. Mindy shook her head vigorously.

"No!" she cried. "And you can't say nothing, Frankie. Not nothing!" Her voice shrilled. "You have to promise!"

"First, tell me what he did," I insisted. Mindy recognized the determination on my face. I could tell she wanted to tell me but couldn't bring herself to say the words.

"He did bad things, and I'll never say what. Not to anyone, not even you." She cried.

"Min. you have to tell—"

"No!" Mindy shrieked. "Frankie, if you tell Mummy or anyone, I'll never talk to you again! Not never!" As I looked into my sister's eyes, I knew she meant it. I had never seen her like this before, and my mind raced, not sure what to do next.

"I mean it, Frankie!" she threatened again, then stormed from the room.

Chapter 25

Joe didn't leave the apartment for the next few days, mostly staying in bed as his wounds healed. The news spread throughout the neighborhood that someone had murdered another man in Larimer. A bar owner had found him behind his bar; someone had severely beaten him up, then crushed his head with a trash can. There was no other person found. There was speculation that it might have been the same person who killed the hobo by the railroad tracks since no one had come forward with any information about who may have done it. No one knew for sure, except for my mum and me.

Then, I woke one morning soon after and made my way to the kitchen, where our mum and sisters sat around the kitchen table, eating breakfast. The coffee percolated on the stove. Our mum crushed her cigarette into the ashtray, pushed up from the kitchen table, turned off the burner, sat back down, and returned to reading the *Pittsburgh Press*. Sometimes, our only neighbor in our building, Elizabeth, would leave the discarded newspaper on the back porch for our mum. Mindy sat at the end of the table, nearest the sink, and I sat opposite her. She didn't seem upset anymore, but she also didn't seem to be her same bubbly self. She got up to pour herself a cup of milk from the refrigerator, and when she had finished, she discovered that Doreen had slid into her chair.

"Get out of my chair!" Mindy demanded.

"Ain't your chair," Doreen said spitefully. "It ain't got your name on it, does it?"

"I mean it, Doreen, get out of my chair!" Mindy warned.

"Make me!"

"Don't think I won't?" Mindy set the cup down on the table to free her hands for battle.

"Oh, Jesus Christ Almighty! Would yinz two quit your yakking and knock it off!" our mum hollered with growing frustration as she peered over the top of the newspaper. "I swear, I can't even read the paper in peace with both of yinz in the room. Now stop it!"

"Well, she started it!" Mindy complained.

"Nuh-uh, you started it!" Doreen shot back.

"Nuh-uh, you started it, and you know it!" Mindy shouted indignantly.

"Nuh-uh—"

"Oh, for Christ's sake, that's it!" our mum yelled, slapping the paper down on the table. "I've had it up to here with both of you. One more word and you both will spend the rest of the day in your room. You hear me?"

They both fought the urge to get in the final word. Instead, Mindy and Doreen both resolved themselves to make derogatory faces at one another when they thought our mum wasn't looking. We heard Joe's slow, heavy footsteps heading toward us from the hall. He entered the kitchen and walked over to the sink. We glimpsed the torn sheets wrapped around his waist with blotches of blood seeping through the front. He set down his coffee cup in the sink, then turned and stared directly at us. Me, Mindy, and Doreen lowered our eyes, not daring to look in his direction.

"If I hear another word out here, I'm going to crack every one of you upside the head. Got it?" Everyone sat in silence. Satisfied, Joe grunted, then turned and lumbered slowly back down the passageway to his bedroom. My sisters and I exhaled a sigh of relief.

I continued making my sugar bread for breakfast. I buttered two slices of bread, got a spoon full of sugar, and carefully sprinkled sugar over them. I took a bite and chewed the sweetness slowly.

"Mum?" I finally whispered.

"What is it, Frankie?" our mum whispered back.

"Do you know what the Ten Commandments are?"

She shot me a puzzled look. "Of course I do, Frankie. Why?"

"Do you know what God considers one of the most important commandments?"

Our mum narrowed her eyes in contemplation. "Let's see. Probably 'thou shalt not kill,'" she speculated.

I gave a slow shake of my head. "Nope." It was something Honeymarmo had taught me. "It's 'Thou shall not take the name of the Lord in vain,'" I whispered accusingly.

Our mum blushed slightly. "Well, I suppose I need to be more careful then."

"Yeah, Mrs. Piper at school said if you use the Lord's name in vain, he might strike you dead with lightning," Doreen interjected.

"Well, I'm sure God won't strike anyone dead with lightning, Doreen, but I get your point, Frankie, and in the future, I'll try and be more careful," our mum promised. "Now, keep your voices down." She picked up the paper and again began to read.

"Hey, they got something in here about Larimer," she announced. We all looked over at her attentively, and I took another bite of my sugar bread.

"Another indigent man was found—"

"What's indigent mean?" Doreen asked.

"It means he doesn't have no home, like a hobo, stupid!" Mindy clucked.

"I ain't stupid," Doreen shot back.

"You are too." Mindy sang out, "Stupid, stupid...*stupid!*"

"What did I tell yinz? You both want to spend the rest of the day in your rooms, or worse?" our mum again warned over the top of the paper, staring them into silence. She continued to read.

"'Another indigent man was found dead near the woods on the east side of Larimer early yesterday morning.'" Our mum paused and sipped her coffee before continuing. "'A group of boys, who lived nearby, discovered the body while playing near the railroad tracks not far from Larimer Bridge. It appears that the man had been dead for several days. Although the cause of death is still undetermined,' stated county coroner Vince Olasky 'the preliminary cause of death appears to have been from natural causes.'"

I abruptly stopped chewing, and the sweet sugar bread that stuffed my cheeks soured in my mouth. My stomach constricted, and I forced myself to breathe. Nausea gripped me. I stood, hurried to the open kitchen door, ran across the back porch, and made it to the railing just as my breakfast spewed from my mouth and stomach. Behind me, I could hear disgusting noises coming from Doreen and the sound of a kitchen chair scraping across the linoleum floor as our mum pushed away from the table and hurried to my side.

I sat alone under Larimer Bridge a little while later, distraught and deep in thought. I had spent the better part of an hour searching the entire wooded area, hoping I had been wrong. Even now, I was trying to rationalize that the indigent man found could in no way be Honeymarmo. Yet my heart and intuition told me otherwise. Just the possibility that it might have been Honeymarmo created in me a sense of loss, which was more profound than I had ever known. Despite my betrayal of Honeymarmo, I still held out hope that somehow we would reconcile. I had convinced myself that I would eventually seek him out and tell him how sorry I was for what I had done. If this dead hobo found was Honeymarmo, that meant I would never have that chance, and I would never know if he would have ever forgiven me. And without Honeymarmo's forgiveness, I knew I could never forgive myself.

My anguish deepened. I had rehearsed my apology a hundred times in my mind, and the need to see him and tell him was powerful within me. Gradually, a dark truth slowly emerged. Even if this dead hobo was not Honeymarmo, I doubted if I even possessed the courage to seek out my friend to apologize for what I had done. I was a coward; I had proven it. My shame was as fresh and powerful as the day I betrayed him. But what was most agonizing for me was that if the man found dead was indeed Honeymarmo, then it probably was my treachery, my cowardice, and not the rock that had killed him. It was too much for me to bear. If Honeymarmo was dead, then it was too late, and not even God could help me now. Still, not knowing what else to do or where else to turn, I bowed my head and prayed for his help.

In another week, summer vacation would come to an end, and the school would open its doors, and the distraction of being able to busy my mind and thrust myself into schoolwork carried a much-welcomed appeal to me like never before.

*****

On the first day of school, the classroom was buzzing with excitement. All of us students looked spiffy in our new school clothes. We were all giddy with anticipation at being reunited and spoke of our summer activities as we waited for the bell to ring to start class and a new school year. As the desks filled up, I was disappointed that Donald, Ronald, or Marco was not in my class. I told myself I was glad Bunny wasn't in my class either, but secretly, I longed to see her again. Then, Leroy strolled through the door, and my spirit lifted. Leroy spotted me and immediately made his way over to an empty desk in front of me. A couple of minutes later, we spotted Lulu walking through the door with a nylon stocking tied in a knot stretched over his head. Leroy and I looked at one another.

"Ringworm," we both said at the same time, then started laughing.

Lulu heard me and Leroy laughing, gave us a sour look, and then hurried to the last empty desk in the classroom's far rear corner. The bell rang at last, and from the back of the room, our new teacher, Mrs. English, walked to the door and pulled it shut. She strolled across the front of the classroom with a dignified and graceful posture and faced us. Some were still talking, so she clapped her hands twice to gain their attention.

"Be quiet now," she said firmly. All the chatter ceased, and everyone stared up at her, wide-eyed with curiosity. She was a relatively young black woman, and although her stern voice commanded instant obedience from all in the classroom, her eyes were gentle and kind. I have to be honest; I got a warm mushy feeling inside the first time she spoke.

"Now, children, when we hear the bell ring to begin class each day, I expect you to be in your seats, sitting up straight with eyes facing toward the front and your hands folded on your desk in front of you." The entire classroom instantly folded their hands on their desks. "That's it. Also, once you hear the bell ring, there will be no more talking. Does everyone understand me?"

"Yes, Mrs. English," everyone chimed in cadence.

"Good." She then gave us the most approving smile I had ever witnessed, and as her eyes roamed around the room to get a good look at her new students, I swear, they settled on me longer than anyone else. Pleased, I responded with the broadest crooked-tooth smile I could manage. "Starting tomorrow, we will have milk available in the morning, so don't forget to bring in your nickel, or you can pay for the entire week starting on Monday. Does everyone understand?"

"Yes, Mrs. English."

"Very good, children," she said, again giving the entire class an approving smile. The rest of the morning, she covered the subjects, passed out our textbooks, and handed out papers that had to go home with us students to be signed by our parents. There was something different about being in Mrs. English's class. I decided right there and then, on that very day, that I wasn't going to mess up as I had in previous years, but instead, I would become the best student ever so that Mrs. English would like me. I decided to make a real effort in all my subjects and buckle down on the required work for the first time. I had never given school much effort before, but I decided this year would be different, especially since I had promised Honeymarmo.

Mrs. English made it easy for me, and she seemed to like me too. Her genuine affection for all her students, coupled with a devoted passion that she poured into teaching, seemed to stimulate me and created a thirst within me for discovery like I had never known before. I'm not ashamed to say that I fell madly in love with Mrs. English from the start.

Often, as she would pace the classroom while the students worked on their assignments, I would sometimes, as a ploy, raise my hand, pretending to need her assistance so she would get next to me. Mrs. English would come to my desk and lean over my shoulder to help resolve my fictitious problem. I would sit motionless, as if under a spell, as she whispered to me in a soft, hypnotic tone while secretly

I inhaled her intoxicating perfume. A soothing sensation would flow through me that lingered even after she had moved on to another student. And when that calming sensation eventually dissipated, it left within me an emptiness.

Mrs. English would line us students up each afternoon, march us through the hall, and dismiss us for lunch. Student safety guards would strategically be placed at different street corners to ensure students' safety as we crossed the streets while walking home for lunch and back again.

Most days, I would hang around the schoolyard during lunch, playing on the monkey bars and swings, waiting for my classmates to drift back from their homes after they had eaten lunch, so we could play together before the bell rang to start the afternoon school session. My choosing to stay in the schoolyard was not solely because of the scarcity of food at home, but mostly I didn't go home because of Joe and his irrational and unpredictable behavior. There had been times when Joe had discovered me home during lunch and had locked me in my room the rest of the day, forcing my mum to write a note the following day as to why I hadn't returned to school.

A few weeks into the new school year, as everyone lined up for lunch, Mrs. English pulled me aside. "Can you stay behind a few moments?" she asked. After the rest of the class had gone, she returned to the room and walked to her desk. She pulled up a chair, smiled at me, and motioned for me to sit down.

As I slid into the chair, Mrs. English focused her attention on me. "It seems like almost every day during lunch when I look outside, I see you playing by yourself when all the other students are home eating lunch. Is there a reason you don't go home, Frankie?" she asked with concern.

I quickly searched my mind for a lie. But looking into Mrs. English's compassionate eyes, I couldn't lie to her. I couldn't tell her about Joe because our mum made me and my sisters promise never to tell anyone about him, and I was too embarrassed to mention that sometimes we didn't have any food in the apartment, especially near the end of the month. So instead, I just shrugged.

"Is there anyone home at lunch? Does your mother work?"

I shook my head. "No, she don't work. We live on relief," I mumbled. I had never given much thought to being on welfare, but the prospect that Mrs. English might like me less because of it made me suddenly self-conscious and even embarrassed.

"Oh, I see," Mrs. English said softly. "Is that why you never have milk money?" I shifted uneasily in my chair and nodded.

Then, she studied me for a moment and retrieved her purse from under the desk. She reached inside and pulled out a quarter. "I wonder if you wouldn't mind doing me a favor, Frankie?" she asked.

"Sure," I said. I liked how she said my name, and I would do anything for her.

"Most of the time, I don't have the chance to eat lunch because I have to catch up on grading papers. Do you think you could run down to the little store on the corner and get me one of those little packs of cheese crackers?"

I sat erect in my chair. "Sure."

"That's wonderful," she exclaimed, smiling as she handed me the quarter. I jumped up from my chair and hurried toward the door. "Be careful crossing the street," she warned, knowing the safety guards were gone.

"I know that," I assured her, although it seemed silly to me since I had been running the streets of Larimer since I was practically a baby. I quickened my pace through the hall, and once I reached the front doors, I broke out into a full sprint.

"That was fast," Mrs. English said, seeming surprised when I returned only moments later. She was pleased, which made me beam. I handed her the packet of cheese crackers, and her fifteen cents change, and I felt proud of myself that I hadn't even short-changed her. "Thank you, Frankie, you're a lifesaver," she said pleasantly. "Here, this is for you." She grabbed my hand and pressed a dime into my palm.

"For real?" I exclaimed.

"You know, I'll probably need you to run to the store for me a couple of times a week, maybe more, since I just love these things," Mrs. English informed me as she tore open the package. "That is if you promise to save the money you earn for your milk money. This way, you can drink milk with the rest of the class when the milk lady comes around in the morning."

I stared at the dime intently. "Okay," I finally agreed, handing the money back to her.

"No, you can keep it—you earned it," Mrs. English said.

"Nuh-uh, I'll probably spend it on candy if I keep it." Mrs. English stared amusedly at me before finally taking the dime back.

"Okay," she chuckled, "I'll put it in your milk fund right away." I was relieved that she had taken it because I was pretty sure that I would have spent it on candy before paying for my milk like Mrs. English wanted, and I shuddered at the thought of disappointing her.

"You know, you're doing very well so far in all your subjects, and I have faith in you that you are going to do even better for the remainder of the year."

Before today, Honeymarmo had been the only other person to tell me that they had faith in me. I missed my friend, and the guilt resurfaced whenever I thought of him. I was suddenly struck with a thought, a question, and I had to know the answer. "Do you believe in God, Mrs. English?" I asked.

Mrs. English looked inquisitively at me. "Well, actually, yes, I do, Frankie, very much so."

"Me too!" I cried out giddily, now knowing we had something in common. "I knew you did," I said. I thought a lot about God lately and found myself not wanting to disappoint him. It is why I gave Mrs. English the correct change back, something I would have never done before. I turned and walked from the classroom, feeling a newfound kinship with my teacher.

The following day, and for the first time that year, when the milk lady stopped by our classroom carrying a crate filled with pints of milk in cardboard boxes, she called out my name. I rose from my seat, walked to the front, and the milk lady handed me a pint of milk and a straw. I walked back to my desk, peeled open the corner with the aluminum foiled edge, plunged in the straw, and slurped down the entire carton. Milk had never tasted sweeter to me or been more satisfying. Afterward, I stood with my empty container and disposed of it in the wastebasket by the door. On the way back to my seat, I noticed Mrs. English looking at me. We exchanged grins before I sat down and anxiously waited for the next subject of the day to begin.

*****

Early fall that year carried with it an Indian summer. Leroy's and my friendship grew closer, and we began spending more time together. Sometimes, after school, we would hang out on the playground. I was never in a hurry to get home; however, Leroy always had a strict time limit.

One day, Leroy turned to me. "You want to come over to my house instead of hanging out in the schoolyard?" he asked.

It was the first time Leroy had invited me over. "I have to go home and change out of my school clothes first," I said.

"Okay, see you in a little bit." Leroy gave me the address, and we walked off in different directions. I started across Larimer Avenue in front of the school.

"Hey! No jaywalking!" yelled one of the safety guards. I glared over at him. He wore a white harness-like belt that stretched diagonally across his chest and looped around his waist. I considered ignoring the safety monitor's command and running across the street anyway but decided against it. I didn't want to get into trouble with Mrs. English. Reluctantly, I shuffled over to the corner. The safety monitor, who took his job seriously, looked both ways, stepped into the intersection, then waved me across.

At our apartment, I quickly changed out of my school clothes. My mum was in the hallway on her hands and knees, scrubbing along the baseboards. The smell of ammonia lingered heavily in the air. I watched as she plunged an old rag into a bucket of black sudsy water, then gave it a light wringing. Suds and excess water ran down her forearm and dripped from her elbow onto the floor. She brushed strands of her curly hair away from her eyes with the back of her wrist. She looked tired as she gave me a weary smile.

"How was school today?"

"Good. Mrs. English is the best teacher ever," I said. "She's really nice."

"Good, maybe you'll keep up your grades this year," my mum hinted humorously.

"Maybe." I shrugged. "I'm going over my friend Leroy's for a little bit. I'll be home later." I hurried through the apartment toward the kitchen door.

"Be home for supper," my mum yelled after me. I heard the rhythmic sound of the sopping wet rag as my mum scrubbed.

A few moments later, I knocked on Leroy's front door. A stout black woman opened it and stared down at me. She wore a faded floral house dress and a white apron. Although she had a motherly face, there was a no-nonsense demeanor about her that promptly told me to tread lightly.

"Can I help you?" she asked.

"Yeah, is Leroy here?" My eyes probed past her into the house.

Her one eyebrow immediately rose almost disapprovingly, as if I had said or done something wrong. "And you are?"

I shifted uncomfortably under her stare. "Frankie."

"Oh, you're the new friend Leroy told us about. Well, come on in, and I'll call him for you." I followed her into the house. Just inside the front door was a staircase. "Leroy?" she yelled up the steps.

"Yes, ma'am?" Leroy hollered back from upstairs.

"Your friend Frankie is here, sweetie."

I heard Leroy running across the upstairs floor, and then he appeared at the top of the steps. "Come on up," he yelled down. I sprinted up the steps two at a time and followed Leroy into his bedroom.

Leroy's room was a sight. He had a twin bed with a lamp on a nightstand. There was a dresser by the window and a clothes hamper in the corner. Against the wall, across from his bed, was a table with a small television with rabbit ears. As I stood looking around, I felt suddenly awkward.

"Want to play Rock 'Em Sock 'Em Robots?" Leroy asked.

"For real? Yeah," I said. I had seen the game advertised on the small black-and-white television that Joe and my mum had in their bedroom, but I had never actually known anyone that had one. Leroy went to his closet and pulled the box from the top shelf. He set it on the floor, opened it, and pulled it out of the box. We both lay on the floor and began to slug it out. It was evident that Leroy had played many times because his red robot kept knocking my blue robot's block off. We heard Leroy's mum walking up the steps in a little while, and she appeared in the doorway.

"Leroy?"

"Yes, ma'am."

"I made some hot biscuits for you and Frankie. They're on the kitchen table," she announced, smiling warmly.

"Okay, Mama, we'll be down in a minute." She disappeared from the doorway, and we heard her walking back down the steps. Leroy knocked my block off one final time, then he put the game away and told me to follow him. We descended the stairs, made a U-turn at the bottom, and walked down a hallway into the kitchen. The smell of fresh-baked biscuits made my stomach growl. I sat down at the kitchen table while Leroy pulled out a couple of plates from the cupboard. Leroy set them on the table, walked to the refrigerator, and pulled out some butter and maple syrup. I watched with anticipation as Leroy sat down at the table, buttered a biscuit, poured maple syrup onto his plate, and dipped the buttered biscuit into the thick brown sweetness before stuffing it into his mouth. I followed Leroy's lead. It melted deliciously in my mouth. We both attacked the remaining biscuits as if we hadn't eaten for a week. Leroy's mum came into the kitchen to check on us.

As she looked over at us, she frowned disapprovingly. "Leroy, chew with your mouth closed," she said sternly. I had never heard of such a thing and had no idea there was an actual etiquette to chewing. I became suddenly conscious of the entire biscuit stuffed in my mouth, ensuring I now ate it with my mouth shut.

"But Mum, I was—," Leroy started to protest in between chews.

"Don't you sass me, and don't you be talking with your mouth full neither," she corrected him again. Leroy swallowed his food.

"Yes, ma'am."

As Leroy's mum spoke, I listened attentively, not wanting to be corrected, taking mental notes to ensure I was doing everything correctly. While Leroy's mum bustled about the kitchen, Leroy and I finished the entire pan of biscuits, and we both stood.

Leroy walked over to his mum and hugged her. "Thank you, Mama," Leroy said. Not wanting to be impolite or corrected for not doing things the right way, I walked over to Leroy's mum and threw my arms around her thick waist.

"Thank you," I said.

"Well, um, Frankie…you're welcome, sweetie," Leroy's mom replied awkwardly. I let her loose, turned, and noticed that Leroy was giving me a peculiar look before exchanging a similar look with his mum, which I immediately interpreted it as approval.

"C'mon, let's go out on the front porch," I suggested happily. I headed down the hallway toward the front of the house. Leroy followed.

Leroy had become my new best friend, and over the next several months, we spent a lot of time together over Leroy's house, playing, eating, doing school homework, and doing class projects together, but mostly, we would just hang out. My only regret was not recip- rocating by inviting Leroy to our apartment. I could never bring friends over to our apartment for fear of what Joe may say or do if he was home, especially if Joe was drunk or loaded on drugs. Even worse, I would have been too mortified to show any of my friends, especially Leroy, my empty room with the broken window, no furni- ture, and a bare, pee-stained mattress. The very thought of any of my friends ever seeing my bedroom filled me with anxiety.

Leroy's dad worked for the city at the water and sewer plant. He mostly sat in the living room wearing his light gray city uniform when home. An emblem with his name "Marvin" was on his shirt pocket, and another insignia that read "Pittsburgh Water and Sewer" was on the other. Mr. Sampson was always reading the Bible or the *Pittsburgh Press* or watching the news. He was friendly and quiet, but everyone in the Sampson household perked up when he spoke, and all were usually quick to obey, especially if he gave an order.

Harold was Leroy's older brother, who had just graduated high school the prior year. Most of the time, Harold didn't want to be bothered by Leroy and me, but he would come into the bedroom or out in the kitchen where we were and talk to us on occasion. His dad was always asking him if he had decided what he was going to do. Leroy told me in confidence that his dad had told Harold he either had to go to college or a trade school or get a job. Leroy also confided in me that his dad had told Harold that he was a man now, and he couldn't just sit around the house doing nothing. Leroy said that Harold would complain and shut himself in his room. I found myself spending much more time over Leroy's than I did at our apartment. Something about being at Leroy's made me feel safe, so I adopted them as mine without much thought or fanfare.

Chapter 26

J oe staggered up Larimer Avenue on the outskirts of Larimer near East Liberty Boulevard. Late October carried a cold front that brought an abrupt end to the Indian summer, turning the air frosty and bringing the possibility of overnight snow. The alcohol and barbiturates had taken effect, and it showed. He wore a thinly knitted shirt, and he seemed impervious to the eye-watering cold. In his left hand, he gripped two thick ropes. At the other end of the ropes, tugging hard, were two large black Doberman pinschers. He stopped in front of a corner bar and grill and gave the makeshift leashes a hard yank.

"Whoa! Stop, you stupid mutts!" Joe barked in his graveled voice. The dogs responded instantly to his command.

"Sit!" he commanded. One of the Dobermans promptly obeyed. The other stood, distracted by something up the street. Joe stepped behind the distracted dog and punched him hard on top of the head. "I said, sit your ass down!" The dog yelped as it cringed to the pavement, and it let out a low guttural growl.

"Who the hell are you growling at?" Joe lifted the front of his shirt, pulled out a pistol from his waistband, and aimed it at the dog's head. He gave the dog a sharp kick to its hindquarters. Once again, the dog yelped and tried to flee, but Joe constrained him with the rope. Realizing its hopeless predicament, it laid its head submissively on the pavement. "Go ahead, growl at me again, and I'll blow your damn head off." The pistol swayed in Joe's hand. Satisfied that he didn't have to shoot the dog, he lifted the front of his shirt and shoved the gun back into his pants. His black eyes were glazed, and his eyelids drooped. Now that both dogs were entirely under his control, Joe tied them to a telephone pole and walked into the bar and grill.

It was dim inside, and Joe slid into an empty booth. The bartender took notice of the large muscular man as he entered the bar and sat down. The man staggered slightly, and there was something about his aggressive features and dark, brooding eyes that made the bartender uneasy. He came out from behind the bar and walked over to Joe.

"Good evening. What can I get you?" the bartender asked pleasantly.

Joe barely glanced in his direction. "You have hamburgers?"

"Sure do. Our hamburger special comes with fries and a pickle."

"Give me three hamburger specials, then."

The bartender seemed confused. "Three hamburger specials?" he repeated to clarify.

Joe shot him a menacing look. "What, are you deaf? Did I stutter or something?" Joe's threatening and aggressive tone caused the bartender to step back. Noticing the apprehension in the bartender, Joe changed his strategy and softened his tone. "I have a couple of friends who'll be joining me in a few minutes—here at this fine establishment," Joe said flippantly, pointing around at the interior of the dingy bar.

The bartender swallowed nervously, then nodded. "Oh, okay. Something to drink?"

"Yeah, bring me three drafts of Iron City."

"Okay, you got it," the bartender said. Once he was behind the bar, the bartender disappeared through a door leading to the kitchen. A few moments later, he reappeared at Joe's booth holding three glasses of beer. He placed the mugs on the table in front of Joe, and Joe picked up one of them and took a long gulp without speaking. The bartender walked back to attend to his other customers sitting at the bar. When Joe had almost finished his beer, he heard a bell ring from an open window behind the bar leading to the kitchen. The bartender once again appeared at Joe's booth carrying three plates.

He set the hamburgers specials on the table, one in front of Joe and two across from him.

"Anything else I can get you?"

Seemingly annoyed, Joe shook his head dismissively. The bartender frowned and made his way back behind the bar. This large muscular man was unfriendly and stoned on something, so he decided to keep a watchful eye on him.

Joe took a bite of his hamburger, and as he began to chew, he pushed himself out from behind the booth, stood, and walked to the front door. He disappeared outside, and in less than a minute, the door flew wide opened, and a rush of frigid air filled the bar room. Two ferocious black Doberman pinschers charged through the open door, followed by Joe, tugging them back by the two thick ropes. Once the Dobermans saw the people seated at the bar, they lunged toward them, growling, gnashing their teeth, and barking viciously. The customers leaped from their stoles and ran behind the bar and into the bathrooms. The bartender stood speechless in utter disbelief at what he was witnessing.

"Shut your freaking mouths," Joe scolded the dogs. "Now, that ain't very friendly of you." He led them over to his table and jerked the ropes toward the open seat across from his. The two dogs jumped up into the booth, and Joe sat down opposite them. He shoved the plates with the hamburgers closer to them and ordered them to eat. The dogs attacked the food, ravenously devouring their burger and fries in a feeding frenzy; food scattered messily over the table.

"Don't eat like pigs. You're embarrassing me," Joe said, turning toward the bartender who also stood behind the protection of the bar and who continued to stare wide-eyed in disbelief, his mouth agape. "I apologize for my friends' table manners. They've never been taught how to eat properly," Joe said mockingly. He picked up one of the glasses of beer and held it in front of the dog directly in front of him. The dog lapped at it greedily. Then, Joe set the mug down, picked up his hamburger, and calmly took a bite.

Finally, the bartender, red-faced from anger, worked up enough courage to speak, but from behind the bar's safety. "Hey, you need to get those filthy dogs out of here. What the hell's the matter with you?" he shouted.

Joe set his hamburger down slowly, wiped his mouth with the back of his hand, and turned toward the bartender. "First of all, these are my friends and my guests, so don't insult them by calling them filthy. You'll hurt their feelings. You ain't filthy, are you?" he asked them. "Now, what you need to do is apologize to them." He stared coldly at the bartender, waiting for his apology.

The bartender stood flabbergasted. "I ain't apologizing to no dogs. Now get them out of my bar before I call the police."

"The police?" Joe looked over at the dogs. "Did yinz hear that, you mutts? He's going to call the police." He turned his attention back to the barkeep. "Yeah, okay, sure, I'll take them outside," he gave the bartender a sarcastic smirk, "right after they finish eating." Joe picked up his hamburger and took another bite.

The bartender was now enraged, but sizing Joe up, he knew he would be no match for him. Besides, this guy was plain crazy, maybe some kind of psychopath. He stood indecisively for a moment, weighing options before finally marching into the back to call the police.

Two police cars arrived with lights flashing and sirens screaming. Four policemen entered the bar, approached Joe but prudently kept their distance from the vicious-looking dogs. After several unsuccessful attempts to reason with Joe, the police called for dog catchers. With extreme caution, the dog catchers approached the snarling canines. Skillfully, they slid nooses attached to long poles around each of the dogs' necks and tightened the rope. Once the dog catchers secured the dogs, they dragged them outside and shoved them into cages in the back of a van.

Once the dog catchers safely removed the canines, one policeman grabbed Joe by the arm to pull him from the booth. Joe hit the policeman right between the eyes, sending him sprawling across the barroom floor. The place erupted into chaos. It took all four police officers to subdue Joe long enough to clasp a set of handcuffs on him. They dragged him outside, threw him in the back of a squad car, and took him down to the police station to spend the next couple of days in the local jail. It turned out that Joe had stolen the Dobermans from a backyard somewhere in the neighborhood of Homewood, next to Larimer. He was also charged with assault and battery on the police, resisting arrest, and carrying a concealed weapon without a license. Joe's court-appointed lawyer negotiated a plea deal, so Joe pled guilty, and the judge sentenced him to six months in the county jail.

*****

Our mum sat at the kitchen table; dark circles had formed under her bloodshot eyes. She wiped her nose with toilet paper, sniffled, and rubbed her face.

Mindy strolled into the kitchen and immediately noticed her mother's distress. "What's the matter, Mummy?" she asked, sitting next to her.

Our mum dabbed at her eyes, "Joe's sister, Aunt Claudia, stopped by and told me the judge gave Joe six months in jail for getting in a fight with those policemen at the bar the other night." She sobbed. "What am I going to do now with the baby on the way and everything? He'll be gone for a whole six months."

Mindy sat quietly. Inside, the absolute bliss of knowing Joe would be gone for six months was almost intoxicating. She forced herself not to smile. Staring at her mum, she felt the need to comfort her.

"I'm sorry, Mummy," she said. "But don't worry. Frankie, Doreen, and me will help you. It'll go fast, you'll see. Don't cry."

Our mum sniffled and wiped her nose. "Thank you, Min. I'll be all right." She pushed herself up from the table. "I'll start supper now," she said weakly.

"Okay. Mum, if you need help, let me know," Mindy said. Then she ran through the apartment to find Doreen and me so she could give us the triumphant news.

*****

Life in the apartment without Joe proved to be pure bliss for me, Mindy, and Doreen. One day, I came home from school and found my bed made up, sheets and all. My mum had even found a pillow for me to use. But even more surprising, I took to school like never before, and Mrs. English took a shine to me and talked me into participating in school events for the first time.

In music class, all the students at Larimer Elementary were encouraged to learn how to play a musical instrument, at least at a rudimentary level. After some consideration, I concluded that bigger was always better, so I settled on the base cello. My teacher, Mrs. Jensen, would have the class practice their instrument almost daily in the music room. I found learning to play the cello was tolerable, except for my sore fingertips from smashing down on the thick metal strings. However, when I discovered that Mrs. Jensen had planned a school performance and expected us to take our instruments home to practice every day, I realized what a severe error in judgment I had made.

For several days, I dragged that monstrosity of an instrument home after school along with the music stand and then back again the following morning. At home in my room, I practiced fervently with the determination of a virtuoso. Still, the torturous shrills that screeched from the strings of my cello assaulted the ears of my sisters and mum and sent them scurrying behind closed doors or to the safety of the back porch. Though not very convincingly, Mindy and my mum attempted to encourage me, while Doreen bluntly exclaimed that she preferred the spine-shivering sound of fingernails scraping across a chalkboard. That's when I reluctantly admitted I had a complete lack of musical aptitude. However, I did find solace in the fact that I had a real knack and talent for applying just the precise amount of rosin on my bow, which I seemed to do quite often.

So after a week of practicing at home, and to the absolute delight of my mum and sisters, I dragged my cello into the music room for the last time, informed Mrs. Jensen I had permanently retired from the cello playing business, and walked out.

*****

Joe being in jail was the best Christmas present my sisters and I could have hoped for that winter.

Every year, we erected an artificial Christmas tree that Mindy, Doreen, and I decorated with old, worn-out bulbs and reused icicles. In front of the Christmas tree on the floor was a motorized red, blue, yellow, and green cellophane turn-wheel that spun slowly over a light bulb casting its changing colors onto the tree. For the three of us, it was magical.

That Christmas, Mindy and Doreen seemed to get along wonderfully without incessantly fighting, which was a Christmas miracle in itself.

I abandoned my room nightly and squeezed into bed with my sisters. We sang Christmas carols to one another during the week leading up to Christmas as we lay in bed. We would twirl one another's hair and sing until we fell asleep. Mindy sang like a nightingale, and when it was her turn to sing, I would always request "Silent Night." It was my favorite.

There was a heavy snowfall that Christmas. On Christmas Eve, I lay awake, listening to my sister's shallow snoring. Late into the night, I slipped out of bed and tiptoed over to the window. Freshly fallen snow had blanketed all of Larimer that now glistened white under the street lights. Frozen icicles of all sizes hung from the rooftops like elongated diamonds. On the outside window ledge, the snow had piled high. I unlocked the window and pushed it open. Cold air rushed in at me as I scooped a handful of it before quickly pulling the window shut. The icy snow felt good in my hand, and I squeezed it into a firm ball and popped it into my mouth so I could get the most enjoyment from it, letting it melt refreshingly over my tongue.

I rested my chin on the wooden window sill painted green with lead paint that was severely chipped. I pressed my nose against the frozen pane. As I stared out in wonderment at the breathtaking scene before me, I inhaled deeply, and the musty smell of old wood, lead paint, and crumbling window putty filled my nostrils. It was glorious, and a sense of fulfillment engulfed me. With my sisters gently snoring in the background, I huddled by the radiator, absorbing Christmas's warmth like never before.

On Christmas morning, we opened our presents under the tree. Each of us got a new toy and a new pair of shoes. Our mum baked a ham with yams and cranberry sauce, mashed potatoes, gravy, and rolls. For dessert, we had pumpkin pie with whipped cream. But for me, Mindy, and Doreen, the best part was not our Christmas presents or the mouthwatering delicacy of such a grand meal that made that Christmas special; it was the serenity of knowing that at any moment, Joe would not walk through the door and ruin it for us all.

Chapter 27

I t was February, and a bitterly cold wind bit through my thin coat as I walked home from school. I plunged my hands deep into my pockets and hunched my shoulders as I tried to control my shivers. I rushed up the stairwell steps and burst into the apartment through the front hallway door. I yelled out, "Mum, I'm home." Then, I darted into my room to warm myself by the radiator.

Mrs. English had talked me into joining the choir at school, and since there was no heavy lifting involved, I agreed to give it a try. I found that I liked it, and my music teacher seemed to enjoy my singing. Tonight, the school was putting on a musical for the parents, and she had chosen me to sing a solo. Our mum was so far along in her pregnancy that she would be unable to attend, but Mindy and Doreen said they would be there.

I shed my coat and plopped down in front of the hot radiator to do my homework. I opened a book to memorize my weekly spelling words, and then I heard something I hadn't heard for quite some time. I felt my muscles stiffen as fear surged through me for the first time in a long while. I listened to the slow, menacing footsteps move across the wood floor, approaching my room from across the hall. My door crashed open, and Joe, shirtless, stepped inside. His thick, bulging muscles seemed even bulkier than before as he stared coldly down at me sitting in front of the radiator. I quickly averted my eyes to the floor, and he moved closer.

"Well, if it isn't the creep. Tell me, creep, did you miss me? Huh?" Joe twisted his thin lips into a cynical smirk.

I did not respond. Joe was setting a trap, and I knew it.

Then, without warning, he forcefully shoved his foot into my chest, pinning me against the scalding hot radiator. My thin shirt offered no protection, and I yelped as the hot metal scalded my back. Frantically, I squirmed out from under Joe's foot. I lay on my side writhing in pain; my back arched away from the radiator. It felt as if my back was on fire.

"I asked you a question, bonehead. Did you miss me?" Joe again asked truculently.

My eyes were now brimming with tears from the pain; my skin burned with an intensity that made it hard to focus. But I knew I had to answer. With considerable effort, I nodded.

"Good," Joe grunted. He again reached out with his black, hard leathered shoe and stepped on my face, slowly grinding my face into the floor until I finally let out a painful whimper as my teeth cut sharply into the soft flesh inside my cheeks. "Cause I sure missed you," Joe said sinisterly. The threat in his tone was unmistakable. He lifted his foot, walked over to my bed, yanked all the sheets and covers from the mattress, grabbed my pillow, and walked from the room. For the first time in months, I heard the despairing sound of Joe locking my bedroom door, and along with it, the harsh realization that things had once again returned to the way it was before.

As I raised myself to a sitting position, I knew that I would not be going to my school musical. Every day, for weeks, I had practiced my solo, and I had finally memorized an entire song, but now I would never get to sing it. But what troubled me most was the prospect of disappointing Mrs. English. Earlier that day, she had expressed how excited she was to hear me sing that night with unbridled delight. What would she think of me now when I didn't show? *She probably won't like me anymore*, I thought.

I gingerly lifted the back of my shirt, craned my neck, and strained to see the bright red burns branding my back. Anger and frustration consumed me, and I felt helpless. Then, inexplicably, I thought of Honeymarmo. It seemed almost natural now that I also thought about God when I thought of him. I knew what Honeymarmo would tell me to do if he were here with me. So in desperation, trying to ignore the searing pain, I bowed my head and prayed to God for his help.

God's answer came in about an hour, as our mum went into labor a week ahead of schedule. It turns out that the county jail had released Joe early, and since he had come directly to the apartment, he had not yet had the opportunity to get drunk or find drugs. As a result, when our mum's contractions started, he was available to drive her to the hospital. I listened to the commotion unfold from their room. Our mum started groaning, which turned to screams as she pleaded for Joe to hurry. Joe left the apartment and returned a short while later. Through muddled conversations, I understood that Joe had borrowed a car so he could drive our mum to the hospital. A few moments later, Joe walked her out the front door. I followed their footsteps down the stairwell until they were gone. Mindy and Doreen were standing on the stairs, and when they heard the sidewalk door below slam shut, they rushed back into the apartment.

"Mindy. Doreen. Come here. Let me out," I pleaded.

"I don't know, Frankie. You know what happened to us last time, and we didn't even do it," Mindy answered timidly.

"Okay. Just never mind, I'll get out myself. How's Mum?" I asked.

"How are you going to get out by yourself?" Doreen interjected.

"She didn't look too good, Frankie. I'm scared," Mindy said.

"Come on, Frankie, tell me how you do it?" Doreen persisted.

"None of your beeswax!" I shouted at Doreen. "Both yinz go to the kitchen because I don't want you to see how I do it."

"Okay," Mindy agreed.

"Okay," Doreen said. I heard their footsteps fade toward the living room. I stepped over to the box filled with old television vacuum tubes and dug out my hidden piece of cardboard, and just as I started to work it between the door and door jamb, I heard a floorboard squeak. I stopped. I eased myself down and pressed my cheek and ear against the floor so I could both listen and scan the outside hallway from under my door. I didn't see anything at first, but then I spotted a pair of shoes off to the right near the passageway leading to the living room as I adjusted my position. There was no mistaking whose shoes they were.

"Doreen, I know you're out there. I swear when I get out of here, you're going to be sorry," I threatened. I heard the faint creak of the floorboards as she crept toward the living room. Once again, I slid the cardboard between the door and the frame. I forced the latch from its locked position with a flick of my wrist, and the door swung freely on its hinges. I hurriedly placed the piece of cardboard back into its hiding place and stepped out into the hall, latching the door behind me. My sisters sat together on the couch in the living room, speculating whether they would have a new baby brother or baby sister. Their mouths gaped open when they saw me come down the hallway.

Doreen asked, "How'd you do it?" I smiled smugly, ignoring her question.

"How was Mum doing when she left?" I asked again.

"Not too good," Doreen answered. "She kept holding her stomach because of the pain, and she was making all kinds of weird faces and stuff. I thought she was going to throw up."

"Yeah!" Mindy agreed, biting her nails.

"I have an idea. How about we pray for her," I suggested. My sisters both gave me a strange look, then shrugged.

"Okay."

"Sure."

We looked at one another, not sure who would do the praying. I was about to volunteer when Doreen spoke out, "You're the oldest, Mindy, so you say the prayer."

"What should I say?"

"You know, that please God don't let Mummy and the baby die and stuff like that," Doreen said matter-of-factly.

Mindy climbed down off the couch, dropped to her knees, and folded her hands in front of her chest, just like she saw it done in pictures. Doreen and I looked at one another, then dropped down in front of Mindy in perfect imitation. We closed our eyes.

"God, please don't let our mum or our new baby brother or baby sister die. Help keep them safe in the hospital, and don't let our mum be in too much pain," Mindy whispered reverently. I squinted through one eye to look at my sisters. Mindy had shut her eyes tight, her face taut with sincerity. Doreen, on the other hand, looked like a barnyard owl. One eye was closed, while the other was open wide, and her head fitfully swiveled on her shoulders as she looked around the room and between Mindy and me. "Amen," Mindy said.

"Amen," Doreen and I repeated. Together we opened our eyes.

"Is that it?" Doreen asked.

"That's it," I said, rising to my feet. "I'm going to get ready for the school performance tonight. Are yinz still going with me?"

"I don't think I should…just in case," Mindy said.

"I'll go." Doreen jumped up eagerly.

"Okay, I'll be ready in a minute." I raced to my room to change back into my school clothes. In ten minutes, Doreen and I walked up Larimer Avenue toward Larimer Elementary School. Later that evening, to Mrs. English's delight, I put on the singing performance of my life.

When I had finished singing my solo, everyone sprang to their feet and erupted into applause in the only standing ovation of the night. After the program, backstage, I found myself the center of attention as my classmates, teachers, and parents surrounded me so they could compliment me on my singing. Even Doreen gave me a rare tribute of approval. At one point, I thought I would pass out from the pain when one of the parents gave me a congratulatory clap on the back.

Doreen and I made it back to the apartment before Joe had returned. I made a bologna sandwich, heavy with ketchup, before letting Mindy lock me again in my bedroom for the night.

It wasn't until after school the following day that I discovered we had a new baby sister who our mum named Rose Elizabeth Desimone, after herself. Joe had insisted that little Rose not be given his last name of Gallucci. If his name was on her birth certificate, Social Services might track him down and force him to pay child support. Instead, little Rose was given the same last name as me and my sisters, Desimone, ensuring that our monthly food stamps and welfare check would continue. However, because our mum had listed baby Rose's last name as Desimone, Social Services located mine, Mindy's, and Doreen's father somewhere in California; they attempted to make him pay support for little Rose. Our baffled father, who had not seen our mum in years and did not know anything about a baby, adamantly denied paternity and refused to pay any support. In the end, because he lived in another state, they couldn't force him. Ultimately, the welfare benefits increased, and the government did not pursue Joe to fulfill his parental responsibilities.

Our mum came home from the hospital with our new sister a few days later. Mindy and Doreen took to fussing over our new little sister like two mother hens. They changed her diapers, fought over whose turn it was to burp her, and took turns singing to her. I didn't understand all the fuss. All little Rose did was scream her head off at all hours of the day and night, eat, sleep, and make a mess of herself, which increasingly looked and smelled awful.

When our mum or sisters were around, I mostly ignored the baby. However, sometimes when I found myself alone with her, and there was no one nearby to observe, curiosity got the best of me, and I would give her a good looking over. She would stare up at me with wide eyes and a smile, almost as if she recognized me. I would lower my guard reluctantly, smile back, and find myself spewing nonsensical phrases such as "goo-goo" or "ga-ga" while tickling her belly.

Joe decided to go out and get loaded a couple of weeks after our mum and little Rose came home from the hospital, which was bad news for the rest of us.

It was Friday after school, and when I walked through the kitchen door, I knew immediately there was trouble. Our mum stood at the kitchen sink, and she had been crying. Her face was puffy, the rims of her eyes were red, and she sniffled to keep her nose from dripping.

"He's high on some kind of pills, or something, Frankie," she whispered. "Maybe you should go back out for a little while."

"How about my school clothes?"

"It's okay," she said weakly. I set my school books down on the kitchen table, then heard Joe's footsteps coming toward us from the front of the apartment. Before I could run out of the door, Joe appeared and gave us both an accusing look. His eyelids drooped, and he swayed like the branch of an oak tree pushed by the wind.

"What's all the whispering about?" he slurred reproachfully.

"I wasn't whispering. I was just talking to Frankie," our mum replied. Joe looked over at me. The familiar sadistic glint appeared in his black eyes. My eyes darted quickly away, hoping that I had been fast enough.

"Oh, I see, so we got secrets now, is that it?" Joe persisted.

"No, Joe, we were just talking, that's all," our mum pleaded, attempting reason. She softened her tone to assuage his anger, but I knew it was already too late, and I braced myself.

"Do I look stupid to you?" Joe asked. He turned his attention fully on me. "So we just want to talk about me behind my back, is that it, freak?"

I swallowed hard, hoping he didn't see it. I knew the slightest movement could set him off. I didn't answer but only stood motionless, staring down at the linoleum floor.

"What? Oh, you don't want to answer me now? Huh, bonehead? You just want to ignore me, is that it?" Joe's teeth clenched. I felt powerless. Joe had again craftily put me in a box. If I answered, he would manipulate my words to justify the abuse that would follow in his warped mind. I knew I would still incur Joe's wrath by standing silent, but I hoped that it would be to a lesser degree. So I continued to say nothing, cowering under Joe's hateful glare.

"Get to your room, you little imbecile," Joe growled. I had expected the words, and it was a relief to me when they came. I knew with certainty that when I passed Joe, I would feel the thump of his heavy hand against the back of my head, but it would be worth it to escape the humiliation of having my spirit whither under Joe's depraved and sadistic gaze.

"Joe...," our mum started to speak, but a fierce look quickly silenced her. I walked tensely toward him.

"Oh, let's just take our time, huh?" Joe snarled. He struck the back of my skull with an open hand that sent me sprawling to the floor. Stunned, I scrambled to my feet. But before I could get away, I felt the heel of Joe's shoe jam against my lower spine, causing it to hyperextend unnaturally. I yelped from the sharp stabbing pain as I lurched forward, smashing my face against the hard plaster-of-paris wall, then slid to the floor. Blood trickled from my nose, and a knot formed on my forehead. Panicked, I scrambled crab-like down the hall before reaching my room. I shut the door behind me, praying that Joe would not pursue me inside. My breath came in spasms, almost to the point of hyperventilation. Trembling, I waited to see if the onslaught would continue. Joe's shoes scuffed the floorboards outside his door, and then I heard the sound of Joe setting the latch in place. My breathing slowed with relief. Gradually, the numbness returned until I felt nothing inside. I pulled off my shirt and held it to my nose to stop the bleeding. I settled back against the wall, staring angrily into space.

A little while later, just before dusk, the radiator in my room went cold. I whispered the information to my mum as she passed by my door, and she immediately sent Mindy downstairs to inform our landlady, Mrs. Natalutti. When Mindy returned, she gave our mum the bad news that the steam pipe leading to my room had broken, and it may be Monday before anyone would be out to fix it. It was the coldest time of the winter, and it didn't help that the broken glass in my window still hadn't been repaired. I felt the frigid air blowing through the large opening without meeting any heat resistance. As darkness engulfed my room, I sat on the bare mattress, shivering. When I exhaled, my breath turned to frost, and my teeth chattered with increasing frequency. I pulled my knees to my chest to keep myself as warm as possible and waited for my mum to walk by so I could whisper out to her. Before long, I heard footsteps. I jumped from the bed and hurried to the door, lay flat with my cheek against the cold floorboards so I could see for sure whose they were.

"Pssst. Mindy!" I whispered as I spied her shoes. Mindy stopped and came to the door.

"What, Frankie?" she whispered back nervously.

"Tell Mummy it's freezing in here. Tell her to bring me a blanket or something."

"Okay, Frankie, as soon as I can get her alone, I will," Mindy promised. It seemed like forever before I finally heard my mum approaching, and she fumbled with the latch, but just as the door cracked open, Joe's hard shoes scraped the floor as he stepped out into the hallway from their bedroom.

"What do you think you're doing?"

"His radiator ain't working, so I'm giving him a couple of blankets so he doesn't freeze," our mum explained.

"The little imbecile doesn't need any blankets. He ain't going to freeze. Put them back!" Joe's deep raspy voice reverberated in the hallway.

"But, Joe—"

Joe cut her off. "What, are you deaf? You heard what I said. He don't need them! Now put them back!" I saw the door shut, and I heard my mum reset the latch, then her footsteps faded away. For the first time, I felt panic. My face was stinging, and my fingers were as cold as icicles; even my toes through my tennis shoes started to numb. I knew that as the night dragged on, the temperature outside and in my room would plummet further. I was in deep trouble.

In a couple of hours, the cold had become intolerable. On my mattress, I curled myself so tightly into a ball to generate as much body heat as possible that my muscles went rigid, and I could not seem to straighten myself out, nor did I want to. My entire body shook and convulsed, and my jaws ached from the pounding they were taking from my chattering teeth. I found myself making ghastly sounds with each breath I took, and I began to lose my ability to focus. Soon, even being curled into a ball no longer provided any warmth. Things were becoming desperate. Then, I noticed a small tear in my mattress, and in full survival mode, I devised a solution. I fought my body's instinct for self-preservation with considerable effort and forced myself to uncurl.

The icy air quickly engulfed my entire body. With every muscle quaking, especially my hands, I worked my stiff fingers into the small tear and ripped it open further. I began to pull out chunks of cotton and straw until I eventually created a cubbyhole large enough to accommodate my curled-up body. Slowly, I squeezed inside the mattress up to my neck, my body fully insulated, except for my exposed head. The stale, musty odor of urine was strong. My body soon began to warm to the point where my muscles relaxed, and the convulsions slowed. I was still cold, but I knew that it was now survivable. As I lay there, my senses began to return, and my mind again began to focus. I became acutely aware that if Joe walked through the door and saw me buried up to my neck inside the mattress, it would end disastrously for me, but at the moment, I didn't care. I was surviving now, and later was only a possibility that existed in the future.

I became drowsy because of the amount of energy my body had expended to fight the cold, coupled with the warmth that now engulfed me. I tried to resist it, primarily out of fear that Joe would walk into the room at any moment, but my fatigue was too great, and before long, I had fallen into a deep sleep.

I heard a baby crying. I opened my eyes groggily and thought I saw a shadowy figure in the doorway, but my mind was too foggy to recognize it as a person. I couldn't yet tell if I was awake or dreaming in my tired and confused state.

The silhouette moved toward me, and instantly my mind became lucid as I grasped the reality of my situation. I was awake. I attempted to climb out from inside the mattress but only managed to get partway before Joe reached me. He grabbed a fistful of my hair and yanked me the rest of the way out of my cubbyhole. Once on my feet, Joe slammed me to the floor. He loomed menacingly above me. "You ungrateful little creep!" Joe slurred. "We get you this nice mattress, and look what you do to it." White breath spewed from his mouth as he spoke. He snatched the mattress up off the metal springs as if it was weightless and carried it from the room. He was shirtless, and his back muscles bulged and rippled. When Joe tossed the mattress onto the hallway floor, our mum, carrying little Rose, stepped out of her bedroom.

"This is what your imbecile son does to the nice things we get him." Joe pointed angrily at the gaping hole in the mattress. Our mum, still half asleep, looked groggily down at the bed.

"From now on, he can sleep on the bedsprings," Joe declared bitterly. He stepped back to the doorway and glared in at me. "You hear me, you little creep?" I remained motionless on the floor and didn't answer. Joe gave a demented grunt, then shut and locked the door.

After a few moments, my heart stopped racing as the adrenaline began to ebb, and once again, I felt the frigid night air attack my body. The shivers returned more intensely than before, and I pulled my knees to my chest again. By the dim gray light that had replaced the blackness, I knew that dawn was not far off and would bring the morning sun and hopefully some relief. But pre-dawn carried a bitter cold as I had never felt before. As the temperature continued to drop in my room, my muscles convulsed so violently that my eyes rolled back in my head, and once again, I found that I could no longer focus. It was then I was sure I was going to freeze to death. I wondered if, in the end, it would be warmer than this. I hoped so. As I lay on the floor, my body convulsing, an unexpected calmness came to me, and I surrendered to the biting cold, hoping, praying, for the warm embrace of death.

Chapter 28

Death didn't come. The following day, Joe left and was gone from the apartment for three days on another of his drug binges. Our mum let me out of my room and allowed me to sleep in my sister's bed, and I slept most of that day and through the next night.

When I arrived home on Monday after school, someone had fixed the steam pipe, and my radiator once again seethed with heat. I discovered my mum had repaired and sealed my broken window with tape and a large piece of cardboard, which helped lessen the cold.

In mid-March, the winter snow melted away, and Larimer felt the first warm breath of spring as it stirred from its cold slumber. Buds pushed out through the tree branches, and birds began to arrive, their songs announcing the changing season. This change awakened in us the promise of summer, and a yearning for the end of the school year. As the days warmed, the school's closed windows were pushed open, and the vitality of spring teased us to come outside to play. I grew restless, and I found it harder to concentrate on schoolwork. The open windows constantly drew my attention outside, and I found my mind wandering. Then, when finally, I saw the first robin redbreast as it perched itself on the window sill, I knew for sure that summer was near, and the school days would soon come to an end.

Mrs. English stood at the chalkboard, going over our assignment for the day. For English class, we had been studying different types of poetry, and today we were learning about a kind of Japanese poem called a haiku. Mrs. English had drawn three lines on the board and had written five syllables on the first line, seven syllables on the second line, and five syllables on the third line. The class assignment was for each of the students to write their own haiku, and then Mrs. English would choose the best one to be read to the class, and that student would get a much-coveted gold star pasted to their forehead.

As I sat at my desk next to the window staring out at the luring spring day, I tried to think of something, anything, to write. It seemed useless. Then, I remembered something Honeymarmo had once said to me as we walked the tracks, watching a glowing orange sunset that melted over the horizon like poured out honey. That sort of thing excited Honeymarmo, but it was only a stupid sunset to me. I never understood Honeymarmo's fascination with these ordinary things. "Don't just look *with* your eyes, Frankie," he had said to me, "but look with your heart and your soul. This way, you will not only see it, but you will feel it." Now, as I stared out the window, remembering those words, I felt myself smile as, for the first time, Honeymarmo's words made sense. I suddenly understood. Gazing out at the budding elm tree just a few feet away, I experienced a flash of inspiration. I picked up my pencil and effortlessly wrote my haiku, then turned my paper over on my desk and scanned the room. Watching the other students' faces as they struggled with their work was amusing. I peeked over Leroy's shoulder, and Leroy had his first line written, which started with "Batman and Robin." I looked down at my paper and thought about crumbling it for the wastebasket because it suddenly seemed silly. Mrs. English appeared unexpectedly next to my desk.

"Frankie, this has to be your poem, no one else's," she whispered reproachfully, believing that I was trying to copy from Leroy.

"I'm already done," I mumbled.

"You're finished, already?" she inquired, picking up my paper from the desk and reading it silently to herself. I shifted uncomfortably in my seat. She stared down at me when she had finished, and I lowered my head.

"You wrote this?" Mrs. English asked. I turned my head and looked out the window at the large elm tree just a few feet away, with its branches exploding with new leaves. She glanced where I was

228

looking, then back at me. Finally, I mustered up the courage to peek in her direction. Mrs. English was smiling. She gently laid the paper back down on my desk, face down, and walked away.

After the allotted time had expired to complete our poems, Mrs. English collected them, and as she sat at her desk reviewing, everyone sat quietly, hands folded, hoping she would pick their poem. That is, everyone except for me. As I sat and wrote it, there was a sense of fulfillment that had washed over me like I hadn't experienced before, but now I desperately hoped Mrs. English wouldn't select my poem. I wanted no part of her to read it aloud to the class.

Finally, Mrs. English's chair scraped the floor as she scooted out from behind her desk and walked to the front of the room, holding a single sheet of paper.

"Frankie, could you come here please." The words made me cringe. Every head in the classroom snapped in my direction, most with a shocked expression. Even Leroy turned fully around and looked curiously at me. I slid out from behind my desk with dread and shuffled reluctantly to the front of the room, taking my place at Mrs. English's side.

"First, let me say that I have had students write haikus in my class for three years now, and this is one of the best haikus that any-one in any of my previous classes has ever written," Mrs. English announced. My face flushed hot, and I desperately wanted to step behind my teacher and hide from my classmates' probing eyes. But, then, she began to read:

> The wonder of it
> New leaves from a simple branch
> Beautifies the world

I stood staring down at the floor as she read, and after she had finished, I snuck a glance toward the class. To my surprise, no one clucked or laughed, but encouraged by Mrs. English, everyone applauded. After Mrs. English had licked and pasted the gold star to my forehead, I hurried back to my desk, and Leroy immediately spun around to face me.

"You wrote that, Frankie?" I nodded. "Man, I wrote some stupid thing about Batman and Robin. "That was really good."

For me, schoolwork had always been difficult. Praise and affirmation from my teachers never happened before, so it made me uncomfortable. It wasn't that I didn't care for the attention, I liked it, but I simply didn't know how to process or respond to such things. Joe had always told me that I was stupid, a bonehead, or an imbecile, and I always believed it. Honeymarmo was the first person to tell me differently, to tell me I was smart. Maybe there was a chance that Honeymarmo was right. By picking my poem, wasn't Mrs. English saying the same thing as Honeymarmo? Still, I couldn't shake my doubts so easily. For the remainder of the day, even with the gold star on my forehead, I struggled with my worthiness. I kept thinking that maybe I just got lucky, or perhaps it was a fluke. That scared me most of all.

*****

April arrived, and by the end of the first week, there was still no sign of the rain that usually accompanied it. I had developed the habit of doing my homework when I got home from school. One day, after finishing my homework, which took me longer than usual because it was fractions, I hurried to Leroy's house, which had become an afternoon ritual. I arrived at Leroy's and knocked softly on the front door. Mrs. Sampson answered. Her expression was gloomy, and it was apparent she was surprised to see me at the door this late. She stared down at me pensively. Finally, she smiled weakly and pushed open the door.

"Come on in, Frankie, everyone's in the living room," she said.

"Thanks, ma'am," I said, hurrying past her. Since I had first started coming to Leroy's house, I had adopted all of the manners established within their household.

I stepped into the living room and immediately felt everyone's somberness as they focused on the television. Mr. Sampson was sitting in his armchair, still in his work clothes, puffing thoughtfully on a pipe. The room smelled of black cherry tobacco. Harold was on the couch, resting his forearms on his thighs as he leaned toward the television. Leroy lay on his stomach on the floor, propped up on his elbows, just in front of the TV. All shot me a glance before returning their attention to the television. I hurried over to Leroy without saying a word and dropped to the floor next to him, propping myself up on my elbows.

The evening news was having a special report on some guy named Dr. Martin Luther King Jr. The news anchor, some man named Walter Cronkite, said someone had just assassinated him. On the streets, crying and angry witnesses, mostly Negros as the news called them, were being questioned by reporters about what they had heard or seen at the site where the shooting took place. Reporters were interviewing civil rights leaders. Some spoke with great sadness and the need for calm, while others spoke with bitterness and unrestrained anger. Across the nation, as other reporters talked to blacks in their communities, many broke down and cried, while others raged with the threat of revenge and riots against whites. I wondered if that meant me too? As we watched these events unfold before us, even in this small living room in the middle of Larimer, the growing tension in the nation poured from the television screen with such intensity that we all felt its presence.

An image of a man appeared, and I suspected it was Dr. Martin Luther King Jr. even before the newscaster identified him. The broadcaster spoke about some of the significant accomplishments that the "late Reverend King" had made in civil rights.

It then showed a black-and-white news film of protesters, some white, but mostly blacks, marching peacefully, arm in arm, with signs that demanded justice and equality. The news clip switched to other protesters, sitting passively together while police officers dragged and beat them with clubs. Men, women, and children alike of all ages had powerful water hoses turned on them. Some black men covered the woman, children, and the elderly with their bodies to absorb the clubs' blows and protect them from the devastating effects of potentially lethal water streams. Dogs on leashes were allowed to attack demonstrators with great viciousness without provocation as they sat passively huddled together. Some fought off the dogs as best they could, but they did not rise up against those who initiated the attacks.

As I lay next to Leroy watching these tragedies unfold, my heart ached for these people, and I felt such intense anger toward the police and against those who stood by watching and did nothing.

Harold jumped to his feet and shouted angrily at the television. "Why don't they fight back?" Everyone turned and looked at his livid face. Mr. Sampson pulled his pipe out from the corner of his mouth.

"They were fighting back, son," he responded calmly.

Harold's agitation grew. "How, by sitting there letting them white policeman bust their heads wide open?" Harald snapped belligerently. In the months that I had been coming over to Leroy's, I had never heard anyone in the family speak to Mr. Sampson this way, and I felt the rising tension in the room, making me feel suddenly uncomfortable.

Mr. Sampson took a long, thoughtful drag from his pipe. "What those men and women and even children did took greater courage than you know. Those people were willing to sacrifice their lives for all of us Negros, their people, so the world would see and know the kind of injustice and indignities our people suffer every day, just because of our skin color. There are other ways of fighting than just with your fists, son."

"I disagree, Pops. I'd have to start swinging back if one of them cops came after me with a club," Harold exclaimed.

"And what would that have got you, son, except maybe dead? If those folks would've fought back, then the news would have just reported it as just another violent riot started by some Negro agitators. Those white policemen would've been seen by many as just doing their job and keeping the peace. And many white folks across this country would have just confirmed in their minds what they already believe about us as a people. No, son, what they did was show the world that we could be nonviolent people who just want to be treated with respect and that we deserve our equal share of the American dream. Those people showed the world that we are a people of character who are willing to stand up peacefully for those rights that we have fought and died for in this country, the same as white folks. They showed this country and the world that they have nothing to fear from us. Like them, we are just people who want to live peacefully and with dignity and want to have the right to raise our children in safety and with the same opportunities as anyone else. That's what Dr. King was showing the world, son, that Negros are just folks like them, who should be judged by our character and not by the color of our skin."

Harold listened to his father, then glared boldly over at him. "And what did it get him, Pops, except dead?"

Mr. Sampson's expression became suddenly perplexed by the directness of Harold's remark. His eyebrows furrowed, but he seemed unable to find an answer. He settled back in his chair. Finally, Harold stood and walked toward the stairs. As he reached the bottom, he turned toward his father.

"And Pops, I ain't colored, and I ain't no Negro neither. I'm Black," he proclaimed, then turned and bolted up the steps to his bedroom. Mr. Sampson stared after his son thoughtfully, then took a puff from his pipe.

Leroy and I looked at one another, not fully understanding everything that had just taken place between Harold and his dad. Finally, the voice of the Reverend Dr. Martin Luther King blared out at us from the television, and we turned our attention back to the screen where he stood on a platform before thousands of people, blacks and whites together. As we perched ourselves in front of the television, Leroy and I were mesmerized by Dr. King's charisma and his words. He was magnificent. Lying there on the floor next to Leroy, I absorbed Reverend King's words and filed them deep in the recesses of my heart and mind. *Honeymarmo would like him*, I thought. I remembered something Honeymarmo had said: "Beating someone out of anger or hatred doesn't accomplish anything. As a matter of fact, it usually has the opposite effect." I also remembered Honeymarmo talking about how hatred can poison the soul. Now I saw it unfolding before me in real life. Honeymarmo was right about so many things. Now, thinking of him, the sting of my betrayal resurfaced, as it always did, and I forced my attention back to the television to push the shameful memory away.

Mrs. Sampson made a big pot of black eye peas, a ham hock, some spinach, and cornbread for supper that night. Leroy and I shook a healthy portion of ketchup onto our plates. Mrs. Sampson sat across the table, shaking her head disapprovingly at our unusual culinary taste. Usually, when I ate supper over Leroy's, the conversation was lively and plentiful, but tonight, we all sat in a stupor that I could only describe as mourning.

Chapter 29

The next day classrooms were buzzing with the news of Reverend Dr. Martin Luther King Jr.'s death. The students offered their opinions in class, most of which were regurgitations of what they had heard from their parents at home. The faculty attempted to carry on with the daily curriculum and activities. Still, it was apparent that not even the teachers could stay focused on their subjects. Before lunch, teachers handed out notes to the students for their parents, explaining that the school district had decided to close school for the remainder of the day, and since it was Friday, all students would not be required to return to school until Monday morning.

At home, I hung out with my sisters in their bedroom. We talked about all the things we had heard at school that day, and Mindy, who was now in her second year of middle school at Dilworth, said that she had heard that there might be some riots taking place around the country, maybe even right there in Larimer.

Our mum carried little Rose into the room as we shared rumors and opinions. She laid her on the bed along with a cloth diaper, rubber pants, and baby powder.

"Mindy, little Rose pooped, so I need you to change her while I go wash some diapers," our mum said. "Doreen, the hallway needs sweeping, then I need you to go clean up the living room and empty the rubbish in the kitchen." She turned and walked from the bedroom. The three of us gathered around little Rose, who smiled up at us, making gurgling noises and blowing spit bubbles. Mindy pulled off her plastic pants and carefully unhooked the large diaper pins.

She opened the soiled diaper, and immediately we winced with disgust at the mess and the foul stench that permeated our nostrils. Little Rose giggled. I shrewdly announced I had something to do and quickly made my escape. I ran through the apartment, down the back steps, and straight toward Leroy's house.

Leroy opened the front door, and we both sprinted up the stairs to Leroy's room, searching for something to do. Leroy pulled out a couple of wooden spinning tops from his top drawer, a green one and red one and two long strings. He handed me the green top, and we both stomped down the steps.

"Boys, quit running in the house," Leroy's mum shouted from the kitchen.

"Yes, ma'am," Leroy and I both hollered back as we bolted out the front door. Out on the sidewalk, we wound the strings around the cone-shaped tops and then, at the same time, flung them skillfully to the pavement. Their metal tips hit the cement spinning, and both darted smoothly across the sidewalk, barely avoiding a collision. If they collided, the one knocked off its axis would be the loser. In a while, Leroy's mum came to the door and called him in for supper.

"Can Frankie eat over?" Leroy asked.

Mrs. Sampson gave me a pitiful look. "Of course he can, but make sure you both wash your hands before you sit down at the table." We picked up the tops, set them on the porch, and disappeared into the house to wash our hands. When I sat down at the table, Mr. Sampson gave me a peculiar look, as did Harold. Mr. Sampson said grace as he always did, and everyone began to eat. A few minutes into supper, Mr. Sampson set down his fork and looked reflectively over at Harold.

"Harold," he began, "I've been thinking about what you said yesterday, about fighting injustice with violence, an eye for an eye. I asked myself, could Dr. King have been wrong? Then, I remembered something that Reverend King said. He said, 'Darkness cannot drive out darkness; only light can do that. Hate cannot drive out hate; only love can do that.' Dr. King understood that violence would only create fear and resentment toward us as a people. He understood that protesting with nonviolence would heap burning coals upon the heads of most white people as they watched us being mistreated for no reason other than our skin color. He knew you first had to change people's hearts because that is the only way a community living together in peace and harmony can endure. No, son, a community created out of violence will only alienate and deepen resentment on all sides."

"Yeah, well, I got news for you, Pops: There are some white folks who hate us so much that their hearts will never change, and violence is the only thing they'll understand. It probably won't change their hearts, but maybe it's time they know what it feels like to live in fear," Harold snapped.

"You're right, son." Mr. Sampson nodded. "There are some people whose hate for us will never change. For a lot of people, hate has been taught to them and passed down from generation to generation. They don't know why they hate us. They just do. But if hate can be taught, it can be untaught. If fear is the end goal for us, then maybe violence is the answer. But it's not. The end goal is to find a way to live together as equals in peace and harmony. Dr. King awakened the consciousness and hearts of most in the white community to our injustice, and now is the time to show them that we are good people who can be good neighbors." Mr. Sampson reached over, rested his hand gently on Harold's arm, and probed into his son's eyes. "But violence, son, will plant the seeds of bitterness and resentment and distrust. Regardless, the courts will enforce this land's laws, but we will hinder the degree and speed of our acceptance as equals through violence. I fear that if we fuel the fires of anger amongst our own people through violence, then there will be little or no healing between us and whites, at least not for a very long time. No, son, Reverend King was killed not because his methods failed but because they were working. He was killed by an evil that saw the hearts of many in this nation beginning to change. Dr. King dreamed that we would come together as Christian brothers and sisters in love and understanding, not by force of will but by the spirit of acceptance. Change must come from the inside if that change is to last."

Harold pushed at his corn, searching for a response. Finally, Mr. Sampson picked up his knife and fork, then cut into a piece of chicken. Everyone at the table followed his lead and began to eat. While Leroy and I stuffed our mouths full, Harold picked at his food, taking small, thoughtful bites.

"Pops, I know that Dr. King was a good man," Harold finally answered. "I mean, I think we all know that," Harold said, "but what many of the black leaders are saying is that Dr. King's way wasn't working like you say. Or if it was, it was just too slow. You know, Stokely is calling for us to stand up and fight back—to riot."

Mrs. Sampson perked up and gave her son a quizzical look. "Who's Stokely?" she asked.

"Stokely Carmichael, Mum," Harold answered incredulously.

"Carmichael? Marvin, do we know the Carmichaels? Where do they live, son? What's his mother's name?" Mrs. Sampson asked concernedly.

Mr. Sampson cleared his throat, suppressing a chuckle, and Harold shook his head at his mother's blatant ignorance. "Stokely Carmichael is one of them civil rights activist, Esther," Mr. Sampson informed her.

"Oh," Mrs. Sampson mumbled embarrassingly.

"Son, to some extent, I agree with you, but rioting is not the answer. That's why I think Dr. King was a great man. Through non-violence, he has dragged our plight into the public arena for all the world to plainly see and, in doing so, forced most people to take a stance. He used peaceful demonstrations and the Word of God to prick the social conscience of this nation. I understand that some states, mostly in the south, are deeply rooted in the sin of racism. But that's not true of all states or all people in this country. No, those other states and those other people, especially whites, are guilty not so much for racism but the sin and shame of apathy. They've seen the injustice inflicted on our people for years, yet they've turned a blind eye for the sake of convenience. I'll tell you something else, son, and this pains me to say more than anything else, but it's the truth as I see it, and that is it's the white Christian churches and white Christian people across this nation who bear the greatest shame. From the pulpits to the congregations, they saw God's laws and Christian values being violated against us every day, yet they stood idly by. As our nation's moral conscience, their lukewarmness and compromise to racism may be the greatest sin of all. Just think about what I'm saying, son."

Harold's eyebrows furrowed as he weighed his father's words against his preconceived notions. Finally, he nodded. "Okay, Pops, I promise to think about it," Harold agreed. "But one more thing, Pops—I wish you'd quit referring to black people as coloreds and Negros," Harold said. "That's not who I am, and that's not who you are. Those are the names given to us by white people. We are black and should be proud of it. You're a black man, Pops—that's who you are—and I'm a black man—that's who I am," Harold exclaimed.

"Son, you can call yourself whatever you want," Mrs. Sampson interjected, "colored, Negro, black, but don't ever think that's who you are. Black is what you are, not who you are, son. Who you are has to do with your character and beliefs and how you treat other people, and what you make of yourself in this world. Be proud that you're a Negro, or black, but your identity is not in the color of your skin. It's in your heart and your mind and your soul. That's why Dr. King said that he dreamed that someday his own children would be judged by the content of their character and not by the color of their skin. If we begin to identify who we are foremost by our skin color, how can we expect the world not to identify and judge us the same? That's what the racist of this world do now, and that's what we should be fighting against."

"That's right. I heard Dr. King say that on the television yesterday," I exclaimed. I don't know why I spoke up, I hadn't planned it, but it just came out. Either way, everyone was now staring at me, and I immediately regretted my forwardness.

Harold pointed his fork directly at me. "What do you know?" he retorted. "All you do is come over here almost every day and eat our food anyway."

"Harold, that's enough," his mum barked.

"Aw, Mum, you know it's true. I heard you and Pop say it yourselves. You think this white boy would be coming over to black folk's home if he weren't poor and on welfare?" Harold said cruelly.

Mr. Sampson raised his voice and gave Harold a sharp look. "Son, your mom said that's enough, and now I'm telling you the same. Frankie is your brother's friend, and he's a guest in this house." Harold grimaced, picked up his fork, and stabbed it into a piece of chicken.

Harold's words pierced somewhere deep inside me. I felt suddenly like an unwelcome intruder at their table. I hung my head, set my fork down quietly, and stared into my lap, afraid to move, not daring even to blink. My embarrassment was so profound that I was scared to chew the food I held in my mouth. My face flushed as all eyes around the table bore down on me, and if it weren't for the humiliation that fastened me to the chair, I would have crawled under the kitchen table to hide.

"Frankie, baby, don't you pay no mind to Harold. You go on and eat your supper now. Let me get you another piece of chicken," Mrs. Sampson said, trying to comfort me as she stabbed a fork into a plump fried chicken thigh and plopped it down on my plate. I remained still, and I heard the clinking of silverware on plates as everyone else again began to eat. Finally, Mrs. Sampson stood and began to clear the table. Mr. Sampson and Harold got up and left the kitchen, and Leroy nudged me with his knee.

"Come on, let's go up to my room," Leroy said. A great relief washed over me as I scooted away from the table and walked quickly from the kitchen with Leroy. We skirted past the living room, where Mr. Sampson and Harold sat. Mr. Sampson was reading, and Harold was watching the news. Once we reached the bottom of the stairs, Leroy climbed the steps.

"Leroy?" I whispered. Leroy stopped on the stairs and turned toward me. "I have to go home now."

Leroy looked disappointed. "How come?"

"I promised my mum." I turned and pulled open the front door. "Tell your mum I said thanks for supper." I stepped out onto the porch and pulled the door shut behind me. Outside, it had begun to drizzle, and the April rains had finally arrived. I descended the porch steps and barely made it to the sidewalk before I heard the front door open.

"Frankie?" I turned to face Mrs. Sampson. "Here, sweetie, you take this piece of chicken with you that you left on your plate," she said, holding out the chicken wrapped neatly in aluminum foil.

"No, thanks, I'm already full," I lied as I spun and began to walk up the wet sidewalk. Something was gnawing at me, though, and I knew I had to say something. So I turned and faced Leroy's mum again.

"Mrs. Sampson?"

"Yes, Frankie," she answered warmly.

I had to let her know that Harold was wrong. "Even though I'm white, I still would've come over to your house if I weren't on welfare," I said.

Mrs. Sampson smiled uncomfortably. "I know that, baby," she said.

"And I'm sorry for eating all your food," I added quickly. Before Mrs. Sampson could respond, I turned, plunged my hands deep into my pockets, squinted against the rain, and walked briskly from their house toward our apartment, leaving Mrs. Sampson alone on her porch to stare after me.

Chapter 30

I walked home from Leroy's in the dark, feeling foolish, and inwardly admonishing myself for believing that I had actually become a part of his family. How could I be so stupid? Leroy was my best friend, and that wouldn't change; I liked Leroy's mum and dad a lot, and it bothered me that they didn't care for me in the same way. Their family bond was special, and I had convinced myself I had become a part of it. Even when Mr. Sampson became angry, there was an underpinning of love and purpose to his tone that was foreign to me. At home with Joe, anger and violence were the same. Mr. Sampson's anger did not generate anxiety in me like Joe; to the contrary, it manifested within me admiration. The only anxiousness I felt was the possibility that Mr. Sampson might reject me. I now understood I was never really a part of their family, and I had become a victim of my own lie. Coming to terms with the truth, I experienced a profound feeling of gloom and rejection. "What's wrong with me?" I scolded myself as I walked.

As I approached Martha's store, the windows to our apartment across the street came into view. A light glowed inside my mum's bedroom through the darkness, and Joe's ominous silhouette appeared. Other than Joe, this was where those who loved me most lived. There was not the same semblance of warmth and security that existed in Leroy's household, but it was mine, and it was all I had.

*****

The following evening, just after dusk, clusters of black men, women, and teenagers assembled on Larimer's streets. Soon, angry shouts filled the night air, and the groups gradually merged into an agitated mob that ebbed and flowed on Larimer Avenue. Then, as the anger-fueled screams grew in intensity, smashing bottles against brick and pavement could be heard. The shouts morphed into a single roar, followed by rioters' violence and the obscene sound of shattering plate glass windows.

I huddled with my sisters in their bedroom. Gunshots rang out. In the distance, sirens from police cars and fire engines moved closer. Rioters set fire to tires and vehicles, sending thick columns of black smoke into the air. They dumped heaps of garbage along the sidewalks, and some of it was also set on fire. The stench was putrid. The three of us watched in horror as our neighborhood was transformed into what our mum called "a war zone."

Mindy, Doreen, and I pressed our noses against the window. Joe suddenly appeared in the doorway, shirtless, a gun dangling in his hand.

"Get away from the windows, imbeciles," he growled. We scrambled from the window and jumped on the bed. Joe disappeared from the doorway; we heard him jiggling doorknobs to make sure they were locked. I was glad that Joe was in the apartment for the only time ever.

We got very little sleep that night. I slept with my sisters, and when we woke the following morning, we all sensed that something had changed with our community, only we weren't yet sure of its magnitude.

Our mum walked into my sisters' bedroom and looked down at us as we stretched awake. "The radio just said that everyone, especially all the kids, should stay inside because of the riots," she informed us, looking directly at me. She knew I would be eager to go outside and explore.

Me, Mindy, and Doreen sat on my sisters' bedroom floor, whispering our opinions when Joe appeared in the doorway wearing white boxers. He tossed Mindy a comb. "Come on and comb my hair." Mindy picked up the comb. "Well, any day!" Joe growled. He turned and walked toward the living room. Mindy snuck me a crest-fallen look, stood, and trailed behind Joe.

Mindy sat at the end of the couch in the living room while Joe stretched out on his side and snuggled his large head obscenely in her lap. Mindy dragged the comb through Joe's thick black hair with dread, just the way he liked it.

In a little while, I became thirsty and walked to the kitchen. When I reached the living room, I began to tiptoe. Mindy looked helplessly up at me. Joe had closed his eyes, and although he wasn't snoring, his breathing was rhythmic and shallow. Joe often made Mindy comb his hair like this, and she was not allowed to stop, not even if he fell asleep, which would usually be for an hour or more. I gave Mindy an empathetic look and continued to the kitchen.

As I sat at the kitchen table sipping water, there was a light knock at the kitchen door. I hurried to answer it before it could disturb Joe and was surprised to see Leroy standing there. He had never come to our apartment before, and I knew better than to invite him inside.

Leroy looked curiously past me. "Can you come out?" I peeked over my shoulder to ensure no one was there.

"Yeah, hurry up. Let's go before my mum catches me," I whispered, stepping out the door and pulling it quietly behind me. Leroy gave me a puzzled look.

"You ain't going to ask your mum?" he asked.

"Nuh-uh," I answered. "If I ask her, she'll probably say no. Let's go."

We hurried down the back steps and ran to the front of the apartment building on Larimer Avenue. The stench from smoldering tires and burnt debris still lingered heavily in the air. About a half-block up Larimer Avenue toward Larimer Bridge, the remains of a burnt-out car, scorched black, still smoldered. In the opposite direction along Larimer Avenue, rioters had smashed most of the plate glass windows from the businesses and stores for as far as I could see. Debris from inside the stores littered the sidewalks and streets everywhere.

"Ain't it a mess?" Leroy said.

"Jeez-o-man!" I answered, almost in disbelief at what I was witnessing. It no longer looked like Larimer Avenue. Slowly, we walked up the sidewalk, crunching glass. I skirted close to the apartment building so Joe or my mum wouldn't see me from the upstairs windows. In front of us, Mr. and Mrs. Cosenza stepped out from inside their store. Mr. Cosenza had his arm around his wife's shoulder, and Mrs. Cosenza's hand covered her mouth as she looked on with horror. She was crying. When we reached them, Leroy and I peeked inside their exposed store. Looters had destroyed it. Shelves were overturned and stripped clean, and in the back, the mob had smashed the window to the meat display case. There were discarded food boxes and wrappers everywhere. It barely resembled a grocery store.

Mr. Cosenza's brother, Pauly, carried an empty cardboard box out of the store, and he set it down and walked back inside with his brother. Mrs. Cosenza wiped her eyes, bent down, and began to pick up large chunks of broken glass. I felt terrible for her, and I looked over at Leroy, and his expression told me he was feeling the same way. We squatted down without saying a word and began to help Mrs. Cosenza pick up chunks of broken glass.

As we worked to clear the sidewalk, a group of black teenagers gathered across the street. When Mrs. Cosenza saw them, she stood up and glared in their direction. I had known Mrs. Cosenza all of my life, and even when she occasionally caught one of us stealing candy from her store and scolded us, I never saw her angry like this. Now, her eyes burned with indignation.

She took a step toward the curb. "How come you did this to our store, huh? What did we ever do to you?" she shrieked. "I know some of your mums. Why would you do this to our store? Tell me!" Her face flushed with anger. Mr. Cosenza and his brother Pauly quickly reappeared from inside the store and stood next to her.

Mr. Cosenza put his arm around his wife's quaking shoulders. "Come on, Linda," he whispered, walking her back inside.

As Leroy and I watched, one of the boys stepped to the front of the crowd, raised his fist high in the air, and shouted, "Black power." Those behind him began to laugh and joke amongst themselves. Then, I noticed that Leroy's brother Harold was amongst them. He was standing toward the rear of the horde with his hands shoved into his pockets. Leroy saw him too.

Leroy and I resumed picking up the broken glass from the pavement, placing them carefully in the box. One of the boys asked Harold why his little brother was helping those white people across the street.

"Hey, Leroy, get on over here!" Harold shouted. Leroy stood, squared his shoulders, and gazed deliberately at his brother. He raised his chin, his wide nostrils flared slightly, and I immediately recognized the hard glint in my friend's eyes from that day we had fought on the basketball court. It was a proud look of defiance that had informed me that day that no matter what, he would never back down or be afraid of me. As I looked up at Leroy, I realized how much he had grown since last summer. He was not only taller but was more muscular. If I were to fight him now, the outcome would probably be very different. As Leroy boldly stared at his brother and the other boys, I felt a sudden sense of inferiority and unexpected envy. He was stronger than me, and he would never bend to the will of the mob. The truth was, he had a strength of character that I lacked, and I now knew it. No, he most definitely was not one to follow the crowd. Despite my feelings, I was glad that Leroy was my friend, and I felt a kinship toward him like never before. Satisfied that he had made his point, Leroy stooped next to me and once again began to pick up the broken glass.

"Hey, Uncle Tom! Yeah, you!" one of the boys shouted at Leroy. The crowd of boys broke out into laughter, except for Harold, who stood silent with his hands still shoved into his pockets. I understood that somehow this was an attempt to insult Leroy, but I had no inclination as to what the name meant, and by the indifferent look on Leroy's face, I was pretty sure he didn't know or care either. He simply ignored them. As we picked up the broken glass, I suddenly realized the source of Leroy's strength of character. He was his father's son.

Later, as Leroy and I sat on the stoop of Cosenza's store, there appeared in the distance, rolling toward us, several massive, drab green military trucks full of soldiers. We could hardly believe our eyes. The trucks' roar grew louder as they approached until they finally squealed to a stop directly in front of us. Soldiers armed with rifles jumped from the trucks and began strategically disbursing themselves along the streets and corners. Once the men were in place, an important-looking soldier in a jeep announced with a loudspeaker that there would be a 9:00 p.m. curfew. It was both scary and exhilarating, and Leroy and I dared one another to talk to one of the soldiers, but neither of us did. Instead, we just watched, wondering what it would be like to wear such a uniform that instilled respect and even fear in others.

To be honest, we didn't understand the political or social reasons why any of this was occurring. Initially, the best we could figure was that black people around the country were angry because of Martin Luther King's assassination. They blamed the white people and expressed their anger by rioting against them in the streets. But as Leroy and I discussed and pondered our theory, we eventually concluded that there had to be something else since black rioters also destroyed the stores owned by black businessmen along Larimer Avenue as well. Besides, the Cosenza family were good people who extended credit to Larimer's black families, just as they did to white families. They had never treated blacks or whites differently. None of it made sense to us as we tried to connect the dots between Dr. King's senseless death and the senseless destruction of Mr. and Mrs. Cosenza's store, along with all the other businesses on Larimer Avenue. It was a mystery.

There was one thing we agreed on, though, and it was that the man who shot Dr. King needed to die in the worst way possible. The only disagreement between us was how to accomplish the execution.

Leroy was partial to the idea that the assassin should be lowered into a giant pot of boiling oil, inch by inch. On the other hand, I thought the best way would be to bury him in the ground up to his neck next to a giant anthill, pour honey over his head, and then let the ants slowly eat him alive. I had seen this done by Apaches on an old cowboy and Indian movie, who, I explained to Leroy, knew a thing or two about torture.

Eventually, we grew content to sit on the curb outside Cosenza's store and watch the soldiers with rifles pacing the sidewalks.

"About the other night at supper," Leroy spoke up at one point. "My mum feels bad for what Harold said to you, and she told me to tell you that you're welcome at our house anytime."

"Tell her thanks." I nodded. I had already decided never to go back, but I didn't want to tell that to Leroy.

"There's something else," Leroy said, staring at the sidewalk. "I was wrong, man." I shot him a curious look.

"What do you mean?"

"I should have said something when Harold said those things to you. But I didn't. I was wrong, and I'm sorry."

"It's okay, man."

"No, it's not. When you left, my mum and dad let Harold have it good, and I took a swing at him."

"Get out!" I clucked.

Leroy grinned. "No, really, my dad grounded me in my room because of it. Anyway, I just wanted to let you know."

"It's cool, man." I grinned. We both turned our attention back to the soldiers.

Finally, Leroy announced he had to get home. We stood, slapped each other five, and said goodbye.

That night, the soldiers, whom our mum called the National Guard, patrolled Larimer Avenue. Occasionally, a helicopter with its thumping blades roared above our rooftop. The soldiers remained through the rest of the weekend and were still there when I went to school on Monday. Then, when I awoke on Tuesday, they were gone.

I soon discovered that Mr. Sampson was correct; not all things were the same as before. In a couple of weeks, things in Larimer began to settle down. Most of the businesses made repairs and began to reopen for business. Some, though, never opened their doors again. Signs began to appear in windows that read, "No Credit," and store owners no longer welcomed the black kids in the store, as they did previously, but instead scrutinized and watched them closely. Before, the young black kids who stared at the penny candy display wishing they had money drew sympathy from the store owners, who would, in turn, give them a piece of candy for free. But now, the store owners quickly shooed them away.

Cosenza's Italian grocery store and meat market was the exception. As resentment and distrust crept into the community, their store had not posted a "No Credit" sign in the window. Instead, the Cosenza family decided to do business the same as before and would continue to extend credit to all families in good standing, both black and white alike. They were a family with good hearts, and despite what had happened to them, they decided the best way to move forward, and do their part to help heal the community they loved, was to forgive and forget.

*****

It rained almost every day the latter half of April, and many of the lessons taught by Mrs. English had to do with racial healing and coming together as a community. For me, it seemed as if she and Mr. Sampson had much of the same thoughts on the subject. Then, the month of May brought much warmer weather, and the racial discussions amongst the students seemed to be replaced by talks and anticipation of summer and the freedom it would bring. Like most other students, I became restless with each passing day as the school year neared its end. It was increasingly hard to focus on school work. The teachers sensed our eagerness too, and it took all their experience and skill to keep us attentive through the last days of school.

As the weather warmed, I found myself at Larimer Bridge more often. Although it had been several months, the memory and guilt of my betrayal of Honeymarmo had not diminished. I still hoped that maybe it wasn't Honeymarmo that had been found dead along the tracks, and if I sat long enough, Honeymarmo would appear on the horizon. I craved to tell him I was sorry, but even more, I needed to know that he forgave me. So for hours I would sit, and wait, and hope. During these times, I found myself having long conversations with God. He never spoke back, but I began to feel his presence, just like Honeymarmo had said.

Then, at last, the final day of school arrived. I lagged behind the others being dismissed for summer vacation to say a personal goodbye to Mrs. English. Unlike Lulu, I had graduated to the next grade. As I stared at my report card with five As and one B, my promotion brought mixed emotions. I was glad to be promoted because I knew that next year offered new and exciting things, but it also meant that I would be leaving Mrs. English behind, the one teacher who planted the hunger for learning within me. She was the reason for my good grades. I could not leave without telling her how grateful I was, and that I thought her an excellent teacher, and that I would miss her next year. So when the bell rang, and everyone jumped up from their desks and scampered toward the door, I sat firmly in my seat.

"Frankie?" a surprised Mrs. English chirped when she turned in the doorway after she had dismissed her class, noticing me still sitting at my desk. "Is everything all right?"

I nodded, "Yeah." I slid from my chair. When I reached her, I felt suddenly awkward, and the words I had rehearsed inexplicitly left me. With patience, Mrs. English smiled calmly down at me, waiting for me to say something. Finally, knowing the words wouldn't return, I sucked a deep breath and returned her gaze.

"I promise to visit you next year," I said clumsily.

"Well, I hope you do too, Frankie," she responded. I stood awkwardly, still unable to find the words to express further what I was feeling. I wanted to reach out and hug her around the waist and say, "Thank you." But the fear of rejection was high, so I turned and stepped into the hallway. As I hurried along, everything I wanted to say came flooding back, and I felt angry with myself. I tried to tell her that I was glad she had been my teacher, and I had learned so much from her. I needed to let her know she was the reason for my good grades, and I regretted her not being my teacher next year.

I had not gotten in a single fight all year, and although Honeymarmo was mainly responsible for that, she too had a lot to do with it. I wished to say so many things, but I said none of them; I didn't know why. "Next year," I whispered to myself. Next year, I would visit her and tell her how I felt. I hurried down the hall toward the front entrance of the school. Outside, dark threatening clouds were gathering above Larimer. As I stared at the sky, a gust of wind pushed against me. I rushed down the cement steps and sprinted through the playground toward home.

A storm was coming.

Chapter 31

Shortly after school had let out for the summer, our mum sat my sisters and me down at the kitchen table to give us the news. "I'm three months pregnant. Yinz are going to have another little brother or sister," she beamed.

"I hope it's a boy this time," Doreen said giddily.

"Yeah," Mindy agreed.

I rolled my eyes.

"It doesn't matter, as long as the baby is healthy," our mum said.

I didn't get why the news made my sisters so happy, and I thought it was a lousy break. Another baby meant more crying at all hours of the day and night and more of that disgusting smell. I stood and walked toward the open kitchen door.

"Where are you going?" our mum asked.

"Over to Martha's store to see what Phyllis thinks about you having another baby," I answered flippantly.

"Don't you dare! That's none of her..." was all I heard my mum say as I stomped down the steps.

*****

That summer, Joe became worse. Almost daily, he walked around the apartment loaded on some kind of drug, and he had become more irrational, more unpredictable, and more dangerous than ever before. My sisters and I thought we would be okay if we made ourselves more scarce than usual, but we were fooling ourselves.

In late June, a week after my twelfth birthday, Joe roamed about the apartment in the morning wearing only his boxers, and my sisters and I had already detected the unstableness in his walk. We had withdrawn to Mindy's and Doreen's bedroom and had shut the door to keep out of sight. We played as quietly as mice.

Joe banged open the door, causing it to rattle on its hinges. Me and my sisters cowed together on the floor. He stood in the doorway, staring with contempt.

"What are you little imbeciles being so sneaky about?" We sat silently and didn't move.

"Get in the bathroom," Joe growled. The three of us scrambled quickly past him. My mind raced at what Joe might have planned for us, and all I could think about was Fluffy's kittens. In the bathroom, my sisters and I huddled together. Joe followed us inside and stopped abruptly in front of the wall above the bathtub.

"Which one of you little creeps did this?" he snarled. With growing trepidation, we all stared blankly at the place on the wall where Joe was pointing, but there was nothing there.

"Somebody better open their filthy mouth!" he threatened. Confused, Mindy, Doreen, and I stood dumbfounded, unsure what to say. We had no idea what we were being accused of as we searched the wall for a clue, but there was nothing there, not a single mark.

"Oh, I see," Joe grumbled, "no one knows nothing, is that it? We just want to play like we're stupid. All right then, have it your way." He stepped over to the medicine cabinet, opened it, pulled out a box of razor blades, and set it down on the top of the white porcelain toilet tank.

"I want all this paint scraped off the walls, and I mean every last bit of it!" he commanded, gesturing with his beefy hands. "You don't stop for nothing until it's done." The three of us stood motionless. "Well, what are you jagoffs waiting for?" he snapped. We each picked out a razor blade from the box. Satisfied, Joe left us to our task.

"There ain't nothing on that wall," Doreen whispered.

Mindy sighed. "No, kidding!" The three of us looked around the bathroom. The entire room, except for the ceiling, was a dingy yellow.

"Frankie, you start on that wall, Doreen, you start over there, and I'll start on this wall," Mindy instructed.

"Why do you get that wall? Why can't I start there?" Doreen objected.

"Because it's bigger," Mindy snapped impatiently. "If you want the bigger wall, then go ahead, be my guest." Doreen sized up Mindy's wall and then looked at hers, then at Mindy's wall again.

"Never mind," Doreen acquiesced, walking to her assigned wall, where she began to chip away with the razor blade. Mindy's wall was next to the bathtub, so she climbed inside and began scraping as I walked to my wall near the window.

The old paint was thick and hard. After a solid hour of scraping, our fingers were sore, and our arms grew fatigued. We stepped back to compare our progress. I had scraped away the most, which was an area about the size of my fist. As we exchanged looks, we recognized the hopelessness on each of our faces. Panic set in.

"This will take forever!" I complained.

"At least," Mindy added. Although we now realized how impossible our task was, we also knew that we couldn't stop no matter what. We stepped back to our walls and once again returned to the senseless job before us.

We worked diligently through the pain of blistered fingers, cramped arms, and stiffening legs and backs for the next three hours. As our pain and frustration increased, so did our groans and whispered complaints.

Close to exhaustion, we again stepped back from the walls. Each of us had scraped off an area no bigger than the size of our heads. We felt each other's fear. If Joe came in now, we knew what he probably would do.

"This is so stupid!" Doreen whispered.

"We know that," Mindy whispered back. "Just get back to work. If Joe catches us not scraping, it will be a lot worse."

Sucking an anguished breath, we went back to our tortured labor. Three more hours passed, then tears and muffled sobs began to emanate from both Mindy and Doreen. I too felt the strong urge to cry from both the pain and frustration of such a futile task, but I would not succumb; I would not give Joe the satisfaction of my tears.

Nine hours after we had first begun, Mindy was the first to break. She leaned heavily against the wall as she stood in the bathtub. The pain in her raw and bleeding fingers was excruciating, and her cramping body was exhausted and weak. The last of her resolve and strength drained from her, and she slid down the wall. As she lay collapsed in the tub, sobbing, I rushed to her.

"Shhhh, Mindy, Joe will hear you," I whispered. But when I saw my sister's vacant and distant stare, I knew trying to reason with her was useless. Now, scared for her, I placed my hand over her mouth to muffle her sobs. After a few moments, Mindy's crying dwindled into low whimpers.

Knowing there was nothing else to be done for her, I hurried back to my task, leaving Mindy lying in the tub, and once again, Doreen and I began to scrape at the wall with our bloody fingers. Doreen's razor blade was the next to stop. I turned and saw her sitting on the floor, her back against the wall, tears streaking down her face.

"I ain't doing no more," she announced, her typical indomitable spirit broken. "I don't care if he kills me dead, Frankie. I ain't scraping no more." I stared at her for a moment and knew that nothing I could say would change her mind, so I didn't try. Instead, I turned and went back to work.

It wasn't long before I heard Joe's heavy footsteps creaking loudly across the floorboards. I held my breath, praying Joe wasn't coming to us. I glimpsed him from the corner of my eye as he appeared in the doorway.

"What do you think you're doing? Get up off that floor and get to work!" Joe growled at Doreen. I was scared that she might defy him, and I knew what that would mean. To my relief, I heard Doreen get to her feet, and once again, sobbing sporadically, she began scraping the wall.

"That goes for you too!" Joe hissed. He was talking to Mindy. She didn't move. "Are you deaf? I said, get up, you little whore!" Joe growled. He stepped toward the tub. Mindy lay sobbing and did not respond. Joe reached in, grabbed her by the hair, and jerked her to her feet in one motion. Doreen and I scraped faster. Joe pulled Mindy from the tub, almost lifting her off her feet. With only the balls of her feet touching the floor, Joe walked her from the bathroom into her bedroom. Now, I was scared for her.

In a moment, we heard the horrifying sound of the thick board as it repeatedly smacked against Mindy's bare flesh. She screamed in agony from the onslaught, gasping for air as the pain sucked away her breath. I heard our mums' footsteps, followed by tearful pleas for Joe to stop. Then, I heard the smack because of her interference and the door rattling as she stumbled against it. Joe's massive figure once again loomed in the bathroom doorway.

"I better not catch yinz stopping again—either one of you imbeciles," he warned. Then, he dropped the board on the floor in the doorway as a reminder of what would happen if we disobeyed. He grunted, then walked away. I fought to control my fear and anger, and I pushed back against my emotions until the tears that had begun to blur my vision were gone.

My entire body cramped up and ached with pain, but I knew it was worse for Doreen. I would scrape for a while with my right hand until I could no longer hold up my arm; then, I would switch the razor blade to my left hand. After a while, I didn't even care if I was scraping paint off the wall. We had not eaten all day, and my hunger pains were sharp. I ignored them. I looked out the bathroom window and realized for the first time that it was dark. I stared out into the blackness. Soon, I was yawning, and my knees sometimes buckled, but I would catch myself, lean all my weight against the wall, and continue. The pain in my legs was unbearable. My eyelids had begun to droop, and my head nodded from exhaustion, and I repeatedly caught myself falling asleep. I shook my head vigorously to keep myself awake, only to become drowsy again. As I fought off sleep, I turned to see how Doreen was doing and saw she was curled up on the floor, snoring softly. I considered waking her, but I was too tired, and my legs hurt too much to walk to her. I decided that I would hurry to kick her awake only if I heard Joe coming. I turned wearily back to my wall and now scraped with a useless pawing motion.

"Frankie? Frankie? Wake up now. You need to go to your room and get to bed." I looked up from the bathroom floor where I lay. At some point, I had slid to the bathroom floor and had fallen asleep. Hovering above me stood our mum; a soft glow from the ceiling light bulb surrounded her head like a halo. Groggily, I squinted up at her. She helped me to my feet, and as her face came into focus, I could see that the rims of her eyes were red from crying. I looked across the bathroom floor; Doreen was no longer there. "I'm sorry, Frankie!" my mum whispered. "I'm so sorry. He's just so doped up." She whispered, "Come on now." She held me against her side, and we walked to my room, where she had spread several blankets on the metal box springs for me to sleep. I crawled on top of the blankets, and the tiredness was so great within me that even the stiff metal springs felt good. My mum stood over me, running her fingers through my hair.

"Mummy?" I whispered sleepily, almost too tired to speak.

"Yeah, Frankie?"

"I think I peed, Mummy," I mumbled, feeling the wetness as I shut my eyes, drifting toward sleep.

"That's okay. Just go to sleep. We'll take care of it tomorrow." Her voice was distant and fading as I again felt my mum brush my hair away from my eyes with her fingers. That was the last I remembered before slipping into a deep, deep sleep.

Chapter 32

June ended, but for me, the summer continued to invoke memories of Honeymarmo. I missed my friend, and this summer felt different without him. I often shuffled down the trail leading under the bridge, plopped down in the dirt, and stared down the tracks. My hope was always the same: that I would see Honeymarmo appear on the horizon, walking toward me. Just in case, I would rehearse my apology in my mind, hoping we would reunite our friendship. I sometimes searched the woods nearby for signs that would show where the kids found the dead hobo the previous year. But mostly, I would lean back on my elbows, stretch out my legs, cross my ankles, like Honeymarmo used to do, and stare down the tracks and wait.

I remembered once asking Honeymarmo where the seemingly endless stretch of railroad tracks led. I wanted to know if it was what I had imagined.

"I guess I've traveled these tracks over half my life," he answered thoughtfully. "They've taken me to more cities and places than I can count. I guess you could say they've taken me just about everywhere there is to go in this country. Yes, sir, and I've had some interesting adventures over the years. They've taken me to good times and to bad times—mostly bad if I were to be honest." His shoulders slumped forward, and his voice softened with regret. "You ask me where they lead to, Frankie? Well, I'll tell you. Where they lead, in the end, is to an aimless, lonely, and wasted life. You know, Frankie, the good book says that our life is a vapor that appears for a little time then vanishes away. I know that you, being young and all, well, that probably doesn't mean much to you. But one morning, you're going to wake up, look in the mirror, and realize that you've become old, and you're going to wonder where all the years have gone. When that time comes, besides having God in your life, it's important to have a family of your own and to have accomplished something worthwhile in this world, or else life will have little meaning for you. It will have lost all of its luster, and you will become tired far beyond your years. Places you've dreamt about going to, like Big Rock Candy Mountain, will no longer matter, and with each passing day, you'll find yourself longing to catch that last train on the Indian Valley Line."

I scrunched my face. "What's the Big Rock Candy Mountain or the Indian Valley Line?" I asked.

Honeymarmo chuckled. "Well, Frankie, for us hobos, the Big Rock Candy Mountain is a place where there are no worries about anything. Where chickens lay soft-boiled eggs, fruit trees are everywhere, and the sun shines every day. It's a hobo's paradise, where you don't have to do anything, and there's no police or railroad bulls to bother you. It's where you live an easy life."

"Sounds like a make-believe place," I said cynically. When I daydreamed of leaving Larimer for good, not even my imagination had conjured up such a thing.

"Yeah, I suppose it is, Frankie. But it's sure nice to think about." Honeymarmo grinned.

"What's the Indian Valley Line?" I asked. "Is that make-believe too?"

"Well, the Indian Valley Line has a train that can take you to the Indian Valley. The Indian Valley can be any place where life is better for a hobo, where there are jobs, good panhandling, and nice people. But sometimes, when you catch the Indian Valley Line train, it takes you to the other side. Sometimes, when a hobo catches the Indian Valley Line train, it means that the hobo has died and moved on from this world."

"Sounds like make-believe to me," I clucked.

Honeymarmo turned from me, clasped his hands behind his head, and lay back in the dirt. "There are stories that some of the old-timers tell about the Indian Valley Line train, and these old hobos swear they're true, that once you climb on board, you go into a deep, peaceful sleep, and you never wake up." He paused, glanced over at me, and saw I was sporting a skeptical smirk.

"I know what you're thinking because, for a long time, I never believed it myself. I always thought it was just one of those tall tales that hobos like me told around a campfire." Honeymarmo paused again, searching for words. "I had a friend once, an old road dog by the name of Slick Willy-Nilly. He was from somewhere in Nevada—Reno, I think. Anyway, we had been on the bum together for maybe a month when Slick Willy got real sick with a really bad cough. We were outside San Antonio, and after a couple of days, he said he was feeling a little better, good enough to jump a slow train and move on, although he still looked pretty sick to me, and his cough hadn't gotten any better. In fact, I thought it had gotten worse. Well, we were in this wooded area, much like here, and we heard a train coming down the tracks, and sure enough, it came around a bend, and it was just a chugging along as slow as could be. When it got to us, we started running next to it so we could jump aboard one of the boxcars, like we did a thousand times before. Just as easy as pie, Slick Willy jumped on first and climbed into an open box, but wouldn't you know it, my foot slipped off the steel ladder, strange like, almost as if the train didn't want me to climb aboard, and I fell to the ground and damn near broke my ankle. It was the closest I ever come to greasing them there tracks. Anyway, ole Slick Willy-Nilly stayed on board, and I figured to meet up with him at the next station or somewhere down the line. So I hobbled down them tracks for about a mile or so before I stumbled upon a small jungle with four other hobos. They were all set up right next to the tracks, and when they saw me hobbling up, a couple of them ran up to help me. After I told them what had happened, they just stared at me queer-like. Finally, one of them spoke up.

"'Brother,' he says, 'we don't know what you're talking about. We have been right here since last night, and there ain't been no train come by here.' They studied me like maybe I wasn't quite right in the head or something. But you know what the funniest thing of all was, Frankie? I never saw Slick Willy-Nilly again. Sometimes, I would run into old road dogs that me and Willy knew, and not a single one had ever seen or heard from him again either. You know, I used to feel sorry for old Slick Willy, but now, well, now I envy him. Now, it seems more and more, as of late, I find myself hoping that the next train I catch will be on that Indian Valley Line and that it will be the last train for me too. I'm just tired and worn-out, I guess. Sometimes I feel as if I've been all chewed up by this world, and I'm ready for it to finally spit me out." Honeymarmo's demeanor became melancholy, and he shut his eyes.

*****

The first week of July came and went, and Joe continued to be just as mean and vindictive as ever. He was high on something almost every day. It was the second week, and I had spent part of the day with Marco and his neighbor Gino. In the southeast part of town were woods we occasionally explored, and on this day, we located a wild crab apple tree bursting with green apples that were deliciously sour. We climbed and pillaged the tree and ate until our stomachs bulged. Afterward, we drank cool water from a natural creek that percolated from the hillside.

I arrived home late afternoon, and my mum was standing over the stove, stirring something in a big pot. She looked haggard when she glanced over at me as I burst into the kitchen and sat down at the table, and I knew something was wrong.

"Frankie, where've you been all day?" she asked weakly.

"Me, Marco, and Gino were down in the woods," I said. "We found a crab apple tree, and I think I ate too many because now I have a stomachache."

"Well, it serves you right. It'll be another hour or so before the ham and cabbage is ready, so maybe your stomach will be okay by then."

"Don't worry, even if it's not, I'll still eat some," I mused. I looked at my mum's tired face, and she didn't seem like herself. "You okay, Mum? You don't look so good," I said.

Our mum grinned weakly at me. "I'm okay. The baby is just being disagreeable today, that's all," she assured me while rubbing her stomach.

Before I could respond, we both heard footsteps coming down the passage toward us. My mum's expression became stern as she got up from the kitchen table, walked back over to the stove, and began to stir in the pot. Joe stepped into the kitchen.

"Well, if it isn't, Frankie," he slurred. I stared down at the table. It was rare that Joe used my actual name, and it scared me.

"Frankie, go out and play for a while," my mum interrupted. I detected a hint of anger in her tone.

"Now, wait a minute Rose, you said you wanted me to be nicer to the little creep—I'm sorry, I mean to Frankie." His voice dripped with sarcasm, and he gave a demented cackle. He grinned crookedly at me.

"Joe, you promised," my mum begged.

"What? I'm being nice here, ain't I, Frankie?" I knew there was only one way to answer, so I nodded.

"See," Joe said. "Come here, Frankie. I want to show you something." Joe turned and walked toward the front of the apartment. I knew I had no choice but to follow. As I rose from the kitchen chair, I concluded that I would much rather have Joe show his typical open contempt for me because at least then I had some idea what to expect.

In the bedroom, Joe had me sit on the bed. He walked over to the dresser, opened one of the drawers, and reached inside. He pulled something out and turned to face me. Immediately, I went pale, and my leg began to tremble. Joe was holding his gun.

Doreen and Mindy burst loudly through the kitchen door from the back of the apartment.

"I won," Doreen shouted.

"Yeah, only cause you cheated," Mindy retorted.

"Nuh-uh, did not!"

"Ya-huh, you tripped me on the steps, and you know you did!"

"Nuh-uh, you tripped over your own big feet," Doreen shouted.

"I hate you!" Mindy barked.

"I hate you more!"

Then our mum whispered something, and Mindy and Doreen went quiet.

Joe held the pistol loosely in his hand. It hung down by his thigh. He seemed amused at the fear he was creating in me. His lips curled into a grin.

"Have you ever seen one of these before?" Joe asked balefully. I nodded. "So you know what it is, huh? Well, let me tell you, these things are dangerous and should never be pointed at anyone. You know why?" I shook my head. "Because it might be loaded, and if you were to accidentally pull the trigger, you could shoot someone, say, like in the head," Joe said. "Then, their head might explode, kind of like a watermelon. Did you know that, Frankie?" he asked as he raised the gun and pressed the barrel into my forehead. I squeezed my eyes shut, and my entire body quaked.

"Would you like to shoot it?" Joe asked. "Maybe you'd like to shoot me, huh?" He gave a demented cackle. "Maybe I'll take you out to shoot it some time, just you and me, deep in the woods, somewhere." I felt the barrel of the gun press harder against my forehead.

"Joe! What are you doing?" my mum cried as she ran into the room, sat down, and wrapped her arms around me. Joe lowered the pistol.

"What? See, there you go again. I was just asking the boy if he would like me to take him out shooting some time, just like a father, ain't that right, Frankie?" Joe asked sardonically.

"Yeah!" I nodded. Joe walked over and tossed the gun back in the dresser drawer.

"Joe, you're stoned out of your mind," my mum screamed as she began to cry. Joe grunted and walked from the room.

"Are you okay?" she asked. I nodded. "Why don't you go out and play for a little while until supper," my mum suggested. Together, we walked through the apartment, past Joe, who was now sitting in the living room, taking apart our old toaster.

Everyone ate at the kitchen table a little while later, except for Joe. Halfway through supper, Joe staggered into the kitchen carrying his half-eaten plate of food, tossed it disgustedly into the sink, and turned toward our mum.

"Don't ever feed me that slop again."

"That's not slop! You always liked my ham and cabbage before!" our mum shot back.

"I said it's slop, and don't get mouthy with me!"

Our mum jumped angrily to her feet. "I'll get mouthy if I want to get mouthy, jagoff!" Joe stared incredulously at her, almost in disbelief at what he had just heard. His face tensed as he deliberated on whether or not he should crack her one across the mouth. Me, Mindy, and Doreen all sat in terror at the mounting tension. Finally, Joe grunted and walked back into the living room. We all breathed a sigh of relief. Then, our mum walked over to the sink and slammed her plate loudly into it. The plate shattered.

We heard Joe rising from the old worn couch from the living room. The sound of his walk had a purpose and ill intent. He stepped into the kitchen and glared at our mum. "You have a problem?" he barked.

"Yeah, I have a problem!" My sisters and I had never heard our mum speak to Joe like this before, and we instantly became scared for her. "You, you're my problem! I cook for you, wash your clothes, do everything for you, and all on what little I get from welfare. And what do I get back from you? Nothing. You don't like my slop? Go let someone else cook for you then!"

We all knew it was coming, especially our mum, but she was so angry she didn't seem to care. The back of Joe's hand struck her across the mouth with such force that it sent her crashing back against the sink. Blood burst from her bottom lip and trickled down her chin.

"Oh, big man, hit a pregnant woman, why don't you," fumed our mum as she straightened. I wanted to run over and tell her to stop before Joe got really mad and hurt her bad, but fear held me in place. "Why don't you go pop some more damned pills or shoot up some more dope and get higher?" she goaded him further. Then, abruptly, without saying a word, Joe reached out and grabbed a fist full of our mum's thick brown curly hair and began to drag her through the kitchen toward the back porch.

"How about I throw you over the freaking railing instead," Joe threatened. Our mum pawed helplessly at his hand. I sensed the level of danger my mum was in, and I was suddenly afraid for her life. I knew what Joe was capable of, especially in his current state. At that moment, I thought for sure that Joe intended to throw our mum over the railing sending her plunging three floors to her death.

When Joe had dragged my mum past me, I jumped up from my chair and sprinted to the front of the apartment to my mum's bedroom. I pulled the pistol from the dresser drawer, flipped off the safety, and ran through the apartment back into the kitchen.

What I saw froze me in place. Joe had picked up our mum and was holding her over the railing; her arms and legs thrashed as she dangled in midair above the graveled parking lot below.

"Joe! Joe! Please, don't do it. You're going to hurt the baby. Please, please, don't!" she begged as she struggled to grab hold of the railing.

Mindy was sobbing as she hugged little Rose, her eyes fixed with horror on what was unfolding before her. No one took notice of me. Then, I raised the gun from across the kitchen and aimed it at Joe's massive chest.

"Put her down," I yelled, "put her down, now!" Joe looked over at me as our mum continued to flail helplessly. Then, he noticed the gun, and his eyes became sober. He jerked our mum back and set her down on the cement porch. She collapsed to her knees and grabbed her stomach, crying uncontrollably. Both of my sisters glanced in my direction and, for the first time, saw me pointing the gun at Joe. Mindy was still holding little Rose on her lap at the kitchen table, and Doreen had moved across the kitchen and was standing by the stove. I stood between my sisters in the middle of the kitchen, not taking my eyes off Joe. I paid no attention to Doreen as she edged closer to the open doorway.

Joe took a step forward. "It ain't going to fire, you little—"

"Little what?" I shouted. "Little imbecile? The safety's off, creep!" I said coldly. Joe's eyes darted between me and the gun, then he swallowed. I saw my mum put her hand over her mouth and gasp as she noticed me for the first time, pointing the gun at Joe.

"Oh god, no, Frankie, don't!" she begged. I ignored her and continued to stare at Joe. Joe took another step, and with both thumbs, I pulled the hammer back until it locked in place. Again, Joe froze.

"I wasn't going to drop her. Ask your mum. She knows I love her, and I was only scaring her, that's all. Now, take your finger off that trigger," Joe said nervously. He smiled as if the whole thing were just a joke. "And put the gun down before it goes off."

Slowly, I raised my aim from Joe's chest to his head. "If it does, maybe your head will explode, like a watermelon," I said coldly. The blood drained from Joe's face, and his fake smile vanished. For the first time ever, I saw fear in Joe's eyes.

"Frankie…," Joe started to say.

"Shut up!" I shrieked.

Then, in a flash, Doreen rushed through the door and plunged a steak knife into Joe's right thigh. Joe grimaced in pain as he staggered backward. Then, in one swift motion, he reached down, grabbed Doreen, and flung her. I gasped, then shouted, "No," as I watched my sister disappear over the railing.

The explosion of the first shot was deafening as it reverberated in the small kitchen. Mindy immediately clapped her hands over her ears. Joe lurched backward against the railing as the bullet struck him high on the left side of his chest. Then, another explosion. The second bullet ripped through the right side of Joe's chest. He collapsed on the porch and lay motionless against the railing.

"Oh god, no! No! No!" our mum sobbed into her hands. Little Rose was squalling loudly, and Mindy, still holding her, was now crying hysterically. I slowly walked toward the open kitchen door. I set the gun on the kitchen table, not taking my eyes off Joe, as I edged closer toward him. He wasn't moving, and there were two bullet holes in his bare chest, leaking blood. Then, remembering, I sprinted past Joe and my mum and hurried down the steps.

Doreen laid face up in the gravel parking lots, her left arm grotesquely bent underneath her, and her left leg had twisted in an unnatural angle away from her body. I stopped and looked on in horror. Blood seeped from her nose and ears, and it soaked her hair as a small crimson puddle formed under her head. I rushed over to my sister.

"Doreen? Doreen?" I cried. I couldn't believe what I was looking at and needed confirmation that it was her. I knelt beside her.

"Frankie?" Doreen mumbled; her eyes were scared, and her voice was panicked.

"Yeah, Dor, it's me."

"Frankie! Joe killed me, Frankie!" she cried. "He killed me dead!"

"No, Dor, he didn't. You'll be okay, honest. He just broke you a little, that's all."

"Really, Frankie?" she asked, with a trace of hope. Then, in the distance, I heard the faint sound of sirens.

"Doreen! Listen, that's the police coming to get you and take you to the hospital. Don't worry, Dor, they'll fix you up good."

"Okay, Frankie. Frankie? I didn't tell no one about our secret."

"What secret, Dor?"

"You know, about the pop bottles, Frankie," Doreen whispered.

"I know, Dor, you did good. I knew I could trust you."

Doreen smiled weakly. "See, I ain't no blabbermouth. You can tell me any secret like you do Mindy."

"I know that, Dor," I answered. "I'll tell you all of them from now on. I swear I will."

Doreen shut then opened her eyes. "Tell me one now."

"Sure, Dor, I got one, a real big one, that I ain't even told Mindy." I bent over my sister and began to whisper in her ear. Then, after a moment, I straightened up.

"Frankie? Is that the truth?" Doreen murmured, barely audible.

Frankie nodded. "Really, Dor. It's the God's truth."

"Okay, Frankie, don't worry, I won't tell no one," Doreen whispered, her voice weakening.

My vision blurred as I stared down at my sister. Then, I watched Doreen's eyes glaze over, her breathing stopped, and then she was still.

"Dor? Dor?" I cried out. I wanted to reach down and grab her but was afraid I would break her more. A police van and two police cars turned on Shetland Avenue, then sped into the parking lot. Two policemen jumped out of the police van and ran toward us, while two more policemen from the second car ran toward the steps leading to our apartment, where Mindy was still crying hysterically. A small crowd had begun to gather on the sidewalk, and two more policemen from the third car walked in their direction to keep them away.

"Call an ambulance!" one of the policemen shouted out, looking in the direction of the policemen keeping the crowd away.

"Give us some room, son," the other policeman said as he bent over Doreen to examine her. "It doesn't look like she was shot," he observed. Both policemen nodded. In a moment, he stood erect, looked over, and stared sadly at me.

"What happened here?" the policeman asked. "We received a call that there were gunshots." I stood mute. "Is this your sister, son?" he asked. I looked blankly at him and nodded.

"What's your name?"

"Frankie."

"I'm sorry, Frankie, but your sister is gone. What happened here?" he asked again.

"You mean she's dead?" I asked numbly.

"I'm afraid so. I'm sorry," the policeman whispered, placing his hand on my shoulder to comfort me. I felt nauseous. I wanted to cry, I needed to cry, but no tears would come.

"I think he might be in shock," the other policeman said, looking at me. He studied my face, which showed little emotion as I stared down at my sister.

Just then, from above us on the porch, one of the policemen leaned over the railing and shouted down.

"Hey, we have a man up here who has a knife sticking out of his leg, and he's been shot twice. The lady up here said her son Frankie shot him. You better call another ambulance."

"Okay," the policeman standing closest to me shouted back. He grasped my wrist and gave me a curious look.

"And you better hurry, Jack," the policeman yelled down again. "I don't know how, but this guy is still alive."

Chapter 33

Dan Kelly, East Liberty Police Chief, sat at his desk reading the report given to him by the two detectives sitting across from him. Finally, he leaned back in his chair and sighed.

"Well, we sure got a mess on our hands, don't we?" The two detectives looked at one another, then nodded.

"That's an understatement," Phillip White said, the detective to his right.

"So let me make sure I understand this whole thing. This guy Joe was stoned on some kind of drugs, got into a fight with the lady he lives with, and threatened to throw her off their apartment's third-floor porch. The lady's kids thought he meant to harm their mother since he had actually picked her up and, at one point, had dangled her over the porch railing."

Both men nodded in agreement; Detective White spoke out again. "Yeah, but for the record, the mother, Rose Desimone, insists that she instigated the entire fight." Chief Kelly nodded that he understood. "So at some point, the boy, Frankie, ran and got Joe's gun just to scare him—at least that's what he claims—so Joe would stop. Meanwhile, the daughter, Doreen, decided to protect her mom by attacking and stabbing Joe in the leg. Joe then picked up the girl and threw her over the railing, killing her."

"Yeah, but Joe claims it was an accident," Bob Sweeney, the other detective, interrupted. "We spent quite some time with him at the hospital, and he claims once the girl stabbed him in the leg, he reacted instinctively. He was afraid she was going to stab him again, so he grabbed and tossed her away from him in self-defense but didn't realize he was so close to the railing, and she just went over."

"How bad did she stab him?" the Chief queried.

"It was deep," Detective White answered. "The doctor that pulled it out said it was a steak knife, and she buried it in his leg to the hilt."

Chief Kelly furrowed his eyebrows. "Geez. And the guy's name is Joe Gallucci? Why does that name sound familiar to me?"

Detective Sweeney opened a notebook on his lap. "You remember last year when that guy assaulted four police officers in that bar in East Liberty, broke one of their noses?"

"You mean the one with the stolen dogs and was feeding them?"

"Yep, that's the one," Detective Sweeney said. "That was Joe Gallucci."

"No kidding," the chief said. "Any other priors?"

"Oh, yeah, this guy has a laundry list of priors going all the way back to his teenage years," Detective White said. "He's been arrested for assault and battery, drugs, drunk and disorderly, robbery—the list goes on. Do you remember about three years ago when that miniature horse went missing from the Pittsburgh Zoo, and we found some guy walking it down the middle of Larimer Avenue, stoned out of his mind?"

"That was this Joe guy?" Chief Kelly asked.

"Yep, that was him."

"Holy crap," Chief Kelly clucked. "This guy's a regular model citizen, ain't he?" he added flippantly.

The two detectives chuckled. "Not exactly," Detective Sweeney said.

Chief Kelly continued, "All right, so the boy, Frankie, sees Joe slapping the mom around and threatening her life, gets the gun to scare him, but when he sees Joe throw his sister over the railing, he snaps and shoots him twice in the chest."

"That's about it," Detective Sweeney confirmed. "Only, the boy swears he doesn't remember firing the gun. And the court-appointed psychiatrist that examined him says that he was so traumatized by what he witnessed that not remembering something like that was not unusual."

"Meaning he's probably not responsible for his actions," the chief concluded. "Geez, what a mess," he sighed. "We can't charge the mother with anything just for instigating an argument. When the little girl stabbed this Joe guy in the leg with the steak knife, he claims he was defending himself, and her going over the railing was an accident. So what do we charge him with? I don't think manslaughter charges will stick here. Maybe assault and battery for hitting the mother?"

"Maybe," Detective White chimed in, "but the mother was adamant that she wasn't going to press any charges against him. She claims that since she started the whole thing, it wasn't his fault." Both detectives gave one another an exasperated look, then turned back to the chief. "One more thing, the mom claims that from her vantage point, it looked to her like Joe didn't throw the girl over the railing on purpose. She said to her it looked like an accident, pure and simple."

Dan Kelly shook his head. "Even though he killed her kid? Unbelievable." He sighed disgustedly. "So the son was not only protecting his mother but witnessed his sister being killed, shoots Joe, but can't remember doing it. I just don't see us charging him with anything, do you?"

Both detectives looked at one another, shrugged, shook their heads, and stared vacantly at the chief.

"Okay, boys, I'll get with the district attorney and go over this with him and see what he thinks. I'll let you know." Both detectives stood and headed toward the door.

"Hey guys." They both turned back to face the chief. "Great work." They both smiled thinly, then walked out the door.

*****

The week after the shooting was hectic, mostly because of the funeral services for Doreen. Our mum brooded most of the time, emotionally detached, even lethargic at times, obviously depressed. Our Aunt Daphne, her sister, drove in from Ohio to help with the funeral arrangements and manage the household. She was a fearless, no-nonsense, direct-speaking woman who spoke her mind regardless of who she was addressing. But beneath her hardened exterior, she could be tender and kind and had a good heart. I liked her a lot. She stomped around our apartment, barking orders like a drill sergeant when my sisters and I needed to get things done. But when we accomplished our tasks to her satisfaction, she was warm and cordial and even affectionate. She seemed annoyed at my mum that I had no mattress. And one day, when I arrived home, I found that she had bought me one secondhand and had it delivered to my room. There were no urine stains or foul odors; it was the best mattress I had ever had.

Doreen was laid out at DeRosa Funeral Home on Paulson Street, in Larimer, for three days. I attended the viewing the first day with my mum and Mindy, but I refused to go back inside the funeral home after that. Instead, I sat outside on the front stoop the last two days, reluctantly greeting people who came to pay their respects. It was mainly neighbors and Doreen's friends who came to say goodbye, but very few family members. Our aunt Connie showed up the first day with her husband, Pete, but they left their kids home. I was sitting in a chair next to the casket when they arrived.

"Oh, Rose, how are you holding up?" Our aunt Connie asked as she rushed over to embrace our mum. "We are so sorry for your loss, and we were so shocked to hear about Doreen. Why I just saw her last summer at Saint Rocco's festival, and it hardly seems possible." She sighed sympathetically.

"Thank you, Connie. It was nice of you to come." Our mum smiled.

"What about our dad? Is he coming?" I asked, rising to my feet.

"Oh, Frankie, your dad is sick to death about Doreen. When I called and told him, he couldn't stop crying. He wanted to come, but he's working through some issues right now, and he just got a new job as a security guard. If he were to come, then he would lose his job."

"What kind of issues?" I asked bluntly.

"Well, sweetie, let's just say grown-up issues," Aunt Connie said.

"Oh, for Christ's sake, Connie," our uncle Pete interceded, "your father likes to drink a lot, Frankie."

"Pete!" Aunt Connie scolded.

"Oh, come on, Connie, your brother couldn't even bother to come to his own daughter's funeral."

"That's not fair!" Aunt Connie snapped. "And besides, this is not the place nor time for that right now."

Uncle Pete forced his mouth shut, shook his head, and walked away. Connie turned back toward our mum. "I'm sorry, Rose. Pete liked Doreen and is just upset about everything. I'm going to go talk to him, and I'll be back in a little bit," she promised.

"That's okay, Connie. I understand. I'll see you in a bit," our mum answered. We watched as our aunt Connie trailed after her husband. I plopped back down in my chair, feeling both hurt and anger rising within me. I knew how much Doreen loved our father and wanted to be with him when she was alive, and now, our father wouldn't even come to her funeral when she was dead. Finally, I stood and stared down at my sister. "I'm sorry, Dad's not coming." I reached out and touched her arm. It felt like wood. "Goodbye, Dor," I whispered, then walked outside and never saw her again.

*****

For the next couple of weeks, I moped around the apartment in a malaise. All I could think about was Doreen and how much I missed her. The apartment felt empty and was so quiet without her. Then, on one occasion, after waking suddenly, I could have sworn I heard her voice through my grogginess. Even after realizing it was probably only a dream, I felt her presence.

One morning, Mindy plopped down next to me as I sat alone on the back porch. It was apparent she had been crying. We sat quietly; I waited for Mindy to speak first.

"I keep thinking that Doreen thought I hated her," Mindy finally whispered.

"Min, Doreen didn't think no such thing," I reassured her.

"You don't understand, Frankie. We had one of our fights that day over something stupid, and the last thing I remember saying to her was that 'I hate you.' But, Frankie, I didn't hate her, honest I didn't."

"Min, Doreen knew you didn't mean it. How often did she tell you the same thing, that she hated you? How many times did she tell me that? We said a lot of things when we fought that we didn't mean, Min. Doreen knew that more than anyone. I'm sure she knew deep down that you loved her."

"You think so, Frankie, you really, really think so?" Mindy began to cry. I wanted to reach out to my sister to hug her for comfort, but I couldn't do it for some reason. So instead, I touched her arm.

"Of course, Min!" I again reassured her, which seemed to make Mindy cry harder. I sat there with her for a long time.

"Min," I finally said. "I think there's something wrong with me."

"Why?" Mindy asked, wiping her face. "What do you mean?"

"Sometimes, it's like I don't feel anything inside. I can't cry anymore. I mean, I want to, especially for Doreen, but I can't. I've even tried to force myself, Min, but no tears will come. What kind of brother doesn't even cry for his own killed sister? I keep thinking maybe I didn't love her like I was supposed to, or something, but I know that's not true, Min, because I miss her bad—really bad."

Mindy wrapped her arms around me. "I just think you're still in shock, Frankie, like that doctor said, that's all. Give it some time, and you'll be okay. You just wait and see."

I hung my head. "I'm not in shock, Min. After I shot Joe, that doctor the courts made me see kept asking me if I remembered pulling the trigger, if I remembered shooting him. He told me that people who sometimes experience or do something terrible in their lives go into shock and can't remember what they did, so they're not responsible for their actions. So I told him I didn't. I told him the last thing I remembered was getting the gun from the drawer, and everything after that was blank until I was in the parking lot with Doreen. That's when he told me he thought I had gone into shock. But the truth is I lied to him, Min, because I remember everything. I remember how the gun felt in my hand. I remember everything I said. I remember each time I pulled the trigger. I remember how loud it was and the smell of gun powder. I remember Joe falling down on the porch. But mostly, I remember how good I felt when I thought he was dead, when I thought I had killed him." I sighed. "So you see, I'm not in shock, Min. I never was."

*****

It wasn't long before most of Larimer heard that I had shot Joe. Most had no clue who Joe was or had any insight into the circumstance surrounding the shooting, but that didn't stop them from jumping to their conclusion, which was especially true of most parents around the neighborhood. Me shooting Joe only confirmed their suspicions that I was wild and somehow dangerous. Now, they forbade their children from associating with me. All the neighborhood kids now avoided me, even those I had been friends with most of my life. Even Leroy's mum and dad no longer allowed him to loaf with me. It wasn't fair; I knew I wasn't a threat to anyone. I felt like an outcast, like someone who had a terrible disease, and everyone was afraid to catch it from me. So most days, I took to walking the streets of Larimer, alone.

A couple of weeks after Doreen's funeral, I glanced inside while passing my mum's room. My mum stood in front of her dresser mirror, wearing a loose-fitting dress to accommodate her swollen stomach. I watched as she leaned toward the mirror and carefully smeared on red lipstick. Finished, she puckered, made a popping noise with her lips, and dropped her lipstick tube into her purse. Next, she unwrapped a Band-Aid, lifted her dress, and carefully covered up the small tattoo on her thigh that bore Joe's name. Then, she tugged on some nylon stockings and slipped into an old pair of high heels before spotting me in the mirror. She smiled. It was rare for my mum to dress nicely, and I had forgotten how beautiful she could look, even if she was pregnant.

"Where are you going?" I asked.

"I'm going to go visit Grandma Desimone," my mum answered pleasantly. Grandma Desimone was our dad's mother, who lived in a small apartment on Larimer's outskirts. She always seemed nice enough to my sisters and me whenever we happened to run into her, which was seldom, but she rarely went out of her way to visit us. In fact, it had been more than two years since I had last seen her.

"Why are you going to go see Grandma?" I asked. My mum walked over to me and gently muffed my hair.

"No reason," she said, "she's getting old, and I just haven't seen her in a while."

"Oh," I mumbled, but it seemed odd to me. "Okay, tell her I said hi."

"I will." She brushed past me and opened the front door. "Mindy?" she yelled through the apartment.

"What?"

"I need you to watch the baby while I'm gone."

"All right, Mum," Mindy hollered back.

"I might be gone a while," my mum informed me, "so if I'm not home by supper, there's some leftover beans and weenies in the fridge. Just heat them up." She strode out the door and disappeared down the stairwell. I listened until I heard the apartments' street door slam shut.

Our mum walked briskly up Larimer Avenue. Almost a block behind, across the street, I trailed behind her. I skirted close to the buildings so I could duck into a doorway for concealment in the event she turned in my direction.

In fifteen minutes, she turned right on Broad Street. After a couple of minutes, she found herself on Centre Avenue and turned left. A few yards further, she stopped until the coast was clear of speeding cars at Penn Avenue intersection, then dashed across the street remaining on Centre Avenue.

I continued to trail stealthily behind her, praying she wouldn't spot me. Thankfully, she seemed to be more focused on where she was going. I got held up at Penn Avenue, waiting for the traffic to clear, before finally making it across the street. I lost sight of her and started sprinting, thinking I had lost her. In a couple of moments, my mum again came into view.

After twenty minutes, she stopped in front of a building with large glass doors and disappeared inside. I closed the distance and looked up at the letters on the building above the doors. It read Shadyside Hospital. I stood staring at the door my mum had walked through, first confused, then as the reality of where she was going struck me, I felt the rage bubble up inside. Without thinking, I smashed my knuckles into the bricks of the building next to me, causing me to wince from the pain, but I didn't care. I debated whether or not to follow her as she visited Joe but decided against it. Instead, I started the long jog home.

Our mum regularly disappeared all that week, and she never mentioned where she was going other than that first day, which was a lie. My sadness from missing Doreen deepened every day, but no one seemed to want to talk about the tragedy in our kitchen, especially what Joe had done to Doreen. It was almost as if it never happened. The daily anxiety and stress in the apartment were absent with Joe gone, but in its place, lingering beneath the surface, I now felt a foreboding I couldn't shake. Mindy seemed oblivious to it. Then, on one of the days our mother returned from one of her long absences, she sat Mindy and me down at the kitchen table.

"I was in East Liberty today talking to Chief Kelly. He told me he had talked with the district attorney's office, and they have decided not to file any charges against anyone."

"You mean, not even Joe for killing Doreen," I blurted out angrily.

"No, Frankie, they determined that what happened was just an unfortunate accident, and that's all," our mum explained. I clenched my teeth. It wasn't right. How could the police let him get away with killing our sister?

"Also, yinz know I've been gone a lot this week," our mum continued, her tone more staid than usual. We nodded. "I've got news for both of you."

"What news?" I asked.

"Well, I've been spending time over at Grandma Desimone, and she's been talking to your dad in California." She turned her full attention to me. "Frankie, your dad wants you to go live with him in California, and Aunt Connie and Uncle Pete are buying you a plane ticket. You'll fly out there in a couple of weeks." Our mum's tone was business-like as she reached across the table and rested her hand on my arm. "We have a few things to do between now and then. Grandma Desimone has given me money to buy you some new clothes. After all, we can't have you going to California looking like some kind of orphan," she mused, grinning thinly in an attempt to lighten the conversation. "In the meantime, you can start saying your goodbyes to all your friends."

"What friends?" I shot back. "I ain't got no more friends."

"Well, that's even more of a reason moving to California is probably best," our mum said. Then she turned her attention to Mindy.

"Mindy, I'm going to need your help a lot more now with the new baby on the way," our mum said. Then she looked past Mindy, shifted uncomfortably in her chair, and cleared her throat.

"There's something else I need to tell yinz both as well. I've been going to Shadyside Hospital to visit Joe," she said. "That's another reason I've been gone so much. He's doing a lot better. They moved him from ICU to the third floor, so he'll be getting out of the hospital in the next couple of weeks, and, well, he wants to come back to the apartment."

It felt as if our mum had kicked me in the stomach. I looked over at Mindy and saw the pain and fear in her eyes. She stayed quiet. "How can you even think about letting him back into the apartment after he killed Doreen?" I shouted.

"Like I said, and like Chief Kelly said, that was an unfortunate accident, Frankie, and Joe is out of his mind sick about what happened to Doreen, even sicker about it than we are, and he blames himself for you shooting him. He knows it wasn't your fault. He wants to tell you himself that he's sorry. Joe's a changed person now, and you probably wouldn't even recognize him. He's stopped doing drugs, and he promised me he will never do them again. You have to understand, little Rose and the new baby are his kids, and I can't just let them grow up without their father, not if I can help it. That just wouldn't be right," our mum exclaimed.

I stared at my mum in disbelief. There was no way she could believe everything she was saying, especially about what happened to Doreen being an accident or Joe changing.

"We'll talk more about this later," our mum said, standing up. "I'm going to get supper ready now. Come on, Mindy, set the table."

I walked into the living room and sat down on the couch, trying to digest and make sense of everything. In case Joe hadn't changed, and I know he hadn't, then I understood why I had to leave since I was the one who had shot him. But what about Mindy? Now that Joe would be returning, I felt sick that Mindy would again be in the same apartment with him. No, Mindy needed to go with me; that was all there was to it. I hated to betray my promise to Mindy, but I had to do it.

Mindy appeared in the doorway. "I have to go pee so bad," she whispered as she hurried down the passageway. I stood and walked into the kitchen. My mum was sitting at the kitchen table, and I slid into the chair opposite her.

"Mum, I have something to tell you," I announced, holding her eyes.

"What?" our mum asked when she saw the serious look on my face.

"It's about Joe." I searched for the right words. "Mum, he's been doing things to Mindy, I mean, bad things. Mindy can't stay here with him in the apartment—she needs to come with me to live with dad. You need to talk to Grandma and Aunt Connie about getting her a plane ticket too."

My mum listened, and I was surprised at her apparent indifference. But then, her eyes dulled. "Even if he did that before, and I'm not saying he did, I told you he's changed now, and he wouldn't do that no more," she said dismissively. I sat stunned. *Why hadn't she asked me, "What bad things?"* I thought.

"What do you mean, he's not going to do it no more?" I snapped at her angrily. "You sound like you already knew what he was doing. Mum, did you?"

My accusing stare caused our mum to break eye contact and look down at the table. Then, she snapped her eyes back up at me.

"You know how crazy he got, and the awful things he was capable of when he got loaded on that dope? He doesn't even remember half of what he did when he was on that stuff. It's different now, Frankie. Mindy will be safe. She has nothing to worry about. He regrets everything he did to all of you, and he's clean, completely clean. he's done with drugs—I know it," our mum said.

"You're lying to yourself, Mum. Mindy can't stay here. Deep down, you know he ain't going to change," I said soberly.

Our mum stared uneasily at me, and I saw guilt flicker in her eyes like someone just caught in a lie. She stood. "I know no such thing, and I just think this way is best for everyone, that's all."

"You mean best for you," I said coldly. "Joe once told me you would always want him, more than me. I guess he meant Mindy and Doreen too. I know now that he was right."

"No, that's not right!" my mum snapped. "Now, I don't want to hear any more about it. Go find something to do until supper." She turned her back to me and stepped over to the stove. I stood and walked to my room. It had been a while, but I felt the familiar urge inside return.

Chapter 34

I walked briskly, carrying a brown paper bag. I had been walking for nearly an hour, and sweat matted my hair and trickled down my temple and neck. Mt. Carmel Road was steeper than I remembered causing me to sweat more, which meant the cemetery was close. A few minutes more, and I reached the opening. There was a big sign that read "Mount Carmel Cemetery." As I walked into the entrance, to the left of the driveway was a white statue of Jesus, and on the other side was a white statue of Mary. I stopped between the figures to get my bearings and then marched through the graveyard in the general direction they had buried Doreen. It took me a little while, but I found the grave. There was no headstone, but a plaque read "Doreen Desimone," and under her name, it read 13 July 1955 to 10 July 1968. Then, below that, in big letters, was RIP.

I dropped to one knee, set the bag down, pulled out an empty pop bottle, and laid it carefully below the plaque. Again, I reached in and pulled out a smaller bag with five cents worth of penny candy from Martha's store. It included a couple of strawberry licorice laces, Doreen's favorite. I carefully set it next to the pop bottle. Then I reached into the bag one final time and pulled out two *Archie* comic books featuring Veronica and lined them up next to the bag of candy. Satisfied, I stood.

"Hi, Dor, I've brought you some things. The candy is from Phyllis. I told her I was coming to visit, and she gave them to me for free and asked that I bring them to you. I brought the pop bottle to remind you of one of our secrets, and I brought the Veronica comic books because I know she was your favorite. I have to tell you something about that. I lied to you, Dor. I always thought Veronica was way prettier than Betty. I just took Mindy's side out of spite, and I'm sorry I didn't tell you the truth." I looked away, then turned back. "Mindy and Mom and little Rose are doing good. But I think you might know that already. Mindy thinks you hated her when you died, but I told her it wasn't true. I told her you loved her. I hope you don't mind me saying that." I paused thoughtfully for a moment. "The other morning, I woke up in my room real sudden like because I thought I heard your voice, and even though I didn't see you anywhere, I knew you were there with me, Dor. I felt you. I don't know how this whole thing works with you being in heaven with God and then sometimes being with us here on earth, but I miss you, Dor. I miss you a lot. Sometimes it hurts real bad. It's so quiet around the apartment without you." I paused, then took a regretful breath. "There's something else I got to tell you. I think by now you know I shot Joe for what he did to you, only he didn't die. God, Dor, I still can't believe you stabbed him in the leg with that knife." I shook my head and grinned. "Anyway, I was hoping he would go to jail for a long time, but it looks like he's going to get away with it, and even worse, it looks like Mum is going to let him back into the apartment to live with us, just like nothing ever happened. It makes me sick to my stomach. The thing is, Dor, they're sending me to California to go live with Dad, and I'm afraid for Mindy if I leave. I don't know what to do. But I have to do something, don't I? If you were here, I think you would do something." I took a step back, crumpled the paper bag, and shoved it in my pocket.

"I have a long walk home, so I better go. I hope you visit me in my room again, Dor. It made me happy the whole day."

I turned, then maneuvered through the headstones toward the front entrance and home.

*****

Nurse Cathy Bream yawned, then rubbed her eyes. Another nurse sitting next to her at the nursing station smiled. "It sure has been a long night," she said. "Hang in there, Cathy, just a couple of more hours, and we can go home," the nurse promised.

Nurse Bream chuckled. "Thank God for that, Maggie. It seemed like we barely had any time for a break." She reached down and rubbed her foot through her shoe. "My bunions sure are acting up, and I can't wait to get home and kick these things off."

Nurse Maggie Pellegrini picked up a clipboard and scanned over it. "Well, that's odd."

"What?"

"Our patient in room 308, Mr. Gallucci, was awful quiet last night. Usually, he's buzzing us two or three times a night, demanding more morphine. I'll go check in on him, but I have to tell you, that guy scares the hell out of me. There's something about him that just doesn't seem right."

Nurse Bream nodded. "I know what you mean. He's not the friendliest patient we've ever had, that's for sure." She took the chart and looked it over. "It looks like he got his last shot at nine thirty last night, so he's overdue. You just sit tight, Maggie. I'll take care of it."

"You sure?"

"Yeah, besides, my bunions seemed to throb more when I'm sitting still. Walking some will make them feel better," Nurse Bream said. A couple of minutes later, with a tray in hand containing a hypodermic needle with morphine, Nurse Bream walked gingerly down the hall on aching feet toward room 308.

"Thanks, Cath," Nurse Pellegrini shouted out from the nurse's station.

Nurse Bream dismissed her friend's expression of gratitude with a wave of her hand as she walked into the darkened room. She slid back the curtain at the foot of the bed, then stopped. Something seemed off. She didn't hear any of the usual sounds from a sleeping patient, like snoring or heavy breathing. She squinted down at the man cloaked in shadows, then noticed something odd about his neck. She leaned closer.

Nurse Pellegrini was startled when she heard the scream and the clatter of a tray falling to the floor. She jumped out of her chair and hurried to room 308, where Nurse Bream had just entered. Her first thought was that the scary patient in the room had done something to hurt her friend. Her heart was racing when she reached the open door.

Nurse Beam stood at the foot of the bed, her hands cupped over her mouth. Nurse Pellegrini edged toward her until she was by her side, then looked at where Nurse Bream was staring.

"Oh my god!" she shrieked, then ran from the room toward the phone on her desk to call the police.

*****

Joe's two older sisters, Claudia and Beatrice, walked in silence. They were both thick in stature and had a rough look about them. Both applied a substantial foundation of makeup, Beatrice more so in an unsuccessful effort to cover the pockmarks on her face. They both wore heavy black eyeliner and had dark purplish circles under their eyes. Beatrice was the younger, with puffy black hair, stiff with hair spray. They wore tight shorts and loose tank tops that showed tattoos on their forearms and thighs.

They strode across the gravel parking lot, stopped at the bottom of the metal steps, exchanged glances, then climbed the stairs.

"Rose?" they both shouted into the apartment as they stepped into the kitchen. Their voices were harsh and raspy, a Gallucci trait.

"I'm in the bedroom," our mum shouted back. It was still morning, and she was dressing to go to the hospital. Mindy and I were within earshot in Mindy's room, reading comic books.

"It's Aunt Claudia and Aunt Beatrice," Mindy whispered. Our mum had insisted that we call Joe's sisters aunt, but I couldn't bring myself to do it. Sometimes they would come over to the apartment, and they and our mum would sit around the kitchen table, drinking coffee, smoking cigarettes, and swearing up a storm. Our mum usually didn't swear much, but she displayed a whole new vocabulary that I never knew she possessed around them.

"What are you guys doing here?' our mum chirped when they entered her bedroom. "I was just getting dressed to go to the hospital." She noticed the somberness on their faces. "What's wrong?"

"Come on, let's sit down," Claudia said as she grabbed our mum's arm and led her to the bed. Our mum refused to sit. "What is it? What's wrong?"

"It's Joe, sweetie. He's dead," Claudia said soberly.

"What? That's not true. He's not dead."

"We got the call from the hospital just a little while ago," Beatrice said.

"I don't understand. I was just there yesterday and spent half the day. When I left, he was fine. He was doing good—he was getting stronger. They were talking about releasing him maybe next week. How can he be dead?" our mum cried, a hint of hysteria rising in her voice.

Claudia and Beatrice exchanged glances. Claudia sucked a deep breath. "He was getting stronger," she said, "but he didn't die from his injuries."

"What do you mean? I don't understand."

"When one of the nurses checked in on him early this morning, she found a knife sticking out of his neck. Someone stabbed him."

"Yeah, someone stabbed him through the throat," Beatrice added.

Our mum's legs wobbled. She reached for the bed and sat down. Did Claudia just say someone stabbed Joe in the neck? No, that couldn't have been what she said. She looked blankly up at Claudia and Beatrice, and both were wiping tears off their face. "I got to go to the hospital to see him," our mum finally said.

"No, sweetie, they already took him out of the room. He's not there anymore," Beatrice whispered.

"But he can't be dead. Did you say someone stabbed him?" our mum asked. The sisters nodded.

"Why? Who would do such a thing?"

"Right now, no one knows. The police are there questioning people at the hospital to see if they saw anything, but so far, no one seems to know anything. From what they told us this morning, since he was no longer in ICU, he wasn't hooked up to any monitors to alert the nurses that anything might be wrong."

Our mum crawled onto the bed, laid her head on a pillow, and pulled her knees to her chest. "Can we get you something?" Beatrice asked. Our mum shook her head, then closed her eyes.

"I'm going to put on a pot of coffee," Claudia said. "Me and Beatrice will be in the kitchen if you need us for anything. Try to rest for a while." They walked from the room.

Mindy and I sat in silence on the floor, listening to the conversation that came from our mum's room. Now, we studied each other, probing curiously into one another's eyes.

"Who do you think did it?" Mindy finally asked.

"I know what you're thinking," I answered, "but it wasn't me."

"I didn't say it was."

"I know, but the way you were looking at me…"

"I wasn't looking at you in any particular way," Mindy said. "Besides, even if it were you, I wouldn't want you to tell me."

"Min, I said—"

"I don't care!" she snapped at me. "I don't care who did it, or why, or anything else. I don't think we should talk about it." She stood and marched from the room.

I watched her leave, then leaned my back against the bed, unaware I was grinning.

*****

A couple of mornings later, there was a knock at the front door. A policeman stood in the stairwell. "Rose Desimone?" he asked.

"Yeah, that's me," our mum said.

"Chief Kelly asked me to come to tell you he needs to talk to you down at the police station."

"What about?"

"Ma'am, that's not for me to know. He just told me to come let you know and to wait for you if you needed a ride."

Our mum bit her bottom lip, thoughtfully. "Okay, give me a couple of minutes, and I'll go with you."

"And ma'am, he wants to see your son Frankie as well."

"Frankie? What for?" she asked. The policeman shrugged.

"Okay, won't you come in and wait?"

"No, thank you, ma'am. I'll wait right here."

"Frankie!" our mum yelled through the apartment, leaving the door slightly ajar.

*****

Chief Kelly's office door opened, and Chief Kelly appeared in the doorway. He squinted down at my mum and me sitting on the bench outside his office, and he smiled. "Won't you please come in?"

We stood and followed him into the office. He motioned for us to sit in the two empty chairs in front of his desk before walking around his desk and sitting down. Our mum watched him nervously while I shifted uncomfortably in the wood chair.

"As you know, your boyfriend, Joe Gallucci, was murdered in his sleep while in the hospital a couple of days ago, and we are investigating it."

"Have you found out anything yet?" our mum asked.

Chief Kelly shook his head. "No, not yet. We're questioning everyone on duty in the hospital that night and anyone we think could be a potential suspect—including both of you."

"Me? You can't be serious!" our mum said. "Joe was coming back to the apartment to live once they released him from the hospital in a couple of weeks. So I had no reason to kill him."

"No, ma'am, I don't believe you did," he said, then glanced over at me. "But since it was your son who shot him in the first place, we needed to talk to him so that we can eliminate him as a suspect. You understand?" Chief Kelly asked craftily.

"We were both at home in our apartment when this happened, so I'm sure my son knows nothing about this."

"And I'm sure you're probably right, but we have to do our job."

Our mum pushed stiffly back in her chair and gave a reluctant nod. Chief Kelly opened a drawer, reached inside, and pulled out a large manila envelope with something inside it, and he emptied it on the desk in front of us.

"This is the knife we found sticking out, well, the knife that killed your boyfriend. Have either of you ever seen it before?"

Our mum leaned forward and scrutinized the knife. "No, I've never seen that knife before in my life."

I sat slumped in my chair, disinterested. Then, finally, I felt the eyes of both Chief Kelly and my mum boring into me, so reluctantly, I slid to the edge of my chair to look at the knife. Before I could stop myself, I gasped.

"What is it? Do you recognize it?" Chief Kelly, who had been studying my face for any reaction, asked.

I knew I had to think fast and fight the emotions and adrenaline surging through me. I had made Chief Kelly suspicious and knew it. I swallowed as I stared at the hunting knife with the brass blade guard and stag handle with the letter *H* carved into it.

"No, I ain't never seen it before. It's just that it's so scary-looking. I ain't never seen a knife that killed someone," I said, trying to sound convincing.

Chief Kelly continued to study me. "Are you sure you've never seen it before, either of you?" My mum and I shook our heads.

"I'm sure," my mum said.

"Yeah," I lied again.

After a few seconds, Chief Kelly returned the knife to the manila envelope. "Okay, that's all we have for now. I'll let you know if anything else turns up. I'll have one of our officers drive you back home. Before you leave, we will need to take both of your fingerprints." We stood. He walked around his desk and opened the door. "Thanks for your cooperation," he said as we left.

As Chief Kelly sat at his desk a few hours later, a detective appeared in the doorway and knocked on the door jamb. "What is it?" Chief Kelly asked.

"It's about the fingerprints on the knife. We couldn't match it against any on record," the detective said.

"Are you sure? Not even the boy's fingerprints?"

"Not a match."

"Damn, I thought for sure it was him. Okay, thanks."

The detective disappeared from the doorway; Chief Kelly slumped back into his chair and stared into space.

*****

My mum and I climbed from the police car. "Thank you for giving us a ride," my mum said. The police officer doffed his hat from behind the wheel before speeding away.

"I got to go," I yelled as I ran toward Larimer Bridge.

"Frankie!" my mum hollered after me; I ignored her and ran faster.

I hurried down the path and searched under the bridge. I had hoped Honeymarmo would be sitting waiting for me, but he wasn't. I rushed to where the concrete arch jammed into the abutment and searched for Honeymarmo's bindle. Still, there was nothing.

I scurried down to the tracks and began to jog, probing carefully into the woods while shouting Honeymarmo's name. After almost an hour of searching in both directions, I found myself again under the bridge. Exhausted, I sat down in the soft dirt. It didn't make sense. Honeymarmo still had to be alive, especially since his knife had killed Joe. He must have been lurking in the shadows, following me all this time, waiting for the right moment to kill Joe. I remembered his cold eyes when he had killed Grub, so I knew he was capable of doing it. He had protected me then, so why not now? Nothing else made sense. But why was he hiding, especially from me?

Then, I remembered the story Honeymarmo told him about Slick Willy-Nilly and how he climbed on what seemed to be a ghost train and never was seen again. Could it have been Honeymarmo's ghost that killed Joe? I shook away the notion as absurd and very little made sense. Eventually, still confused but hoping that Honeymarmo was still alive, I climbed the path and walked up Larimer Avenue toward home.

My mum was sitting at the kitchen table when I walked through the door. She had been waiting for me.

"Sit down, Frankie," she said soberly. I lowered myself into one of the kitchen chairs. My mum stared intently at me.

"I want you to tell me the truth. No lies. Did you do it? Did you kill Joe? I saw the look on your face when you saw that knife, and it sure looked to me like you recognized it. Did you do it, Frankie?"

"No, I didn't kill him, Mum. But I wish I had. I hated him that much, but I didn't do it. You want me to tell you the truth? Okay! The truth is, I'm glad he's dead!"

"Don't say that!"

"I already did, and I meant it. And not just for me, but for Mindy and Doreen," I snapped.

My mum continued to hold my eyes. "What about the knife?" she asked.

"What about it? I already told Chief Kelly I never saw it before, and now I'm telling you. Do you know what you saw on my face, Mum? You saw my satisfaction that I was looking at the knife that killed that jagoff. That's what you saw!" I said bitterly. I stood and marched from the kitchen, leaving my mom sitting alone.

Mindy was sitting on her bed when I strolled in. Mindy looked at my angry face, then smiled. It seemed to have a calming effect on me, and I smiled back.

"I heard you talking to Mummy," Mindy began, "and I'm glad you didn't do it, Frankie. I know you were thinking about it, and don't ask me how, but I just knew you were. If you would've done it, they would have caught you and sent you to jail for sure, and I couldn't stand it if that happened."

I stared warmly at my sister. She was the only one in the world who cared for me this much. "Thanks for believing me, Min."

Mindy squinted. "So who do you think did it?"

"I thought you didn't want to know," I reminded her.

"That was before."

I shrugged. "I don't know, Min. I mean, Joe hung out with some pretty bad people, like drug dealers and such. Maybe one of them did it. Maybe he owed money or did someone wrong. I doubt if we'll ever really know."

Mindy nodded. She slid off the bed, then hugged me. "I need to go help Mummy get supper ready." She whisked past me and out of the room.

Alone in the room, I wondered why I hadn't ever told Mindy about Honeymarmo. If I had, I could share my suspicion that he was still alive and was probably the one who killed Joe. I didn't know why I hadn't told her; we shared everything, especially secrets. The only person I told about Honeymarmo was Doreen, and that was just before she died. It was my last secret to her. If I shared my secret with Mindy now, it would be as if I was betraying Doreen, and I couldn't do that. No, Honeymarmo would just be my and Doreen's secret.

*****

A week later, our mum woke me early in the morning. "Come on, Frankie, it's time to get up. I ran a bath for you, and your clothes are in the bathroom."

"Okay," I said, sitting up in my sisters' bed and rubbing the sleep from my eyes. I walked into the bathroom, undressed, then slipped into the bathtub. Thirty minutes later, I emerged from the bathroom, fully dressed in my new clothes and feeling both excited and scared about the day.

Sitting by the front door was an old suitcase that our mum had borrowed from our grandmother. It contained all of my clothes. From the kitchen, I could hear the clatter of silverware and plates. The tantalizing smell of cooked bacon filled my nostrils. I walked past the suitcase, down the passageway, through the living room, and into the kitchen. On the table waiting for me was a plate of dippy eggs, crisp bacon, and a stack of buttered toast.

"Well, don't you look nice," my mum said as she hugged me.

"Look, Frankie," Mindy beamed, pointing to the kitchen table. She held baby Rose on her hip. "We made you breakfast."

"I'm starving," I said, sitting down at the table. Mindy and our mum fussed over me, refilling my glass with milk and scooping a second helping of everything onto my plate.

"Oh, look at the time," our mum said suddenly. "Grandma Desimone will be here soon to take you to the airport, so we better get downstairs and wait for her. Mindy, you can clean the kitchen later." Together we walked through the apartment to the front door where my suitcase was waiting.

"I'll get it." With baby Rose on her hip, Mindy picked up the suitcase. "This is light," she exclaimed as we stepped into the stairwell.

A summer rainstorm had begun forming in the sky as we stepped out on the sidewalk, turning the morning a dreary gray. Mindy sat the suitcase down on the curb, and our mum pulled me close as we waited for my grandmother.

Mrs. Cosenza stepped out of her store and looked over at us. "So you're leaving us for California today, Frankie?" she asked.

I nodded. "Yeah."

"Well, you say hello to your father for me, and maybe you can send me some oranges, yes?" she half-teased.

I grinned. "Okay." My mum pulled me tighter, which caused me to stiffen. Mrs. Cosenza walked back into the store.

"Look, Frankie." Our mum pointed across the street toward Martha's store. I looked, and Phyllis, who had just opened for business, stood in the doorway, waving vigorously at us.

"Bye, Frankie!" she yelled cheerfully. "Have fun in California."

"I will," I hollered back. Phyllis disappeared inside the store.

We waited for ten minutes before a yellow cab pulled up to the curb, and our grandmother climbed out of the back seat. She was old and thin with gray hair and a typical Italian nose that looked just a little too big for her face. She wore wired-rimmed glasses and repeatedly squinted and blinked as she pushed them back on her nose.

"Well, you ready to go?" she asked with a slight Italian accent. I nodded. The taxi cab driver slid out from behind the wheel, snatched my suitcase from the curb, and tossed it in the trunk.

"He's ready," our mum announced. As she hugged me tightly, I could feel her body shake as she tried to bottle up her emotions. Her eyes moistened, and she began to sniffle. I looked over at Mindy, who was doing the same.

"It's okay, Rose, he's 'a going to be all right," Grandma Desimone said, attempting to comfort her. "We need to hurry before the rain'a comes," she added, looking up at the darkening sky. Finally, we drifted over to the open door of the taxi cab. Our grandmother got in first and scooted across the seat.

"Now, you be good. I'm going to miss you so much," my mum said, kissing me on the head and face, and I could feel her tears wetting my face as she pressed her cheek against mine. She squeezed me one final time. Then, finally, she let go, stepped back, and wiped her tears from my face. Mindy handed the baby to our mum. She stepped up and gave me a quick embrace.

"Write me," she said.

"I will, Min," I promised.

"I sure wish I was going to California with you instead," Mindy quipped. "Oh, I almost forgot. I have something for you. Wait just a minute." Mindy disappeared into the apartment building. A moment later, she reemerged, carrying a small cardboard box tied shut with a piece of twine.

"Here."

"What is it?" I asked curiously. Someone had written my name and address on it.

"You'll see. Just don't open it now. Wait until you're on the way to the airport."

I studied my sister's face, then nodded. "Okay, Min."

I climbed in the taxi, and Mindy slammed the door shut. Our mum reached inside the open window and brushed my hair away from my eyes. Then, I glanced up at the old apartment, this time without dread or fear.

"Bye, Frankie, don't forget to write," Mindy said.

"Bye, Min," I said. "I won't."

The cab slowly pulled away into the early morning traffic. I turned, facing the front, a little scared of what lay ahead as we picked up speed. Then, I thought I heard something just outside the window, and it sounded like a faint clicking sound.

I jumped to my knees and stuck my head out the window. I craned my neck back and forth, but the sidewalk was empty. I considered what it was that I thought I had heard, then I grinned knowingly. "Goodbye, Dor," I whispered. I slid back into the cab and settled into my seat. The first of the raindrops spattered on the windshield, so I rolled up the window.

I untied the twine and opened the box that was in my lap. At first, I thought my eyes were playing tricks on me, so I blinked hard. With the stab hole from Charles's knife, Honeymarmo's Bible was inside. I caressed it to make sure it was real, and I didn't understand. On top of the Bible was a folded piece of paper with my name on it. I lifted it out, opened it, and immediately recognized Mindy's handwriting. I began to read.

Frankie,

At the end of last summer, I found this box and what was inside. Someone left it in the hallway under our mailbox, and it had your name on it. It was from someone named Honeymarmo. You never told me about him, Frankie. I know I should have brought it to you, but I opened it instead and decided to hide it in one of the empty apartments for just a little while. I know it was wrong, and I'm sorry for not giving it to you right away. After a while, I didn't know how to tell you that I had kept it from you, and so I never returned it—until now. I was afraid you would be mad at me. I hope you forgive me? I did read some of it, and I didn't throw it this time, I promise. I also read the note this Honeymarmo person left you. He sounds like a very nice man. Well, brother, it looks like we both have kept secrets from each other, but I think mine was the biggest secret of all. I hope you will not think badly of me. Frankie, I did what I thought was right. Have a good life in California, and don't worry about me because I know everything will be fine now. Always remember us, Frankie. I love you, brother.

Mindy Desimone

I stared curiously at the letter. I wasn't mad at Mindy for holding on to Honeymarmo's Bible; how could I be? Why would she ask me not to think badly of her for such a small thing? She knew me better than that. I was a little confused, and what note did Honeymarmo leave me? I lifted the Bible from the box and opened it. On the inside of the cover was a shaky handwritten note in pencil. It read,

Frankie,

I pray that this Bible gets to you safely. It is one of the few things of value that I have to give. I know that by now, you are full of guilt and regret for what happened, but I am writing to tell you that you need not be sorry, for I have forgiven you many times over. Remember our talks about grace and forgiveness? God has forgiven me more times than I deserve, so how could I do less. A mob is a cowardly beast without a soul made from people with weak minds and weaker spirits. They can be a powerful influence and a destructive force, so stay away from them. Always be an individual, and you will find your courage. God has made you special, Frankie, and he wants purpose for your life, seek it, stay within his will, and don't waste your life like I have wasted mine. Always reach out to him as he has reached out to you. I am just a tired old man now, and you getting this means I know I will probably soon be taking the Indian Valley Line, my last train ride, but I will be waiting for you in heaven, my friend. Until that day, God bless you and your life. I will miss you.

PS: Good luck with your whittling.

Your friend always,
Honeymarmo

I sunk further into my seat, hugging the Bible tight against my chest. The inside of the cab blurred as tears welled up in my eyes. I knew now that Honeymarmo had forgiven me for my treachery, for my betrayal, but the downside was that I now knew that my friend was dead, which meant he couldn't have killed Joe. Honeymarmo had saved my life twice, and now, even in death, he was giving me life again. I knew I now had the strength to give up my hate and anger and to forgive—and not just Joe. It had already cost me too much. After a moment, the pitter-patter from the rain turned to a thunderous downpour. This time I didn't fight my tears; I no longer could.

"What's a matter, Frankie? Why 'a you cry?" my grandmother asked.

"He forgave me, Grandma! He really forgave me!" I sobbed.

"Who forgave you?" she asked.

I could not answer. My emotions, all of them that I had fought to keep buried for so long, erupted as I emptied myself of guilt and pain and sorrow. I wept for Snowball and all of Fluffy's kittens. I cried for my love for Bunny and how she had broken my heart. I wept for what I had done to Honeymarmo, and because he forgave me. I sobbed for Doreen because of how she had suffered and died and because I missed her terribly. I cried for what Joe had done to Mindy, and finally, I wept for the injustice of being rejected by friends and neighbors and the loneliness I felt.

As the rain pounded the cab like spilled rice, streams of hot tears poured from me until I felt empty inside. I gently touched my wet cheeks; warmth spread through my chest. From now on, things would be different in my life; things would be better. My life would have a purpose with God in it.

But if Honeymarmo was dead, then who? I thought as I returned the Bible to the box. It was then I noticed something that the Bible had hidden. I reached inside and pulled it out. The green etching of a deer stared up at me. It was Honeymarmo's empty leather knife sheath. I held it in my hand, my mind racing, then it dawned on me. I quickly opened Mindy's letter again, and this time her words jumped out at me: "Well, brother, it looks like we both have kept secrets from each other, but I think mine was the biggest secret of all. I hope you will not think badly of me. Frankie, I did what I thought was right."

Her words sunk in for the first time as I now understood. How had I missed it before? Chief Kelly had our mum and me come to the police station for fingerprints so he could match them against those found on the knife. He never even considered Mindy. Why would he? Why would anyone? I thought about how repulsed Mindy had been at impaling a worm on a hook that day we went fishing or how she had made me carry cockroaches out of the apartment so that I wouldn't smash them. How could I think badly of her now? Mindy was good, she was the best person I had ever known, and the fact that she killed Joe didn't change that. Now, because she felt compelled to confront and destroy the evil in our lives, to protect us, she had changed. More profound grief settled within me, much like I felt when Doreen died. How hard that must have been for her, I thought. I was overwhelmed with regret. If only I had made sure Joe was dead when I shot him, then Mindy wouldn't have had to save herself and feel the need to seek justice for us. My guilt returned, and I again began to weep. Joe had taken away most of Mindy's innocence when he was alive, and now, he had taken the rest with his death.

I slumped back in my seat and stared sullenly out at the stormy day. I listened to the thunder and watched the lightning light up the dark, angry-moving clouds. Then unexpectantly, something came to mind. I remembered Honeymarmo had said something about how the rain was God's tears and that they would wash away sadness until there was again more happiness in the world. I knew it was a silly notion, but somehow, I took comfort from it. I looked toward my new life in California and how fresh and clean everything would be, especially once the storm had passed. I thought about how everything would be better for Mindy, and even our mum, even if she didn't know it.

Mindy's letter lay open in my lap, so I picked it up and reread it, this time focusing on one particular line. "Always remember us, Frankie."

"I will, Min. I promise I will," I whispered. I wiped the tears from my face, then, as I stared out at the storm, I noticed my reflection in the window, and I smiled.

THE END

About the Author

Anthony Michael Yallum was born in Pittsburgh, Pennsylvania, and spent his early years in one of the city's rougher neighborhoods. He has also lived in Morningside and Wilkinsburg, outside Pittsburgh. He later moved to Ohio, where he graduated from Rocky River High School. After graduation, he attended Ohio University for a semester before moving to California to attend Cerritos College as a journalism major. He became an editor for the college newspaper, winning awards for the most improved journalist and the most inspirational writer on staff. But before he could complete his studies, circumstances forced him into a different direction, and he joined the United States Marine Corps. He fell in love with the Corps, and what was supposed to be a four-year enlistment turned into a twenty-eight-year career. He retired in 2012 as a master gunnery sergeant. While in the Corps, he married, and he and his wife raised five children together. He now lives in Bluffton, South Carolina.

CPSIA information can be obtained
at www.ICGtesting.com
Printed in the USA
LVHW022234211022
731281LV00001B/4